PRAISE FOR T. KINGFISHER

"Dive in...if you are looking to be charmed and delighted."

— LOCUS

"...[A] knack for creating colorful, instantly memorable characters, and inhuman creatures capable of inspiring awe and wonder."

— NPR BOOKS

"The writing. It is superb. T. Kingfisher, where have you been all my life?"

— THE BOOK SMUGGLERS

PALADIN'S FAITH

BOOK FOUR OF THE SAINT OF STEEL

T. KINGFISHER

ARGYLL PRODUCTIONS

Paladin's Faith

http://www.tkingfisher.com

Published by Argyll Productions

Dallas, Texas

www.argyllproductions.com

ISBN 978-1-61450-609-6

First Edition Hardcover December 2023

For Uncle Roy

CHAPTER 1

Breaking into the Bishop of the White Rat's office was far more trouble than it had any right to be, and Marguerite was a bit annoyed by it.

To start with, the room where the Bishop saw petitioners was not actually her private office but a suite of rooms set aside specifically for that task, so Marguerite spent three days staking out the wrong room entirely. Secondly, her actual private office did not have windows, but instead a series of ventilation slits that could not have been infiltrated by anything larger than a ferret. (Not that Marguerite wanted to break into a third story office from outside. She had done such things before, but they did not rank among her fondest memories.) Thirdly, the only way to reach the office was to go through the offices of a whole cadre of staff, all of which were fanatically loyal and most of whom worked late.

All of these issues might have been surmountable, if Marguerite could have, say, bribed the cleaning staff, but even that proved difficult. The Temple of the White Rat solved problems. That was their god's entire purview. They were staffed with lawyers, social workers, healers, and organizers.

Apparently one of the problems they had solved was bribery. You couldn't bribe a Rat-priest. (Well, you probably *could,* but only by offering to donate the money to the poor.) They were all genuinely good people who wanted to make the world a better place, and how obnox-

Rigney's and the aide's, with only a narrow scarf-like vestment to indicate her rank.

"I am concerned that she may be an assassin, Your Holiness," said Rigney. He filled the doorway, not letting her pass, while his eyes traveled over Marguerite. Spectacles or no, Marguerite suspected that he didn't miss much.

The Bishop sighed. "If she was an assassin, I'd probably already be dead by now, Rigney. The only reason I'm alive is because I'd be so much more trouble for everyone dead."

Marguerite put her hands flat on the table. "If you'd like to search me for weapons, you may. I've got a knife strapped to my left calf and a bodice dagger. I feel underdressed without them, but I'm telling you they're there as a sign of good faith."

Rigney narrowed his eyes. The Bishop thumped his shoulder. "There, you see? Gesture of good faith."

"Also exactly the sort of thing that someone would say to make you let down your guard...Your Holiness."

"Then she's done so much homework that she knows exactly how much trouble I'll be dead. Come on, Rigney. Marguerite and I are old... ah...what would you call us, my dear?" She smiled over her secretary's shoulder. "We were not adversaries. I don't know that we're even acquaintances, given that we've never actually met. But you did me a very good turn once, and I have not forgotten."

"Colleagues?" asked Marguerite, who had found herself in similar positions with other operatives in the past.

"Colleagues," said the Bishop, inclining her head. "I like that. Move aside, Rigney, if she murders me, you can say 'I told you so' to my corpse."

Rigney's sigh conveyed a vast amount of information about his approval, lack thereof, and the things he was expected to put up with. He stepped inside and held out his hand. "If you could remove the knives, for my own peace of mind."

"As you wish." Marguerite extracted the bodice dagger, while the secretary gazed politely at the ceiling, and then the one strapped to her calf. (Her hairpins were also more than sharp enough to kill a man, but she left them in place. There was no sense in giving everything away.) She placed them on the table.

"And now," said the Bishop, "I believe you're in my chair. May I trade places with you? And then you can tell me why you are here, when you have been content to be officially dead for the last three years."

Marguerite took a deep breath and rose. "I need your help," she said.

CHAPTER 2

If the Bishop was surprised, she gave no sign. She sat down and leaned back in her chair and steepled her fingers together. "It is very likely that your intervention saved the lives of my borrowed paladins, once upon a time. I had been wondering when you would call in that debt. Nevertheless, we serve the Rat and even if a debt is owed, we cannot go against His will. I will have to know more."

"I thought as much." Marguerite had researched Beartongue quite thoroughly some years back. She was ethical to a fault, although her ethics were occasionally ruthlessly utilitarian. "I do not propose to keep you in the dark, although there are some limits on what I can say. I will not lie, my plan may put your people in danger. But I believe it is worth it."

The Bishop made an inviting gesture with one hand. "I'm listening."

"Well. I'm not sure how much of my history you managed to ferret out, but I took the name Marguerite from a fellow operative in Anuket City. I used to work for a consortium there, powerful merchants who...let us say...did not feel that the Merchant's Guild was entirely representing their interests."

Beartongue's lips quirked. "I take it that matters did not end well, if you had to flee and take on a dead woman's identity."

"An understatement for the ages. My patron within the consortium was found hanging from a beam. It was ruled suicide, but it was not. His information network was thrown into shambles, and several were picked off before we knew what was happening."

"And you're certain it was murder?"

"I would bet my own life on it. And *yes*, I understand that when someone commits suicide, everyone stands around wringing their hands and saying, 'But he would never have done that!' But Samuel truly would not have. His sense of duty to his operatives would never have allowed it. He would have crawled over broken glass for one of his people, and too many of us were left exposed by his death." It required no effort for her voice to fill with cold anger. The best roles had real emotion behind them, and this emotion was as real as anything she had ever felt.

Beartongue's lips made a flat line. *You understand,* Marguerite thought. *You would be right there on the broken glass beside him. You would never leave your people out to dry. And unless I have lost my touch completely, it's one of your fears, too—that someday you will become so politically inconvenient that an assassin puts a knife in you, and what will happen to your people then?*

She took up the thread of her story again. "At any rate, we were in disarray. We fled in all directions. Some of us took jobs with other groups. I did so myself. It was only later that I discovered that I was working for a branch of the very people that had killed my patron, and that there was still a price on *my* head."

"I can see how that would be uncomfortable, yes."

"You have no idea," Marguerite said dryly. "I was actually doing quite well in my new position when another branch of it showed up and tried to kill me. It was quite a shock to my employers as well. Fortunately I was able to escape while they were still thrashing out the details."

"Are you at liberty to tell me the name of this group?"

Marguerite licked dry lips. *And here is where you throw the dice and hope that the good Bishop is not already compromised. Though if they can suborn the head of the White Rat's temple, what chance do you possibly have?* "The Red Sail."

Beartongue frowned, but not in a hostile fashion. "The merchant fleet company? I thought their primary business was supplying salt from Morstone's Sealords to the rest of the continent. I can well believe that they want to keep abreast of Anuket's dealings, but I am surprised that they maintained a dedicated spy network in this area."

Her puzzlement seemed genuine. Marguerite relaxed slightly. The bishop might be a very good actor—almost certainly was, in fact—but if she had been in the Sail's pockets, she would likely have chosen a different tactic than ignorance. And she was entirely correct in her assessment. Anuket City, the fabled city of artificers, was arguably the greatest power in the region, but the Red Sail had access to dozens of regions and had only a passing interest in a small group of inland city states. "It was not what I'd call a dedicated network until fairly recently. I was the only one in Archenhold, so far as I know, and they were content to keep it that way. I passed information from here to the Sail, and if they did not tell me otherwise, on to a few old contacts in Anuket City. When things became a trifle...ah...heated here,"—Beartongue's lips twitched in acknowledgment that she had been some of that heat—"I became a traveling trader, moving among courts and sending information back. At least I did, until someone realized that 'Marguerite Florian' was a loose end and decided to kill me."

The Bishop frowned. "Obviously I'm sympathetic. If you need help getting away, or assuming a new identity, I suspect I can be of service. But I confess, Mistress Florian, that I don't see what the Temple can do for you that you could not just as easily do for yourself. Particularly since if we do it, there will be a paper trail and a dozen people who might accidentally let something slip."

Marguerite was already shaking her head. "That's not why I came. I've tried that. I've even tried simply going to my contacts in the Sail and asking for amnesty. They were suitably appalled and tried to help, but the Red Sail is an immense organization. There are a dozen individual fiefdoms who are all scrabbling for power. If one group wants me forgiven, another will want me neutralized simply to spite them."

"The right hand does not know who the left is killing," murmured Rigney.

"Precisely. And unfortunately, the group that wants me dead have seen their star ascendant recently, so..." She spread her hands.

Beartongue sighed. "Just like politics between religious orders, then. Still, as fascinating as all this is, I am certain you did not break into my office merely to complain about a merchant company's organizational flaws. Although given a bottle of wine, I'd be happy to expound on a few flawed organizations I know as well."

"No, not just for that," said Marguerite. *Although I suspect that would be a* delightful *conversation.* "Something is happening. The Red Sail has sent delegations here recently. *Very* recently. And it isn't regular trade they're after."

Beartongue glanced at her secretary. Rigney shrugged. "There *was* a trade delegation from Morstone to the Archon last month, Your Holiness. We thought nothing of it at the time. Archenhold only produces a few things that they would be particularly interested in trading, and none in any great volume."

Marguerite nodded. "I doubt they did anything of note. But it and a half-dozen others were cover for a much more serious delegation to Anuket City."

"I don't particularly like them," said Beartongue dryly, "but it's not a crime to trade with Anuket City. They have a great many things we don't. So why would they require cover?"

Marguerite leaned forward. "Word has it that an artificer there has invented a device that will convert sea water into salt...and do it far more cheaply than the Sealords can beat it out of their populace."

She watched the Bishop's face as the implications sank in. Beartongue's secretary let out a low whistle. "That would destabilize the Sealords...the trade fleets..."

"Half the continent," said Marguerite crisply. "Enormous political upheaval. More than a third of the income of the Toxocan Confederacy comes from salt taxes imposed on vessels passing through their strait. If the salt trade stops, they, too, will be scrambling to survive."

"And they're the haven for half the pirate fleets in the south. That tax is protection money as much as anything else." Beartongue's gaze became unfocused. "The Sealords are monsters...if they could be removed from power, I can only consider that good...but when a trade network fails, people starve. Violence breaks out. The cure may be as bad as the disease...and yet..." Her voice was soft, as if she was talking mostly to herself. Then she seemed to remember where she was. "Very well. I understand why the Red Sail wants it stopped. What do you want?"

"I want the Red Sail to be in such hopeless disarray that they stop bothering with minor players like myself." Marguerite met Beartongue's eyes squarely. "I want to have friends again without worrying that I'm painting a target on their backs. I want the Sail confused, bankrupt, and out of commission."

And I hope you believe me, because that is the actual truth, and if you try to ferret out something behind it, we'll both be disappointed. She ran her fingers over the surface of the desk. It was polished to glass smoothness here, unlike the oiled softness of the underside.

The Bishop pursed her lips. "So your solution to one faction of an enormous organization hunting you is to destabilize the economy of half the world."

"I *did* try to find a civilized solution first." When the other woman snorted, Marguerite added, "Honestly, if I hadn't been in Anuket City and quite literally overheard someone in the Artificer's Quarter talking about it, it would never have occurred to me to try. But when something like that falls in your lap..." She spread her hands. "This is an extraordinary opportunity. But I can't do it alone."

Beartongue stared off into the distance. "Rigney. How much does the Temple spend on salt?"

"I do not have the exact figures, Your Grace, but it is a significant expense, both directly and in terms of spending on food." He ticked off points on his fingers. "We must salt our food, of course, and items such as cheese require salt in their preparation." One finger. "Anything being stored or transported any distance must be pickled or salt-preserved." Two fingers. "Although it is likely a small quantity compared to the other two, livestock require salt in their diets, particularly over winter. Most of our wool comes from upriver, and the farther into the hills you go, the longer the winters. Sheep require salt blocks, and that is reflected in the price of wool." Third finger. "Industrial processes. Tanning leather, making soap, and papermaking all require salt. We use leather as much as wool, and we go through truly epic quantities of soap and paper." Fourth finger. "Well over a third of our parishioners ascribe to the folk belief that the dead must be buried with a handful of salt to keep evil spirits from inhabiting their bodies, and it has been the policy of the Temple to provide this for the grieving who cannot afford it." Thumb. "Finally, we tithe five percent of our annual income to establishing other temples of the Rat and offsetting their operating costs. The temple in Morstone has been soaking up the lion's share of that for a number of years, largely because of the unbridled power held by the Sealords." He dropped his hand. Marguerite waited to see if he was going to start in on the other hand, but he did not.

"God's whiskers," said Beartongue, passing a hand over her eyes. "How much money would we save if salt was cheaper?"

Rigney began to scratch numbers on a ledger. "I cannot even begin to calculate without knowing the cost of the technology, but assuming the cost of salt was halved...leaving Morstone's Temple as an unknown quantity...mmm..."

Marguerite and the Bishop exchanged looks and waited.

"Based on reduction of shipping costs and the lack of the Toxocan salt tax, we might well see a three to five percent savings in total annual food expenditures across all our temples in this region."

"That," said Beartongue, after a long pause, "is *real* money."

"Indeed, Your Holiness. And there is the additional effect, though difficult to quantify, that if salt is less expensive but prices remain stable, many smallholders will turn a larger profit and thus require less assistance from the Temple for major investments."

The Bishop turned back to Marguerite. "All right, you've definitely got my attention. And I can see why the Red Sail would want this invention suppressed. So is this device real?"

"They believe it is. They went so far as to blow up the artificer's workshop over it. She's gone into hiding now, but they're hunting for her."

"Do *you* think it's real?"

Marguerite smiled. "That is what I'm hoping you'll lend me a couple of paladins to find out."

CHAPTER 3

"Paladins?" Beartongue's eyebrows shot up. "*Why*—forgive me, but if you were planning a covert spy mission, I don't think our paladins would be my first choice." She considered this. "Or my second choice. Possibly not even my third."

"There is a certain bull-in-a-pottery-shop quality to the late Saint's chosen," Rigney observed.

Marguerite sank back in her chair. *She's interested. She's going to help me.* It was important not to show the depths of her relief. The Sail had been baying at her heels for so long that even this first small step felt like a victory. "People are already trying to kill me," she said. "Ruthless people with very deep pockets. When they learn that I'm trying to get to this artificer before they do, I imagine that it will get even worse. What I need are people who cannot be bought and who are very, very hard to kill. People that I can trust."

Beartongue grunted. "Well. When you put it that way...the paladins it is."

The two paladins were as different a pair as Marguerite could imagine. One was a woman a bit taller than she was, and—there was no getting around it—rather dumpy. Frizzy hair, soft chin, muscle and fat in equal quantity. You would not look at her and think *paladin.* You would likely not look at her and think much of anything, until you noticed that she was carrying an axe strapped to her back. Marguerite was immediately delighted.

The other one was tall and well-muscled, rather more like her stereotypical view of paladin-kind. His eyes were a blue so pale they were almost white, and the rest of his face had been devoured by a beard that had passed *scruffy* and was firmly lodged in *regrettable.* Like many blonde men, his beard had come in red. It was not a good combination. It looked as if a woodchuck had latched onto his jaw.

"Shane and Wren are both paladins of the Saint of Steel," said Beartongue smoothly.

"Former paladins," said Shane. His voice was deep and very calm, despite passing through the beard.

"Your god may be dead, but you still serve," said Beartongue. "Do not make me break out a theological argument, Shane, I'll do it."

Wren grinned. "We'd never argue with the bishop of a god of lawyers."

"Never? That's news to me. You argued with me last week."

"Yes, and I was right, too. You should have let me kill him."

"Everyone gets a fair trial, Wren."

"We caught him eating that old man's face! I saw it with my own eyes! So did you!"

"It was," said Beartongue heavily, "a particularly eventful trip to the library."

Shane's beard assumed an expression of saintly forbearance. Marguerite did not wince, although it was a near thing. *Well, you wanted a paladin. Looks like you got one. Complete with stick in uncomfortable places.*

"At *any* rate," said the Bishop, "you will be accompanying Mistress Marguerite to the Court of Smoke. Wren, I apologize for what I am about to ask you to do, but do you think you can impersonate a noblewoman at court?"

"Technically I *am* a noblewoman," said Wren a bit dryly. "I can't say I relish revisiting it, but in a good cause, certainly. What do you need?"

Beartongue gestured to Marguerite, who said, "Information. We are trying to locate an artificer who has done a very impressive disappearing act. We know that artificer has a patron at the Court of Smoke, and that they have thrown themselves upon said patron's mercy. Unfortunately, we do not know who that patron is. They are likely to be the only one with knowledge of the artificer's current whereabouts."

"Hmm," said Wren. "I can definitely pretend to be an airheaded noblewoman and listen for gossip, but the sort of circles that I'd be moving in aren't necessarily going to have the information you want."

Marguerite nodded. "It's a long shot," she said. "But I don't need much. Even a bored wife dropping a line about how her husband spends his money hiring artificers could be enough to set us on the right track. I'll be there as well, in my usual role as perfume seller to the rich and idle, but I move in...ah...slightly different circles." She nodded to the male paladin. "Which is where you come in."

He lifted an eyebrow at her, waiting.

"Shane, you will stand as Mistress Marguerite's bodyguard," said Beartongue. "You've attended me at court often enough that your manners are impeccable and you won't cause an international incident. Also, of course, you'll be spying on her in case she decides to double-cross us."

"Naturally." Marguerite had suspected as much, but having it out on the table was oddly refreshing. She recognized the same impulse that had her setting out her weapons as a show of good faith. "Though I'd be a great fool to let something incriminating slip in the presence of my bodyguard."

"Naturally." The Bishop raised her mug of tea in a gesture that was more than half salute.

Shane cleared his throat. "I do not wish to second-guess you, Your Grace," he said, "but I suspect that I am familiar to those at court who have seen me in your retinue. If any of those attend the Court of Smoke, will they not recognize me?"

"Not once you shave off that disgusting mop you call a beard," said Beartongue. "And the barber will do something with your hair. The people who will recognize you after that are few, and they would likely learn that the Rat is involved in this venture by some other method anyway. I shall leave it to Mistress Marguerite, in the moment, to decide what use to make of that."

Shane's beard looked dismayed. Wren slapped her fellow paladin on the back. "Don't mope," she said. "*I'll* probably have to wear a dress. Which reminds me, Bishop, I haven't *got* a dress."

The indefatigable Rigney coughed politely. "We can arrange a certain amount of travel clothing," he said, "including what might be considered appropriate for a minor noble from—forgive me, Lady Wren—a small backwater holding."

"It's fine," Wren said, wrinkling up her nose. "It's all true. It'd be strange if I showed up looking fashionable. Come to think of it, I'm not sure if I'd recognize if I was fashionable or not. How long should we expect to be gone?"

"Court lasts three months," said Marguerite. "If the gods are kind, we won't have to stay that long, but if we receive a good lead on the artificer's location, I'll want to leave from the Court and go there directly." She glanced at Beartongue, who nodded. "Can you both ride?"

The paladins exchanged glances. Marguerite raised her eyebrows.

"Technically," said Wren. "I used to, anyway. Horses don't care for berserkers much, so it's been a while. Shane?"

"I was trained in riding in my youth," said Shane. Marguerite placed him in his late thirties, possibly even early forties, but his hesitant manner of speaking made him seem oddly young.

"We will find you reliable horses," said Beartongue. "You'll only need them for a few days up river anyway. Court is in the western mountains this year, and I presume you'll go by boat most of the way?"

Marguerite nodded. The Court of Smoke was where the elite went when the weather got too hot to stay in the city. Those who had chateaus or estates somewhere more pleasant went to them. Those who could not afford such, or who did not wish to leave the glittering swirl of court life, went instead to the Court of Smoke, which was held in a fortress in the highlands and hosted by whichever courtier was currently most fashionable and wealthy enough to afford the extravagant expense. It was a summer-long party that hosted the scions of multiple nations. A spy could hardly miss it. Too many deals were brokered there, alliances made and broken, fortunes lost and won and lost again.

Marguerite had attended almost every year, in her guise as a perfume broker, and even though by mid-August she was ready to chuck the whole job and become a dirt farmer, by the next April she was already planning her journey again. The past two years, she hadn't dared risk attending, and the knowledge of how much she must be missing itched at her like a nettle.

"Make your preparations," said the Bishop. "Be ready for a long stay. If there's any duties here that need to be handed off, you know the drill." And as both Wren and Shane moved toward the door, "And for the Rat's sake, if you need new equipment, tell someone. I realize complaining is practically anathema to you people, but if your boots are about to wear through, we can *fix* that!"

Wren chuckled. Shane's beard looked martyred.

The door closed behind the paladins. Marguerite transferred her gaze to Beartongue, who had the fond look of a teacher whose pupils have performed well. "I think they'll do fine," she said. *Better than fine. I might actually be able to sleep if I know those two are on guard.* "But tell me, Your Grace, is there anything I should know about them in advance, to make this all go more smoothly?"

Beartongue steepled her fingers. "Not a great deal. They're both superb fighters, of course, but you presumably know enough about the Saint of Steel to know that once the battle tide takes them, you won't get them back easily. So don't point them at anything you don't want turned into mince."

Marguerite thought of Stephen, the gloomy but good-natured paladin that her dear friend Grace had fallen madly in love with. "I'm familiar with the type, yes."

"Then as to specifics...Wren will never tell you if she is injured or overmatched. If you ask her to fight an army singlehandedly, she'll salute and march out to do it. Shane will tell you if he thinks she's suffering, but that is probably the only thing he will volunteer information about. He is actually a far keener observer than he gives himself credit for, but he will not offer his opinion unless you ask." The Bishop tilted one hand back and forth. "He is polite, self-effacing, apologetic, and you'll probably want to throttle him before too long."

"Oof." Marguerite rubbed her eyes. "Well, good to know. But decent court manners, you say?"

"Impeccable, and he keeps his mouth shut. Like a very polite shadow. Although he's a terrible liar, so do *not* put him in a situation where he has to flatter someone." She grimaced. "I learned that one the hard way."

"Oh dear."

"Other than that...well, they're both loyal unto death, but that goes with the territory. They cannot be bought, they cannot be intimidated, and I assume that's why you wanted them in the first place."

Marguerite traced a circle on the polished wood of the desk, feeling the smooth gloss under her fingers. "If you were up against an enemy who could meet almost anyone's price, who would *you* want to watch your back?"

"Precisely. That said, you will have to pull rank if you want to do something...ah...expedient...in front of them. They will argue with you, but they will probably obey."

"Probably?"

"There are some things that a wise woman doesn't ask a paladin to do," said Beartongue. The Bishop held her gaze and Marguerite had the feeling that they understood each other very well indeed.

CHAPTER 4

"So that was the famous Marguerite," said Wren, as she and Shane descended the stairs to the courtyard.

"So it seems." Insomuch as Shane had ever thought of the woman who had saved all seven of the Saint of Steel's paladins a few years earlier, he had pictured someone rather like the Bishop, a tall, spare, civil-servant type. He had been very wrong.

Well, no surprise there, is it?

This time, though, it was a pleasant surprise. Marguerite had tawny skin and dark, blue-black hair, and to say that she had curves was an understatement that bordered on a venial sin. Her breasts were nearly the size of his head. Individually. He wondered if she frequently found herself having to repeat things to men two or three times, or if people often walked into walls and doorframes when she was around.

The less-pleasant surprise had been how nervous she was. Perhaps it had been Shane's imagination, but when the door had opened, her eyes had shot to it like a woman expecting armed warriors to pour through. *Which, in fairness, we did, but she knew that we were coming.*

It was odd. The legend of Marguerite, who had locked horns with the Bishop and gotten away with it, did not quite mesh with his first impression.

Though my impression is more likely to be wrong than not, Dreaming God knows.

"Wonder why we're trying to track down this artificer," mused Wren.

"I imagine we'll be told the reason in private. Or as much of the reason as the Bishop thinks we need to know."

"Probably." Wren rubbed the back of her neck. "I can't believe I'm going to have to wear a dress again."

"I can't believe I'm going to have to *shave.*"

Wren grinned. "It's been so long since I saw you without that starving badger attached to your face that I may not recognize you."

Shane sighed deeply. "*Why* does no one like my beard?"

"Do you really want me to answer that?"

"...no."

Wren hooked her arm through his. "Between my skirts and your bare face, we'll take the court by storm. You'll see."

Shane knew that neither he or Wren was the sort to take a court by storm—unless charging in with blades flashing counted—but thinking back to Marguerite and the lazy gleam of assurance in her eyes, he suspected that there might be one brewing nonetheless.

And I am no longer the man to hold back the storm. Possibly I never was. Perhaps I should go to Beartongue and ask her to assign someone else. Someone who is not so unreliable.

He doubted that she'd let him get out of it, but fear of failure churned in his gut. He had not yet failed the White Rat, as he had failed two gods before Him, but perhaps it was only a matter of time.

I can ask. And when she tells me no, I will respect her judgment.

It is bound to be superior to my own.

Marguerite bit her lip. She was, for the first time that day, nervous.

If the audience with Beartongue had gone badly, she would have been annoyed, frustrated, and facing a great deal of extra work. If the Bishop had been in the pay of the Red Sail, she would have been downright terrified. But neither one of those things would have *hurt.*

If *this* meeting went badly, though...

It's been three years. And you didn't come to her trial, even though you tried to make it right.

She'd had to leave. It wasn't safe. The memory of what had happened to her patron had been too fresh. She'd made herself too obvious, and if she didn't cut and run, it was only a matter of time until someone realized who she really was. At the time, she hadn't known that the Red Sail was behind the attack on her patron, and the world had been full of faceless enemies. Then it had turned out that having a face to put on the enemy didn't help. *I had to go. There was too much danger to Grace if I stayed.*

Guilt stabbed at her. She bowed her head.

This is what comes of caring too much for people who aren't in the game. Either they become targets or you cut them off because you know what happens to targets. Her patron had taught her that lesson and its corollary: that you must care for your own operatives and use them ruthlessly nonetheless. She had broken the first rule three years ago, and it haunted her still.

The door to the room opened, and Grace stepped through, her head turned to speak to someone over her shoulder. "Fine, I'm going, but this better be important. I was in the middle of a distillation and..."

"Well," said Marguerite, "if you're in the middle of distillation, I can always come back later."

Grace's head snapped around so fast that Marguerite heard vertebrae crackle. *"Marguerite?!"*

Grace charged into the room. Marguerite braced herself, not sure if she'd earned a warm embrace or a punch in the jaw but willing to accept either.

Grace's arms went around her and the knot in Marguerite's chest loosened. She hadn't broken things past mending. She'd left before Grace became a target, and Grace had forgiven her. She took a deep breath, smelling the scent that her perfumer friend was wearing, something tantalizingly familiar that she couldn't quite put a name on.

"What on earth is that perfume?"

Grace's laughing sob, or sobbing laugh—Marguerite doubted that she knew herself—broke against her shoulder. "It's supposed to be petrichor."

"Isn't that a level of hell?"

"No, silly." Grace stepped back, wiping at her eyes. "It's the smell right before a rainstorm. You know it."

"Oh." Marguerite leaned in and sniffed. "That's it. How on earth did you make a scent like that?"

Grace shook her head. "Never mind any of that. You're here! You're back! Are you staying? I've moved into the upstairs, but there's still a bed in my old room."

"No, no. I'm only here for a day or two. Until the Bishop has her people ready to ride."

"Will you stay with us until then?"

Marguerite winced internally at the hope on Grace's face. She hated to say no, but the thought of that small, narrow room, with only one door, and no way to escape if someone came through... "I'm sorry. I'd love to, but I have to be here for all the last-minute arrangements, not sending runners halfway across the city." She grasped Grace's hands more tightly. "But tell me everything that's happened with you!"

"Me? I haven't done anything special. I work, I make perfumes, some of them sell, some of them flop. I have a deal with a minstrel who attends all the fancy parties and takes orders, but he's not half the agent you were. Tab is the same as ever. He gets into Stephen's yarn and rolls around and makes a horrible mess, and Stephen sighs and extracts him again."

"And are you still happy with your paladin, dear heart?"

"Yes," said Grace. "Gloriously, foolishly happy." She smiled down at her friend. "I go about my work and I sell perfume and everything is normal and then he turns up and I think *my god, I love you so damn much.* And it's just...easy. I know that everyone says that love is hard work, but when I compare it to what life used to be like..." She shook her head.

Marguerite knew that Grace had been in a particularly dreadful marriage with a particularly dreadful man named Phillip some years earlier. She had also arranged for the information of Phillip's death to be brought to her friend last year. (She hadn't arranged for the death itself, although she'd certainly considered it.)

"I was grateful for your letter," Grace said, as if reading her mind. "Not just to know about Phillip, but to know that you were still alive. We worry about you, you know."

Marguerite waved her hands. "I'm fine. Always am."

"Yes, but *I* don't know that!"

"I'd rather not bring anything down on your head," said Marguerite. "You know what kind of business I'm in. The fact that I lived here for so long is trouble enough. It had to look like a clean break. I'm sorry."

Grace sighed. "I know," she said. "Or rather I don't know, but I know you're doing what you think is best. And you *would* know. So, what do you need?"

"Some samples. They don't have to be anything you actually want to sell. It's just my cover story. I'm peddling perfumes to the nobility again, and fell in with a noblewoman who needed an escort to the Court of Smoke. That's Wren."

"Oh, that'll be delightful," said Grace, laughing. "You'll like her. *I* like her, anyway."

"Right. And I'm taking another one along as a bodyguard. Tall fellow, regrettable beard."

"Shane." Grace nodded. "I can't say if you'll like him. He's...very paladinly."

"What, clanky and judgmental?"

"Oh no, not at all. More like apologetic furniture. He doesn't talk and when he does, it's usually to apologize for interrupting."

Marguerite groaned. "Joy. Still, what I want is an obvious bodyguard for the court, and apparently he's good at that."

"Yes, very. The Bishop takes him everywhere. And I hear that he's the one most likely to overrule the Bishop on matters of her own safety."

"Not *that* apologetic, then?"

Grace grinned at her. "Eh, I've seen you charm customers who were ready to burn the building down. I'm sure you'll have no trouble getting him to warm up."

Marguerite accepted this statement as her due. "I'll see what I can do." She hooked her arm through Grace's. "Now tell me more about how Tab is doing. I haven't seen my best civette boy in far too long..."

Shane climbed the steps to Beartongue's offices. The outer rooms full of clerks and civil servants, all working with great intensity, still seemed familiar and foreign all at once.

In the Temple of the Dreaming God, there were also scribes and clerks, many engaged in the work of writing and copying, reading reports on demonic activity, and dispatching paladins and priests to deal with it. His father had been one such clerk, and one of Shane's earliest memories was of rooms of pale stone, the scratch of quills and the murmur of voices, and in the far distance, the sound of the litany being chanted.

But there the similarity ended. There were twice as many clerks here, many of them sharing desks, and three more rooms just like this one, plus a cadre of lawyers and organizers with quarters in the White Rat's temple compound. The Rat had bigger problems than the occasional demonic possession. The Dreaming God's people carried themselves with an air of solemn purpose, whereas the Rat's always seemed to be cheerfully bailing the tide.

He waited outside the Bishop's chamber, listening to the familiar sounds of reports being issued and reviewed.

"...says we need another healer assigned south of..."

"...ten gold will fix the problem..."

"...haven't got enough. I can send an apprentice with her on rounds..."

"...lawyers don't grow on trees, you know. Not even around here..."

After about five minutes, the door opened and two servants of the Rat came out, holding thick folios in front of them. He slipped in behind them. "May I request a moment of your time, Your Holiness?" It occurred to him belatedly that he should probably have asked for an appointment.

"Not if you're going to 'Your Holiness' at me," said Beartongue. She gestured to a seat, then leaned back in her chair, sharpening a quill with a pen-knife. "Is there a problem?"

"Ah...not exactly a problem, but..." He sat, wondering how to phrase the question.

Her eyes moved over him and she sighed. "You're wondering why I'm sending you off with Marguerite and not someone else?"

Shane ducked his head ruefully. "Am I that predictable?"

"Desperately so. It's part of the reason I'm sending you. I predict, in fact, that you will do brilliantly, succeed in circumstances that will likely prove far more muddled than anyone hopes, and bring yourself and Wren back in two pieces." She cocked an eyebrow at him. "Second-guessing yourself all the way, of course."

"Ouch. Would you like to stab me in the heart as well?"

Beartongue grinned. "Am I wrong?"

Obviously not, or I wouldn't be here. It was simply a little embarrassing to be so transparent. Shane muttered something into his beard. After a moment he asked, "Do you trust her? Marguerite?"

"Trust," mused Beartongue. "A complicated notion, isn't it? I trust her to be acting in her own best interests. I trust that she is a very intelligent woman. And she and I both know that she proceeds with the understanding that, should her actions reflect badly on the Rat, I will claim to have been grievously misled."

"Istvhan always says that trust is faith plus predictability," said Shane. He missed his brother-in-arms a great deal, and more so lately. *Istvhan could always make everyone laugh. The day we are dependent on my sense of humor to carry us through is the day that we will all be in a great deal of trouble.*

It wasn't that he didn't have a sense of humor. He did. It was just that he kept it to himself rather than inflict it on other people.

Beartongue's face softened slightly at the mention of Istvhan. "He's not wrong. Let us say that I have a good deal of faith in Marguerite's goodwill, but very little in my ability to predict her. Which is why you are perfect for the job, as you are, as we have established, very predictable."

"Istvhan would be better at this than I am."

"I wish he were here," she admitted. "I know that you are not comfortable in this role. But he is happy in the north, traveling with his lady friend, and any word I send will take weeks to reach him."

"What about Marcus?"

"There is a chance that he would be recognized. And since he has chosen to let his family believe he is dead—well, I do not agree with his decision, but I respect his wishes."

Shane sighed. "Stephen, perhaps?"

"Working with Galen and Piper to track down more information about the death of the Saint."

He bowed his head. Galen's husband, Piper, was a lich-doctor, possessor of a rare wild talent. If he touched a dead body, he could relive their last moments. A few months earlier, he had laid hands upon the altar cleared from the rubble of the burnt temple of the Saint of Steel, and to the shock of everyone, he had felt the god's death from the inside. Since no one knew how or why the Saint had died, they were trying to unravel as much as they could from that flash of insight. "I suppose there is no information to be gleaned about that at the Court of Smoke?"

"If you mean, are nobles likely to be casually discussing dead gods in the corridors? I shouldn't think so. Then again, stranger things have happened. Keep your ears open, but don't blame yourself if you don't hear anything relevant." Beartongue's gaze lingered on him sympathetically. The only remaining paladin, the one that they had not mentioned, was Judith, and she had simply left after the revelation of the god's death. Looking for something, perhaps. Running away from something. No one knew for certain.

He grunted.

"To that end," Beartongue said, ignoring the grunt, "I have a message for you to deliver. Lady Silver dwells at the Court of Smoke for most of the year. She is favorably inclined to the Rat, and I have reason to believe that a message to her might not go amiss." She slid a fresh sheet of foolscap in front of her and wrote quickly. Her hand was neat and clean, a testament to early training as a scribe, and Shane looked away so as not to risk reading the words.

"Deliver this to Lady Silver," said Beartongue, sprinkling sand on the letters to dry them, then sealing it with wax. "Whether or not you tell Marguerite of this, I leave to your discretion."

My *discretion? I'm a berserker. I hit things with swords until they fall down. That is not discreet.*

His alarm must have shown, because she smiled. "If you truly don't know, then it rarely hurts *not* to tell everything you know."

Shane groaned. "And then I will—"

"Feel guilty?"

His sense of humor was well-buried, but not completely dead. He gave her a wry look. "I was going to say, 'worry that I am withholding vital information.'"

"Well, it's always a concern." She leaned over the desk and patted his hand. "You are the only possible choice," said Beartongue. "And you are far more competent than you believe yourself to be."

Shane squared his shoulders. "I pray that I may not fail you, Your Grace."

"You won't," she said. "In that, I have faith."

CHAPTER 5

Dawn's gritty grey light was spilling over the courtyard when they assembled to travel north and west. Five horses awaited them, along with a groom to care for them. Four were saddled, and the last horse was clearly a pack animal.

Marguerite was not a particularly skilled rider as such things went, but she had learned to judge horseflesh because you could often tell a great deal about a person by their mount. These animals were well-cared for, sturdy, and no noble would be caught dead on any of them.

"Dreadful beasts, aren't they?" asked Beartongue cheerfully. The Bishop had come down to see them off, although Marguerite suspected that the woman had already been up and working. "It's the berserker problem. You have to get a horse so placid that they don't care that the person on their back smells like violence."

"Does violence have a smell?" asked Marguerite.

Beartongue shot her a wry glance. "You know it does."

"Mmm," she said noncommittally. *Yes, it does. When you cut Samuel down from the beam, you could smell it on his skin. You've smelled it too many times of late. It lingers in some places. If it's not a smell, it's something close to it.*

"So we end up on plowhorses," she said, turning away from that line of thought. "Fair enough. I'm not such a magnificent horsewoman that I'll complain."

"Indeed." Beartongue lifted a hand to wave to two people approaching. They both wore leather and chain and carried weapons. Wren had an axe and a cheerfully bloodthirsty expression, but Marguerite almost didn't recognize the other paladin.

As they came closer, she frowned, trying to place him. He had a massive sword slung across his back, the hilt sticking up past his ear, and a shorter blade at his waist. They'd definitely met before, but surely she'd remember someone who looked like *that.* He had a square jaw and a full lower lip and truly elegant cheekbones. Marguerite had always been an admirer of good cheekbones.

It was the pale, pale blue eyes that finally tipped her off. *This is* Shane? *Really? And he deliberately went around looking like...like whatever that was?*

"Good god," she said, eyeing him with frank admiration. "Are you sure you're not one of the Dreaming God's people?"

He flinched. She hadn't expected that. But still, absent that regrettable beard, the man was downright beautiful. *And if you see a beautiful paladin, odds are good it's one of the Dreaming God's. But clearly that touched a nerve.*

"I'm sorry," she said, with her most contrite smile. "I just put my foot in it, didn't I?"

"I served in the Dreaming God's Temple until my eighteenth year," he said. "But the god did not see fit to take me into service."

Ouch. From what Marguerite knew of paladins, which admittedly wasn't a great deal, this was akin to being jilted at the altar, only by your god instead of your bride. She wondered how long ago that had been. Without the beard, she reassessed his age. Mid-thirties at most. There was the slightest suggestion of lines at the corners of his eyes, but that was all.

If the god didn't take him, it certainly wasn't because of his looks. But I don't think I'll say that out loud.

"That temple's loss is clearly my gain," she said, instead. "Glad to have you with us. Both of you." She nodded to Wren, who now had a fashionable haircut and appeared to resent it.

They both saluted. Marguerite winced. "Oh yes," said Beartongue, as the pair went to their horses, "they're saluting types."

"I really should have guessed."

"You *are* their commander."

"I don't want to be their commander. I just want to be the one in charge."

Beartongue laughed at that. "I have been saying that for years now. Let me know if it works out any better for you."

Marguerite shook her head, eyes still following Shane. "Damn, he cleaned up nice."

Beartongue leaned over and murmured, for her ears only, "It would be a gross violation of power to force an underling to modify their appearance for my amusement. So believe me when I say that I have wanted an ethical excuse to make him shave that miserable beard for *years*."

"You don't have a barber, you have a miracle-worker," said Marguerite, at roughly the same volume.

"Your Holiness," Shane called.

The Bishop looked up inquiringly. Marguerite watched the paladin stride toward them, then drop gracefully to one knee before her.

"I request your blessing, Your Holiness."

"Rat's tail," said Beartongue. "You know you don't need to get on your knees for that."

An almost imperceptible smile crossed the man's lips. Marguerite suspected that she was the only one at the correct angle to see it.

"Very well," muttered the Bishop, holding out her hand. "May the Rat walk with you and clear the way before you, and may your problems contain the seeds of their own solutions. And for the love of all that's holy, don't die." (Marguerite suspected that last bit was not actually part of the formal blessing, but then again, the Rat was *very* practical, so she couldn't swear to it.)

Shane rose as gracefully as he had knelt. She filed that away in the back of her mind. She did not know a great deal about the Saint of Steel, but she knew that His paladins were not generally knighted. Nevertheless, something about the way Shane moved, the practiced ease of his deference, made her think of the knights that she knew.

Well, if he was in the Dreaming God's temple, he may well have been. They do tend to knight their people, if only because it makes life easier for someone to have secular authority when a demon shows up.

He went over to where the other paladin was standing next to a horse, and knelt again, offering her his laced hands as a stirrup. She climbed onto the animal with the set expression of a woman climbing a very tall ladder to a very great height. Shane stood up and said something to her that Marguerite didn't catch, but which made Wren laugh.

Were they lovers? They seemed absolutely comfortable with each other's bodies, but it was impossible to tell if that was from the intimacy of battle or the bedchamber.

"Oh, I should warn you," said Beartongue, as she turned to leave. "One last thing."

Marguerite braced herself. There was a glint in the other woman's eye. It wasn't quite malice, but it was definitely mischief. "Yes?"

"Shane can do the voice *really* well."

"The voice? What voice?"

The glint became a gleam. "I suspect you'll find out." And then she was gone in a swirl of vestments, while Marguerite stared after her, wondering what on earth she was talking about.

The first leg of their journey was deeply uneventful. They took the road by slow stages for the riders who were not accustomed to time on horseback. Marguerite felt her nerves slowly settle. The Red Sail's attempts to murder her had mostly occurred in places where they were already established. While it would be simple enough for someone to lie in wait with a crossbow, it would require them to know which road she was taking or to stake out every possible road. Marguerite was quite certain that she simply wasn't worth that kind of effort. She was a loose end, not an active target.

Being a loose end is quite unsettling enough, thank you very much.

Wren was cheerful and chatty and Beartongue had been right—she really didn't complain. Even when she was slapping about in the saddle with her teeth gritted and lines of pain around her eyes, she didn't ask for stops. Marguerite found herself calling for an early halt out of pure sympathy.

Truth was, she was grateful for the frequent stops herself. While she often worked with the mounted nobility, riding out for a few hours of flirtation was rather different than day after day on horseback. She was not exactly sore, but she was certainly very stiff.

Though not as stiff as some *people I could name.* Her eyes drifted to the tall blonde man beside her.

Shane was courteous, answered her questions politely, and volunteered nothing. Marguerite's attempts to draw him into conversation failed utterly. He was from a town southeast of the Dowager's capital. Had he grown up there? No. Had he been back? No. Did he miss it? No. Was the landscape similar? Yes, but the trees were different. Whenever she left a silence and waited for him to fill it, he allowed the silence to grow.

He didn't laugh at her jokes. (She didn't take it personally because he didn't laugh at anyone else's jokes either, and their groom, Foster, made quite a good one about a chicken.) He watched everything and said nothing unless spoken to.

She didn't think that he was unintelligent. It seemed more like he was paying very close attention to the world and filing it all away somewhere behind those ice-colored eyes and simply had nothing to say.

For many people, this might have made him unreadable, but Marguerite had made her life's work out of reading people, and the day that she couldn't read a silence was the day that she retired and took up goat farming. The key was usually the eyelids. *People* say *the eyes are the windows to the soul, but windows don't actually have expressions. But you can sure tell a lot by how someone closes the blinds.* The little twitchy muscles in the lower lid, the fine lines at the outer edge, the startled blink—those were the tells that she watched for.

Sadly, it was extremely difficult to watch someone's eyelids when you were both on horseback, on different horses, facing the same direction.

I'll figure it out. I've got a week, and we won't be riding all the time. And in the meantime, I can just ask Wren.

The first night on the road, she bespoke two rooms, one for Wren and herself, one for Shane and Foster. "Forgive me," she said to Wren. "I was hoping to have you in the same room at night, in case someone comes through the window, but I realize that might be awkward with you and Shane. Are you two…ah…?"

The other woman looked blank. Marguerite made explanatory hand gestures.

"*Oh.* Saint's balls, *no.* He's like an older brother. They're all like older brothers. All six of them. Including Judith."

"Having that many older brothers sounds exhausting."

Wren put her head in her hands. "You have *no* idea."

Marguerite smiled. At least one of the paladins was easy to read. "I'll have a tray sent up," she said. "I'm guessing you would rather not brave the stairs down again."

"I can if I have to," said Wren, who could not currently stand without her legs trembling.

"Yes, but you don't have to."

"It's no trouble."

If Marguerite had not been familiar with berserkers, she would have been worried that she might end up guarding her bodyguard. Absent a full-blown berserk fit, though... She decided to try diplomacy. "Actually, I wanted to get a tray for myself, so if you don't mind eating with me? Rooms full of strangers are a little...ah...dicey at the moment."

"Oh, *that's* different. By all means."

"Won't be a moment," Marguerite assured her. "Let me just check on the boys."

She checked to make certain the hallway was empty, then hurried to the stairs down. The taproom was bustling, which was a relief. It was surprisingly easy to murder people in a crowded room, but not when you had a paladin with you.

"How is Wren?" asked Shane, the first question that he had asked directly all day.

"Sore," said Marguerite, joining the two men at the table. "She tells me it's been years since she was on a horse, and that was an elderly pony."

Foster nodded, wiping foam from his ale from his upper lip. "Doesn't matter how fine a shape you're in," he said sympathetically. "All the wrong muscles used in all the wrong ways on a horse."

Shane nodded. Marguerite rubbed her sore thighs surreptitiously under the table. "We'll take it easy on the road to the river," she said. "There's no point in hurting ourselves for an extra day or two. Everyone arrives fashionably late to the court anyway." *And the longer the patron is there, the more chance that they'll let something slip that we can pick up from someone else later.* Like most spycraft, Marguerite was happy to let someone else do the work for her whenever possible.

Shane nodded again. Marguerite thought about trying to engage him in conversation, decided that it had been a long enough day already, ordered two trays, and went to go eat with Wren.

CHAPTER 6

"So how did you wind up a paladin?" Marguerite asked two days later, when Wren was comfortable enough that she wasn't clinging to the saddle horn with an expression of impending doom. (Her horse ignored this. Her horse had, so far, ignored everything that did not involve food or Foster.)

Wren's lips twisted. "You mean, how does someone who looks like me become a paladin?"

"As a fellow member of the society of chunky women, I trust you'll take that in the spirit that it's offered."

Wren gave her a frankly skeptical look. "Except that you're gorgeous."

"No, I just dress well and have large breasts. It's not the same." She looked Wren over. The other woman was less an hourglass than a muscular apple. "I won't lie, your shape isn't the easiest to work with, but a good tailor could do work that will astound you."

"It would still be me inside the clothes," said Wren, gesturing to her relative lack of endowments.

"Well, yes. Attitude is very important."

"Exactly. And you carry yourself like you're gorgeous." Wren shook her head. "I don't know how."

"You are my sister-in-arms," said Shane behind them, "and it is my honor to fight beside you."

Did he just say that? Marguerite stared briefly heavenward and thought about letting it pass but...no, there were times you just had to intervene.

"Shane," she said, turning to look at the paladin, "when a woman is lamenting that she doesn't feel attractive, you're supposed to tell her she's beautiful. Not that you're honored to kill people with her."

He looked at her blankly, then said, "Oh."

If she'd had any remaining doubts that he and Wren were not lovers, they would have been put immediately to rest. He had the exact expression of a man whose little sister has hit puberty while he wasn't looking. She should probably have let it go there, but it offended Marguerite's sensibilities that Wren was tasked with killing enemies of the gods and had to do it while feeling unattractive. "Now start again. Try, 'Wren, you are beautiful.'"

"Wren," said Shane, as grimly as if he were pronouncing a blood-feud upon an enemy, "you are beautiful."

"Very good."

"And I will fight anyone who says differently."

Well, that's progress, I suppose.

Wren giggled helplessly. "Right," Marguerite said, nodding. "Next time, we'll work up to a specific compliment. Perhaps something about your eyes." Shane looked appalled, which was a vast improvement over inscrutable. "Now then, you were saying?"

Wren wiped her eyes. "Ah...what was I...oh, right! Well, I was twenty and went out to take some medicine to a crofter. The neighboring clan are a bunch of low-life thieves, and a group of wolfsheads...uh, I don't know what you call those here...Shane, help me out."

"Criminals cast out of their clans or tribes, who were either too well-connected to execute or who fled the axe. Frequently deserters will end up there as well. Or those who are simply unlucky and must fall in with criminals or risk being their prey."

"Yes, that. Well, the wolfsheads knew that the neighbor clan chief would turn a blind eye to them if they raided everybody else's lands and left his alone. They were making enough of a nuisance of themselves that the Saint of Steel had gotten involved—they burned a monastery and you just don't *do* that—and unbeknownst to any of us, they'd chased the group practically to that poor family's doorstep. We heard fighting and the mother was trying to bar the door and the grandfather was yelling to get him his sword, he could still fight if she'd just prop him up in the doorway. And then the battle tide rose for the Saint's chosen." She spread her hands. "And the next thing I knew, I grabbed the old man's sword, went out through the window, and was charging across the field at the enemy. I was in skirts and I'd never held a sword in my life."

Marguerite felt her eyes go wide. "You must have been terrified."

"Not in the slightest. The god was with me, you see. It was all this marvelous golden fire and everything was...*right.*"

The soft noise behind them came from Shane. It sounded like pain.

"Anyhow, the tide ran its course and I came to surrounded by corpses. I'd killed a couple of them myself. My arms hurt so badly I could barely lift them. Fortunately all the other paladins had seen baby berserkers before. Istvhan—have you met Istvhan? No? Pity, you'd like him—he bundled me up and took me back home and explained the whole situation, both to my husband and me."

"Husband?" Somehow it was hard to picture Wren as having been married.

"Of convenience," said Wren cheerfully. "Poor fellow married me to secure water rights from my father, and didn't know what to do with me, I'm afraid. He's dead now. Err, from fever, not anything I did."

"Good to know," said Marguerite. "And so you decided to become a paladin?"

"Not much deciding involved. The Saint takes you and that's the end of the matter. Next thing I knew, I was being assigned weapons and a bunk and spending my days learning how to swing a sword without wanting to die the next day."

Marguerite ran the reins through her fingers, grounding herself in the grain of the leather and the raised bumps of stitching. *I wonder if all the Saint of Steel's people had a similar experience, simply going into a battle rage with no idea what's happening. And how did they come out of it after?*

Did some of them never come out again?

She glanced back at Shane, riding behind them. His expression was very still. She wondered how it had happened for him, and what scars it might have left behind.

"And now you work for the White Rat," she said, carefully skipping over the awkward intervening bit where the Saint of Steel had died.

"That always struck me as unusual, I admit, though it obviously worked out well."

"They needed us," said Wren, shrugging. "I mean, I love the Rat's people, but the vast majority are so busy fixing things that it doesn't occur to them that they might be in physical danger."

Marguerite thought of Beartongue's surprising security. "Mm," she said noncommittally. "Well, if you ever get tired of working with the Rat, I'm sure you could set up as bodyguards."

"We owe them," said Shane.

Marguerite turned to look back at him. "Beg pardon?"

"We owe them," he repeated. "When the god died, they cared for us. Dozens of us fell into a stupor. Most didn't wake up again."

Wren stared at her hands. Marguerite thought, *So much for skipping over the awkward bit.* "They're good people," she said aloud. "And you can't tell me that Beartongue kept some kind of ledger for that."

"God, no," said Wren, making a gesture as if to avert the evil eye. "She would never."

"Still," said Shane quietly. "We owe them. For the living and the dead."

You cannot buy that kind of loyalty. If I were to turn against the Rat, these two would cut me down without thinking twice. On the bright side, it also means that no one is going to be able to bribe or suborn them against me, so long as I stay on Beartongue's good side.

"All right," said Wren, obviously changing the subject. "Now your turn. How does one wind up an...er...?"

"Operative," said Marguerite, lowering her voice. Spies generally did not lie in wait on deserted stretches of country road in hopes of overhearing something incriminating, but old habits died hard. Foster was riding a few lengths back, not that Marguerite was really worried about him, either. "I fear it's not nearly as exciting a story as yours." She sorted mentally through a half-dozen cover stories, and settled on one that was more or less true, though it glossed over some of the grimmer details. "I was a page in the Merchant's Guild in Anuket City. Most of the pages there are by-blows of the various members, so presumably I was as well." This was true, in fact, although she knew exactly whose bastard she was. Her grandfather had been a shipping magnate, and when his son had the poor taste to sire half a dozen children on the wrong side of the sheets, they had all wound up as pages. It was a way to care for them without having to acknowledge anyone, and if any of the youngsters showed talent, they were within easy reach.

Marguerite had indeed shown talent, although not for business. At least, not for the business of trading physical goods. "I was very good at listening. Pages are nearly invisible, and even people who should know better let things slip in front of us. Eventually that talent attracted notice from certain factions within the Guild. First they pay you for information, then they start sending you out specifically to collect more information..." She lifted a hand from the reins and waggled it back and forth. "There's not a specific point where you wake up and realize that you're an operative. You just keep going along and meeting more people and chatting to them and learning who is interested in buying what information, and then it's twenty-odd years later and you're off to the Court of Smoke, trying to figure out where a stray artificer has gotten off to."

This was also true, so far as it went. Mostly. If you squinted.

Wren cocked an eyebrow at her. "I doubt it's as simple as you're making it sound."

"No, but I doubt learning to swing a sword was that simple, either." Wren's expression made Marguerite want to laugh. "Honestly, being an operative is frequently very boring. For every time you're smuggling information out of a powerful warlord's bedroom, you spend a month sitting and watching one particular bar, waiting to see who shows up." (This was not a lie, but the truth was that these days, Marguerite paid people to sit in bars for her.)

Shane surprised her by offering a comment. "We often marched a great deal," he said, "and waited a great deal, merely to be in place for a battle that might last less than an hour."

"Yes," she said, turning to nod at him. "Exactly like that." Internally, she exulted that she'd gotten the man to talk at all. *Perhaps he simply needs time to warm up to new people. He might even be shy.*

A shy berserker. Well, why not?

She would have liked to draw him out more, but unfortunately the road grew busier as they approached a market town, and they went back to riding single-file.

They were passing a drover with a line of bored-looking cattle when disaster struck.

A dog came out of nowhere, barking at the cows. Most of them ignored the animal, but one youngster made a deep sound of alarm and kicked up his heels. The drover turned to get him back in line when the dog darted forward and nipped savagely at another cow's hocks.

The cow jumped forward, startled, swinging her head to look at the dog. Marguerite's mare was sufficiently placid that neither the sound nor the motion bothered her much, though she did manage a rather graceless sidestep. Marguerite tightened the reins just as the cow kicked out in a panic.

The cow's aim was good, if slow. The dog was fast enough to dodge, but dodging put it practically under the mare's hooves, and suddenly there was a barking dog and a kicking cow and the mare was no longer feeling placid at all. Marguerite had time to think, *Oh shit* and then the horse went up on her hind legs to avoid stepping on the dog and crow-hopped sideways and the dog went nuts and the cow kicked again and the drover was yelling and she lost her seat on the saddle and the horse came down and Marguerite fell off and the ground came up to meet her.

CHAPTER 7

"Easy..." someone said in her ear. "Easy. Don't move. I'm right here."

Marguerite wanted to say that she was fine, she hadn't even lost consciousness in the fall, but her head was still ringing and adrenaline was a cold wash through her veins. She wasn't quite sure how long it had been. She didn't think she'd blacked out, but there had been a long few seconds when the world was going *whommmmm* around her and she had been carefully not moving, in case it didn't stop.

The horse hadn't stepped on her. That was the important thing. It would be extremely annoying to have dodged the Sail for several years, only to have her career ended with a badly placed hoof.

"Easy," he said again. A man, but she didn't quite recognize his voice. "Easy. Hold still. I'm going to check your neck. Don't move. It's okay. I'm right here."

Of course you're right there, she thought. She would have been annoyed but there was something incredibly soothing about the way he spoke. She could not remember the last voice she'd heard that was so gentle, so trustworthy. She wanted to trust that voice, to believe that everything really was okay.

Strong fingers moved down the back of her neck. "Does this hurt at all?"

She tried to shake her head and the hands immediately locked into place, holding her head still with unexpected strength. "No, don't do that. Tell me. Can you talk?"

"I can talk," she said. Her mouth was full of sand and more got in when she opened it.

"Good, good." That voice made speaking sound like a great accomplishment. "You're doing good. Tell me if anything hurts."

"My knee hurts like the devil."

A deep, sympathetic noise. "We'll get there in a minute. Can you wiggle your fingers?" Marguerite wiggled them obediently. "Good girl. Does your head hurt?" He slid his hands across her skull. "Any sore spots?"

"There."

He fell silent, fingers gently working over the soreness. "Nothing soft," he said after a moment. "Nothing bleeding. Can you focus your eyes?"

He's a healer. Of course. I should have realized before. That was the kind of voice it was. Calm and kind and absolutely in control of the situation. Marguerite could recognize it now, but that didn't stop her from enjoying it. There was a nagging familiarity to it, though. Had they met before? And where were the paladins when she was lying injured on the dirt with a strange man poking her head?

"I can focus just fine," she said. "There's a pebble in front of me shaped vaguely like a goat. I can't say it's terribly interesting. Can I move yet?" She hadn't slept on her stomach since she was thirteen and her breasts were squashed in uncomfortable ways.

"Just a little longer. You're doing very well." She felt his thumbs settle on either side of her spine, moving lower. His forearm brushed her back. There was nothing remotely sexual about his touch, but Marguerite was incredibly aware of his presence. *Those hands...and that* voice. *Damn. He's got to be taken. Men who sound like that never stay on the market for long.*

She really wanted to see his face. Maybe she'd be lucky and he'd have a face like a frog's ass and the other women in his life had all been terribly shallow and she could sweep in and prove to him that looks were all a matter of attitude anyway and what mattered was who you were on the inside and...*dammit all, we're on a deadline, we have to go save the world's economy, I don't have time for dallying along the way. Crap.*

"I don't feel any breaks," he said after a moment. He took her left arm and stretched it out. "Does this hurt?"

"Angle's a little awkward, but no."

Wren's voice intruded. "Foster caught the horse," she said, from somewhere over Marguerite's head. "Is she okay?"

"She's doing fine," said the healer.

"Hi, Wren," said Marguerite. "I fell off my horse."

"Yes, I saw. It was pretty spectacular. You did an amazing shoulder roll."

"Did I?"

"Does this hurt?" Her left leg this time, though he wasn't rubbing his hands over it the way he had her neck. *Damn.*

"Nope."

"Yeah, it was really impressive," Wren said.

"I bet. Is everyone else okay?"

"Oh, yeah, fine. You just got unlucky. The drover's very sorry."

"Does this hurt?" Right leg. He was coming up on the right side now. She rolled her eyes down to see if she could get a look at him, but the angle was still bad. Then he hit a sore spot and she hissed.

"Easy, easy..." He rolled up her trouser leg and those strong hands settled on her calf. "Here?"

"That's the spot."

He worked his way along the shin. Marguerite had not previously considered the erotic qualities of the human shin. *Okay, yeah, that's definitely the adrenaline. Nobody's* that *into shins. Maybe I can convince him to check a bit higher.*

"No breaks that I can feel. You may have a bruise there."

"How's my horse?"

Wren shrugged. "Still a horse? I dunno. Foster says she's fine too."

"Oh, good." *And where exactly is Shane in all of this? Giving that dog a very stern look?*

"I'm going to lift you up," the healer said. "Tell me immediately if anything hurts, or if anything goes numb." He got his hands under her armpits and picked her up. She helped as much as she could and found herself sitting upright with her back against his chest as he knelt behind her. "There you go," he said. She could feel that voice rumbling against her back, a very agreeable sensation. "How is your head?"

"Sore, but I think I'm fine." She looked ruefully at Wren. "Now where did Shane get off to? He's supposed to be my damn bodyguard."

Wren's eyebrows shot up. The healer went very still.

Did I just put my foot in it?

"Errr..." said the healer. His voice was suddenly a little less deep and much less soothing. It sounded apologetic. More than that, it sounded *familiar.*

Fighting a sudden sinking realization, Marguerite wriggled around to see the man's face.

One arm still around her shoulders, close enough to bite or kiss, Shane looked down into her eyes.

"Well," said Marguerite. "This is awkward." She got hastily to her feet, slapping dirt off her backside. "I...ah...didn't realize it was you."

Shane inclined his head and said nothing, but his jaw was drawn so tight that she wondered if he was in pain.

"Must have still been a little dazed from the fall." She swallowed, looking down at him. He was so tall and she was so short that the difference in their heights was actually rather less when he was kneeling. "I apologize. I shouldn't have implied you were shirking your duties."

"No," said Shane. "No, you are correct. It is my place to keep you from harm, and I have already failed."

Wren winced. Marguerite's sinking feeling intensified. *Oh god, only the third day on the road and I've already set off the paladin's self-loathing.* "What could you possibly have done? Leapt off your horse to break my fall? And I didn't come to harm, so it's fine."

He rose to his feet. "I can only assure you that I will do everything in my power to keep it from happening again."

"But this wasn't really *within* your power."

He turned away. Foster was holding the reins of her horse, looking as embarrassed as Marguerite felt. Wren looked from one to the other and sank her teeth into her lower lip.

"Welp, I'm an ass," Marguerite said out loud, to no one in particular.

"You'd just been hit on the head," said Wren. "I don't think you can blame yourself for that."

"If he's going to blame himself for a dog spooking a cow, I get to blame myself for this."

Wren snorted. Marguerite watched Shane take her mare's reins and lead her back. *How the hell did he do that anyway? He sounded like a different person! He sounded like...like...*

Damn it all.

The paladin always sounded so diffident. He prefaced things with apologies, if he spoke at all. She couldn't believe that low, soothing, trustworthy voice came from the same man.

And then, like a bolt from the blue, she remembered Beartongue saying, "He can do the voice really well."

Was that *the voice? Is that what she meant? Gods above and below. If Grace could bottle that, we could make a fortune.*

Shane brought the mare to her and dropped to one knee in front of her. Marguerite bit back a curse. *If he's going to go all knightly at me, this is going to be a really long trip.* Then she saw that his hands were clasped to make a stirrup.

"Oh," she said. "Thanks. It's hard without a mounting block." Shane nodded, staring at the ground. When she stepped into his hand, he didn't yield an inch.

He's either angry at me or at himself or both of us. Damn, damn, damn. You were wrong, Grace, I may not be able to charm this one after all.

When Marguerite had fallen from the saddle, time had slowed to a crawl. Shane had seen her fall, known that he could not possibly reach her in time, and everything had gone silent, except for the little voice that said, *Failed already. It was only a matter of time, but this was quick even for you. You might as well just have kicked her down the stairs on the first day and saved everyone the ride back.*

He was on the ground and throwing the reins to Foster before she had even stopped rolling. When he went to his knees beside her and saw that she was still breathing, it felt as if his heart had started beating again. Had he been granted a reprieve?

Oh good, a longer ride back for everyone when you inevitably fail to protect her. Do you think you can hit the exact midpoint of the journey next time?

He'd touched her then. He hadn't meant anything by it, truly, beyond the fear that she had broken her neck. He'd used the paladin's voice, because if she had injured herself, any sudden movement could make it worse. He'd seen it before, in the temple. Demons did not understand the fragility of human spines, and after one was exorcised, sometimes they left such injuries behind.

Fortunately the voice was the one thing that still came easily to him. You reached down into some deep internal well, and out it came, the voice of a brother, a confidant, a reliable friend. A voice that anyone would trust. You needed to project authority but also kindness. When a civilian staggered up to you, hollow-eyed and exhausted, and gasped out that there were demons in the fields, that was the voice that they needed to hear.

It was not until he was sliding his hands up Marguerite's thigh that the reality of the situation had struck him suddenly, that she was lying there and he had his hands on her body in a position of incredible intimacy.

He fought it down at once. It was unworthy to even think such a thing, and certainly unworthy to notice the muscle of her legs, or to think of how those legs might feel wrapped around his waist, or—

The direction of his own thoughts shocked him. He would have sworn that he had left such thoughts behind. But even now, an hour later, riding close beside her, he could not keep his thoughts from drifting back.

No matter how strong he was, lust was always waiting in the wings, watching for a moment of weakness. It was why the paladins of the Dreaming God tended to be promiscuous. A demon could hardly tempt you with something that you were freely and frequently given.

But you are not a paladin of the Dreaming God, and never were. You are a failure and she was injured and all you can think of now is the feel of her flesh under your fingers. That is revolting and you should be ashamed.

No, even more ashamed than that.

Shane wondered if there was a term for feeling guilty about not feeling sufficiently guilty. It seemed like a useful word to have. If he was still at the Temple, he would have asked one of the scholars. Not that knowing the name would help much.

Perhaps there would be a temple in the town they stayed at tonight. Somewhere that he could pray alone, surrounded by holiness.

Even a little roadside shrine would serve in a pinch. *Do penance. Clear my head.*

Rub one out somewhere in private, feel guilty, and do even more penance.

God, Beartongue was right, he *was* predictable.

His horse was crowding Marguerite's mare. She gave him an annoyed glance and drew her mount further out of the way. Shane reined his back a little, fighting back the urge to close the gap. He had been given a reprieve, however unearned. He had a second chance not to fail, if he could just keep her safe.

Assuming that she doesn't decide to send you back as soon as we stop for the night, both for failing to protect her, and then for running your hands over her like that.

There is no chance that I will be that lucky.

His punishment was to continue on and to try desperately to avert the inevitable, while the voice in his head sang like the chorus of an ancient tragedy, predicting ruin.

Perhaps it was no more than he deserved.

CHAPTER 8

Shane insisted on going ahead of them into the bedroom that night, presumably to check for assassins hiding under the bed. Given that the fashion in this part of the world was for very low beds, they would have to be remarkably flat assassins, but he checked anyway. Marguerite and Wren exchanged looks behind his back. *And I thought* I *was becoming paranoid.*

"Clear," he said, very seriously, stepping back.

Marguerite bit back a sarcastic remark. *Flat assassins, who somehow knew which inn we'd be stopping at, and which room I would take... No. Be good. You already put your foot in it once today. If it makes the man feel better, there's no harm in it.*

"I will accompany you downstairs," he informed them.

"I don't think we're going to be attacked on the stairs, brother," Wren said.

Shane grunted. Marguerite's growing glossary of Shane Grunts translated this one as "You may be correct, but I am not altering my behavior." She stifled a sigh. *I brought this on myself. If I had realized who was talking to me...*

Yes, but how on earth was I supposed to know that he *could sound like* that?

She waited until the door had shut and then turned to Wren. "What on earth was *that?*"

"Shane takes his duty very seriously. I don't think he ever got over being left at the altar by his first god. And then later, when the Saint died—"

"No, no." Marguerite waved her arms. "I meant when he was picking me up. The way he *sounded.*"

"Oh, *that.*" Wren grinned, no longer so serious. "That was the voice. Shane's really good at it."

"Beartongue warned me, but I had no idea. Is that magic?"

Wren considered this. "Not exactly? I think it's more like the black tide. The berserker fits, I mean." She gestured to herself. "Anybody can learn to fight, and some people go berserk, but only some people go berserk for a god. But now that the Saint is dead, we all still go berserk, unfortunately." One corner of her mouth crooked up. "Well, not me that often. Some of us are closer to the edge than others."

Marguerite filed that away as interesting information for later, but at the moment she had other fish to fry. "So a divine gift of sorts?"

"Right. Except you have to have a certain amount of potential to do the voice in the first place." Wren cocked her head and then said, in a kind, sympathetic voice, "I hope that it didn't upset you. He would never have intended to cause you harm."

It was the voice of a friend, the one who held you when you cried because you'd spotted your lover with another woman, the one who picked you up when everything was broken past all mending. "Not really," said Marguerite, "it was just a surprise, and then I felt bad because... *hey!*"

Wren burst out laughing. "That's the best I can do. I'm not in Shane's league, or even Istvhan's. It works a lot better when you sound like an authority figure, and I'm no good at that."

Marguerite suddenly remembered hearing Stephen talk to a young would-be assassin, a few years and several lifetimes ago. He'd sounded so calm and so trustworthy, but she'd assumed that it was because he *was* genuinely calm and trustworthy.

Sweet Lady of Grass, if I could sound like that, I'd be the greatest spy the world has ever known. People would fight to tell me their secrets. As it is, I just make sympathetic noises and top up the wineglass.

"I don't suppose you can teach me...?"

"Nope." Wren shook her head. "Most of us can do it, but not that well. Galen—have you met Galen? No?—he can't do it at all. He just sounds like himself. But most of the Saint of Steel's people didn't need it anyway. You use it most when you're dealing with civilians. If you find survivors, or if you're trying to get people out of an area where things are about to get really ugly, it helps to have someone who can sound trustworthy explaining the situation instead of just screaming at people to get the hell out."

"Huh." Marguerite considered this. "I can see how it would be useful." She thought back to her interactions with Stephen. He'd always seemed patient and trustworthy. On the other hand, he actually *was* patient and trustworthy, so that might have a lot to do with it. *Most of the paladins are. It's why they're paladins and the rest of us aren't.*

"Anyway, the people who can *really* do the voice are the Dreaming God's people," said Wren. "They have to. It's all tied up with how they compel demons. So since Shane was trained in His temple, he's really good at it." She paused, then gave Marguerite a concerned look. "It's not like mind control. You can't make someone walk off a cliff or anything. Hell, half the time you can't even convince them to move off a battlefield. It's just good at calming people down and making them actually stop and listen to you. And you can't lie in the voice, either."

"You can't?"

Wren shook her head, getting to her feet. "You have to mean what you're saying. Really and truly believe it. That's why it works."

Marguerite abandoned her dream of becoming the world's most persuasive spy. *Ah, well. Easy come, easy go.* "Thanks for explaining. Let's go see if Shane has found any assassins standing between us and dinner, shall we?"

There were no assassins, although Shane was out of his room and planted in front of them the instant their own door opened. "I can bring you up food," he said.

"You can, but I'd rather eat down below," said Marguerite. "We might pick up something worth knowing."

That was definitely a skeptical expression. Marguerite exulted that she was able to read it. Wren elbowed him in the ribs and said, "If you bring us up a tray, somebody might poison it, you know. Or a bird could come through the window and attack us."

"I have confidence that you could dispatch a bird."

"A *rabid* bird."

His lips twitched. "Birds don't get rabies. Are you implying that I'm being overly cautious?"

"Just a tad."

He glanced at Marguerite, who attempted to shrug as diplomatically as possible.

"Very well." Shane bowed his head and led the way downstairs, although she noted that he was still wearing the massive sword across his back. *That can't be comfortable. Though I wonder if he even notices it anymore.*

She discovered on the way down that she was extremely sore. Falling off a horse was no joke when you were over thirty. She limped until Shane stopped at the bottom and looked back up the steps, then stiffened her spine and gritted her teeth.

The inn was half-full of people, a mix of travelers and locals. There was also a paladin in one corner, with his eye swollen shut and his arm in a sling.

"Demon," he said cheerfully, when Marguerite and her two paladins made their way over to him. His good eye traveled over Wren's axe and Shane's sword. "It's in a damn big steer. I took out one of its legs, or thought I had. But you know how they are—they don't understand that a broken bone means you shouldn't use it. So it kicked me with the damn leg that was broken and gave me a broken arm to match. Probably hurt it worse than it hurt me, though that's not much consolation."

Marguerite winced. "Can we buy you dinner?" she asked. You treated demonslayers well as a matter of principle, but it also occurred to her that her own two paladins might appreciate the show of solidarity. *And I certainly don't have to worry about them having been bought.*

The injured paladin grinned at her. His tabard had the closed-eye sigil of the Dreaming God on it, but there seemed to be nothing more to his voice than rueful good humor. "The innkeeper's already taken care of that, but the sympathy of a pretty lady is always appreciated if you'd like to join us for dinner...or dessert." He winked at her.

Marguerite chuckled. "You have all my sympathy, but don't get any ideas. I'm afraid I might hurt you worse than the demon did."

He put his good hand over his heart. "Cut to the quick. Do you see this, Ramsey?"

Ramsey, who was apparently the priest sitting next to him, rolled his eyes heavenward. He was older, his dark, tightly curled hair cropped close and threaded with gray. "Do you see what I have to put up with?"

"Where's the demon now?" asked Shane, who had clearly not stayed in the Dreaming God's temple long enough to understand the fine art of conversational flirtation.

Ramsey signaled for more drinks as the trio pulled up chairs. "Still wandering around the pastures. We've got spotters on it, but we'll have to wait for the temple to send out another paladin."

"Could we be of any assistance?" asked Wren.

"Saint of Steel?" The priest looked from one to the other. "I don't know. Can you fight demons?"

"I was trained in the Dreaming God's temple until my seventeenth year," said Shane quietly. "I cannot speak well in the imperative mode, but I can help to bind."

"I don't know jack shit," said Wren cheerfully, "but I can chop the legs off a bull one at a time if I have to. And we've both helped the Dreaming God's people before."

Marguerite wondered what the hell *speak in the imperative mode* meant, and filed it away to ask about later. *I am acquiring quite a number of things to follow up on when I get the chance.*

The priest shared a glance with the paladin, then smiled across the table at them both. "Then my friends, you may be the answer to my prayers."

CHAPTER 9

"You know, we *do* have the fate of the world's economy resting on our shoulders," said Marguerite, as they got up entirely too early the next morning. She was sore from her fall and she knew that it was probably making her cranky, but she couldn't quite stop.

"I apologize for the delay," said Shane. "Truly." He was armed and armored and gave every appearance of having been awake for hours. Marguerite considered pushing him down the stairs just on principle.

"It's a demon, though," said Wren. "*You* know."

"I know." Marguerite sighed. Apparently one of the things you didn't ask paladins to do was to walk away from situations where they could help. Shane, at least, had asked permission. Wren had just looked at her like a small child who has been promised a day at the fair. *Still, if I didn't give permission, the Dreaming God's people have the authority to deputize damn near anyone in pursuit of an active demon. And I really don't want to start off with my hired muscle resenting me.* "Just don't get killed or grievously injured, I beg of you."

"We'll try to avoid it," said Wren happily.

"Truly, it should be easy enough," said Sir Xavier, the paladin of the Dreaming God. "It's already on three legs. If my sword arm wasn't broken, I could do it without breaking a sweat."

Marguerite hoped it was really that easy. *This is what they do. This is their job. They know how to do this. And I really do not want to go back to*

Beartongue and ask for replacements. If one or both of the paladins died in pursuit of their mission, Marguerite would grieve and move on, but she was hoping to at least reach the Court of Smoke before the bodies began racking up. Losing a paladin before they were even halfway there would look extremely careless. *And I would really prefer to have two at court, thank you very much.*

"Can I watch?" she asked. "I've never seen a demon exorcised before."

Shane frowned. "Certainly not. It's much too dangerous."

"Eh..." Ramsey shrugged. "It's a weak one, so I doubt it can jump unless we kill the steer, and that only with physical contact. I don't object."

An actual expression flicked across Shane's face. This one resembled a scowl. Marguerite suspected that he wanted to argue the point, but wasn't quite willing to go up against a senior member of the Temple. *I should never have implied that he wasn't protecting me well enough. All it did was make things worse.*

Then he bowed his head. "I should not question your judgment, sir. I apologize."

"Don't," said Ramsey. "You're doing exactly what a responsible guardian would. If I hadn't already come up against this one, I wouldn't allow it either."

"Don't fret. I'll stand with her," added Xavier. He winked at her. "Sweet deal for me. I get to stand around with a pretty lady while the youngsters do all the heavy lifting."

"I'm thirty-six," said Shane.

"I'm forty-five. You're a youngster."

Wren, who Marguerite had pegged as being in her late twenties, muttered something. Foster gazed at the ceiling and whistled.

"I'm fifty-seven, so all of you can be quiet," grumbled Ramsey.

They rode out until they reached an area that looked exactly the same as all the other areas to Marguerite, except that there was a fence on the other side of the field.

Behind the fence was a very large cow. *Or steer, I suppose. Not that I imagine it matters much, now that it's a demon.*

It didn't look particularly demonic. It looked injured and exhausted. One of its hind legs dragged and its sides heaved as it breathed. One side of its body seemed larger than the other. Were cows supposed to stick out to the sides like that?

"Bloat," said Wren. "It's going to die soon anyway."

"If we want to bind it with the animal's death, we'll have to do it now, then," said the Dreaming God's paladin. Shane slid off his horse and moved to assist the injured man in dismounting, with the same unobtrusive courtesy that he used on Wren.

They left the mounts in the trees on the far side of the field, out of sight. Foster preferred to stay with the horses. "I've seen a demon," he said laconically. "I don't need to see another one in this life."

The paladin of the Dreaming God stopped well back from the fence, on a slight rise in the ground. "We'll get a better view from here."

"I bow to an expert." Marguerite turned to follow him, but Shane put a gauntleted hand on her shoulder.

He had not touched her since he had helped her up from her fall. She was briefly surprised, and then even more surprised when he gripped her other shoulder as well and leaned down to look her in the eyes.

"Lady Marguerite," he said quietly, and it was the voice again, the healer's voice, and even though she knew what he was doing, it felt like warm water being poured down her spine. Comforting. Trustworthy. *Safe.* She could not remember the last time that another person had made her feel safe.

Ice blue eyes gazed intently into hers. "Lady Marguerite," he said again, "if the demon charges the fence, I want you to run. Run for the horses. If Wren or I am slain, run. Above all else, if any of us begin to act strangely, run. There will be nothing that you can do to help, and you may be in terrible danger. Will you give me your word?"

In other circumstances, she might have felt patronized. Did the man think that she was such a fool that she wouldn't run from a demon? It was the knife in the dark that she feared, not a possessed cow in broad daylight. But there was nothing in his eyes but concern and his voice was so earnest and she remembered Wren saying, *You have to mean it.*

"Yes," she said. "I promise. Are you sure this safe?"

He released her, rubbing his heavy leather gauntlets together. "It is dangerous, but no more so than stopping a mugging in an alley. And I would insist on doing that as well." A rueful smile flashed across his face, so quickly that she half-thought she'd imagined it, and then he stepped back and drew his sword.

"Was that necessary?" Marguerite asked the injured paladin in an undertone.

"It was all good advice," said Sir Xavier. "He's being conscientious." The older man paused, and the humor left his eyes as well. "He's right, though. I'm fairly certain we're safe over here, and I ought to be able to see a demon jump, but if I got it wrong—and especially if *I* start acting bizarre—run like hell and don't look back. Get to the nearest temple and have them send out an army. A demon that can take a paladin is a walking nightmare."

"Has that ever happened?" Marguerite watched as Shane hopped over the fence, drawing his sword. Wren had pulled out her axe and unslung her shield.

"Yes." Xavier's voice was grim. "I knew Lord Caliban, many years ago. He was the best of us, and then a demon grabbed him somehow. He murdered half the temple before the other paladins brought him down."

"My god."

Shane and Wren circled the demon steer. It limped pathetically on three legs, bloated and bedraggled. For a moment, Marguerite wondered if they were simply showing an abundance of caution, and then the thing charged.

It was blindingly fast and it moved completely wrong, throwing its legs forward in a way that no mammal should ever move. Marguerite was reminded of a roach's scuttle. She put her hand to her mouth.

The two paladins dove in opposite directions. It focused on the bigger target. Shane danced backward while Wren buried her axe in the steer's hind leg with the air of a woman chopping wood. The steer screamed in a keening voice that was never meant to come from an herbivore's throat and wheeled around.

Marguerite was already regretting her desire to watch. "This looks very difficult."

Sir Xavier snorted. "This is the easy kind. It's when they get into humans that you're in real trouble."

"How does that happen?"

"Nine times out of ten, it's in an animal and someone kills the host thinking it's rabid," the Dreaming God's paladin explained. "Once the host is dead, they either go back to hell unbound, or if they can they jump to another host. They usually can't jump very far—most can only go by touch—but if the farmer or the hunter comes up to check if that animal is dead..." He sighed.

"What happens the tenth time?"

"The tenth time, they're smart. Maybe they've lived long enough to possess multiple people, learned how to hide that they're there. Then it's a *real* problem."

"Do you have to kill the human host?"

"If we can't save them, yes. Usually we can bind the demon, and then we offer the victim a choice of exorcism or the sword." He kept his eyes on the steer and the paladins dodging it.

Exorcism, Marguerite recalled, involved drowning the victim in cold water. The demon would flee and there was a chance, albeit a slim one, that the victim could be revived. It was not anyone's idea of a pleasant experience, though the priests of the Dreaming God were supposed to be very, very good at it.

"You can't make them jump back out of the victim?" she asked.

"It's not a kindness. Demons are like barbed arrows. If you drag one out, you do...well, a lot of damage."

"How much damage?"

He glanced at her. "Lady Marguerite?"

"Yes?"

"If the situation arises? Choose the sword before that."

"Noted," she said. Sir Xavier went back to watching the Saint of Steel's paladins. Wren's attack on the hind legs had been successful. The demon was dragging its back half behind it now, lurching and writhing like a broken-backed snake.

"So you send them back to hell, then," said Marguerite, disgusted but not daring to look away in case something happened to her companions.

"Yes, but we bind them first. You have to get up close for that, which is why we don't just shoot them with crossbows. Once they're bound, the demons don't come back. If they're not bound, though, they keep trying to come back from hell."

"I wonder why."

The paladin's expression was wry. "It's hell. Wouldn't you try to get out?"

"Fair enough."

Shane approached the fallen demon, holding his sword upright before him. It was a strange, ritualistic pose, not at all like the one he'd had before. The steer screamed again, louder, a scream that seemed to have words in it. Marguerite jumped, startled, and the paladin of the Dreaming God put out a hand to steady her. "It's all right," he said. "It's nearly done."

Shane bowed his head and spoke.

She could not quite catch the words, but her ears popped and the demon went to its knees as if its strings had been cut. Shane stepped back.

"Oh, very nicely done," murmured the Dreaming God's paladin, almost to himself. Ramsey the priest clambered over the fence and approached the demon. "I'm surprised the god let that boy go."

Marguerite would have asked about that—from what she'd heard, there was no letting go and a lot more never-having-chosen-in-the-first-place—but Ramsey walked forward. The steer began to flail on the ground, but it could not seem to push itself up again. Ramsey uttered another sharp phrase and Marguerite's ears popped again, harder, and the steer froze, then began to speak.

"Yaahaa n'gaaaah kalaak kalaak nhai!"

Its voice sounded like rotting meat smelled. She wanted to spit to get the taste out of her mouth, except that it was in her ears. She wanted to run and keep running, to get away from that thing and that voice and a world where such things were allowed to exist.

The priest set his palm on the steer's broad forehead. Her nerves screamed in alarm, even knowing that the priest was an expert and wouldn't have done it if it wasn't safe.

Ramsey spoke quietly. She could not make out the words. Shane stood to one side, his sword still held before him, showing no sign of strain.

The demon's voice cut off as if a door had been slammed, and it lowered its horned head even further, until its muzzle touched the earth. Ramsey stepped back and nodded to Shane.

The paladin lifted the sword high overhead and brought it down in a sweeping overhand strike. Marguerite looked away before it landed. She was no stranger to death, but she preferred not to watch it closely.

When she turned back, the steer had been separated from its head and blood was soaking into the thirsty ground. Ramsey went to Shane, reached up, and caught his head. He pulled the paladin's face down until it was only a few inches from his. Marguerite wondered if the priest was about to kiss him. *Seems a trifle odd, but then again, demonslaying is clearly very complicated.*

Ramsey did not kiss him. Instead he stared into the other man's eyes for a long moment, then nodded and released him. He went to Wren and performed the same gesture, though he had to bend down to do it.

"Checking to make sure the demon hasn't jumped," Sir Xavier said. "If I may, madam?"

"Go ahead," said Marguerite, torn between horror and amusement. "You can tell by the eyes?"

"On a demon like this, we'd probably notice because you were screaming in tongues," he said. "But we check anyway." He leaned forward, gazing deeply into her eyes. "Oh, dear..."

"What?"

"I fear that you have remarkably lovely eyes."

She snorted. "How unchivalrous of you, sir. You're injured, so I can't smack you for that."

He grinned, clearly unrepentant. Ramsey approached, clambered over the fence, and checked his partner's eyes. "This man is a shameless flirt," Marguerite informed the priest.

"Dreadful, I know. If he's bothering you, tell me, and I'll inform the nuns when we return to the temple."

"Oh god, not the nuns!" Sir Xavier put his good arm over his face. "I shall be as humble and silent as a novice. Anything but nuns."

Wren and Shane joined them. Ramsey cocked an eye approvingly at them. "That was good work, you two."

"And you said you couldn't use the imperative mode," said Xavier, slapping Shane on the back with his good hand. Shane didn't quite stagger, but it was clearly a near thing.

"I can't," he said. "Not truly."

"It knelt, didn't it?"

"But it tried immediately to get back up again." Shane shook his head. "A few seconds, that's all."

"Sometimes a few seconds is enough."

Shane sighed. "My heart is not pure enough," he said simply. "The god was right not to choose me."

Ramsey and the Dreaming God's paladin exchanged a look.

Not pure enough? If Shane's *not pure enough, how do the regular paladins even function?*

Apparently Sir Xavier agreed with her, because she heard him mutter, "You're a damn sight more pure of heart than I am, youngster," not entirely under his breath.

"All right," said Ramsey, shaking his head. "We've kept you long enough, friends. We'll see you back to the river, though."

They collected the horses, although Wren looked at hers as if she would prefer fighting possessed livestock to mounting again. Marguerite glanced at the position of the sun, decided that they hadn't lost a significant amount of time, and tapped the reins across her mount's neck. "All right. Let's get a move on, before we trip over another part of the world that needs saving."

CHAPTER 10

Foster took the horses and bid them a good journey, then rode away, whistling tunelessly between his teeth. Marguerite, Shane, and Wren waited by the dock for their ride upriver to finish loading supplies. Shane was still keyed up from the fight with the demon, but he suspected that the adrenaline would wear off soon.

They had done well. Even the little voice nagging him that he should have been able to make the demon kneel longer couldn't quite drown that out. There was one less demon in the world, and that was an unalloyed good thing.

Yes, but it certainly doesn't make up for all the terrible—

Shut up, Shane told it wearily. *I promise I won't develop any self-confidence while your back is turned.*

"A word in your ear, before you go," said Ramsey. The priest and the paladin had accompanied them to the dock, leading their own horses. "Might not be useful, but then again, it might."

"I'd never turn down a good word," said Marguerite, pushing herself up onto a crate. Her legs dangled girlishly, but no one would ever mistake her for anything but a grown woman. Her shirt was modestly cut, but *modest* in her case still revealed a significant expanse of flesh. Shane averted his eyes. He had found a shrine in the town to the Four-Faced God, and offered up prayers last night, but he had not been comfortable leaving his companions for long. Wren was more than capable of standing up to most threats, but if she had to face them alone, the guilt would have eaten him alive.

Vigil on my knees at the next available opportunity. Whenever that may be.

"I don't know where you're going, other than upriver," said the priest. "And I don't want to know. I'm not asking, and I'd rather you didn't tell me. I smell secrecy on all three of you."

Shane glanced back at Marguerite, who smiled guilelessly. "Secrecy? I don't know what you mean."

"Of course you don't," said Ramsey.

For some reason, her response disappointed Shane. It would have cost nothing to admit that they were traveling with a purpose in mind, but she was lying to a priest out of...what? Out of reflex? *What a terrible reflex to have—No. No, you are on a clandestine mission, and she is in command. And she knows more of this than you do. You have no right to judge.*

"But if you happened to be going into the highlands to the north," said the priest, "which, the Dreaming God keep you, you will not, be warned." His eyes caught Shane's. "There are rumors of a demon out there with human accomplices. An old and subtle one."

Shane's blood ran cold. Most demons were young and stupid and did not know how the world worked. You could spot them easily. They moved wrong, they spoke in demonic tongues, they had a tendency to levitate. They did not understand hunger, so they ate dirt and stones, and they did not understand pain, so they broke their own limbs and barely noticed. But the ones that lived long enough to learn better, the smart ones, the old ones...those became much harder to spot. And if a human worked with one willingly...well. They could see a paladin coming from a mile off and sink into their human host, hiding behind human eyes. Those were the temple's worst nightmare.

"What sort of rumors?" he asked, through dry lips.

"The kind that get through when a demon's too smart to leave an obvious trail." Sir Xavier rubbed absently at his injured arm. "It's not doing anything obvious. No grisly murders. No unholy miracles. Lots of little cults pop up in the wilds, whenever someone charismatic enough comes along and promises people a better life following orders. We don't assume all of them are demons."

"But you think this might be?" asked Marguerite.

"A view not shared by my superiors." Ramsey grimaced. "The Temple says we don't have enough evidence to go haring off into the wilds looking. We're spread too thin already. Ever since whatever was keeping demons free of Anuket City stopped working, they've been coming through fast and furious. And we don't have your brethren to call on any more—sorry, you two—so it's all the Forge God's people now, and most of their smiths aren't warriors."

Shane bowed his head. It was an old, old pain, long scarred over, but like many old wounds, it still ached, even though he knew that Ramsey's comments weren't directed at him. In another life, where he had been worthy of the Dreaming God, he would have been in Anuket City himself, binding demons before they could do harm.

"Keep an eye out," said Ramsey. "It may be nothing. I hope to the God it's nothing. But if you find yourself out that way..." He trailed off.

"And now we should take our leave," said Sir Xavier. "Since I believe that they are about to begin loading your trunks, and my arm won't let me assist with that." He saluted Shane and Wren, then bowed over Marguerite's hand and kissed each knuckle with maximum dramatic effect.

"Get on with you, you shameless reprobate," she laughed, swatting at him. "Ramsey, keep him out of trouble."

"Set me an impossible job, why don't you," muttered the priest. He signed a blessing in their direction, waved, and scurried off after his partner.

And in that other life, I would be the one kissing her. And perhaps thinking no more of it than either of them did. The thought sank Shane's spirits even lower. He picked up Marguerite's trunk of perfume samples and followed the two women to the end of the dock, where the captain of their barge was waiting. She was an older woman with a mouth full of gold teeth and a grandson who looked capable of picking up the entire barge and carrying it to the Court of Smoke. "Well, don't tha stand there gawping," she said to the grandson in question. "Take tha trunks and put them in the cabin, afore I box tha's ears."

"Yes, gran," mumbled the bear-sized young man. He picked a trunk up under each arm and carried it off. When he came back for the others, Marguerite had already stepped aboard, and the adolescent colossus stopped dead, staring at her chest.

Shane swung his own trunk with rather more force than was

required, and the youngster caught it with a surprised grunt, but didn't drop it. He tore his gaze away from Marguerite, turning dull red, and hastened to stow the remainder of the luggage.

"You alright?" asked Wren, joining him at the railing.

"Fine," said Shane, through gritted teeth. "Why?"

"You're growling."

Vigil might not be enough. Perhaps he could find a hairshirt somewhere, or engage in some hearty self-flagellation. (*Careful with that,* his friend Istvhan used to say. *Flagellate yourself too often, you'll go blind.)*

"Wren?"

"Hmm?"

"Is there a word for feeling guilty that you don't feel guilty enough?"

"Sure," said Wren. "It's called *pathology.*"

Marguerite went down to her knees to enter the low cabin.

"You're still growling," said Wren. "Do you have something in your throat?"

"I'm fine." He cleared his throat and fixed his eyes on the surface of the river. "I don't suppose you packed a hairshirt?"

"I don't think they wear those at court. At least, not unless fashions have *really* changed." She nudged him with her elbow. "Cheer up. We got the demon *and* we didn't miss the boat."

Shane summoned a smile for her benefit. Wren looked at it, shook her head sadly, and left him to his thoughts.

Marguerite was in a sour mood and was finding it hard to shake. Normally her disposition tended toward the sunny, if sardonic, but today she felt off-kilter.

The demon had been unsettling. She'd known they existed, of course, but there was something about actually seeing one, and realizing that no amount of cleverness and negotiation would get rid of the thing. *Oof. At least there's a chance, however small, of buying off an assassin.* She'd done so once, last year, although it had been a very near thing and she'd had to threaten to throw herself and her coin purse off a bridge in the process. *If I can't talk my way out of something, I'm in a world of hurt.*

It didn't help that it was a gray, gloomy day on the water, or that

Shane, who was capable of one of the sexiest voices she'd ever heard, was now communicating almost entirely in grunts.

"This is the last slow leg of the trip," she said, as the team of mules on the shore plodded along and the boat moved slowly upstream.

"Mmmph," Shane said.

"The food will be better once we get there."

"Mmmph."

"Then I thought perhaps we'd bronze one of the donkeys as a souvenir."

"Mmmph."

She gave up. She slept that night in one of the two small cabins, Wren alongside her. Shane slept on the deck, outside the cabin door, as if amphibious assassins might really swarm the barge during the night. The irony wasn't lost on her, given that for once, she *wasn't* worried about the Sail coming after her. There was simply nowhere on the barge for them to hide.

When she got up, Shane was already awake. He nodded to her as she emerged and then left without a word.

Is something wrong? Is it my breath?

He returned a few minutes later, carrying a steaming mug of tea, which he handed to her as formally as a knight presenting his sword to a king.

"Oh! Thank you."

He nodded and returned to the railing. *Well, at least he didn't grunt. And he's trying to be considerate. And at least he doesn't* loom *the way that Stephen always did.* She had to give Shane credit: he was, for a large armored man, remarkably unobtrusive. Beartongue's influence, perhaps. Presumably formal audiences were less awkward if all eyes weren't riveted on the big guy with the sword standing behind the bishop.

Still if I don't find a way to get him talking in actual words soon, I may push him into the water and tell Beartongue a catfish got him.

She joined him at the railing. "So what do you do for fun?"

"Fun?" he said, his eyes darting toward her as if expecting a trap.

"Fun. Pleasure. Not for work. Hobbies."

"I know what the word means."

Marguerite had her doubts about that, but waited.

He was silent for so long that she thought maybe he simply wasn't going to answer, then finally he cleared his throat and said, "I walk."

Marguerite wasn't quite sure whether walking counted as a hobby, but was willing to chance it. "Walk where?"

"Around the city. Sometimes across the river."

She nodded. "There's some pretty countryside over there."

"Yes." And then, after an even longer moment, "I read."

"That's good." *Dear sweet Rat, I might actually be getting somewhere.* "I like dramatic poetry, myself."

He glanced at her again. "Have you read Erneste's *Idylls of Summer?*"

"I have, actually." She was a little surprised. *Idylls of Summer* had been quite popular the last few months, featuring lost loves, traumatic misunderstandings, and an inevitable deathbed redemption. "I thought it was well written, but soppy."

Shane accepted this judgment somberly. She wondered too late if she'd mortally offended him. *Is a man who chops up demons devouring literature where the improbably virtuous maiden dies of despair because she has been spurned by the boy she loved?* "Did you enjoy it?" she asked.

He grunted.

Oh, lovely. You finally got him talking and you immediately insult his taste in reading material. She hurried to salvage matters. "I really liked the sequence where they explore the caverns, though. I could have read a hundred pages of that alone."

"Yes!" Shane turned toward her, face suddenly animated. "The descriptions of the mushrooms, with the glowing insects living in the gills? And the echo creatures?"

"Those were lovely." *Good heavens. He makes a fine-looking wall, but when he's interested in something, he's practically incandescent.* She tried to remember anything else that she knew about recent novels. "Has Erneste written anything else?"

Shane shook his head. "Not under that name. The poet prefers to remain anonymous."

"Hmm. Someone must know who it is. I wonder if I could poke around the publisher and find out."

Indecision crossed his face. "I am torn between intrigue and a desire to respect their privacy," the paladin admitted.

"Ah," said Marguerite lightly. "A commendable virtue. Not one I possess, mind you, but I admire it in others." She winked and left him at the railing, feeling as if she had scored a minor victory.

That didn't go too badly. Now, is there something else we can do to keep him from brooding at the railing for the rest of the trip?

Inspiration struck a few hours later, as she heard Wren chatting with the barge owner in Harshek, a language she was only somewhat familiar with. *Language. Yes.* She rounded up the pair of paladins. "Do either of you speak Dailian?"

"I do," said Wren, in that language, "although my accent is the worst kind of country bumpkin."

Marguerite laughed delightedly. "Where on earth did you learn to talk like that?"

"Growing up, believe it or not. Dailian is what we speak where we live, although it's so far from what they speak in the cities that it's practically a different language. They're very clipped, and we drag our vowels out into next week."

"But that's wonderful! We want people to think you're a minor rural noble, and you sound *perfect.*"

"My humiliation is the Rat's gain," said Wren.

"Bah. None of them will know the real you. You're playing a role, like an actress. Everyone will think you are harmless and dismiss you and that means they won't guard their tongues around you." Marguerite glanced at Shane. "And you?"

He frowned. "I speak...little," he said haltingly. "Speech is taught...in Temple. I listen more than speak."

Marguerite nodded and switched back to the common tongue of Archenhold. "Most people at the Court of Smoke won't actually use it. The higher nobles have taken to it as an affectation lately, claiming it's a more civilized tongue. Might be useful on the job."

"So what is this job actually going to entail?" said Wren. "Daring midnight raids? Blackmail? Torturing the secrets out of someone?"

"We are paladins. We do *not* torture secrets out of people," said Shane sternly.

Marguerite snorted. "I think you have the wrong sort of idea about what I do. I'm not some kind of military infiltrator. I just talk to people and listen to what they say and pay attention to things. Very rarely am I..."

oh...stealing the invasion plans off someone's desk in the middle of the night, say."

"But you have done that?" asked Shane, with the faintest lift of one pale eyebrow.

She chuckled. "Stolen something off a desk? Once or twice, I suppose. Never for an actual invasion, though."

"So you're just *listening* to people?" asked Wren. "That's *it?*"

"Sorry to disappoint."

"Ughhh, fine. Can we still blackmail people?"

Disapproval radiated off Shane so strongly that it was practically visible, like heat haze. Marguerite stifled sudden annoyance. *You used to chop people to pieces for a living. What gives you the right to disapprove?*

"If I have to blackmail someone, I certainly will," she said, hoping perversely that would annoy him. Judging by the lines around his eyes, she succeeded. "The real problem is figuring out *who.* So we'll go to court and listen to a lot of people and hopefully someone will casually drop who Magnus's patron is."

"And then?" asked Wren. "Do we blackmail *them?*"

The disapproving silence from Shane's direction got even louder.

"Well, then it gets trickier. I'll talk to them and perhaps we'll get lucky and they'll casually drop where Magnus is hiding over a cup of tea. Or perhaps they won't, and then yes, anything's on the table. But it all starts with just listening."

"Ugh," muttered Wren. "I had no idea being a spy would be so *boring.*"

Marguerite laughed. "Yes, and I have to pretend to be interested, that's the worst of it. But ninety percent of the job is just learning who to talk to, sifting through gossip, and putting it together in useful ways. For example...oh...we once had a tailor who was bragging that he'd found an incredible new designer and that he was going to be the hottest thing next season. He wouldn't say a word about what the designs were like, just that they were amazing. And he was smart enough not to leave the designs where a cracksman could get to them. So I went in and talked to the people who lived along the same street as his warehouse, and they all wanted to complain about the traffic coming and going. Watching the street got me the name of the people shipping the materials to the warehouse, and some chatting with a driver at a bar told me that they were delivering lace. There are only so many sources of lace in large quantities, so I simply strolled into a clerk's office and asked what their current price was. The third one told me that a buyer had locked up their supply, and when I dropped the tailor's name, they confirmed it. That was enough for my employer. They cornered the market on lace in advance of the season, and when the designs hit big, they made a fortune."

Shane's grunt was definitely disapproving. Marguerite rolled her eyes. "Look, most of the time we're dealing with merchants, not the fate of the world. I prefer it that way."

"But people kill for it nonetheless," said Shane quietly.

"Yes. Often. The amounts of money involved are extraordinary."

"For *lace.*"

Marguerite shrugged. "Or salt. Or food. Or iron. Lace may seem frivolous to you, but to the people making or losing a fortune, it's deadly serious."

Shane grunted again. After a moment he asked, "Will there be others attempting to stop you?"

"There will be agents of the Red Sail there, yes," said Marguerite. "And I'll be listening to them. And they'll be listening to me." She felt her lips twist. "If we're lucky, they'll drop something and we'll figure out what it means before they do. If not...well, we'll see. And there are likely to be other operatives around as well, pursuing their own lines of inquiry, and if they learn something interesting, they may be willing to share it. That's the difficulty of keeping an operation completely quiet. Someone might go to the Sail rather than me because they don't know that I want the information. So one has to weigh how much that they want to make known."

"Could the Sail be dangerous?" rumbled Shane.

"Yes, but that's why I have a bodyguard."

She expected another grunt, but he nodded instead. After a moment he asked, "When you say 'anything is on the table,' what do you mean?"

And here is where you crawl into your armored shell and disapprove at me for the rest of the day, my boy. She lifted one shoulder in a nonchalant shrug. "Bedding, blackmail, breaking and entering...whatever it takes to acquire the information."

She'd definitely startled him that time. *Probably the* bedding *part. As if it's somehow less moral to sleep with another adult than to chop them to little bits.*

Marguerite was determined not to let any of that show on her face. She turned away from the railing. "It's probably worth practicing Dailian as much as we can in the meantime. Now I'm going to go see what we've got in the way of lunch."

CHAPTER 11

The trip upriver was uneventful. Shane was torn between the knowledge that it was much better to have a boring trip than an exciting one, and the fact that at least an attack by river pirates would have given him something to think about other than Marguerite, his own failings, and possible demonic cultists, in that order.

Mind you, any river pirates on this river would have to get in line. Literally.

All the barges going upriver used animals on the river bank to haul, and that made passing each other an extremely delicate proposition. There were designated crossover spots every few miles, but Shane still wasn't sure how they did it without getting everything hopelessly tangled. At night, all the barges would tie up in a line along the bank, the animals would be unharnessed and rubbed down, and gossip and supplies would be swapped between the crews. Shane was pleased to see that their captain was as taciturn with other boat crews as she was with her passengers.

Of course, Marguerite must have chosen this barge specifically for that fact. She knows what she's doing.

Which had him thinking about Marguerite again. *Bedding, blackmail, or breaking and entering.*

The way her lips had formed the word *bedding* was going to haunt his dreams. He tried very hard to focus on the other two.

As a former paladin and, somewhere under all that, a knight, he knew he should object to blackmail and burglary on a moral level. But he also knew that Beartongue had undoubtedly blackmailed many people in a good cause, so it wasn't as if he could claim innocence. And Beartongue had sent him on this mission and told him to use his best judgment.

He blew out a long breath and stared over the river. The sun was hot but the breeze off the river was cold, which meant that his lower half was chilly and his shoulders and the back of his neck were uncomfortably warm.

The difference, of course, was that Beartongue had an entire temple of people to protect her if things backfired. *And it's not as if she's doing the breaking and entering herself, either.* Marguerite had him and Wren. As soon as Marguerite had mentioned blackmail, his mind had filled with visions of dangerous men willing to kill to protect their secrets. Noblemen who can afford guards, troops, even assassins. *How many can I stop? Particularly in a place that I do not know, surrounded by people I cannot trust?*

You will fail, whispered the chorus in his mind. *You can do nothing else. And when you fail, it will all be down to Wren, and Wren has never learned to back down, and so your failure will likely doom you both.*

He turned to look back across the barge, shading his eyes from the sun. Wren was doing weapon drills, the light glinting off her axe blades. Axes that she could hardly carry with her, in her guise as a noblewoman.

Marguerite was sitting cross-legged by the low cabin, working on altering one of the dresses that the Rat had sent with them for Wren. "I can't do much about the fashion," she'd said earlier, "but there's no reason you can't have a decent fit."

Well, Shane thought dryly, *that's covered dwelling on Marguerite and your own failure. Would you like to worry about the demonic cultists some now?*

That, at least, was unlikely to affect him directly, though he would definitely mention it to Beartongue when they returned. Perhaps she could send someone to investigate who had a chance of learning more. The Dreaming God's people were not known for the subtlety of their approach. *Someone probably rode in wearing a white cloak and shouted,*

"Hey! Anyone seen any levitating cows around here?" No wonder they can't get good information.

(Granted, Shane's method would have been to walk in wearing a gray cloak and shout "Excuse me, have you heard of any strange cults around here?" but at least he was aware of it.)

Marguerite leaned back and stretched, which did impressive things to her torso, then grimaced. "These beds aren't my favorite," she said. "At least it's our last night on the river."

Shane considered this, and what he knew of Marguerite's fears. "Does it...ah...bother you?" he asked. "That we will be going to a place that you know holds those that hunt you?"

She snorted. "I'm not exactly being hunted. I almost wish I was."

His eyebrows went up at that, and Marguerite's lips twisted in a rueful smile. "If someone was actually hunting for me, I'd know exactly what to do. I could hire a dozen armed guards and sit in a fortified room and wait for them to come for me. But that's not what's happening. I'm an afterthought. A target of opportunity. Frankly, it's maddening."

"Because you don't know who to trust?"

"I get around that by not trusting anyone." She gave him a wicked grin when she said it, and Shane had no idea if she was joking or not. "No, being an afterthought means that if someone tries to kill me, I don't know if they're going to try again, or if it was just some operative passing through and going, 'Oh, hmm, I remember her, someone deal with that,' as they head out of town. I am just important enough to send some hired thugs after, if they're standing around anyway, but not significant enough to warrant a skilled assassin. Except that every now and again, I run into a member of the Sail who is bloody-minded enough that they get annoyed when I don't agree to die quietly, and then I have to run for it, without knowing whether they'll pursue me, or whether it's enough that I've left town."

"Ah. So if you did hire armed guards and sit in a fortified room..."

"They'd sit around and play cards until I ran out of money and nothing would happen. And then a week later I'd spend the night at a posting inn and someone would come in for five minutes to change horses and spot me at the bar and one of their grooms would come through the window that night and try to strangle me." Judging by her expression, this was not a purely hypothetical scenario. "Fortunately, in the Court, I know the rules, and so do they. I don't know if the branch of the Sail who wants me dead will be attending, or if they'll consider it worthwhile to go after me, but I do have a pretty good idea how they'll go about it if they do. Which is where you come in."

"I live to serve." Shane put a fist over his heart and bowed his head. Marguerite snorted and went back to sewing.

He watched her for a long moment, then turned back to gaze upriver. The mountains had grown steadily closer. *Tomorrow, land. And after that, the Court of Smoke.*

And may the Dreaming God have mercy on us all.

When Marguerite crawled out of the cabin the next morning, she was surprised to find that Shane was not waiting for her. She looked around, puzzled. The mist lay thickly on the water, but the light was starting to break through and he should have had no difficulty seeing her.

And? What, just because he brings you tea a couple of times, you decided that was part of his duties?

She spotted him sitting near the railing a few feet away. He was kneeling with his hands clasped in his lap, gazing downward with an expression of intense concentration.

Is he praying?

She climbed to her feet. He looked up at her, nodded once, and said, "Please forgive me for not bringing you tea."

"It's not your job," she said, mostly to kick her earlier thoughts in the teeth. Was that something in his hands? "What have you got there?"

"I believe it is some kind of swallow," said Shane gravely.

Marguerite was not expecting that answer. She peered down.

Yes, indeed, the man had a small bird clinging to his fingers. It had a forked tail and looked at her with lacquer-bright eyes.

"All right," said Marguerite, "I'll bite. Why are you holding a swallow?"

"It flew right to me," said Shane. "I believe the mist confused it. It is not apparently injured."

Marguerite couldn't help but laugh. With the bird clinging in his hand and the pale, indirect light, he looked more like a marble sculpture than a man. An allegorical representation of Strength, perhaps. Or, given the bird, Compassion. Although Marguerite had seen plenty of allegorical representations of the latter, most of them female, none of which left the viewer wanting to tear the statue's clothes off and see just how much passion there was in Compassion.

Down, girl. You don't know anything about him. He could have a sweetheart back in Archon's Glory for all you know.

"How long have you been sitting there with a bird?" she asked.

"Only a moment." He turned his hand, but the swallow showed no interest in moving.

"It's avoiding a river devil," said the captain of the barge.

Both Marguerite and Shane turned to look at her. The old woman stumped across the deck toward them, her hands shoved deeply into her pockets.

"A river devil?" asked Shane.

The captain nodded. "It's a river swallow," she said. "They go back and forth picking off insects. And the devils pick them off." She pulled one gnarled hand out of her pocket and pointed. "Watch."

Marguerite peered into the mist. Another bird was flying along the water's surface, making long, repetitive arcs that made the fog tremble. She couldn't see anything that resembled a devil, though.

She was just about to ask what she was looking for when the surface of the water broke and something large and flat leaped up after the bird. She had an impression of blunt wings, a pale underside, and an open, lipless mouth, before the devil struck the water again and vanished beneath the surface.

The flying swallow was gone. The one on Shane's hand was perfectly still.

"Did it...?" Marguerite asked.

"Oh, aye." The captain nodded to her. "They mostly eat little bitty fish, but they'll take a bird if they can."

"Are they dangerous to people?" asked Shane. She could understand the question—the thing had been at least five feet across, maybe more.

"Nah. They leave us alone, we leave them alone." She turned to go, then paused. "If you catch one in your net, you got to throw it back, though. It's bad luck otherwise. And iffen one dies in your net, you got to make an offering to the river gods."

"Are they sacred to the gods, then?"

The captain frowned at him. "No, but they belong to 'em. Like a mule belongs to its owner. You kill somebody's mule, you got to make it right with them."

Shane nodded understanding of this fine theological difference, and the captain went back to her perch near the back. Marguerite felt a twitch of amusement. That was more words than she'd ever heard the woman speak willingly. Indeed, she hired this barge specifically because the captain spoke so little and was entirely resistant to gossip.

And I consider that a virtue in her, and not in Shane. What a hypocrite I am. I should simply be glad that he will not gossip to anyone else about our mission.

"You still seem to have a bird," she said.

"So I have noticed." He gazed at the bird with an air of resignation. "I cannot begrudge it the sanctuary, but my hand is becoming cramped."

"Can I get you anything? A perch, perhaps?"

Shane considered this. "I would not object to tea," he said finally. "If I may impose on you."

"Ah yes, a truly monstrous imposition, tea. But I'll allow it." She went to the small galley in back of the raft and returned a few moments later with two steaming cups.

The fingers that touched hers felt like ice. Marguerite wondered if the bird was getting cold as well.

Apparently the bird felt the same way, or perhaps when his hands shifted, it decided it was time to leave. It leapt up in a flutter of wings and was gone into the mist in a heartbeat. Marguerite let out a startled laugh. Shane gazed after it, then dropped his head. She would have sworn that he smiled.

He signed a benediction in the air after the bird, then washed his hands in the river and finally took a sip of tea. "Thank you."

"Glad to help." She cocked her head, studying him. "Are you a knight?"

Shane stilled. "Why do you ask?"

"Curiosity. You move like one."

"How so?"

"You kneel and get up again too easily."

Shane frowned. "I don't follow?"

She smiled. "The only people who spend as much time on their knees as knights are whores and holy men. You're not the latter, though I admit I'm merely guessing with the other one."

He blinked at her. The tips of his ears went suddenly, blazingly scarlet. Marguerite did not know whether to feel guilty or charmed.

"I. Uh." He cleared his throat. "Yes. Technically. I was knighted as part of my training with the...as part of my training."

He might as well have held up a sign saying 'Please Do Not Ask About The Dreaming God.' Marguerite had no intention of doing so. "It's not a bad thing," she said. "I was just curious. Should I be calling you Sir Shane?"

He sighed deeply, and Marguerite wondered how she'd ever thought that he was expressionless. "It would be Sir Shane of Templemarch. And I'd *really* rather you didn't."

"Then I won't." *And now, my finely honed conversational senses are telling me to change the subject.* She scanned the water, but saw no sign of the river devil. "You know, I've gone up and down this stretch nearly a dozen times, and I've never seen a river devil before. I didn't know they were so large."

"I had never even heard of them." He stretched his fingers, shaking out the stiffness. "It is unsettling to think that there are such large creatures passing beneath us."

Marguerite chuckled. "We'll soon be at the Court of Smoke. Fewer rays, but a great deal more going on beneath the surface."

Shane sighed. "I will look forward to being off the boat," he confessed, "but I am concerned about the rest."

"You and me both," said Marguerite with a sigh. "You and me both."

CHAPTER 12

Their final stop before the court was a small town at the river's edge. It was divided into two distinct districts, one full of expensive-looking inns and shops, set well back from the water, and one built on and around a network of docks. They disembarked and made their way to an inn on the edge of the wealthy district, where Marguerite bespoke a private dining room.

Once inside, Shane was surprised and a trifle appalled when Marguerite began to strip.

"Uh," he said.

"Turn your back," said Marguerite, digging into one of her trunks. "We're only staying here long enough to turn Wren into a noble and me into a luxury merchant." She shared an exasperated glance with Wren. "*He* doesn't have to change, the lucky sod."

Shane turned his back and gazed at the wall, trying to ignore the sounds of sliding fabric behind him. He told himself that they might be coming from Wren, and since picturing Wren naked would be tantamount to incest, he managed to hold off any inconveniently erotic images.

"You can turn around," said Wren, after a few minutes. "We're decent."

"Well, as decent as we're likely to get," Marguerite added.

He turned around. Wren was wearing something green that was

probably fashionable. It had ruffles, anyway, and no one would wear ruffles if fashion wasn't involved somehow. Marguerite was dressed much as she always was, except that the fabric was of far higher quality and the bodice was cut rather lower. A panel of lace across her cleavage was presumably supposed to provide modesty, but in Shane's opinion, it was not doing a very good job.

Why did he not own a hairshirt?

"Right," said Marguerite cheerfully. "And now a carriage, and into the lion's den."

The carriage ride took nearly an hour, and by the end of it, Shane's teeth were beginning to ache from being rattled around in his skull. He rode with the Bishop often enough, to and from court appearances, and he was rather surprised at the difference between cobblestone streets and the road.

Marguerite laughed when he confessed this. "Possibly, but I'd bet money that the Bishop's carriage has quite good springs, compared to this rattletrap."

Shane tried not to bridle at the implication. "I cannot imagine that the Bishop would waste money on such a frivolous luxury."

"Frivolous?" Marguerite's eyes had a wicked gleam. "She takes that carriage to court, does she not? To meet with the Archon and visiting dignitaries, to make official appearances on behalf of the Rat, that sort of thing?"

Shane nodded. As the Bishop's guard detail, he had been to more official appearances than he could count, and was always a trifle astonished that Beartongue had no difficulty remembering the name and rank of everyone she was introduced to.

"Tell me, what makes a better impression—stumbling out with your hair mussed and your bones rattled and your stomach roiling, or sweeping in without a hair out of place, looking entirely in control of the situation?"

"Huh." Shane had to stop and think about that one. Obviously the Bishop had to look...well...*bishop-like,* whatever that meant. Possibly an investment in that was not frivolous after all.

"Her robes are very carefully tailored, too, even though they look like standard clerical wear for the Rat. She's not actually as tall as she looks, it's all done with strong lines. Her vestments are about a half-inch narrower than the norm. All of which adds to the impression she's trying to convey. Like the carriage."

He wondered how on earth Marguerite had learned all that. *Perhaps spies simply notice these things. Or she went through the Bishop's laundry.* "I admit that had not occurred to me."

"Of course it didn't. You're a paladin." Marguerite patted his arm. "Physical privation is practically one of your hobbies."

Wren laughed. "We're not that bad. I mean, it's not like we *enjoy* bad food and dumping ice cold water over our heads at dawn. It just works out that way sometimes."

"I enjoy hot baths," said Shane. "And...err...food..."

Both women looked at him. Wren shook her head sorrowfully. "Poor bastard wouldn't know a spice if it drew steel on him," she murmured to Marguerite.

"It's probably not his fault. Raised wrong, I expect."

"I use pepper," muttered Shane, stung. "And salt."

He looked up into identical expressions of pity and decided to stare out the window instead.

"Speaking of salt and jobs associated with it," said Marguerite, following his gaze, "I believe we're here."

They disembarked from the carriage by the shores of a narrow lake. Mountains framed the water on three sides, casting extraordinary reflections that were only slightly marred by wind ruffling the water. Towering above them, battlements raking the sky, stood an immense fortress. It looked ancient and immovable and as if it had been hewn from the living rock itself.

It was also painted bright purple.

"Goodness," said Wren, craning her neck. "That's certainly...uh... *vivid.*"

Careful inspection revealed that the fortress was actually painted in shades of red and blue. One immense tower was ringed with alternating bands, but the colors were so intense that they seemed to vibrate against each other, turning into a violet blur.

"They re-paint it depending on who's hosting," said Marguerite.

"Hosting?"

"Footing the bill. This year I think it's Lord Guillemot, so those are his colors. This isn't bad. One year Lady Millhaven shared hosting with the Merchant's Guild of the Dowager's City, and the place was done up in orange checkerboard on one half and green stripes on the other." Marguerite flagged down a man in livery standing nearby. "Three for the Court." Coins exchanged hands and he began carting away their trunks. Marguerite picked up a single bag and slung it over her shoulder. "Right." She dusted her hands. "We walk from here."

There was a nicely paved footpath leading toward the fortress. Shane guessed that all the wagon traffic went elsewhere. This was borne out a moment later, when they passed a large dock jutting into the lake, which seemed to be for loading and unloading river traffic. A second dock extended out past it, with boats bobbing at anchor, but without the bustle of activity.

"So who rules this place?" he asked. "Is it whoever is hosting?"

"Mmm. Technically we are on the land of the princes of Alta, and no, there is no reason you should have heard of them." Marguerite waved a hand generally cliffward as she explained that generations of princes had ruled the fortress, which controlled the side of the lake that the river drained from, which was, by orders of magnitude, the easiest route into the highlands. Surrounded by high crags and questionable mountain passes, without a great deal of arable land to feed themselves, the princes instead levied taxes on goods passing through.

In the distant past, various kingdoms had either objected to or envied these taxes, and attempted to take the fortress away, which meant that the Prince of Alta had to command a rather large standing army. Of course taxes went even higher whenever there was an attack—and the princes made sure that everyone knew the reason *why*. Rulers who challenged the fortress rapidly found themselves facing both the sheer cliff, the army, and a great many merchants who were very displeased about suddenly being taxed in excess of fifty percent to use the river.

Attacking Alta entered the vocabulary as slang for a self-defeating plan, and no one had attacked the fortress in over a century.

"The last few princes didn't feel the need to keep up the full army," Marguerite said. "Which left them with a fortress full of empty rooms. The grandfather of the current prince started inviting his friends over in the summer, and then a few more friends, and so forth. But it gets expensive to host that kind of party—nobles cost almost as much as armies—so the next Prince graciously allowed people to curry favor with him by footing the bill, and the Court of Smoke was born."

"So we would be subject to the judgment of this prince in the event of an incident?" asked Shane.

"Define incident."

"Somebody takes an axe to the face," offered Wren.

"The guards would frown on that, yes," said Marguerite. "Both the Prince and the hosting lords prefer that things run as smoothly and as... ah...*incident-free* as possible." She glanced from one paladin to the other. "There aren't going to be any lawyers or trials here. The nobility resolves things with sanctioned dueling. People like us are either thrown in a cell or evicted from the fortress."

"So no axes?"

"Not unless you can do it without being caught."

The footpath turned and the shadow of the mountain fell over them. The temperature instantly dropped. Shane tilted his head back to try to estimate the height of the violet fortress. and gave up somewhere at *really quite tall.*

"This is gonna be a lot of stairs," muttered Wren.

"No, no. There's a lift. They don't make nobility climb like pilgrims."

"Oh," said Wren glumly, "joy."

Shane winced internally. Wren was fearless about virtually everything, but she did not have a terribly good head for heights. It was probably too much to hope for that the lift was enclosed. He bumped her shoulder in wordless support.

"I'll be fine," she muttered. "It's fine as long as I'm not actually looking down."

Despite the brave words, she turned a bit green at the sight of the lift, which was a fragile-looking confection of wicker, though large enough to hold a dozen people. From the ropes and pulleys overhead, Shane guessed that it functioned the same way as any other lift. Somewhere inside, there was probably a donkey on a treadmill supplying the power.

The attendant waved them inside and closed the little half-door, latching it. "Don't lean out of the windows," he recited in a bored monotone. "Don't try to climb anything. Don't light any fires, not to cook, not to warm up, not at all."

"Do people actually try to cook in this thing?" asked Shane, aghast.

"Sir," said the attendant, "I have seen people do things that you cannot possibly imagine." He grabbed a pull-rope and tugged, and a moment later, the lift swung aloft.

"Hooooooo boy," said Wren, retreating to the side closest to the wall and closing her eyes.

Shane took her hand. She gave him a wan smile, not opening her eyes. Marguerite stood at the window opposite, looking across the view with interest, but didn't say anything.

The trip up only took about five minutes, but Shane suspected that for Wren, it seemed like a lot longer. The ascent would run smoothly for a few moments, then there would be a series of short, jerky motions, then it would settle down again. At one point a gust of wind set the basket swaying and Wren turned fishbelly white.

"It's fine," said Shane, using the paladin's voice. "All will be well. We're nearly there and we don't need to come back down again unless you decide to go horseback riding."

"Not unless they bring the horse up to me."

"I suspect that attendant has seen it happen before."

Marguerite caught Shane's eye and glanced at Wren, lifting one eyebrow. He shook his head at her. Wren would be fine once she was back on solid ground, he knew, and having Marguerite appear to notice would only deepen her future embarrassment.

At last the basket jerked to a halt. Another attendant opened the door and motioned them out. "We're here," Shane said, tugging on Wren's hand.

"Right," she said, taking a deep breath. She stepped out of the lift, eyes straight ahead. Marguerite followed, with Shane bringing up the rear.

They stepped through an archway into an unexpectedly broad courtyard, the fortress rising on all four sides around it. The courtyard was a hive of activity, porters moving trunks and servants in a dozen different shades of livery running on errands of their own. None of them seemed bothered by the fact that they were so far up, not even when the wind came whistling through the archway behind them, cutting through Shane's surcoat like a knife and tugging Marguerite's cloak loose from her shoulders.

"Ack!" Marguerite fumbled and nearly dropped her bag. Shane caught the cloak as it slid and tugged it back up her shoulders, re-fastening the pin. Marguerite looked up at him with a rueful smile. "I need an extra set of hands."

"Don't we all," he said automatically, but what he truly noticed was that when his fingertips accidentally brushed the side of her throat, she shivered. Just a little. Hardly noticeable, unless it was your job to watch someone for the smallest sign.

If he had been the paladin that he was supposed to be, he would have thought nothing of it. *It's the cold, nothing more.* But he was twice a failure, and so he smoothed the edge of the cloak down and let the back of his knuckles trace the barest line against her skin.

Almost imperceptibly, he felt her shiver again.

Marguerite's eyes met his with a faint, puzzled smile. Something dark and hot flared inside him. Something hungry. He wanted to stroke his finger along the line of her jaw and see if his touch truly had the power to make her tremble.

And who are you to even think such things? Are you that eager to add her name to your long list of failures?

He was not the paladin that he was supposed to be, but neither was he completely lost. He stepped back, gave her a little bow, and turned away.

Probably it was just the cold anyway.

CHAPTER 13

Their rooms were very small. Shane did not know if that was a reflection of their group's lack of standing or if the Court of Smoke only had so many rooms. The suite had a short entryway, barely large enough for the door to swing inward, with two narrow doorways on either side. The main door led onto a room with a large fireplace, a desk, and a dining table, which led to two further bedrooms, no larger than Shane's at the Temple of the Rat.

The two doors in the entry hall opened onto what looked like closets. "Servant quarters," said Marguerite.

"Do they dislike servants here?" asked Shane dryly. "Or just employ the double-jointed?"

"That was very close to a joke." She peered around him into the narrow space. "These are for a maid-of-all-work and a footman. They assume your valet or your lady's maid will stay in your room with you."

Shane digested this. "I fear that I would make a poor lady's maid. I will stay in one of these."

Marguerite's lips twitched. "They didn't teach you to style hair at the temple?"

He was fairly certain that this was also a joke, but he had an actual answer. "I can braid hair in several ways," he said. "It is useful for tucking under a helmet so that the enemy cannot grab your hair and use it as a handle."

Her dark eyes searched his face, perhaps looking for falsehood. Shane wondered if she knew many people who lied about being able to braid hair. *What a peculiar thing to lie about. But spies are complex people, and perhaps there is a reason.*

"You are a man of unexpected talents," she said finally. He bowed his head, accepting this praise.

"And now," Marguerite said, once they had unpacked the trunks that had been brought up, "I am going to do something decadent. Wren, you're coming with me. Shane, you're not."

"I am?"

"I'm not?"

"Yes." She draped a dressing gown over her arm. "We're going to take advantage of the single best feature of the Court of Smoke. Natural hot springs. C'mon, Wren, let's go soak."

"Oh, *hell* yes."

"You're sure it's safe?" asked Shane.

"The walk to and from the bath is the most dangerous part. That's why Wren's coming with me. And at least this way, if they kill me, I'll die a lot less sore." She grinned up at him. "There's a men's side, you don't have to suffer alone."

Shane contemplated the value of mortification of the flesh, and then decided that hot water trumped spiritual development and went to find a towel.

Marguerite leaned back in the hot water and felt her muscles slowly unknot. The smell of mineral salts filled her nostrils and her skin soaked it up with intense delight.

Her mind, alas, was a little less willing to relax. *You're here. You're finally here, and the Sail definitely has operatives here and you don't know if they're from a branch that wants you dead. An assassin could come through that door at any second—*

Stop that, she told herself firmly. *That's why I've got bodyguards.*

One of those bodyguards was currently sitting on the other side of the stone bench, up to her neck in water, with an expression of intense bliss. The baths had both an open general area and a series of enclosed bays for those who preferred privacy. Both women's clothes lay piled up on the floor just inside the door of the bay. For the first time since they'd met, Marguerite was sure that Wren did not have any weapons currently on her.

Fairly sure.

Her paranoia twinged again.

Stop. You've got a paladin berserker with you. You are as safe as it is humanly possible to be. Still, after two years of evading the Sail's clutches, it was difficult to set the anxiety aside completely.

"Wren?"

"Mmm?"

"If an assassin came through the door right now, what would you do?"

Wren turned to study the door. It lasted for so long that Marguerite would normally have wondered if she'd forgotten the question, but finally, in an almost dreamy voice, the paladin said, "If she had a blade, pick up that wooden bathing stool and catch the edge between the legs. A good twist and she'll likely either drop it or the blade will snap. If she holds on too long, assuming she's right-handed, her arm will twist too, and it's easier to snap the elbow backward at that angle. If she drops it, then go in fast with a blow to the throat, knock her down and hold her head underwater."

Marguerite felt a chill despite the heat of the water. *Aren't you glad you asked?*

Isn't this exactly what you wanted, anyway?

Wren coughed and her eyes, which had been worryingly distant, focused again. "It, err, gets a little more complicated if she's left-handed or unarmed."

"That's...uh...comforting?" Marguerite blinked steam out of her eyes. "You keep saying 'she.'"

Wren shrugged. "I assume an assassin wants to blend in as much as possible, so they'd send a woman to kill you in here. Although it would be unwise. Blood would circulate through the whole pool before draining, and people tend to notice if the water turns red."

It was remarkably easy to stop taking Wren seriously as a fighter, particularly with Shane standing around looking like a marble statue of a warrior. Marguerite realized that she'd been in danger of slipping into that mindset herself, and firmly squelched it.

"You're terrifying," she said, with deep admiration.

"Aww, thank you." Wren stretched. "Do people bathe here often?"

"Every day if you want. I try to make time for one. If you're not available for whatever reason, I can use the communal pools, though. They're not going to swoop in and stab me where someone's watching." She eyed Wren thoughtfully. "You, uh, should probably avoid those, though."

"I should?" Wren covered her breasts self-consciously with her hands.

"It's not how you look," said Marguerite. "Or rather it is, but not *bad.*" She shook her head. "It's the scars."

Wren looked down at herself, apparently surprised.

"People are going to wonder about those," said Marguerite gently, pointing to a particularly wicked slash mark across the paladin's left arm. "And nobody gets muscles like that from working on a tapestry."

Wren snorted, stretching her arms out. Her forearms were almost twice as thick around as Marguerite's. "You're probably right. I can explain away some of the scars if I have to, but I don't want to stand out."

Marguerite nodded. "Don't panic if someone notices, just be aware."

The paladin sighed. "There's so much to keep track of," she muttered, sinking deeper into the water. "I don't know how you can keep it all straight."

"Practice," said Marguerite. "I don't know how you can swing a sword for hours on end, so we're even."

"It's rarely *hours,*" said Wren. "More like a few seconds, repeated every few minutes or so, until either the other guys are dead or you are."

"See, that does not sound fun to me."

"I don't know if it's fun, exactly." Wren considered this. "It's more that I'm good at it. And it needs to be done. I don't enjoy killing people, but I do enjoy doing something I'm good at. Does that make sense?"

"Quite a lot, yes." Marguerite decided that she had wrung as much relaxation out of the hot water as she was going to. "All right. Let's get back to our rooms, before Shane frets himself to death, or we turn into prunes."

Shane was not fretting. Not at all. Marguerite was with Wren, and Wren was extremely competent. There was no doubt in his mind that they would both return safely. None whatsoever.

He had seen guards stationed at various points in the corridors, and surely they would leap in to help stop anyone seen attacking a pair of women. Not that Wren would need help. *Unless the guards are in the employ of this group that wishes Marguerite dead. But we have only been here a few hours, so surely that is unlikely.*

I have absolutely nothing to be worried about.

He was so unworried that he spent only twenty minutes in the hot spring. After all, someone as relaxed as he was did not require a long soak to become even more relaxed. It would have been redundant.

Rather than fret when he returned to the suite and found that the others had not yet returned, Shane unpacked all of his gear into the tiny sleeping closet. Then he reorganized it to be more efficient, which he would have done anyway and was certainly not a sign of anxiety.

He was just wondering if he should try to reorganize it again when the door opened and he erupted out of the closet with his short sword in hand.

"We can come back if you're busy," said Marguerite, gazing down eighteen inches of steel.

"Sorry." He let the point drop. "I...was...uh..."

"You were worrying," said Wren, pushing past him. She glowered at him. "Don't trust me to do my job?"

"I have absolute faith in you. It's the rest of the world that I have concerns about."

"Seems fair," said Marguerite. Her black hair clung to her face in damp ringlets. "I'm going to bed. There is a featherbed calling my name."

She vanished through one of the bedroom doors. Shane sat down, avoiding Wren's eyes, but it was difficult to be the picture of relaxation while carrying a naked sword.

"You were *absolutely* worrying."

"I was just going to sharpen this."

"Where's the whetstone?"

Shane muttered something under his breath—even he wasn't sure what—and went to fetch a whetstone.

Wren flung herself into the chair opposite. "You like her."

"I do *not* like her. I mean, I like her fine. I don't dislike her."

"Yes, but you *like* her." Wren wiggled her eyebrows suggestively.

"What are we, twelve?" Shane rubbed his face. "I am an adult. I do not '*like*' people. I am *attracted* to them."

"Oooh, so you *are* attracted to her!" Wren leaned over the arm of the chair, eyes shining. "I knew it."

Shane stared at the ceiling. "She is very attractive. There is nothing strange about that."

"Uh-huh." Wren leaned in closer. "So are you gonna tell her?"

"*No.*" He hadn't meant that to come out quite so vehemently. Wren sat back, grinning like a delighted shark. Shane cleared his throat and said, more quietly, "It's not like that."

Wren didn't say anything, but her eyebrows were eloquent.

"It's *not.*"

"Mm-hmm."

"I'm attracted to lots of people."

"Sure you are."

"I am."

"Name one."

"Uh..." He floundered for a moment. "Errr...how about...Acolyte Melissa?"

"The temple healer's apprentice?"

"Yes. She's very attractive."

"Her husband certainly thought so," Wren said, "when he married her last year."

Shane blinked.

"And then they moved to Aquila-on-Marsh. Six months ago." Wren sat back.

"I said that I was attracted to her, not that I was paying attention to her whereabouts," muttered Shane. "Anyway, it's different. Just because Marguerite is an...an extremely attractive woman..."

"We've gone from *very* to *extremely* attractive," Wren murmured.

Shane put his head in his hands. "Have you been taking lessons from Istvhan?"

Wren beamed. "Now *that,*" she said, "is possibly the nicest thing you've ever said to me." She stood up and patted his shoulder. "I'm going to bed. You should too. Tomorrow is going to be quite a day."

CHAPTER 14

"I feel ridiculous," muttered Wren, adjusting the bodice of her dress for the fifth time. "Everyone will know that I don't belong here."

"You'll be fine," said Marguerite soothingly. She fixed Shane with a gimlet eye and jerked her head toward Wren's back.

"You…uh…look quite nice, Wren."

"You are just the worst liar. Do you know that you can't fit an axe under these skirts? You'd think it would be easy, but no."

Her skirts were a froth of petticoats. They had been the cutting edge of fashion two years ago. The Rat's suppliers had done their best, but high fashion was where they fell short. The result made Wren look like a disembodied torso levitating over a particularly ornate cake.

As they entered the antechamber to the largest ballroom, Marguerite watched Wren steel herself. "You are perfect," said Marguerite softly. "You are supposed to be backward and provincial and on the hunt for amusement, and you are going to play that role magnificently."

Wren flashed her a brief smile. "I'm not sure it's a role."

"It is. Don't forget it."

Shane bent his head and murmured in her ear. Wren laughed abruptly, straightened her shoulders, and lifted her chin. "Alright. Let's do this."

The door opened. The majordomo announced the Lady of Sedgemoor. A few heads turned. Wren snapped her fan open and strode forward into battle.

"What on earth did you say to her?" murmured Marguerite, as they waited their turn to be announced.

"I reminded her that she could kill anyone in the room if need be."

"That might do it." Marguerite watched Wren vanish into the crowd.

The majordomo announced Marguerite simply as "Marguerite Florian of Anuket City, merchant," and omitted Shane entirely. Three more merchants were announced in rapid succession, which, as far as she was concerned, was just fine. She was here to see, not to be seen. At least, not until necessary.

She scanned the room, picking out people she knew, people she liked, people she loathed. And, much more rarely, people she feared. There weren't many of the latter. One dead-eyed courtier that she knew to stay well away from. *He's no part of this, thank god.* One old woman with a shaky smile and an entourage of giddy young things. Marguerite knew for a fact that her web of blackmail extended into three nations. *Only concerned about seeing her granddaughters married off, even if she has to start wars to do it.* Another operative who she didn't fear, but who worked for a man that she did. *Though my best information is that he is in Charlock right now, and the Red Sail does not concern him, so likely not a player in this particular game.*

It was unlikely that any of them would pay much attention to her. Her cover as Marguerite, perfume merchant, was well-established.

Mostly, though, it was the usual swirl of people. Courtiers playing games of rank, merchants playing games of wealth, and scattered spies playing games of information. The three goals crossed and re-crossed, sometimes parallel, sometimes at odds. *But as long as our interests do not overlap, we shall leave each other well alone.*

Perhaps strangely, she felt herself begin to relax. This room felt—oh, not *safe,* exactly, but *familiar.* She had told Shane the truth. She was walking into a den of tigers, but she knew all the tigers by name and which ones she could step over and which she should avoid.

"Who are the men carrying arms?" asked Shane. "They do not appear to be guards or duelists."

Marguerite followed his gaze. "Oh, those. They're chevaliers. Ah... courtier knights."

"Do they know how to use those swords?" asked Shane.

"They're trained in dueling," said Marguerite. Shane gave a noncommittal grunt.

She could understand his skepticism, assuming that grunt had been skepticism. The chevaliers mostly did not look like warriors. They wore silk and velvet and had elaborately plumed hats, and their peace-bonded swords were narrow and often encrusted with jewels. "Don't underestimate them," she warned. "Some of them make a habit of calling other men out for fun."

"I try never to underestimate an opponent."

"I'd prefer you didn't get in any duels."

"I would also prefer that." His eyes moved across the room, lingering briefly on a knot of chevaliers. "Do you know anything of their fighting style?"

"Not much," admitted Marguerite. She was an encyclopedia of information on a great many topics, but armed combat was not one of them. "The duels I've seen all looked very fast and showy?"

"Mmm. Yes, with those swords, that would make sense." He moved his elbow, brushing it against the scabbard across his back and the heavy sword there. Marguerite tried to picture a chevalier fighting a demon-possessed bull with a slender rapier and failed.

"Does that mean that you could beat one?"

"Not necessarily." Shane's eyes continued to scan the crowd. "I am very strong, but my weapon is not made to parry quickly. But by the same token, they could not parry my blade without breaking theirs. It would likely come down to endurance and luck. And the terrain, of course."

The way that Shane said *I am very strong* struck her as amusing. It wasn't boastful. So far as she could tell, the man would rather fall on his sword than boast. It was simply an unremarkable fact. *Squirrels exist. It is raining today. I am very strong.*

She continued her survey of the room, pausing when she recognized a near-friend. "Interesting." Shane cocked an eyebrow at her. "I know him."

"Who?"

"The handsome one charming the ladies over there. That's Davith. He is in something of the same line of work I am."

"Is he a threat?" Shane's voice was pitched so low that she could feel the vibrations in his chest more clearly than his words. A shiver went down her spine and she told herself firmly to stop that.

"Possibly. He could also be very helpful, and he owes me a favor. I am going to go find out. *You* are going to stay here."

"Am I?"

"Yes. You are going to lean against the wall like all the other chaperones and tame duelists are doing."

"How am I supposed to protect you from the wall?"

"If you see anyone stab me, kill them."

"I fail to see how that will help you."

"Oh, it wouldn't in the least. But knowing that you're watching means that nobody's likely to try. If someone's going to do me in, it's going to be in a quiet hallway, not the middle of a ballroom. Anyway, Davith would never stab anyone. It isn't his style."

He grunted again. Marguerite filed this grunt under "grudging acceptance" and went to go see her old friend and enemy.

Davith was that most fortunate of men, one whose boyish good looks were aging gracefully. Marguerite had seen it happen the other way many times. A lad who was strikingly handsome at twenty would lose the glow of youth, acquire a few lines around their eyes and mouth, and suddenly look as if they'd spent their life in the worst sort of debauchery. Usually this happened just when their peers were reaching their prime, too. The good ones bore this with resigned humor. The bad ones became vain and terrified and lashed out at the world that suddenly no longer catered to their every whim. She'd known far too many of the latter, and was sneakingly glad that Davith was unlikely to go that way. The man was far too useful to lose to something so petty, and far too dangerous if he chose to lash out.

He still looked younger than he was—Marguerite knew for a fact that Davith was in his early thirties, even though no one would guess he was over twenty-five—but he had strong bones and the faint grooves at the corners of his eyes were clearly laugh lines. There was no trace of silver in his hair, but that meant little enough. Marguerite knew at least three ways of covering grey hairs. She suspected that when Davith finally allowed it to show, it would involve an artistic touch of silver at the temples, just enough to set off the blackness of the rest, and the elegant amber of his skin.

It will be nearly impossible to see grey in Shane's hair, she mused absently. *It's so pale already that a few white hairs will be invisible. Although they'd probably show up in that awful red beard.*

There were four women gathered around her quarry. As she approached, she could hear Davith's laugh, light and spontaneous and amused, encouraging the listeners to join in on the joke. It took an incredible amount of work to perfect a spontaneous laugh like that. *I wonder which one of them he's trying to seduce?*

At a guess, it was the tall woman in pale green silk. She was standing a trifle farther back and her face was turned slightly away, as if she didn't want to appear too eager. Marguerite assessed the woman's clothes—*moderately wealthy, probably a widow, that's a respectable cut but not too respectable,* very *expensive shoes. Good choice.*

She strolled up to the gathering and nudged Davith in the ribs with her elbow. "Why Davith, what a surprise! I didn't expect to see you here, darling."

He turned, clearly surprised. If he was unhappy to see her, he covered it too quickly for Marguerite to spot. There was an excellent chance that he was working for the Red Sail—among others—but she suspected that he didn't know that his employers wanted her dead. Not that she wanted to be a target, but if he *had* known, that would have told her something. (That was always the problem with other spies. Sometimes it was almost as frustrating when they didn't know enough as when they knew too much.)

"Marguerite!" He bowed to her. "How lovely to see you again. It has been *quite* some time, has it not?"

"*Far* too long," she said, playing along. It would be quite rude to interfere with his work by calling him a liar, but Marguerite was not above a little gentle malice. "I have missed you *terribly*, you naughty man." She turned to the other four women, who were watching her with interest. "Whatever tales you've heard of this man, they don't even begin to do justice to the truth."

Three looked fascinated. The widow in green narrowed her eyes slightly.

And if I was feeling particularly unkind, I'd go on, but I would *like his help.* She therefore did not take his arm or wink saucily at his audience, but only tapped her finger against her lip. "You know, Davith, I'm selling here again this year, and I might have a business opportunity available, if you were interested."

"I don't know...business requires so much effort that might be better spent on pleasure..." He was looking at the woman in green when he said it, and she looked away quickly, then shot an edged look in Marguerite's direction.

"Ah, well. If you change your mind, I'll be...you know. Circulating." She waved a hand in the air and patted his arm. "*So* good to see you again."

It took about ten minutes before he caught up to her at a punchbowl in the next room over. This didn't surprise her at all. Davith was perpetually broke and the notion of profit that didn't come from warming someone's bed was bound to be a draw.

"Marguerite," he said, and this time kissed her cheek. "Thank you for not showing me up too badly."

She chuckled. "Charming that lovely widow, are you?"

"Trying," said Davith. "Lady Sancha doesn't quite believe my claims of undying affection."

"Very wise of her."

"Probably. But she's also the jealous sort, so you might have done me a good turn showing up like that."

"Well, then that's two favors you owe me."

"Ah." His voice was still superficially light, but she saw the sudden watchfulness in his gaze, a coiling of intent. "Are you planning on calling that favor in, then?"

"I might have need of some of your skills. One never knows."

"Interesting." He smiled, although she doubted he meant it. "I don't suppose it's my skill in bed that you'd like to test out?"

She gave him a wry look. "I can't say that's particularly interesting at the moment."

"You wound me to the quick, my dear."

"Yes, you look extremely wounded."

He chuckled. "I'm glad you're here, Marguerite."

"Oh?"

"Yes. One gets so tired of not having someone else to really talk to, when one is charming silly women out of their secrets."

"And their money?"

"Tsk, tsk. The occasional expensive love-gift. They go away well satisfied and I go away with my pockets a little heavier."

"As long as you go away." Marguerite hooked her arm through his to let him know she was joking. They meandered along the refreshment table. "It's not the love-gifts I'm interested in, Davith."

"Ah. Playing the game, are we, my dear?"

"As always. Am I correct in assuming that you're working for someone?"

"You make it sound so commercial." He clucked his tongue. "I suppose it's possible that there's someone somewhere who might be interested in what I happen to turn up." He disentangled from her and picked a plate up from the table. "No different from you. In fact, I imagine we're on the same side."

"Always a pleasure to be on the same side." She eyed him thoughtfully. *Time to roll the dice...* "Would you care to pool our resources?"

Davith turned away, carefully selecting tidbits for the plate. "I suspect that something could be arranged," he said, neatly arranging strawberries alongside a candied snail. "My patron's love-gifts are quite generous, after all." He handed her the plate. Marguerite took it, noting that it contained all her favorites. *Which is not surprising. Davith is very, very good at his job. He probably also knows your favorite flower and what herbs you brush your teeth with.*

"I don't suppose there's any salt to be had...?" she murmured, her fingers brushing his.

Davith stilled. Only another spy would have caught the flicker of an eyelid, the infinitesimal catch of breath. Marguerite cursed internally. The mention of salt had startled him. He knew what it meant, but he hadn't expected her to be looking for it.

The Sail must have told him that he was the only operative sent for this one. Damn and blast. Now I've put his back up, and he has to decide if I'm an enemy or a loyalty test.

He laughed. To any on-looker, they would look like two old friends sharing a joke. Only Marguerite could see that his eyes were deadly serious. "On second thought, my dear, I fear that some widows are far more jealous than others. It would be my balls in a vise should they catch me with someone else."

Marguerite laughed as well. "I've no desire to see you run afoul of such a widow."

"Nor I you. For I cannot imagine they would like being jilted."

"Perish the thought." She took a bite of canape. "Ah, well. A woman can dream."

"Indeed. I'm glad we understand each other, my dear." He gave her a small salute with one finger. "And now, I must go and smooth over Lady Sancha's ruffled feathers. Do you mind being an inconvenient lover from my past who simply cannot let go?"

This time Marguerite's laugh was genuine. "Not at all. Was I very tiresome?"

"Dreadfully tiresome. You wanted us to dress in matching outfits. I think...puce."

"You wound me. Scarlet, if you please."

"Scarlet it is." He winked at her and strolled away. Marguerite watched him go and sighed. He cut a very handsome figure and she quite liked him. It was a damn shame that he was working for the enemy.

CHAPTER 15

Being a bodyguard at the Court of Smoke, Shane realized, involved a lot of leaning against the wall.

Marguerite had explained it all on the long journey to the court, of course. If everyone kept their personal guard with them, the rooms would be far too crowded for anyone to walk. Nobles would try to show their importance by commanding larger and larger armed retinues, and it would have all become quite unwieldy. Every merchant with a formal invitation to the court was therefore allowed one attendant, and every noble was allowed two.

As a result, there were fewer bodyguards than he expected. Shane picked out a half-dozen, all with their weapons peacebonded, all of whom looked as if the peacebond would trouble them for less than four seconds if push came to shove. Some of them probably doubled as duelists, if their employers were prone to picking fights or to having fights picked for them. Formal dueling was allowed at the Court, brawling was most certainly not. They varied wildly in age, appearance, and attire, but they all wore the same look. Shane expected that he wore it himself.

While there weren't many bodyguards, there were certainly a great many chaperones. His post on the wall was flanked by chairs full of old women, all of whom were watching their charges with much the same expression as the bodyguards.

You watched your charge as she moved through the crowd, until she stopped. Every few seconds, your eyes flicked away and you did a sweep of the area, looking for threats. Then you found your charge again, determined that she was still alive and not on the move, assessed her expression for distress, then did another sweep.

It was the same job that he had done for Bishop Beartongue, and it was usually exceptionally tedious. Shane generally amused himself by watching the small dramas playing out all around him, but in a room this large, he was afraid to take his eyes off Marguerite for too long.

Fortunately, watching Marguerite was anything but tedious. Unfortunately, watching Marguerite made him feel things that he had no right to feel.

When she laughed with the too-handsome man that she had pointed out earlier, he felt a stab of...something. Not jealousy, certainly. *I have no right to be jealous. I am her bodyguard, nothing more.* Call it envy, then, that Davith could make her laugh and he could not. An envy that only deepened when she slid her arm through his, and they moved together like old friends or old lovers.

Shane entertained a brief fantasy of wandering over and looming over Davith. He wasn't any taller than the other man, but he was definitely a good deal broader. Plus he had a very large sword on his back, which tended to make looming more effective. Davith was wearing velvet and hose, not armor. *You could cut through that with a butter knife. Well, the hose, anyway.* Loose cloth was excellent at tangling up a blade, although there wasn't anything loose about the man's attire. His clothes looked as if he were sewn into them. Women and no small number of men threw appreciative looks after him as he passed.

It had to be said that Shane did not lack for appreciative looks of his own. At least four chaperones introduced themselves, and he had to run through the rituals of polite conversation while keeping at least one eye on Marguerite. (To their credit, the chaperones were all doing much the same thing with their own charges, so no one went away offended.) At least two young wallflowers noticed him, turned scarlet, and fled to more distant seats. He felt a bit guilty about that, but trying to put them at ease would only make it worse.

After an hour or so, two elderly chaperones began gossiping within earshot. Shane listened in, for lack of anything better to do.

"Now *that's* a handsome fellow. Somebody's man-at-arms, do you think?"

"Doubt he's a wallflower." They cackled. Shane kept his gaze fixed on Marguerite, who was deep in conversation with a group of women wearing the layered brocade of merchants from Baiir.

"Is that Waily's youngest over there?"

"It never was! She was short and had spots, the poor thing."

"No, Harriet, I tell you, it is. She's grown at least six inches, look at her."

"Shows you can never tell how the child will grow up. I saw Lady Octavia at her naming, and that child had ears like jug handles. And now she's a court beauty. They say the Crown Prince of Charlock offered for her."

"Offered for her, aye, but she didn't take him. I hear she's head over heels in love with Doverfrith."

"Doverfrith? He's sixty if he's a day, and she can't be more than twenty."

"That's what they say. P'raps she's merely putting on a good front, though, and hoping he'll die right after the wedding."

"Worse fates than being a widow with a great deal of money."

Shane glanced at the pair out of the corner of his eye. The one named Harriet was fanning herself delicately with a fan of painted vellum. The other one, as yet unnamed, leaned forward. "Who's that talking to your girl?"

"What? Oh, with the oiled hair? Lord Bardulf. Not that he's a lord of anything, as far as I know. A court position, that's all. Master of the Prince's Robes, I think."

"Yes, but which prince?"

"Does it really matter?" The two of them cackled together. "My brother-in-law probably called in a favor to have him speak to the girl for a few minutes and make her appear interesting." Harriet tapped her fan. "I fear it will take more than Bardulf. She's a sweet child, but she hasn't the conversation of a footstool."

"Did any of us at that age?"

"True enough."

"At least yours is sweet. My little Minerva is *damp*."

"Damp?"

"Cries over poems and sunsets. Not even particularly good sunsets."

"Lady of Grass preserve us. What are you going to do?"

"What can I do? Her mother's ordered me to keep her indoors and away from poets. I told her that there's only so much that I can do with a girl so set on tragedy. Particularly when sunsets happen every single *day.*" She sounded deeply aggrieved by this, as if the sun had singled her out personally.

"Oof."

"You don't know the half of it. I thought one of her distant cousins might be coming up to scratch, and then he made the mistake of complaining about the rain. She turned on the lad and told him that the rain was the tears of angels shed for the sins of mankind and the poor bastard said that if that was the case, then the angels had left a foot of mud in the west field and he'd lost a boot in it."

Shane winced. He was not an expert on fanciful young women, but he didn't see that ending well.

"How did that go over?"

"How do you think it went over? He was gone as soon as the rain stopped and she spent a fortnight drifting from room to room and declaring that love was dead."

"Lady of Grass. Well, it could be worse. Did I tell you about Moredena's sheep?"

"Sheep?"

"Sheep. About forty of them. On the ramparts, no less. What happened was..."

Shane felt a pang when Marguerite signaled that she was moving to the next room. Still, duty called. He pushed away from the wall and followed, leaving the saga of the sheep on the ramparts behind.

"Well," said Wren, sprawling across a chair in the main room. "That was certainly a day. That I spent. Somehow."

Shane inclined his head in agreement. He, too, had spent a day. That was about the best that could be said for it. He felt exhausted from sheer inactivity.

Marguerite was the only one of the trio who didn't look worse for wear. She held up a hand and went to the suite's door. "Hello? Is anybody—ah, there you are." A page came to the doorway, dressed in dove gray. Marguerite fished a coin out of her purse and handed it to him. "Please take an order down to the kitchen for a light meal for three." The page nodded and raced away.

"Our maid-of-all-work will be here tomorrow," Marguerite said, closing the door. "She won't stay here overnight, but check before you reveal anything sensitive."

"Do we have anything sensitive to reveal yet?" asked Shane.

Wren shrugged. "How would I know, really? Nothing stands out."

"I'd hardly expect it this early," Marguerite said. "In fact, if information fell into my lap tomorrow, I'd be suspicious of how easy it was."

"Oh, good." Wren sighed. "Because I've talked to a few people who didn't immediately run away, but I haven't found any way to ask gracefully about patronage." She cocked her eyebrow at Shane. "What about you?"

Shane ticked off gossip overheard from chaperones. "A court beauty named Lady Octavia is rumored to be madly in love with an older man named Lord Doverfrith. The Dowager's Master of Horse is not attending this year due to gout, and his wife is reputed to be conducting an affair with both a minstrel and the Eighth Noble Personage. It is believed that the Shadowed Duke poisoned his previous two wives and is now looking for a third. It is unwise for any woman to be alone with Baron Malverstone. Everyone knows that Lady Chadris is being blackmailed, but no one knows about what, though speculation is rife." He paused, seeing that both Marguerite and Wren were staring at him. "Err...what?"

"People *told* you that?" asked Wren.

"No. I just stood there and listened." Shane considered adding the unfortunate Minerva's tendency to cry at sunsets, but couldn't imagine that it was relevant to their efforts. "Chaperones gossip."

"Well," said Marguerite. She shook herself and began to laugh. "Good heavens. That's rather more than I expected. And you remembered it all!"

"The Bishop has often asked me what I have happened to overhear at gatherings," said Shane. Part of him still insisted that eavesdropping was not particularly paladinly behavior, but he tamped it down. *This is my assignment.*

"What's an Eighth Noble Personage?" asked Wren. "I don't know that ranking."

"A diplomat from the Benevolence," said Marguerite. "North and rather far west from here, on the other side of the continent. There's a few mountain ranges in the way and the ocean route is almost unnavigable, so we don't have any significant trade with them, and the diplomats rarely ever go home again. If anyone ever finds an easier way to trade with them, both sides will make a few dozen fortunes, but as it is..." She shrugged.

"Is any of that useful?" asked Shane. "Or mere gossip?"

"That sort of information is always useful," said Marguerite. "Not necessarily relevant to our task at hand, but the sort of thing that may connect to something else down the line." She tapped her finger against her lower lip. "Keep gathering it, anyway. You never know what will turn up."

An hour before sunrise, something did indeed turn up, although in this case it was the maid-of-all-work. She was a middle-aged woman named Ammy, with an expression that indicated she had been born unimpressed and had not seen fit to revise that opinion.

When Shane heard the door open and erupted from his room, clad only in linen braies and the short sword, she looked him up and down, glanced at the blade, and said only, "Eh. I've seen bigger."

"My profound apologies, madam," said Shane, lowering the sword and feeling rather foolish.

"Son, you're not even the tenth strangest thing I've seen since I started serving at the Court." She pushed past him and set to work laying the fire in the hearth.

Shane pulled on a little more clothing and went to warn Wren that there was a stranger in the common room. The lump of blankets containing his sister-in-arms muttered something about not stabbing anyone just yet, then rolled over and began to snore.

Ammy finished the fire, tidied the room, then stomped into Wren's room to repeat the process. Shane wondered if he should warn Marguerite, dithered briefly, then decided that he probably should.

He tapped on the door, heard nothing, then slipped inside. "Lady Marguerite?"

Her head emerged from the blankets, hair tousled by sleep. "Mmm...? Oh, s'you." She smiled sleepily and stretched her arms above her head. Her arms were bare. So were her shoulders. She sat up, pulling the blanket with her, but not before he had a glimpse of her ribs and the side of her breast.

On someone like Marguerite, even the side was a great deal of flesh. Shane blinked several times, then fixed his eyes firmly on the ceiling.

"Is something wrong?" she asked. "Do you need something?"

An extremely base and vulgar part of Shane's soul definitely needed something, and furthermore had suggestions on what that might be and how Marguerite might best provide it. He stomped that part down as furiously as if it had been a demon and continued studying the ceiling. *Carved wooden beams? My goodness. How ornate. And are those ceramic tiles? How interesting. I seem to recall the writer Chandler spending quite a lot of time describing ceramic tiles in one of his works. "A thousand shades of sunset wrapp'd/In fired clay, this chamber to adorn..."*

"Shane? Are you all right?"

"The maid is here," he blurted. "Now. She is cleaning the rooms."

"That's what she does, yes." He could hear the smile in Marguerite's voice.

"Yes. I. Uh. Thought you should be warned. In case you needed to... er..." He glanced helplessly around the room, avoiding the bed at all costs. His eye fell on the small desk, which had letters stacked neatly on it, and he seized the inspiration. "Paperwork. You know."

"Ah. Not to worry." She drew her knees up and even though everything was decently covered, he was suddenly rather desperately aware that her blanket was simply draped across her and could fall down at the slightest movement. Not that he wanted that, of course. Certainly not. That would be deeply unchivalrous.

Marguerite tapped her temple, apparently oblivious to his internal struggle. *Please, gods and saints, let her be oblivious.* "All the important things, I keep up here. My notes are mostly perfume orders. Have no fears on that account."

"Good. Excellent. Right, then." Shane groped behind him for the doorknob and fled with almost indecent haste.

. . .

Paladins. Really. Marguerite rolled her eyes. The man had taken one look at her and turned scarlet. *You'd think the sight of my bare shoulders had led men straight to hell.* She grinned at herself. *Well...maybe a couple of men. But they mostly deserved it, and they* definitely *enjoyed it.*

Maybe I should just haul off and seduce the man. He is very *pretty after all, and even if he wasn't, that* voice... She was a bit hot under the collar just thinking about it. Were paladins allowed to talk dirty in the voice?

No, dammit. You're his commander. More or less. And he still doesn't know if he trusts you. Hard as Shane was to read, she had no illusions on that score. He'd undoubtedly think she had ulterior motives.

Besides, he's apparently genuinely pure of heart. His idea of talking dirty might be "I respect you enormously as a person. Let us pray."

She bit back a laugh at that, shoved the covers back, and went to dress for another day of talking in circles.

CHAPTER 16

Shane waited to be certain that Wren was awake and on guard, then took himself, his sword, and his impure thoughts off to the training rooms. He had scouted them out on the first day but had not been able to put in an hour of sword work yet.

He had to go down several flights, into the underbelly of the fortress. The palace's past as a fortress was on full display down here. There were no windows, no ornamental tiles, only narrow slots carved through the rock to provide ventilation. The rooms were oddly shaped, with bites taken out wherever the space was needed for other purposes. Warm wet air, and the smell of soap reached his nostrils as he passed the laundry. He suspected that room never closed.

The training rooms were long and narrow, with high ceilings. The armory had been repurposed to hold padded staves and wooden training weapons, but that appeared to have been the only change since the old days. Shane took a suitably heavy stave and went to an unused set of pells.

After a few minutes, a pair of fighters sauntered in his direction. One was a tall woman with a hard, raptorial face, and the other was a grizzled man, a head shorter than his companion.

"You're not a duelist," said the man, nodding to Shane's sword, which leaned against the wall nearby.

"No," said Shane, a bit puzzled. He extended a hand. Both of them shook it in turn.

"Ossien."

"Sylla."

"Shane. Are you two duelists?"

"For our sins," said Ossien. "From the Hundred Houses."

Shane had a vague memory of the Hundred Houses, a series of tightly interlocked communities to the northwest of Archenhold. "Is there much call for duelists there?"

"Sometimes," said Sylla. She rested one hand on her sword, which had a long, narrow blade. "Mostly old men deciding that their honor can only be satisfied with blood. So they hire us to spill it."

Ossien grinned. "It's how I can tell you're not a duelist," he said, jerking his chin at Shane's demon-killing sword. "Try to fight to first blood with that thing, and you're liable to take their head off. Then everyone gets grumpy." He had a pair of short, wide blades on his hips, more like long knives than swords. Shane had seen fighters use blades like that, and suspected that Ossien was a good deal more nimble than he let on.

"No," Shane admitted. "I'm here as a guard. If I have to draw my sword, things have already gone badly."

"Heh." Ossien nodded to him. "I hear that." He stretched. "Care for an opponent? I warn you, I'm old and slow, so I'm probably not much of a challenge, but I always like to spar with someone new. I already know what mistakes to make against Sylla." His companion rolled her eyes at this, but didn't argue.

"Certainly," said Shane. He wondered briefly if this was some kind of trap, but it seemed unlikely. If someone was trying to kill him, the training room would be a terrible place for it. There were at least a dozen other people here watching. *I suppose that if they've been hired to take out Marguerite's bodyguard, Ossien could bash me over the head and claim it was an accident. Of course, he'd have to hit me first.*

Ossien dropped off his weapons next to Shane's and returned with a pair of wooden blades with blunt edges. "Fair warning, they're weighted," he said, taking up a sideways stance facing Shane. "Can leave a bruise if I get a good hit in."

Shane nodded. "Mine as well, I expect." He saluted with the tip.

Within a few moves, he began to relax. Ossien was good, there was no question, and for all his claims of being old and slow, he moved fast, though he was slightly unbalanced on his left foot. Shane had strength and reach, though, and while he had to be quick and clever to keep Ossien at bay, it felt like a workout, not like a battle. The black tide muttered a little inside his head, but never tried to rise.

"Enough," said Ossien finally, falling back. "Much more and my back will remind me that I'm not twenty-five anymore." He grinned. "Thank you for the bout, son, even if you were just toying with me."

"Never," said Shane. "You got a few good hits in. If you had a blade, I'd be down a kidney."

"And I'd be down both arms and my head," said Ossien. He returned the weapons to the racks and sat down to change his boots. Shane noticed that one of his feet was made of wood, articulated with a metal swivel at the ankle. *Ah. That explains the balance. Impressive piece of equipment. He doesn't even have a limp.*

Ossien followed his gaze and slapped his knee. "Got this in the Blue Marshes," he said cheerfully. "Miserable place for a campaign. If there was a patch of solid ground big enough to get one foot on, the enemy was standing there and shooting at us."

"You took an arrow?"

"Oh, I took three, but none of those signified. No, I lost my boot in the mud, banged up my foot, and the damn thing took an infection and had to come off." He pulled his boot on over the prosthesis. "Got off lightly, frankly, but that was the end of my mercenary days."

"Mud is the *worst,*" said Shane, with feeling. He still had grim memories of one battle where the Saint of Steel's chosen had been called to clear bandits out of a village that was too deep in mud for horses to get through. They'd done it, but no one's thigh muscles had worked right for a week afterward.

"One nice thing about being a duelist—not a lot of mud to deal with now." Ossien cocked his head at Shane. "Now you...you're a knight, aren't you?"

Shane raised his eyebrows. *Can everybody tell? Do I have a sign on my back?* "Trained as one, although I don't use the title. How did you know?"

Ossien shrugged. "Lotta little things. Your salute at the beginning was a little too crisp to be enlisted, unless I'd pissed you off somehow. And your accent's from over by the Dowager's city, but you don't fight like her infantry. They drill tight together, always keep their elbows in close and they don't make the big sweeps like you did." He held up a hand. "It ain't none of my business, you don't have to tell me. I run my mouth sometimes and I know it."

"It's fine," said Shane, bemused.

Sylla pursed her lips thoughtfully. "If you ever feel like drinking in company some time," she said, "and you don't mind Ossien running his mouth, the place on the other side of the old barracks is cheap and doesn't water the ale too badly." She nodded to him and went back to practice.

Ossien lingered a moment longer. "Most of us tame duelists drink there," he added. "The chevaliers don't bother us there."

Shane paused in the middle of drying his hair. "Do they bother you elsewhere?"

The man hitched one shoulder up in a shrug. "They've got a lot of honor," he said dryly, "and they always seem to think someone's stepping on it." He tapped a finger against his forehead in a small salute. "I'd watch where you step. You're big enough to attract attention."

"Thank you," said Shane. "I appreciate the warning." He watched Ossien stroll away and thought, *Great. Just what I needed, another complication.*

"Oof," said Wren, shifting from foot to foot. "These shoes were not made for these floors."

"If we'd had time to wait on a cobbler, we could have gotten court shoes made for you," said Marguerite sympathetically. "Double thick soles."

"Oh, it's fine." The paladin put her foot down. "I don't mean to complain. I've done forced marches before; it's not like wandering around for a few hours is anything much."

"It is when you're not wearing the right footwear." She looked over her shoulder at Shane. "Of course, Tall, Strong, and Handsome there gets to wear his usual boots."

"Next time we do this, let's put him in the dress and I'll be the bodyguard."

Marguerite grinned. "You know he'd look just devastating in it, though. That's the annoying thing."

Wren paused, tapping her fan against her lower lip. "That is...quite an image."

"Isn't it, though?" Marguerite stepped back and made a slight bow, a merchant to her patron. Pitching her voice up, she said, "Always a pleasure, my lady."

"Miss Florian." Wren sailed off, fan aloft. *I must speak to her about not holding it like a weapon. Though for all I know, it could be. I wonder how many people she could kill with a fan.*

It was easy to see, if you were trained to read people, that Wren was not nearly so confident as she looked. That was a good thing, really. No one would ever think that she was a spy. *The best lies are mostly true.*

"What an odious little mushroom," murmured Davith in her ear.

Marguerite had a strong desire to come to Wren's defense, or failing that, to kick Davith in the shins. She squelched it. "Useful enough, though. One of my top suppliers comes from her town and I was able to convince her to take me along. She was enchanted by the idea of having an entourage."

His lip curled slightly. "Poor you."

"She's not so bad, the poor dear. Just young and completely lacking in airs and graces." Marguerite gave a slight shrug. She did not feel guilty for playing her part well, but she hated the necessity. "Also...well, you know how it is. Anything that saves me money. I have to attend Court to sell perfume, but all my cash is tied up in stock."

Davith grunted. "I hear that," he muttered. "I begin to wish I hadn't set my sights on Lady Sancha. Wealthy and widowed, but she's making me work to get into her good graces. Much longer and I'll be reduced to card sharping."

"Poor Davith. How undignified."

"I don't give a damn about my dignity, I just don't want to get caught. You go to a table where the play is deep and at least one of the players is fleecing the others. If I want to play it safe, I'm playing for chicken stakes."

"Tsk, tsk." Marguerite raised an eyebrow. "And your...ah...other widow isn't providing sufficient love gifts?"

He went quiet for an instant too long. Marguerite could practically hear the wheels turning. Davith was clever and very good at getting into people's good graces, but he did not have her experience in the game.

"My other widow would like results before they send more gifts," he admitted. "Of course, you're familiar with how that works."

"Very familiar." Her current hope was to convince Davith that she was still working for the Red Sail, and that their employer had seen fit to pit them against each other. *Sadly, not as unrealistic as it could be. There are always spymasters who think it's cute to make their people fight.* "I would offer to help, but I would not want your widow to think that you were taking gifts from someone else." She gave him a level look under her lashes. "You know how highly some prize loyalty."

He grimaced. "I do, yes. I suppose I shall simply muddle through."

Just how desperate was he? Marguerite studied the lines of his face; the circles under his eyes expertly concealed with paint. His clothes were quite fine, but if you knew where to look, you could make out signs of expert mending. *His own work, if memory serves. How much is he cutting his coat to fit his cloth, though?*

She examined her nails with studied casualness. "Of course, some would say that what one's paramours don't know won't hurt them. If I were to come across a bauble that might interest your other widow, perhaps I might be convinced to part with it."

"And what would be in it for you? I have little to offer except my gratitude." His smile was equally studied, although there was a gleam of the old wickedness in his eyes. "Mind you, I *have* been complimented on the size of my gratitude before..."

She snorted at him. "I don't require *that* sort of gratitude, thank you."

She *thought* that she waited a sufficient amount of time afterward before glancing in Shane's direction, but Davith always did have a sense for those things.

"Ahhh..." he murmured, "So that's the way of things, is it?"

Marguerite didn't bother to deny it. Denial would only have looked suspicious, even if it was, regrettably, true. "My bodyguard," she said. "Pretty, isn't he?"

"Very. I'd try to bed him myself if I hadn't sworn off men."

"You swore off men?"

"Years ago. We're far too much trouble. I don't know why you put up with us."

"Someone has to reach the high shelves."

He laughed softly. "There's that. I wouldn't suggest you bed that one, though, my dear. He'll disappoint you."

Irritation sparked and she had to work to keep her tone light. "And you wouldn't?"

"My dear Marguerite, it is my job to know what a woman wants." He stroked a fingertip down her bare arm and she repressed the shiver, turning to glare at him. "You want, for once, not to be performing. You want to be in charge, not pretending that some slobbering minor politician is doing you a favor by bedding you."

The problem with other spies was that they were just as capable of seeing you as you were of seeing them. Marguerite shook her head, annoyed with both of them. "And you'd be happy to let me be in charge, I suppose?"

Davith chuckled. "Oh, a few times at least, until the novelty wears off. But that fellow...no, the moody types come in like a storm. Look at his eyes. He is waiting to see who he needs to kill."

"He's a professional killer, what do you expect?"

"An assassin?"

"A knight."

Davith's laugh was startled and unfeigned. "Good god. A knight for a bodyguard? *You?*"

"He can't be bought and he's good at what he does."

"Stone the crows, of course. I don't know why I never thought of it."

"Because you lack imagination, my dear Davith." She stretched up and planted a kiss in the air a few inches from his cheek. "And now, as delightful as this conversation has been, I shall take my leave. Good luck with your widow."

"I am certain that the lady shall yield to my charms eventually," he said, with a mournful glance at his feet. "I only hope that it is before my socks have too many more holes in them."

Marguerite shook her head and went to find other people to mingle with.

CHAPTER 17

For the first time in three days, Shane was not shadowing Marguerite. She had gone to a meeting and bodyguards were, apparently, not allowed.

"It's not that it's dangerous," she said, "it's that there's no room. The largest meeting room they can give us only fits a hundred or so, and we'll be packed in like pickled herring in a jar. There's no *room* to attack anyone."

"Poison could be administered, or a very narrow dagger—"

Marguerite just looked at him. "I'd notice. And since I couldn't get out of the room before I dropped dead, it would make quite a scene."

"But the danger is there. It is my duty—"

"It is your duty to *follow my orders.*"

This was true so far as it went, and it probably wasn't dangerous enough to try to veto it, but Shane made one last stab. "I could pretend to be your apprentice."

She put her hands on her hips and gazed up at him. "Because you look so much like a perfumer's apprentice."

"What do those look like?"

Her mouth suddenly curved in one of those irrepressible grins. Shane had a sudden urge to run his thumb across her lower lip. He froze that thought and set it aside to dispose of later.

"They wear less armor," she said, patting his arm. He could feel the touch through his surcoat, chain, and a layer of padding. "And they don't walk like they're trying to figure out how to murder everyone in the room."

"Not *everyone.*"

"I'll see you in three hours. Wait for me at the door of the meeting room. Go take a walk or a nap or something."

Shane bowed his head in acknowledgment. There was, after all, a second mission that he had been ordered to accomplish, and now was as good a time as any. He only hoped that it did not bring another layer of complication down on all their heads.

"Pardon my interruption," said Shane, approaching two ladies hovering over a punchbowl.

The taller of the two eyed him appreciatively from behind her fan. "You can interrupt me any time."

Shane coughed. "I am looking for Lady Silver."

"Oh, *her,*" said the other one, waving her fan dismissively. "I might have known."

"Do you know where I might find her?"

"She was in the Lion Room, last I saw," said the taller one. "Wearing a green gown."

"You can't miss her," said the short one, "she's a real bitch."

"Martha!" gasped her companion, with a shocked giggle.

"Am I wrong?"

Shane had spent much of his adult life in soldier's camps, and while the language hardly shocked him, the apparent cruelty did. But he could hardly say something without making himself conspicuous, so he bowed his head and murmured something noncommittal, then turned on his heel, seeking the Lion Room.

Is Lady Silver unpopular here, then? Beartongue said to seek her out, and I assumed that she was another operative like Marguerite, and thus would go out of her way to ingratiate herself with the court. But there are many things about spycraft that I do not understand.

He reached the Lion Room. It had a large central fireplace built into a pillar, and the snarling heads of lions emerged from above the mantels. Unlike the ballrooms, the floor here was covered in thick rugs, and even though the fireplaces held only coals, the room was pleasantly warm.

A knot of women were conversing off to one side of the pillar. The tallest of the group had her back to him, and was wearing a green gown over a silvery undertunic and what appeared to be a silver wimple with some kind of headpiece. Lady Silver? Shane made his way toward the group.

"Pardon me," he began, and the woman turned.

Shane's tongue stuck to the roof of his mouth and he forgot what he was going to say.

It wasn't a wimple. Nor was it an undertunic. Lady Silver's arms and neck were covered in short, dense fur that ran down her arms to the backs of her hands, leaving her fingers bare. What he had taken for a headpiece was a pair of stiff, upstanding ears. And her face...

The dog-headed woman smiled at him. The corners of her mouth drew up in a grin, with just a hint of teeth. "You arre! parr!doned," she said. The R's came out high and sharp and explosive, almost a yip.

Shane realized that he was gawking and immediately bowed, half-expecting a nun of the Dreaming God to appear out of nowhere and slap him on the back of the head for his rudeness. "Forgive me, madam," he said. "I was given your name only, and..." He realized that he had no idea how to end that sentence without sounding unforgivably boorish, and stared at the rugs.

Lady Silver laughed. "And you were not warned that I was of the People, yes?" She extended a hand to him and he bowed over it, then straightened. "You may look at me," she told him. "The People do not take offense to humans looking. It is like ourr sniffing. You look and be done and I will sniff and be done and then you need not starrre from corrrners and I need not sniff the ground wherre you have walked, yes?"

"Certainly," said Shane, not quite sure what was going on, but hoping that he was not committing some kind of interspecies incident. He had heard stories of cynocephalic people before, but had always thought that they were found primarily in the margins of illuminated manuscripts.

Lady Silver leaned in, rather closer than Shane was expecting, her nostrils flaring. Her nose was deep gray, a shade darker than her fur. She had large copper eyes and her muzzle was short for a dog, with black lips and flat silver cheeks. She took several deep breaths, then stepped back.

Her forehead had deep vertical wrinkles that gave her a pensive air, but her voice was light and amused. "Metal and incense and many deaths. You are a warrior, are you not?"

"Sometimes," he said. He glanced around at the other women. They were all human, and they were all watching with varying degrees of fascination and humor. One matron was clearly smothering giggles. Perhaps they were used to the impact that Lady Silver had on the unsuspecting. "I am Shane, bodyguard to the merchant Marguerite."

"And I am Lady Silver, chosen representative of the People to the courts of humans." She grinned at him again. "It is a pleasure to make your acquaintance."

"Likewise. Ah..." He suddenly remembered that he had a message and fumbled for it, attempting to regain his composure. "I was tasked with giving you this letter, Lady."

Her coppery gaze flicked to him, then she plucked the letter from his fingers. Shane fell into his formal rest position, hands behind his back, waiting. The other women drifted away, murmuring to each other, occasionally glancing over and chuckling. Shane wondered if he was doing something amusing.

She held the envelope up closely in front of her eyes, clearly nearsighted, then sniffed the paper. "Ah. A message. Verry well." The R was less yip than growl this time, not hostile, but less interested. "I will send a page later if you require a rresponse."

She turned away in clear dismissal. Shane wondered if he had offended, or if Beartongue's name on a letter was unwelcome. He bowed anyway and moved away, wondering what he had set in motion, if anything at all.

CHAPTER 18

Wren dragged herself into the room they all shared and collapsed into a chair with a grunt. "I hate this," she said, to no one in particular.

Marguerite made a sympathetic noise from behind the desk, where she was writing out invitations to a perfume testing. "Long day, I take it."

"I stand and talk and stand and talk and say absolutely nothing," said Wren. She sighed heavily. "I knew it was tiring, from when I was young, but somehow I thought I was misremembering. But I think it's actually worse."

"Any luck?" asked Shane, who was sharpening his sword. He was always sharpening his sword, as far as Marguerite could tell. It was a wonder he didn't go blind.

Wren waved her hand. "Nothing useful. Most of the women here won't talk to me because I'm so terribly unfashionable, but a couple of wallflowers will, mostly because I talked to them first. And Lady...err...I forget her name, sounded like "corrugated"..."

"Coregator," said Marguerite, signing another invitation. "Middle-aged, has outlived two husbands, likes fast men and faster horses."

"She seemed nice," said Wren meekly.

"She's lovely, actually. She doesn't care what anyone thinks of her and she prides herself on being so unfashionable that she's come out the other side. And if she likes you, that goes a long way." Marguerite made a note to add Lady Coregator to the perfume testing.

"She talked to me for nearly an hour," said Wren. "And she was very kind. I think."

"You'd know if she wasn't."

Wren sighed again. "Would I? At least three people have come over and been fake-polite to me so that they could deliver what they thought was a really cutting insult, then scurry away and giggle."

Shane's hands stilled on the sharpening stone. "Tell me their names," he growled.

Wren rolled her eyes and shared a look of mutual exasperation with Marguerite. "That won't work, brother. You can't go rattling your sword at giggling heiresses. For one thing, it'd blow your cover as Marguerite's bodyguard. You're supposed to hold me in thinly-veiled contempt."

The paladin bowed his head as if accused of a severe dereliction of duty. "You are correct," he said. "Forgive me. I am not skilled at subterfuge."

"And for the other thing, I am perfectly capable of rattling a sword at them myself," said Wren. "At least, if I had a sword. But I amuse myself thinking of ways to kill them with the silverware."

"You *are* a bloodthirsty lot," said Marguerite, amused.

"Anyway," said Wren, dragging the conversation back. She began ticking things off on her fingers. "Lady Coregator says that the current fashion for patronage is for painters. Playwrights are completely unfashionable. Sculptors are okay if you can find one. Poets are always acceptable, but I get the impression that when you are the patron to a poet, it's assumed that they are providing...err...extremely private readings."

"It was ever thus," said Marguerite, sighing. "Though it's gotten better since the poet God's Songbird broke her patron's arm for making that assumption."

"I wish I could break someone's arm," said Wren wistfully.

Marguerite snorted. "No word on artificers, then? Not that I want you to ask directly, of course."

"I asked about practical things. Lady Coregator is a patron of a horse trainer and has a friend who patronizes a botanist. I said that sounded more interesting than poets."

"Good!" said Marguerite, setting down the pen. "Very good. Lady Coregator will have it in the back of her mind to find someone for you now. She is a great organizer of things. If you can slip it into the conversation somehow, next time the discussion turns that way...ask if artificers have patrons, make up a story about one inventing a new millwheel or something like that...then we can put her contacts to work."

Wren's smile was genuine this time, and less tired. Marguerite gentled her voice. "You've got the miserable role on this one," she said, "but you've made a good start on it. Certainly you've gotten farther than I have." She frowned down at her invitations. "If this damned perfume demonstration doesn't generate some leads, I may be forced to start breaking into people's rooms and rifling through their accounting."

"Can you do that?" asked Wren.

Marguerite grimaced. "Yes, but not as well as I'd like. I once knew a master in Anuket City who could forge bookkeeping entries in a dark room while the clerk snored in the next, but talents like that are few and far between. So we start with perfume."

She went back to work on the invitations, keeping half an eye on Wren as she worked. The woman's role was clearly wearing on her, and praise could only go so far. *I cannot regret making use of what tools I must, but I could wish that she suffered less for it.* It was all well and good to know that the best performances were rooted in real emotion, and that Wren's pride and vulnerability made her exquisitely convincing, but that did nothing to lessen the hurt.

Her first thought was to ask Wren if she was comfortable continuing, but Beartongue's warning sounded in her head. *Wren will never tell you if she is injured or overmatched.* A direct approach was probably not the best idea, which was a shame. Marguerite quite liked the direct approach. So few people ever saw it coming.

Accordingly, she waited for the chance to speak to Shane alone. He finished sharpening his sword and went off to his tiny servant's room. Wren took a little longer, staring into the fire, before she, too, got to her feet and went to bed. Marguerite finished addressing invitations and closed the desk.

She went to the narrow door and tapped it. "Shane?"

The door jerked open instantly. Marguerite blinked in surprise. Then she looked up at Shane and briefly lost the power of speech.

The paladin was naked to the waist, carrying that short sword again. "Are we under attack?"

"Uh..." Marguerite had to swallow several times. "Uh. No. Nobody's under attack." *Dammit, this is not the first bare chest you've seen,* she told her libido, annoyed. *It just happens to be a particularly fine one. Get yourself together.*

Whoa damn, her libido replied, not listening.

It *was* a particularly fine chest. Shane was so self-effacing and so inclined to fade into the background that you forgot how large a man he really was. His shoulders were easily twice as wide as Marguerite's. Her gaze traveled downward, admiring the sleek indentations of muscle under the skin. A line of dark blonde hair vanished under his waistband. It might as well have been a signpost reading THIS WAY TO THE GOOD BITS.

"Ah..." said Shane.

She realized that she had been staring shamelessly and coughed. *Deflect,* she told herself. *Deflect. Otherwise this will be rather awkward. Pure of heart, doesn't trust you. And unlike Davith, not really the type to enjoy casual ogling.*

"You have a *lot* of scars," she said.

He grimaced. *Ah. Well, now it's awkward in a different way. Well done. Fine smooth-tongued operative you are.*

It was true, though. White lines scored his skin like a playing board, some following the line of his ribs, one slashed down across the left side of his chest from the collarbone almost to the nipple. Her hands itched to touch his skin and feel the texture there, wondering how it would change across the scar, like the nap of velvet rubbed a different direction.

"My shield was low," Shane said, tapping the slash mark with his free hand. "The other fellow's sword went right over the top. I'm lucky it didn't sever the muscle."

"It looks that way." She focused, with difficulty, on his face. "I wanted to ask you about Wren."

"Wren?" He frowned, glancing in the direction of the main room. "Is she well?"

"That's what I came to ask you about. I was...ah..." He put the sword down, and bending brought new muscles into prominent relief. *Goddammit.* "Do you think you could put on a shirt? Otherwise I'm going to stand here ogling your chest and losing my train of thought."

Something flared in his eyes. For a moment, they were no longer the color of ice, but the blue of a very hot flame. Marguerite felt her pulse jump.

Then he took a half step back and the moment passed. She wasn't sure if she was glad of that or not.

Shane reached for his shirt and pulled it over his head. Marguerite gazed at the wall, attempting to think virtuous thoughts and mostly failing.

"How may I be of service?" he said, once he'd gotten his arms through the proper holes.

"Wren's miserable," said Marguerite bluntly. "It's barely been a week and we're looking at potentially months of doing this. Am I going to break her just for the chance she hears some relevant gossip?"

Surprise flickered across his face. He opened his mouth as if to argue, then paused. "I don't know," he said, after a moment. "Wren is excellent on a battlefield. She has quite fine control over the battle tide. That's what we call the, ah, berserker state. I would not have put her up against a demon otherwise."

Marguerite raised her eyebrows. "Are there some paladins that you would suggest not fight demons?"

He nodded. "I would not allow Stephen or Galen to do so. Marcus, I would watch closely. Wren or Istvhan, I would have no fear. Judith..." He trailed off, shaking his head.

Now that's interesting. Possibly not of much use at the moment, but Marguerite could easily see it being so in the future. "Is it all a matter of control, then? Willpower?"

"Not willpower. There is no lack of will in any of them." He rubbed the back of his neck. "The god's hand lay more lightly on Wren and Istvhan, that is all. Or perhaps they are simply better adjusted than the rest of us. Unless their emotions are very deeply involved, the tide is not such a danger to them as some others. Regardless, if you are concerned about Wren going on a rampage through the court, do not be."

"Well, I *wasn't,*" said Marguerite dryly.

Shane actually smiled a little at that. *Somewhere in there is a rudimentary sense of humor, and I will drag it kicking and screaming into the light.* "Honestly, it's not a rampage I'm worried about," she continued. "I'm more concerned that she'll wind up curled in a ball sobbing at night because a pack of spoiled beauties are being cruel to her. Some things cut deep."

His smile was replaced with grimly set lips. "That may happen," he admitted.

"I don't want that to happen."

"Nor do I. Nevertheless, our orders are clear. She will not thank you for removing her from the assignment." He folded his arms. "The cure may be worse than the disease, in this case. She would never admit that someone else's words had so much power over her."

"The whole world is made of words," said Marguerite irritably. "Treaties and contracts and secrets and laws are nothing but words, but everything runs on them. Of course they've got power."

He inclined his head politely. "As you say."

"Right." She sighed gustily. "Well, you know her better than I do. Just...keep an eye on things, and if you think she's starting to crack, tell me immediately. Hell, tell me if you think she just needs a break for a day or two. Beartongue told me that Wren will never admit when she's overmatched, but that you can tell."

"The Bishop places too much trust in me."

"I doubt that." Marguerite reached for the door handle. "The Bishop doesn't strike me as a trusting soul."

"She trusted you on this mission."

"Yes. But only because you're here to watch me." She grinned and closed the door on Shane's sudden startled expression.

CHAPTER 19

Shane lay in bed with his arms behind his head and contemplated the sins of the flesh.

He had not wanted a woman's body so badly in years. After the Saint's death, lust had faded to another merely physical need. A generous servant of the Rat had met those needs, and he liked to think that she had not gone away unsatisfied from the bargain, but it had meant little more than eating or drinking. He knew that she had taken other lovers and he had been neither surprised nor jealous.

And then Marguerite had come along and suddenly those hungers roared back to life as if they had never left at all.

He had done well. He had almost convinced himself that it had simply been too long and that his response when he touched her after her fall was nothing but the aftermath of adrenaline. *You made too much of it. You always do. You drag guilt into every interaction.* Even the moments since were only the appetites of a man working closely with an attractive woman.

Then Marguerite had looked at him with clear admiration and grinned like a cat presented with a bowl of cream and he had been a heartbeat from doing something...rash. Something that he would *definitely* have to feel guilty about.

It wasn't even that she was beautiful. She was, of course, with those curves and breasts and thighs, but she would likely have been beautiful no matter what her body looked like. Marguerite carried herself as if she were beautiful, and the rest of the world simply fell in line behind her.

It was that confidence that drew Shane the most. Having so little of his own, hers blazed like a torch before him. She reminded him of Bishop Beartongue in that regard. Both women had an assurance that owed nothing to arrogance, but to an absolute knowledge of their own abilities and a rock-solid belief that they would never let themselves down.

For Shane, with the constant whisper of failure and ruin in his ears, the pull was undeniable. *Tell me what you want of me,* he wanted to say. *Tell me what you believe I can do. Tell me how not to fail you, and I will serve.*

You could not say such things to another person.

She isn't like Beartongue, though. She's a spy. She tells rich merchants how to corner the market on lace. Just because this time she wants to do something that Beartongue believes is a good idea doesn't mean that she's usually on the side of angels.

She'd also saved all their lives once. Shane felt like an ingrate for suspecting the worst of her, then immediately felt naïve for assuming that she hadn't done it for reasons of her own.

Suppose your wildest fantasies came true and she was willing to take you into her service and into her bed. How long before you were complicit in acts that only served to grind the poor underfoot and make rich men richer? Over something as ridiculous as lace?

If you were an unstoppable killing machine, it was very helpful to have a god providing your moral direction. In the absence of the Saint, the paladins had a bishop. But in the absence of the bishop...

The gods help us all. Shane thought briefly of Judith, wherever she had gone, and prayed that she did not find herself alone in some ethical quagmire. *Though she'd likely handle it better than I would. And at least she wouldn't tie herself in knots being attracted to someone.*

He finally accepted that he was not going to sleep any time soon, got to his feet, dressed quietly, and went to go find the drink that Ossien had suggested.

The bar was exactly as advertised, a small, unpretentious place with a number of tables and a long counter on one side. Ossien was sitting at it, and hailed Shane with a wave when he came in. "Hey, knight. What are you drinking?"

"My sins," muttered Shane, mostly to himself.

"They got beer and whiskey. Either of those answer?"

"Beer."

"Sorry there's no better," said the bartender, sliding a mug across the bar to him. "It's the strike, you know."

Shane didn't actually know. Ossien explained. "The boatmen on the lake are on strike. Say they're done working all hours moving goods for the privilege of being treated like dirt by the Court. So they're demanding better. No goods coming here from the highlands, none going back across until they get it." He tilted his mug. "The best drink comes out of the highlands, though, so we're left with this in the meantime."

"Lowland swill," muttered the bartender, by way of agreement.

Shane raised an eyebrow. "Won't such a strike hurt those on the far side more? It seems like it would be much easier to move goods to the Court by the river than overland into the highlands."

"Oh, aye," said the bartender. "Any other season, they'd be laughed out of the place. But Court's on right now, and either the boatmen get what they want or the fancy lords start to notice that they're running short of beer and meat and dainties among other things. And they'll stay short for at least a month, too. Can't just magic up a full court's worth of meat overnight."

Ossien nodded acknowledgment and lifted his mug in the general direction of the lake and, presumably, the boatmen. "Best time to strike. The big man in charge this year won't want to be known as the one who made his guests eat salt fish instead of...I dunno, pickled partridge, whatever these people eat. So they do it now and they've got him. He'll yowl and threaten but he's stuck and they know it."

Shane knew very little about trade routes or pickled partridge, but lifted his mug as well. "Always strike where the enemy's weakest," he said.

"Hear, hear." Ossien tapped his mug against Shane's. "The hard part is figuring out where that is."

That's not always the hard part. Not for us, anyway. But explaining a berserker fit and the way that one saw the enemy through the black tide's haze would have required far more than a single beer. Shane wondered absently what the equivalent of a berserker fit would be for a trade negotiation. *Perhaps somewhere there's a god that oversees merchants and tradesmen, Whose chosen champion goes into a fugue state and when they come to, they've written a binding legal document about how many barrels of beer can be delivered in a fortnight.*

Actually, that sounds like something a champion of the Rat might do. Shane's old friend Istvhan had joked occasionally about lawyer-berserkers. Beartongue had said, "Don't tempt me."

Still, if you were sussing out the weakness of an enemy economically, rather than simply stabbing them, and you didn't have access to divine intervention, you'd need...well, someone like Marguerite, when you got down to it.

She told you how she worked out the details on that one job, and all you could think was that it was silly to go to that much effort over lace. But is lace any sillier than dainties for a lord's table? And here we are drinking to the men refusing to move those.

"You alright?" asked Ossien.

"Uh?"

"It's just that you've been sitting there with your beer in the air for the last minute."

"Oh." Shane hurriedly took a gulp and set it down. It was nothing to write home about, but swill had probably been an unkind description. "Sorry. Had a thought."

"That happens, yeah. Not to me that often, thankfully."

Shane snorted. "I suspect that you're not being entirely truthful there."

"What, me? Nah. Empty-headed as they come."

"Mmm."

Ossien cocked his head. "Is it a woman, then?" Shane nearly choked on his beer. "Or a man, I'm not judging."

Shane sighed. "Have you ever wanted something badly, even though you know it would be an absolutely terrible idea?"

"Oh gods, yes." Ossien took a long draw on his beer. "My first wife."

"How many have you had?"

"Only the one so far, but I hold out hope." He gazed over the rim at nothing in particular. "Gave me the best years of my life. Then the worst decade of it."

"...I see."

It was Ossien's turn to snort. "They say the gods never give us more than we can handle, but let's just say that the gods had an overinflated sense of my abilities. Ah, well. She's gone now."

"I'm sorry for your loss."

"My loss was someone else's gain. In this case, a tailor who worked down the road." He paused. "Err...not saying that your situation would work out that way, you understand."

Shane had to laugh. "Thanks. I think."

Ossien set his mug down, then winced and rubbed his shoulder. "Bah. I should get a real job instead of working as a tame duelist at my age. Maybe something predicting weather, since half my joints do that anyway."

Shane let himself be drawn into a rambling conversation about joints, injuries that ached when it was going to rain, and how those injuries had been acquired. When both he and Ossien called it a night, he was feeling, if not better, at least a little more resigned to his own confusion. Probably the ale helped.

The keep was quiet at this hour, or as quiet as it ever got. The Court of Smoke was perhaps best viewed as a small, vertical city, with main corridors that encircled each level and dozens of branching hallways off each one. Shane had no doubt that, somewhere below his feet, an army of servants was awake, tending to the laundry or the baking or any of the other hundred tasks that kept the Court functioning. He passed one girl with her arms full of scrolls and another lugging a small keg, but for the most part, the corridors were empty.

Shane turned onto one of the outer walks, where windows had been cut high in the wall to provide a brisk cross-breeze. The cool air chased some of the mental fog away, not that he was particularly tipsy to begin with. Narrow rectangles of moonlight marked the walls, providing plenty of illumination, even though the lamps had been extinguished for the evening.

He had perhaps half a second of warning before someone tried to club him over the head.

If he had been something other than a paladin of the Saint of Steel, it definitely might have worked. If he had actually been drunk, it still might have worked. But half a second was a small eternity, so far as the battle tide went, and the tide rose up and grabbed him and flung him sideways before his conscious mind had even registered the stealthy sound of footsteps.

It wasn't quite enough to avoid the blow completely. Instead of landing square, the club clipped the left side of his head, scraping along his scalp and smacking hard into his left ear. Stars exploded in his vision and he staggered, but didn't go down.

Hitting the enemy in the head is usually a good idea. Even if you don't knock them out, frequently they're stunned and groggy. But it was very unwise to try this on a berserker unless you were very, very certain that you could put them down with one blow.

The black tide poured through Shane. *Spin around, but not toward the blow, they expect you to turn toward the blow, so go the other way, so if they've got a knife in their off-hand, you're not throwing yourself onto it*—His vision was still full of pinprick flashes, but that was fine, he could hear that there were at least two of them. No point in drawing his sword, the ceilings here were much too low to use it. The tide told him that his assailant was here and he reached out and grabbed someone's upper arm in his left hand and that was perfect—*finish the turn, you've got their arm now, right hand slides downward, closes over the wrist, they try to wrench away, good, good, let them, that means your left hand is down by the elbow and all you have to do is push up with one hand and down with the other...*

The crack of bone echoed through the corridor, followed by a hoarse yell of pain. Someone else yelled, "Shit!" The owner of the arm sagged, and Shane didn't feel the need to hold them upright. He heard scrabbling at his feet, then "Come on, *come on!*" and running footsteps.

The tide hissed that he could catch them, break some necks as well as arms, but Shane forced it down. He still couldn't see well. He shook his head, trying to clear his vision, but a wave of darkness obscured it. Had he been hurt worse than he thought?

No, his left eye was burning as if there was something in it. He wiped it clear. His fingers came away black in the moonlight. Blood. Ah, yes.

Scalp wounds, he thought, annoyed. *Always so dramatic. All the epics about people being stabbed in the heart and "the blood gushing forth, as a river in full flood" should have been about being hit in the head.*

Although it's probably not as epic a tale of heroism if the noble knight makes a heroic last stand and the enemy just dings him behind the ear.

He sighed heavily, found a handkerchief, held it to his head, and went to go wake Wren and Marguerite.

"Sweet blithering gods!" Marguerite said, when she entered the common room. "What the hell happened?"

"Someone hit me over the head," said Shane. He sounded almost tranquil about it. Seeing the bloodstained towels strewn about the table, Marguerite was not nearly so calm. It looked as if someone had butchered a hog in the middle of the room.

"*What?*"

"The head," he repeated patiently. "Someone hit me on it. I'm fine," he added.

Marguerite clutched her own head. "Who? Where? *Why?*"

"I don't know, the outer corridor two floors down, and I don't know."

Wren, who had dipped a cloth in water and was dabbing the wound said, "It's not *that* bad. Scraped you all along the side, which is why it's such a spectacular bleeder, but nothing that actually needs stitching up."

Marguerite dropped into her own chair, appalled. "Start at the beginning," she said. "Tell me the whole story."

Unfortunately the whole story didn't shed much light on the matter. Marguerite massaged her temples. "It's not impossible that they were trying to mug you," she said. "That sort of thing does happen occasionally, which is why there are court guards. But if they were trying to lift someone's purse, why go after someone your size?"

Shane shrugged. "Some people think that big men must be slow."

"Well, I think it's safe to say that you disabused them of *that* notion."

"Just bad luck?" asked Wren. "Or someone trying to take out your bodyguard?"

Marguerite shook her head slowly. "I don't know. It could be either." She mistrusted coincidence, but she also knew that her own fears were more likely to have her jumping at shadows and seeing conspiracies under every bush. *They didn't succeed. That's the important thing. Shane is fine.*

"Shall we report this to the guard, then?" asked Shane. Wren had managed to get the bleeding stopped and was wrapping a bandage around his skull.

"I suppose we'd better. Not that I expect them to be much help, but if something else happens, I don't want to be left trying to explain why we *didn't* report it." She snatched up a cloak to cover the dressing gown that she had thrown on when she heard the commotion in the outer room. "Can you walk?"

Wren snorted. Shane looked vaguely offended. "I could jog the whole way in full plate, if you like."

Marguerite rolled her eyes. "We're not all paladins! Most of us would want to go to bed with brandy and sympathy after something like this!"

"Do we *have* any brandy?" Wren wondered.

"I'll send a page for some."

"And the sympathy?" Shane asked.

"I'll send a page for that too."

"I do not know how useful that was," said Shane, as they left the offices of the guard commander an hour later.

"I do," said Marguerite, "and the answer is 'not very.'"

The guard commander had taken their report and made sympathetic noises, but that was as far as it went. His job was to break up drunken brawls and prevent outright murder, so he had promised to increase the patrols in that corridor, but unless they struck again, he clearly wasn't hopeful about catching Shane's assailants.

"I was really hoping he'd say something like "This is the third time this week!" Marguerite said glumly. "Then I'd know that it wasn't targeted at you—and me—specifically."

"Do you think that the Sail is behind it?"

"If it *was* targeted, then probably." Marguerite scowled. "An attack like that means that they've got enough manpower to risk losing three men if they got caught. Only nobles can make that work, particularly if they're bringing along a load of younger relations. No, if another merchant was out to get me, they'd be trying to tamper with my samples or sabotaging my attempts to sell. No one but the big trade delegations can field enough staff to bring actual thugs."

"Why would nobles be involved?"

"Normally they wouldn't be, but the Red Sail could easily buy or blackmail someone to have jumped you. Their pockets are deep enough, and plenty of nobles are light in the purse and the morals. But I'd honestly expect them to use their own people and not make such a sloppy job of it."

"If I were not what I am," said Shane, reaching up to touch the side of his head, "it might not have been a sloppy job at all."

"Ah." Marguerite considered this most of the way back to their rooms. "That doesn't fill me with confidence."

"No." Shane straightened. "Still, I will be more careful about what corridors I use in the future. And if this was something other than a random crime, it cost them a great deal more than it cost us."

"There's that," said Marguerite. She bid the paladin goodnight and went to her bed. He was right. They had come off lightly, and there was no permanent harm done.

But the question that ran in circles around her head, as she stared at the ceiling, was *So how many men will they send next time?*

CHAPTER 20

Wren looked around the great arched room and sighed straight from her toes. Another day of attempting to ingratiate herself with people who looked at her like something they'd scraped off their shoe. Joy.

I am a grown woman, she told herself. *I am not sixteen and on the marriage mart to Father's neighbors. I am an adult. I am on an assignment. I am playing a role.*

Her eyes traveled across a coterie of younger women, all clad in elegant, figure-hugging gowns, with their hair styled into elaborate ringlets. Two of them were whispering to each other behind their fans, and although Wren knew that it was highly unlikely that they were talking about her, she still felt her stomach sink.

I am a grown woman. I do not care what these people think of me.

It didn't help.

I could kill anyone in this room without breaking a sweat.

That helped a little. She glanced around to make sure that Shane was not actually in the room. With the battle tide rendering all else equal, Shane's superior strength would probably carry the day if the two of them fought. He was in one of the other rooms, though, keeping a watchful eye over Marguerite, so the statement stood. *Yes. I could kill anyone in this room, unless one is secretly an assassin. And none of them know it.*

...I just have no idea how to do my hair.

Wren wandered to a window and looked out. These ballrooms were halfway up the great fortress, so the view was an astonishing sweep of countryside, even if she couldn't see the waterfall from here. With the glass pane between her and the open air, she did not feel the usual twinge that affected her in the presence of heights. It reminded her of being young and fearless, standing on the castle battlements able to see halfway to forever. If she stood on her toes, she could just make out the rooftops of the pottery works below, but for the most part, it was all fields and hedgerows, with long strips of woodland between them, stretching across gently rolling hillsides until they reached the mountains on the far side of the valley. Wren thought that it was amazing that the windows weren't packed with people gaping at the view.

Still, they've probably seen it a hundred times. Probably admiring views is unfashionable. Wren turned away from the window and ran her eye over the crowd, looking for anyone that she was even remotely acquainted with.

No one. Bah. Well, what about secret assassins? Surely there must be a couple in the Court of Smoke. I saw one fellow yesterday who was dressed as one of those chevaliers, but if he didn't know his way around a garrote, I'll eat my fan.

She tapped the fan in question on her wrist. It was made of vellum held between two carved wood sticks, meant to be folded and unfolded with an elegant flick of the wrist. Wren didn't know if her flick qualified as elegant, but she could deploy the fan with enough precision to kill flies, which she was secretly rather pleased with.

There was supposedly a whole language to fan signals and where you carried it and how you fluttered it and where your gaze went while so fluttering. Wren had no idea how you learned that language. Her fan had bluntly pointed wooden handles and she was fairly certain that if she held it right, she could jam the closed fan into someone's eye socket with enough force to break through to the brain.

She looked around for potential targets, but if there were any assassins in the room, they were hiding it well. Everyone here moved like... well, like fashionable women in uncomfortable shoes. Small steps, constrained by the hems of the gowns. A sway in the walk carefully calculated to be attractive but not pronounced enough to be scandalous. Wren was doing her best to imitate that walk, and was pretty confident that she had the shoe part down, although the sway was probably a lost cause.

She ambled to the refreshment table. The bowl of wine had fruit floating in it to sweeten the taste, and had been watered down heavily enough that alcohol was a distant memory. Wren would have had to drink her own bodyweight in the insipid stuff to become inebriated. Lady Coregator carried a flask with her and liberally topped up her drinks. Lady Coregator was extremely intelligent. Wren hoped that she would finish her morning ride soon and come up to the court. Then she could talk to someone, or at least stand on the outskirts of the conversation, listening and smiling pleasantly, without anyone looking at her and wondering what she was doing there.

She had just filled a cup with watered wine when something struck her shoulder from behind. Wren spun, started to drop into a crouch—when you were short, coming up from underneath was usually your best bet—saw a sea-green gown and the tall, giggling woman inside it, and had to devote most of her concentration to not slamming her elbow into the woman's solar plexus and following up with a fist to the jaw.

Unfortunately, this left limited energy for holding things, like her fan and her wine cup. The cup fell, splashing across Wren's bodice, and the fan hit the floor.

"Oh, I *do* beg your pardon," said the woman in the sea-green gown, while her two companions murmured behind their hands. "I don't know how I didn't see you down there!"

Like hell you didn't. Wren produced a grunt worthy of Shane. *No, dammit, say something else. Courtly manners. You have them, remember?* "Please don't trouble yourself," she said, trying not to grit her teeth. "Accidents do happen in such close quarters."

"And I'm certain no one will even notice the stain," the woman said brightly.

Given that it had been red wine, however watered, and that Wren was wearing a blue dress, this was absolutely a lie. Wren simply met her eyes steadily. The woman smiled and flicked her fan, and her two companions tugged her away. Giggles erupted as soon as they were out of immediate earshot.

"I hate this," Wren muttered to no one in particular.

"Understandably so," said a man's voice beside her, though not so close as to be alarming. Wren turned, resigned to the fact that her gown probably looked as if someone had put a knife in her ribs, and met the stranger's eyes.

He was taller than she was, although that didn't count for much, since almost everyone was. Not nearly as broad as Shane, and he looked unarmed. He had dark hair and amber skin, and his eyes were nearly black. She took a step back as he bent down, and for a confusing moment, she thought that he was kneeling at her feet, which made no sense at all.

Then he picked up her fan and offered it back to her. *Ah. Yes.* "Thank you."

"It's nothing." He picked up the cup as well, which had broken into several pieces. Wren tried not to feel guilty. The tableware in these rooms was all unglazed bisque from the pottery at the base of the mountain, handsome enough but made to be used only once.

"May I?" he asked, taking a handkerchief from his surcoat.

"May you...?"

"Your dress," he said gently. He had a pleasant tenor voice. Wren watched him dip the corner of the handkerchief in one of the carafes of water on the table. He turned toward her, making a dabbing motion, and she finally realized what he was doing.

"Oh! Err...yes, I...thank you..."

Had she still been that young girl in her father's house, she absolutely should not have let a strange man wipe a cloth over her bodice. But she was a grown woman, dammit, and there was nothing remotely erotic about scrubbing out a stain. Even if it meant that he was bent over her, and that she could feel his breath across the tops of her breasts. Or that he had his other hand on her waist, as if they were dancing, to hold the fabric in position.

"It's fortunate that this wine is so weak," he said, darting a quick smile up at her. "If they were serving the good stuff, it would be another matter."

"If they were serving the good stuff, I would be much less put out by the stain," she said. "At least I could drown my sorrows that way."

He laughed. "Fortunately, my lady, we've caught it before it set." He stepped back, dropping his hands, and Wren felt a pang of disappointment.

"Thank you so much," she said. "I have other gowns, of course, but I suspect that the laundresses in this place are overwhelmed." Was he handsome? She had never been a good judge of such things. Being surrounded by a great many large, muscular men who treated you as a younger sister meant that you developed a somewhat skewed view of masculine beauty. She thought he might be, though. Certainly he was *attractive*, which was something altogether different.

"Dreadfully so," he agreed. *What is he agreeing to? Oh, right, laundry. Something like that.* His dark eyes held hers, and there was a slight smile on his lips.

"I...ah..." She could feel herself flushing. *I am a grown woman, dammit.* "Forgive me, I've forgotten my manners. I'm Wren. Of Sedgemoor." She thrust out a hand, realized it was the one holding the fan, and switched them awkwardly.

He took her hand in his. His fingers were warm and ungloved. She could feel calluses at the fingertips, but not at the base, where a sword's would be. A musician, perhaps? She wasn't sure.

She had expected him to bow over her hand, as men were supposed to do, but instead he brought it to his lips. The actual kiss was so fleeting that she barely felt it, but he rubbed his thumb across her palm in an unexpected caress before he released it. "Lady Wren," he said. "It's been a pleasure to make your acquaintance. I very much hope that I will see you again...soon."

"Yes," said Wren faintly. "I...err...I'd like that..."

He bowed to her then, and smiled as if she was the only woman in the entire room, before he turned to go. Wren watched him leave, then turned herself. The nearby trio of girls led by the one in sea-green were throwing hard-eyed looks in her direction. None of them were giggling now.

"I think," said Wren, almost to herself, "that I will go and change my gown." And she went out the door, feeling a great deal lighter than she had in days.

CHAPTER 21

Marguerite was supposed to be doing paperwork, but she had encountered a definite source of distraction. Namely her bodyguard.

She hadn't minded when Shane was sharpening weaponry or examining his armor or whatever he had been doing by the fire for the last few days. Honestly, she found the small, lethal noises of the whetstone rather soothing after the initial startlement, and there was a certain pleasure in doing your work while someone nearby was doing theirs. The silence had been almost companionable, and when she broke it, frequently, to mutter to herself about names and invitations and who was allied with who, he didn't keep interrupting her to ask what she was saying.

No, the problem was that apparently Shane had *finished* doing all those small lethal things for the time being, and was reading a book. Which, again, would not have been a problem, except that he had taken out a small pair of spectacles and balanced them on the end of his nose.

It was *adorable.*

He turned a page, the firelight highlighting the curve of his neck and shoulder and winking off the small lenses as he turned his head. Worse, she was pretty sure that she knew the book he was reading, and it had been good. She'd enjoyed it. She had to stifle the urge to ask if he'd gotten to the one bit yet.

Really, there ought to be laws against this sort of thing.

She could have handled him being pretty. Marguerite had met a great many pretty men, and most of them weren't worth the trouble. And she could have handled him being brave and trustworthy and responsible, because there were plenty of people like that in the world too, and you just learned to grit your teeth and deal with it.

She could even—probably—have handled companionable silence. She'd come close with Grace, although she rather suspected that she'd driven the other woman up the wall with all her muttering, and...well, all right, Grace was her dearest friend in all the world, but that was fine. There was no reason Marguerite couldn't also have a companionable silence with a man. She was allowed to be friends with men. Even pretty men. Even pretty, brave, trustworthy, responsible men with good taste in books.

Adorable was a step too far, though. She could not be expected to work under such conditions.

A lifetime or so ago, Grace had asked her if she was attracted to a paladin named Stephen. Marguerite remembered replying, enumerating his virtues, and laughing, "What would I do with a man like that?"

The answer, as far as Shane was concerned, was apparently "very, very bad things."

Ironically, it was Stephen who had convinced her that paladins were worth bothering with. Merchant operatives rarely crossed paths with holy warriors. She had spent most of her life believing that the brightest thing about most paladins was the polish on their armor. Then she and Grace had been thrown together with one, investigating a poisoning that turned out to be someone else's political maneuvering. And she'd realized, to her mild chagrin, that Stephen was not stupid, except perhaps when it came to talking to women. He was straightforward and trustworthy and uncomplicated, which people often mistook for simplicity, but he still understood how people *worked.*

Her bodyguards were cut from the same cloth, she suspected. Perhaps all the Saint of Steel's people were. Wren was young and naïve and wore her heart on her sleeve, but having a whole legion of lethal older brothers would probably do that to you, even if you had been married before. Shane...well, the Bishop had certainly been right. He was a much keener observer than she would ever have guessed. In another life, he might have made a fine spy. Except that like many trustworthy people, he was too trusting, and honor had never been something Marguerite worried about much.

He licked his thumb and turned a page. Marguerite followed the flick of his tongue then stared determinedly down at her paperwork. The names swam before her. Did she even know any of these people? Did she care?

It's not like I'd be despoiling the innocent. He was one of the Dreaming God's people. They get around plenty. Bet I could show him a few things they never taught him in the temple, though.

Hell, he could even keep the glasses on.

She stood up. For a moment, their eyes met across the room. "Something wrong?" Shane asked.

"Wrong," Marguerite repeated. She looked down at her papers. *Was* something wrong? *You're frustrated and haven't bedded anyone for pleasure in the better part of a year, that's what's wrong.* "No. Not really. Just going through the replies to my invitations."

Shane waited politely. Marguerite abandoned her fantasies—*Probably for the best*—and waved a piece of paper at him. "A few people sent their regrets who I'd wished would attend, so now I'm going to have to track them down another way."

"Ah."

"I swear that half the people from Charlock are coming, which doesn't surprise me. Most of them are probably genuinely interested in the perfume. But of course the two that I really wanted to have an in with aren't. And apparently Davith's not coming." She went to the table to pour herself a cup of watered wine.

"Your...ah...former colleague? Is that a problem?"

There was some not-very-well-hidden disapproval there. Marguerite shook her head. "Not a problem, exactly. But since I know who he's working for, I could watch him and see who he paid attention to, or didn't, which could lead us in the right direction. Or even just to see if there's anyone he's taking his cues from." She still didn't know if there was a senior Sail operative here in court at all. She scowled at nothing in particular. "But of course he knows that. So possibly he's more suspicious of me than I thought."

Shane nodded gravely at this, closing his book.

"Or possibly he really *did* have a prior engagement that evening. For all I know, the widow he's seducing is demanding he escort her somewhere. That's the problem with intrigue, everything looks significant and almost nothing actually is."

"I don't know how you make sense of it all," Shane said.

"I don't either," she admitted. "I just soak up as much as I can and listen to people telling me their life story, and sooner or later something clicks into place. All this work is just waiting for the click."

Shane raised his eyebrows. "Are you ever wrong?"

"God, yes. Anyone who says their intuition is always right is lying. Frankly, that's why I prefer dealing with merchants and trade deals. People may go broke if I'm wrong, but they're less likely to get killed." She thought of Samuel and winced internally. "Of course, there are always exceptions."

"Which is why we need to find this artificer before anyone else does."

Marguerite nodded.

An actual click came from the door, and they both turned toward it. A few seconds later, Wren came down the short hallway, whistling a merry tune.

"And how are we all doing this evening?" Wren asked.

"You're in a good mood," said Marguerite, amused.

"Mmm." Wren dropped into a chair. "It was a good day, I think."

"Oh?"

"Lady Coregator invited me to visit her chambers tomorrow afternoon, to discuss patronage. She has lists of patrons and artisans they support."

"Oh, very good." Marguerite nodded to her. "See if you can get a look at that list. If there's artificers on it, we may get a lead." She tapped her finger against her lip. "If you can't, I suppose I can always break in and steal it."

"That sounds extremely dangerous," said Shane disapprovingly.

"Yes, well. Needs must."

"I'll try to get a look," said Wren. She leaned back, and then added, with studied casualness, "Ran into a rather nice man today, too."

Shane's head snapped up so fast that Marguerite was surprised he didn't give himself whiplash. *And I hope that Wren is a better liar when it comes to screening patrons than she is when acting casual.* Aloud, she said only, "Stand down, Shane, Wren is allowed to meet nice men."

Shane growled something that sounded like, "No, she isn't."

"Oh, for pity's sake," said Wren, rolling her eyes. "I'd spilled wine and he helped me clean up; he didn't ravish me there on the table."

Shane's second growl contained no coherent words, but appeared to indicate that cleaning up spills was a slippery slope to ravishment.

"So what was his name?" asked Marguerite, not bothering to contain her amusement.

"I didn't catch it."

"Well, maybe I know him. What did he look like?"

"Errr..." Wren bit her lip. "He had dark hair and...err...?"

Marguerite cocked her head. "I'm going to need a little more than that to go on. What did his face look like?"

"Uh. Face." Wren's eyes skittered back and forth. "He definitely had one of those?"

"That's a relief."

"Eyes, nose, the whole works." She nodded firmly. "In all the usual places, too."

Shane put his head in his hands. "Look, I'm not good with faces!" Wren said defensively.

"Would you recognize him if you saw him again?" asked Marguerite, trying not to laugh.

"Oh yes, definitely. Probably. I think." She gnawed on her lower lip again. "I hope?"

"Right," said Marguerite. "I'll keep an eye out for men with dark hair who have faces."

"I think he was tall," added Wren.

"You think everyone is tall," muttered Shane into his hands.

"Was that a short joke? Because if that was a short joke, I will bite your kneecaps bloody."

"You are short."

"I am five-foot-four, which is *exactly* average for a woman from my country."

"Your country is short."

"Children..." said Marguerite.

Wren made a face. "You sound just like the Bishop when you say that."

"My respect for the Bishop grows by leaps and bounds." She laughed ruefully. "Anyway. If you run into your mystery man again, let me know."

"I don't think he meant anything bad," said Wren hesitantly.

Marguerite smiled. "Almost certainly not," she said. "There are some good men out there still, even in this fallen world."

Shane's grunt was practically volcanic, but he didn't argue.

Someone knocked on the door. Shane picked up his sword and went to answer it. Marguerite put down her pen, assuming that it was most likely a page with a message for her. *An invitation, most likely. Or a proposition.* She'd already received several of each and had accepted two of the invitations, and put off the propositions while leaving the door open to the future.

It was a surprise, therefore, when Shane returned, followed by a nervous looking young page. "I have a meeting," he said. "Wren, you're —"

Marguerite cleared her throat and flicked her eyes to the page.

"—absolutely right," Shane said hurriedly. "Right. Yes. Absolutely."

Marguerite stifled a sigh. Beartongue had warned her that Shane was a terrible liar, and she hadn't been wrong. *I assume that was going to be "Wren, you're in charge. Make sure no one stabs Marguerite before I get back." Which is not the sort of thing you say to a lady about a member of her entourage.*

"Of course I'm right," said Wren, slightly quicker on the uptake. "Always. Enjoy your meeting." She waved.

Shane belted his sword around his hips and went into his room briefly, then emerged. "Lead the way," he told the page. The door shut behind them.

"Huh," said Marguerite, putting her chin in her hand. "Now that's interesting. Is our broody friend getting laid, do you think?"

"*Shane?* No, I...huh." Wren wrinkled her nose. "Er. I suppose it's possible?"

"He's a very handsome man," said Marguerite, amused by the dismay in Wren's voice. "Some women might notice."

"I guess." Wren sounded very much like a little sister forced to contemplate her brother's love life. "Huh. I almost wish he was. He hasn't really been interested in anyone since..."

Marguerite lifted her eyebrows. "Since?" There was an odd feeling in her gut. She examined it dispassionately and realized that it felt almost like jealousy.

Now you're just being ridiculous.

"When the Saint died..." Wren spread her hands. "Women were always interested in him before."

"I'm not surprised."

"Yeah. They probably still would have been afterward, but it's like he stopped caring very much. And then he grew that beard."

"Oh god, the beard." No, women probably hadn't been lining up to fight their way through *that.*

Wren shook her head. "Anyway," she said, after a moment, "it took a couple of us that way. Stephen...well, you know Stephen."

Marguerite nodded, thinking of Grace's somber paladin. "I imagine it was very hard."

Wren shrugged one shoulder, clearly unwilling to get into details. "Yeah. But it's been what, almost six years now? We move on or we don't."

"Yes, of course." Marguerite bade Wren a pleasant night and retired to her bed. *Well. That's interesting.*

And none of my business. Shane is probably still in mourning for his god. I don't have the time, the energy, or the patience to compete with a ghost.

And while my ego is extremely well-developed, I also don't know if I can compete with a god.

She thought about this for a few moments, then snorted into the darkness. *If he keeps being adorable and companionable, though, I might be tempted to give it a try.*

CHAPTER 22

Lady Silver's quarters were on another floor of the palace, and Shane was perilously close to lost by the time he got there. The page took him up two flights, then down another one, apparently to save time, but then they plunged into a labyrinth of corridors, some of them clearly older, the walls covered in threadbare tapestries when they were covered at all. *A sign of disfavor?* Shane wondered. *Is Lady Silver disliked? Or does it have something to do with her people—perhaps they are at loggerheads with high-ranked members of the court?*

The Bishop would probably know, but it was the Bishop's job to know. Shane just stood around and listened and looked menacing. Still he made a mental note to ask her, when they finally returned to Archenhold.

It finally occurred to him, as they turned down yet another corridor, just who Lady Silver reminded him of: *Judith.* Strange, enigmatic Judith, oddest of the seven surviving paladins, yet no less loved for all that. Something about the way that both of them moved, just a hairsbreadth too considered, as if, though fluent, human body language was not their native tongue.

Which, for Lady Silver, it wasn't. For Judith, the explanation was doubtless deeper, but Judith never *ever* talked about her past, and no one was cruel enough or fool enough to dig for it. It didn't matter. She'd saved his life any number of times, and he'd saved hers, often enough that neither of them bothered keeping score.

When she'd left after Piper's revelation of the Saint's death, Shane hadn't been surprised, or even particularly worried. It was like her to simply go, with neither explanations nor farewells. Whatever she was looking for, he hoped that she found it. If she did, she'd probably turn up again at the temple as if no time had passed, and look vaguely surprised that anyone had missed her.

He was startled out of his woolgathering when the page stopped at a door, rapped sharply three times, then opened it without waiting. Shane went in.

This suite of rooms was substantially larger than the one that Marguerite had secured, though the ceilings were lower. Bookshelves lined the walls of the main room, while a small brazier provided heat and a strong, pungent scent that reminded Shane vaguely of creosote. A large oak desk dominated the room, covered in papers, but a long side table held a forest of glassware that Shane recognized, surprised, as distillation equipment.

"Ah, Lorrrd Shane," said Lady Silver, straightening from where she bent over the equipment. She nodded to the page, who retreated from the room. "A pleasurrre to see you again."

"And you, madam," said Shane, bowing slightly. "Though I fear that I am not actually a lord. Merely a knight."

"Serrr Shane, then." She smiled, canines just visible, and came toward him. "I must beg yourrr pardon," she said. "I was rrrude earlierr, when you deliverrred your message. It was interrresting, you see, and I have learrrned not to appearr too interrested in things in this place." She lifted a blunt-clawed hand and gestured toward the walls and ceiling, as if encompassing the entire Court of Smoke.

"I can well believe it," said Shane. "I took no offense."

"Good, good." Another toothy smile. "I am a diplomatic guest herrre, and thus am allowed a cerrrtain leeway, but I do not fool myself that I am immune to all that goes on arrround me." Her ears, Shane noted, were eased slightly back as she spoke.

"That seems wise," he offered. "I know that I'm missing most of the undercurrents here, and I don't have diplomatic relations riding on what I do."

"Exactly." Silver nodded to him, her ears coming forward again.

It occurred to Shane, somewhat belatedly, that relations between the White Rat and the city of Morstone might actually be affected by what he did here. *But that is Marguerite and Beartongue's concern, not mine.*

"One moment," Lady Silver said, turning off the heat under a flask. "Let me just finish up herrre..."

Shane glanced at the distillation equipment again with interest. It looked very much like the sort found in his friend Grace's workshop. "Forgive my curiosity, but is this for perfume-making?"

Lady Silver's eyebrow patches shot up. "It is, indeed."

"My current employer is selling perfumes. If you are interested in them, I am sure I could arrange an introduction."

Lady Silver laughed softly. "I apprrreciate the spirrrit of the offerrr, but alas, most human scents do not appeal to me. And I fearrr the rreverrrse is also trrrue." She took a slip of paper from a drawer and dipped the very edge in the contents of the flask. "Forrr example..."

Shane took the proffered sample and took a sniff that nearly staggered him. His eyes started to water. The cynocephalic laughed again. "You see? I have learrrned to tolerrrate the scents that humans wearrr, of necessity, but I do not see these imprrroving my status at Courrrt."

"No," said Shane weakly. The smell had been an unholy mating of fermented manure and burnt hair, with a pungent and startling overtone of pumpkin. He wondered what Grace would think of it.

Probably wonder how she was doing it. I suspect they'd have a lot to talk about.

"I make them forrr my own amusement," his hostess said. "Some I ship back home. Therre arrre ingrredients found herrre that do not exist in my homeland." She made a sweeping gesture. "At any rrrate, you did not come to discuss smells, I think."

Lady Silver waved him to a chair and sat down at the oak desk, tapping a note on the table before her. Shane guessed that it was the one from Beartongue, although he could not read the words at this distance without his glasses. "The good Bishop asks about the death of gods. A most fascinating topic."

Shane inclined his head, wondering if he was about to be plunged into the depths of applied theology. *You don't have to understand it, you just have to remember it so that you can repeat it to Beartongue and Piper.*

"My people's gods die rrregularly. It surrrprised me to learrn that yourrs do not."

Shane's eyebrows shot up. "They do? How? Of what?"

Lady Silver laughed. "Of old age, I suppose you would say. The yearrrs are our gods. Each one is borrrn on the spring equinox and stands between us and the calamities of the seasons. Each one lives long enough to see theirr successorrr borrrn, and then passes away."

It took him a moment to get his head around this. "The year? As a god? You mean, your god was born a few months ago, and you pray to them?"

Lady Silver nodded. "My people mark the calendar differently than yours. We dwell now in the house of Sixth Rising, and next will be Seventh Rising. Then Eighth Waiting, and so forth, on until Twelfth Sleeping, after which a new cycle will begin with First Waking. Twelve year-gods to a cycle, twelve cycles to a Great Year, and so on." She flicked her ears. "Sixth Rising is not quite old enough to say what kind of god He will be yet."

Shane rubbed the bridge of his nose. The notion of worshipping something only a few months old seemed bizarre, but it would be rude to say so. *And unwise to insult a god, in any event.* "Huh," he said. "I've never heard of anything like that."

"And your people's method of keeping gods about, on and on, seems equally peculiar to me," said Silver. "Though we have our ancestors, and the great beasts, who live on and on. We invoke them sometimes as well, in need. But for the little things, the day-to-day things, we call upon the year-gods." She laughed again. "I would be embarrassed to constantly plague my ancestors with requests, calling upon them when I misplace my keys or crack a claw. And to call upon a great beast for such a thing would be most unwise."

Shane's brain was a whirl of gods and beasts. He shook his head to clear it. "Do you have paladins of your gods? Or priests?"

"Priests, yes," Silver said. "And warriors dedicated to the year-god, which I think are the closest we come to your paladins. Some simply dedicate themselves to the next god, year after year, but there are many who find that they are called at the beginning of a year to serve that god only, and not Their successor. But this is all neither here nor there." She leaned forward, tapping her claws on the desk again, her eyes bright and interested. *And I notice that she is no longer growling her words, and her speech is flowing much more eloquently. Is the growling part of her act to seem more dog-like, and thus more harmless, in this palace full of knives?*

"Our gods die in their appointed times. Not like you, my paladin friend, and your Saint of Steel."

Shane knew he didn't quite conceal his surprise. "Did the note tell you?" he asked.

"No." She flattened her ears apologetically. "I guessed. You bear a sword and a note asking for information about gods dying. You ask specifically about paladins. And I have read of a human god dying an untimely death, and what became of His champions."

"Yes, of course," Shane said. One hand rose involuntarily to his sternum, rubbing absently at the spot that had once held a god's fire. "I suppose it was obvious."

"Not so obvious," Lady Silver assured him. "Not unless one had reason to suspect." She made a wavering gesture with one hand that he could not quite interpret. "Still, I would be wary of talking about paladins, if you wish to keep it secret."

"It's not exactly a secret," he said, "so much as just easier." After the Saint had died, the place just under Shane's heart had felt as if it were full of broken glass, slicing him whenever he breathed. Time did not heal all wounds, no matter what the proverb said, but it had scarred over at last. Now it was simply a numb place in his chest that ached occasionally, and a memory of glory—until the black tide rose and swept him away.

The black tide was the reason that the surviving paladins were treated like barely tame animals, as if they might turn and bite at any moment. In Shane's case, that was unlikely, but still, it was easier if people did not know. "It grows wearisome," he said, half to himself, "to always be treated like a wild animal."

Lady Silver laughed. It took him a moment to recognize it as laughter and not as a sneezing fit, but something about the position of her ears gave it away. "Oh yes," she said, "it grows wearisome indeed!"

The tips of his own ears grew hot with embarrassment. "Forgive me," he said, "that was very rude of me. I did not mean to imply—"

"Bah." She cut him off with a waved hand. "You had the right of it. And it is not so hard these days. I am like a tame bear to many of your people, a beast that walks upright and dances and does clever tricks. No one fears the dancing bear. In the early days, when I was not such a fixture here, there was much fear, as if I might suddenly drop to all fours and devour the servants without sauce."

Shane nodded. "The paladins—my brothers and sisters who survived the Saint's death—so many people watched us as if we might run mad and kill everything that moved." Honesty compelled him to add, "Though they had reason, unlike with you. Many of us did, when the Saint died." Shane himself, with his brother Stephen, had attacked the paladins of the Dreaming God that they had been escorting, and only the fact that they had been half-blind with pain and confusion had allowed the others to survive. *And if Istvhan had not simply passed out, I suspect that tale would have a very different ending.*

"That was a hard year," said Lady Silver gently.

"Perhaps the god of that year was cruel."

He was half joking, but she took him seriously. "No, no. The year-god did not do that, friend Shane. The world did it, and Second Waking put herself between us and the world." She studied him intently, her great golden eyes unblinking as a cat's. "There were many hard things that year, and she turned aside as many as she could, and blunted the rest. Our gods are a little like you paladins, I think. The ones who fight for us."

Shane bowed his head, feeling oddly humbled.

Lady Silver took up a pen and began to write. Shane waited, listening to the scratch of pen on parchment. "I do not know how your god was killed," she said, when she had finished and sat waiting for the ink to dry. "Or what did so, or why."

"Killed?" Shane asked, startled. "What do you mean, *killed?*"

Lady Silver's nostrils flared. "But of course, killed. Your god did not simply *die*, paladin, or none of you would be as you are. I have been the servant of a year, and when She died, She slipped out of my soul as kindly as She had come. She did not tear a bloody wound as your god did to you."

"Perhaps your god was less cruel," said Shane, and stopped, shocked by the bitterness in his voice.

"There are many gods that seem cruel to us, who cannot know what They know, and no doubt a few who truly are. But I cannot believe that a god who loved His followers as your Saint must have loved you would have chosen to leave you as He did. No, this was as shocking to Him as it was to you, I expect. And since gods do not fall down the stairs or choke on fishbones..." She spread her hands.

Shane hardly knew what to say in response. *Could this be true? In the first days, I know we lashed out because we thought that our god was taken from us, but that was just the pain, wasn't it? And I know the Temple did their best, but they couldn't turn up anything. We were so busy surviving afterwards that we didn't think about it until Piper laid hands on the altar and felt... something.*

"You seem surprised," said Lady Silver gently.

"I think we'd somehow all agreed that we'd probably never know what happened," Shane admitted. "It was too big and it didn't seem to involve mortals at all. If another god had killed the Saint, we couldn't do anything about it."

But Lady Silver was already shaking her head. "For a god to kill another god is a natural death, of sorts. At least, if one is a god. There are many legends of such things. This was something else. There are stories of heroes with weapons that could slay a god, but that sends a shockwave around the earth, and this did not."

The shockwave it sent through us was quite enough, I suppose. And what would I do if I found out that it was another god? Take up one of these god-slaying weapons in revenge?

He was very afraid that the answer was yes. Not for the Saint of Steel, precisely, but for His chosen, who had suffered and died alongside their god.

"How could a mortal kill a god, without a god-slaying weapon?" he asked.

Lady Silver's eyebrows—or the patches of fur that served as eyebrows—went up. "You think like a warrior," she said. "Think like a courtier instead. How would you kill someone, if you had no blade? If you were weak and they were strong?"

Shane frowned. "Poison," he said finally. "Accident. You say that gods don't fall down the stairs, but can you push a god off a cliff?"

Lady Silver flicked her ears, amused. "I don't believe that's ever been tried." She looked down at the letter before her, then folded it and handed it to him. "For your Bishop. I do not know exactly how it was done, but someone or something killed your Saint. My own meager archives—" she waved her hand at the shelves of books "—contain nothing but hints. You will require a more specialized library for that." She nodded to the letter. "I have listed those that I believe might contain more."

Shane tucked the letter away, and Lady Silver rose to escort him out. "It is an interrresting puzzle," she said, and he guessed by the growling trill that she had remembered to reassume her accent. *No one fears the dancing bear.* He wondered if she realized that he'd noticed. *Probably. I do not think Lady Silver misses many things. I wonder how old she is?* He had no way of knowing. She might have been half his age or a dozen years his senior, even assuming that her race lived the same span as a human would.

"One thing..." Shane paused, one hand on the door. "The weapons that could kill a god. Has anyone ever slain a year-god that way?"

A shiver ran through Lady Silver's great ears. "Once, long ago. The year outside a year."

"What happened?"

"For seven months, there was no one to stand between us and the world. Floods came, and famine. Many, many died. It broke the great cycle, and the next god was declared First Enduring and began a new one."

"Oh." *I'm sorry I asked.*

The cynocephalic's eyes were brooding. "That is why it is important to learn these things. If someone can go about killing gods, what hope is there for mortals?"

She shut the door before Shane could think of an answer for that, assuming one existed at all.

Wren was still awake when he returned. Part of him noticed this in a detached fashion—*of course she stayed awake, someone should be on guard when one of us is out*—but the rest of his brain was a whirl of dead gods, dead priests, and dead years. He dropped into his chair and stared blindly at the ceiling.

"You look like you just took a board to the back of the head."

"That's about how I feel."

Wren considered this, then said, cautiously, "Romantic evening go badly?"

It was such a completely wrong guess that it startled a crack of laughter out of him. "Oh gods and saints! I only wish!" Haltingly, he spelled out the details about Lady Silver, Beartongue's message, and what the scholar had said. Wren's eyes got rounder and rounder as he talked, until she looked like a small, muscular owl.

He finally ran out of words. A minute later, Wren said, in a small voice, "Whoa."

Shane wanted to laugh again, or weep, or both. He put his face in his hands. "What do we do if it's true?"

Fabric rustled and he felt Wren put an arm around his shoulders in a tight hug. "*Do* we need to do anything? Isn't this all...I don't know...god stuff?"

His laugh wasn't entirely humorless. "God stuff. I don't know. Maybe. Wouldn't we want revenge?"

Wren was silent for so long that he wasn't sure that she was going to answer at all. "I don't know," she said finally. "Are humans supposed to avenge gods? That seems like something a priest would know better than I would."

"All our priests are dead," said Shane wearily, dropping his hands. "Maybe they're the ones we need to avenge."

Since she was sitting on the arm of the chair, he couldn't see her face, but he felt Wren go very still. He recognized the flavor of that stillness all too well. The black tide inside him tried to rise in response, and he pushed it back. "Wren."

"I'd avenge you," said Wren, her voice too cold and calm. "All of you who had your god torn away."

He wanted to point out that *she'd* lost the god as well, but he understood too clearly what she meant. It was not in either of their natures to avenge a slight against themselves, only against others. Besides, at the moment, that was not what was important.

"Wren," he said again, and put some steel into it. "Wren, step back from it."

She inhaled slowly, let it out again. The air around her was as charged and prickly as a thunderstorm.

"Wren."

"Right," she said. He felt the tension ease and then she drew away. "It's okay. I'm okay. Sorry. Didn't mean to...well. Sorry."

"It's all right."

Wren rubbed her fingertips together, looking vaguely embarrassed. "I guess maybe we should ask a priest. Maybe Beartongue."

Shane snorted. "Beartongue's probably got three contingency plans in place already."

"Probably. We just swing the swords." She stared into the fire. "Thanks."

"Of course."

Orange firelight licked the side of her face when she smiled ruefully. "I'm glad you're here," she admitted. "You specifically, I mean. Not just one of us."

"I keep thinking someone else would do it better. Istvhan, maybe."

Wren rolled her eyes. "Oh sure, but what if they'd sent Galen along? Can you imagine? He'd make the wrong joke to the wrong person and then pull it all down around their ears."

Shane chuckled. "It'd be spectacular, though."

"Oh yes. We'd all stand on the sidelines and applaud the style with which the battlements came crashing down." Wren shook her head. "Right. I'm going to bed. Some things are above my paygrade."

Shane banked the fire and sought his own bed. His head still felt uncomfortably full, but Wren was right. Some things were simply too large for a single paladin to deal with. *I'll put it to the priests,* he told himself, *and whatever they tell us to do, we'll do. It's just easier that way for everybody.*

CHAPTER 23

The ballroom was full of people, which meant that Wren felt more isolated than ever. The paladin grimaced. Poets always thought they were so clever, talking about how people could be so terribly *lonely* in groups as if it was some special insight, when it was obvious to any fool that other people just made it worse. If you were starving, being surrounded by food you couldn't eat didn't help. It just reminded you how hungry you were.

This was about as much philosophy as Wren could handle on an empty stomach, so she staged a raid on the refreshments. Previous reconnaissance had indicated that anything on a cracker would turn into a shower of crumbs the moment you bit into it. Other people seemed able to eat them without looking as if they had full frontal dandruff, but Wren had no idea how they were managing that. Same problem with the little fruit tarts. The crust would disintegrate at the slightest provocation. They were simply too dry and powdery. Wren had originally thought that maybe it was a failure of that particular batch of crust, but they were all like that, which made her think that the baker just wasn't very good. *This can't be intentional, unless you're supposed to put the whole thing in your mouth at once? You'd practically have to unhinge your jaw like a snake.* Surely that wasn't considered proper courtly manners?

To be honest, none of the prepared foods were very good. The snails were overcooked, the egg butter was oversalted, and the cook put anise in things that did not in any way require anise. Wren liked anise as much as the next person, but there were limits. *A little fennel would work much better here, without turning everything into a weird licorice-flavored endurance test.*

Oh, well. Much as Wren might like to break into the fortress kitchens and demand to know what personal trauma the cook was excising through spices, their mission would probably suffer. She moved on to safer choices. The little rolls of meat were fairly inoffensive, along with slivers of cheese. It wasn't exactly a meal, but if you grazed throughout the day, it kept your stomach from growling too loudly.

She took her food over to the window. The view was spectacular, but more importantly, the sill was nearly a foot deep, which meant that she couldn't see *down,* merely *out.* Distant hills didn't bother her. It was the distant ground that got her into trouble.

This view might have been worth a little queasiness even so. She could see the long curve of the river and the fields that spread across the hills. It looked green and prosperous and well-maintained. The Prince of —whoever the hell the Prince was, the one who owned the fortress, Wren had already forgotten his name—clearly cared for his tiny kingdom. She approved of that.

She nibbled at a bit of cheese. The cheese, at least, was excellent. Wren approved of good cheese. She could have done great things with this cheese, given an adequate kitchen. Not that she often had one of those. The Saint's chosen spent a lot more time around battlefields than bread ovens. Wren had given up on cooking for years. Even now, when she could sometimes convince the Temple staff to let her use a corner of the kitchen, she always felt bad about disrupting the cook's carefully orchestrated chaos.

"What are you looking at?" asked a familiar voice, breaking into her thoughts.

Wren turned, feeling a helpless smile spread across her face. "It's you!" she said, and then cursed herself immediately for her lack of courtly manners.

Her savior from the punchbowl didn't seem to mind. "It is indeed," he said, with a little half-bow. "And Lady Wren."

"Forgive me," she said. "I'm afraid you didn't tell me your name before, when you came to my rescue."

He smiled, his eyes crinkling up at the corners. "Ian."

"Lord Ian?"

He shook his head. "Merely Ian. I fear that there are several cousins and at least one brother in the way before I become so much as a minor noble. And since I quite like my cousins, I'm in no rush to ascend." He leaned against the windowsill beside her, smile still playing around his lips. "But you haven't answered my question."

"I haven't?"

Ian gestured to the window. "What are you looking at, with such an intent expression on your face?"

Wren swallowed. He'd been paying attention to her expression? She hoped that she hadn't been scowling or chewing on her lower lip, a habit which her mother had always chided her about, saying it made her look like a sheep chewing its cud. "The landscape," she admitted. "It's such an extraordinary view. I could look at it for hours." *And a good thing, too, since nobody wants to talk to me.*

He studied her face, oddly intent. "Is that so?"

Belatedly, Wren remembered that anyone familiar with the Court of Smoke had probably seen the view so many times that it no longer registered. She smiled sheepishly. "I know, I know, it is terribly unfashionable to admit to being impressed with the view. Probably anyone who is anyone has seen much better. But I still like it, anyway."

Ian shook his head. "No, no," he said. "Never admit that you have been caught being unfashionable. And never apologize for enjoying something." He leaned his elbows against the broad windowsill and gazed out at it himself. "It *is* beautiful. My home, I fear, is rather flat."

"Mine's all hills," said Wren, turning to look out the window again and wondering when she could steal another glance at his face without being too obvious. *Now? No, too soon. Wait until he says something else.*

He did not say anything else, not for several minutes. When Wren finally gave up and glanced toward him, his eyes caught hers and held them.

"Is there a husband waiting for you, back in those hills?" he asked softly.

Wren's pulse, which stayed steady even when she was trying to put an axe in someone's brain, jumped. "I...err...no," she stammered. *Did he mean that like it sounded?*

Really, though, is there any other way he could *have meant that?*

She couldn't think of one, so she swallowed around a dry throat and asked, "Is there a wife waiting for you, back in your land?"

Ian shook his head, his smile turning wry. "Astonishingly, there is not much market for penniless younger sons without even a courtesy title." He turned back to the window. "But enough of such self-pity. Tell me about your hill country. Is it steeper than this?"

"No," Wren said, "it's more rolling. The mountains are a long way away..." To her mild astonishment, she found herself telling him all about Sedgemoor, about the cold dry winters and the hot green color of the hills in spring and the capricious rivers that were so violently contested by the people who depended on them.

And he *listened*, that was the wonder of it. He listened and nodded and asked intelligent questions and she didn't feel as if she was boring him to tears.

"My...err...friend is holding a gathering to sample perfumes in two nights," she said finally. (Was she supposed to call Marguerite her friend? She couldn't remember.) "You should come! I'm sure I can arrange an invitation."

Ian put a hand over his heart in apparent anguish. "Two nights hence? Alas. I am slated to dance attendance on my aging mother that evening." He gave her a hangdog look. "Believe me, I would far rather be sampling perfumes in pleasant company."

Wren swallowed. *I almost believe him. But maybe that was just a polite excuse?* She dropped her eyes. *Have I been nattering on to him, but he's too polite to leave?*

"When may I see you again?" Ian asked. "If not over perfumes?"

Her heart leapt. She knew that the accepted thing for a lady to do would be to say something flirtatious but noncommittal. She wracked her brain for something flirtatious, but all she could think of was Istvhan, who would probably have said, "Here's my room number, I'll be there all night." Istvhan did not *do* noncommittal.

Instead she said, "When would you like to?" and felt her heart leap again when he smiled.

CHAPTER 24

It had taken Marguerite an entire week to set up the perfume sampling, and now that it had arrived, it was going better than it should have.

People streamed in, chattering. They chattered to each other, they sniffed samples from tiny, cut-glass bottles, they chattered about the samples. They drank wine and chattered about the wine. They sniffed more, they chattered more. The room filled up with sweet scents and gossip and Marguerite circulated through it, smiling warmly, listening hard, and watching people watch other people.

She had, in truth, been braced for something to go wrong. Something always did. Someone would mortally offend someone else, a duel would break out, one of the bottles of wine would have gone to vinegar, a minor noble would have an allergic reaction to one of the perfumes and need to be rushed to the healer.

But so far nothing had gone wrong. It was almost uncanny. Marguerite didn't trust it. Sure, her feet ached from the shoes, which added three inches to her height and took three years off the lifespan of her ankles. Sure, her hair had been scraped and teased into a confection with multiple combs that made her scalp feel as if it was caught in a vise. Sure, she had smelled Grace's perfume selections so many times that she could no longer detect any of them, and her commentary was based on having memorized the color of the paper strips.

But she had expected all that. It was the lack of the unexpected that was throwing her.

One of the people who had refused the invitation had shown up anyway. She suspected that his previous engagement had proved dull. Unfortunately, he proved even duller. After admiring his latest medal and listening to an interminable tale of how he'd acquired it, she crossed him off her mental list. There were operatives who worked by being stultifyingly boring, but his was clearly an impressive natural talent. She eventually excused herself to speak to one of the cloth merchants from Baiir, not without a certain relief.

"Lovely," said Fenella, as Marguerite approached. Her shawl was embroidered in a hundred colors, like a peacock's tail, and she was making distinct inroads on the wine. "Simply a lovely selection, Mistress Florian. We'll certainly want to place orders."

"You are too kind," said Marguerite warmly.

"Lovely gathering, too," Fenella said. "Such handsome men at Court, and you've invited so many of them." She winked at Marguerite, who laughed.

"I fear that reflects more to the Court's credit than mine, madam."

"Bollock—" She coughed. "I mean, *balderdash*. Look at that fellow over there. Do you think he's available?"

Marguerite followed Fenella's gaze and coughed. "I fear that is my bodyguard, madam."

"Oho!" Fenella nudged her in the ribs. "Wouldn't mind him guarding *my* body. I don't suppose he's available too?"

"Sadly, it's only the perfumes."

"Ah, well." Fenella lifted her wineglass in salute. "I'd probably break him anyway."

"I don't doubt it in the slightest." Fenella was clearly slightly tipsy. Too clearly? Marguerite had no reason to suspect her, except that she suspected everyone.

"Oh my," the other woman said suddenly, "now where's he going?"

Marguerite turned and saw Shane stalking across the room with the heavy tread of a man bent on mayhem. *Oh, hell. I knew everything was going too well.* She followed his gaze and found that Baron Maltrevor had cornered Wren and was breathing heavily in her direction.

People got out of the way of a man in armor. They did not get out of the way of Marguerite, but she was a great deal closer. She slid between the Baron and his victim and said, with feigned delight, "Why, Baron Maltrevor! You come to my party and don't even greet your host?"

Maltrevor turned, startled. His eyes focused on her, dropped immediately to her cleavage, and stuck there. "Marguerite! My dear, how long has it been?"

"Far too long," said Marguerite warmly. "Three years, at least. I'm so pleased that you could make time for my little event."

"I wouldn't miss it for the world."

Wren mouthed *thank you* over Maltrevor's shoulder and slipped away. Marguerite hooked her arm through the Baron's and positioned herself between him and Shane. Shane stopped. Marguerite shot him a quelling look, then turned her attention back to Maltrevor. "Now, you must tell me exactly what you think of these new scents. I know that a man of your sophistication will know which is most suitable for a lady."

"Oh, certainly. And perhaps someday soon, you could give me your opinion on the most marvelous little clockwork baubles I've been collecting..." The Baron closed his hand over hers, still talking, and rubbed it in what he probably thought was an erotic fashion. Maltrevor was lecherous to the core, and while Marguerite knew several extremely charming lechers, he was not among them. Unfortunately he was also wealthy and well-connected, and she was at pains to cultivate his goodwill. *At least this is a problem that I know how to handle.* She steered the man toward the closest perfumes, scattering light flirtations like caltrops around him. When she was finally able to disentangle herself, her arm was damp where he'd been clasping it.

She kept an eye on the Baron for the rest of the evening. She only had to intervene once, and then, to her eternal gratitude, Fenella wandered into his orbit and distracted him with a discussion of the trade routes that passed through the Maltrevor lands. Marguerite made a mental note to give her a very, very good deal on the perfume order.

Finally, mercifully, it was over. She thanked the few stragglers as they left—Maltrevor breathed heavily in her ear and she manufactured a giggle—and then there was no one left but the servants that she hired to serve wine and clean up. Marguerite made her way swiftly between them, pressing coins into hands and gratitude into words, and finally reached the doorway where Shane waited.

"Are you as tired as I am?" she asked, as he fell into step beside her.

"Likely not. I only stood there, I was not required to talk."

"There's that." She rolled her shoulders. "It went well, anyway."

His expression soured. "You should have let me throw Maltrevor out on his ear."

"That would have caused an incident. We are trying to *avoid* incidents."

"He deserved it."

"I'm sure he did, but we're here for a very specific reason, and that reason does not involve policing the behavior of lecherous nobles."

"I am willing to expand the scope of our mission," he said, absolutely deadpan.

Marguerite narrowed her eyes. *I* still *can't always tell when he's joking. Dammit.*

"We'll come back next year and make a point of it," she promised. He inclined his head.

They reached their rooms and Marguerite was very glad when the door closed behind them. She let her shoulders sag and yanked off her shoes. "Oof."

"Tell me about it," said Wren, who was lounging barefoot in front of the fire. "I haven't had blisters like this since my first forced march."

"Are you all right?" Marguerite asked, collapsing into a chair. "Apart from the blisters, I mean."

"I'm fine," Wren said. "The perfume gave me something to talk about, even if I was mostly just gushing that my vassal was a genius."

"Good. I was a little worried when Maltrevor cornered you."

"Oh, he tried to grab my ass," said Wren cheerfully.

Shane, who had been sitting, stood up again. Marguerite groaned and put her hand over her eyes.

"Sit down, brother. I said *tried*. He got a very nice handful of tablecloth for his pains. Then he just panted on me for a while." Wren rolled her eyes. "I don't know why, there were plenty of other women there."

"Wrong place at the wrong time," said Marguerite. "It was nothing you did." Shane was still looking murderous. She and Wren shared a look.

"Did you learn stuff?" asked Wren, clearly trying to change the subject. "I mean, useful stuff?"

"I did not magically learn the location of our artificer, but I did rule out a few people as being involved with the Sail." Marguerite grimaced. "Which is extremely useful, in that it lets us concentrate our efforts, but is not as satisfying as providing an actual target. Still, it helps to narrow things down."

Wren sighed. "I wish Ian had been able to come."

"Ian?"

"The man I...err...met. It would be nice if you could meet him too."

"Hmmm. I don't know anyone here named Ian..." And then, when Wren looked suddenly worried, "No, that's *good,* that means I don't know anything *bad* about him."

Shane muttered something that neither of them could make out. Marguerite thought that was probably for the best.

"Right," said Wren, getting up. "I just waited up until you got in to make sure that I didn't need to search the halls for your bodies. Night, all."

Marguerite leaned back in the chair with a sigh. Now that her feet hurt less, her scalp was beginning to complain. She cursed the fashion that had turned against hats in the last few years. She'd liked hats. They covered a multitude of sins in the hair department.

She began pulling out combs. Shane watched in silence, then finally said, "No click, then?"

"No click." She sighed heavily and yanked a comb out with a bit more force than necessary. It came out, trailing several dark strands.

"Perhaps it's still too early," he offered.

"Probably. I was hoping, though." *More than I'm willing to admit, actually.* In her heart of hearts, she'd been hoping to swoop in, have the critical information fall into her lap, and go out after the artificer while the Sail was still trying to figure out if she was the person from the wanted posters. The longer it took, the more danger that the operatives at Court would actually communicate with one of the branches of the Sail that wanted her dead. *Not to mention the chance that they'll locate the artificer and have them quietly shoved off a cliff, which would be extremely detrimental to both their health and my plans.*

One of the combs didn't want to come out. She pulled harder on it, annoyed.

"Here, let me," said Shane behind her. She hadn't heard him move. "It's caught up on a hairpin."

Gods above and below, he was using the voice. Marguerite let her hands drop as the words poured over her, soothing as warm honey.

If I could bottle that, I would make so much *money.*

"Just a bit of a tangle," he murmured, coaxing the pin loose. "I don't want to take half your hair out with it."

"That's fine," said Marguerite, with only a vague idea what she was agreeing to. His fingers were very deft and she felt a shiver going through her as he worked. *Oh yeah. That's the stuff, right there. If I was a cat, I'd be purring.*

He removed the offending comb and then carefully began to pluck out the remaining ones. Her hair fell down across her neck, and she shivered again.

When the last one was out, Shane rested his hands on the back of her chair. She tilted her head back slightly, looking up at him, wondering if he was going to do anything, or she was.

If he'd kissed her then, she would have dragged him into the bedroom, never mind how tired she was or what Wren might think of the noises.

But he did not, and the moment stretched long enough for Marguerite to remember that he did not approve of her, and also for her feet to remember that they ached. She sighed and patted one of his hands as if she were an old lady. *And at the moment I feel like one.* "Tomorrow," she said wearily. She got to her feet, wincing. "And maybe we'll be lucky and out of the blue, there'll be a click."

"May the gods will it so," said Shane politely. Marguerite felt his eyes following her as she went to the bedroom, but he didn't say anything more, and neither did she.

CHAPTER 25

Three days later, Marguerite's feet hurt and her back hurt and she was tired. Again. *Story of my life, really. Although usually my feet aren't in quite this bad a shape.*

She had spent most of the evening at a ball thrown in honor of somebody powerful by somebody even more powerful. (She had notes somewhere, but had filed the people involved as *not currently my problem.)* Normally mere merchants wouldn't dance at such an event, but unfortunately the honoree actually *was* a merchant, so the entire event had been arranged to allow nobles and bourgeoisie to intermingle. Marguerite had only danced when asked by someone that she either wanted to cultivate or didn't want to offend, but unfortunately that was a rather large number of people, and two of them had stepped on her feet.

She envied Shane. He was on an upper balcony, alongside the wallflowers and pet duelists. Nobody stepped on *his* feet.

That's got to be enough dancing, she thought, as she let an eager young puppy escort her from the floor. No one had spilled any immediately relevant information, although she'd picked up the latest scandal from one dance partner and was fairly certain, by the way that one of the others had been staring at another woman over her shoulder, that he was trying to make someone jealous, which was worth filing away for later use.

He'd been one of the ones who stepped on her foot. Several of her toes felt as if they were permanently flattened.

She limped up the steps to the balcony, looking for Shane. He was never hard to find, but this time, it was particularly easy, because everyone around him had drawn back and a chevalier was gesticulating furiously at him.

Oh gods of my mothers, what now?

She recognized the chevalier immediately as Sir Lawrence of Elked. *Too hot-headed for his own good, and* far *too old for that to be cute any longer.* Aching feet forgotten, she rushed forward to save her paladin.

She arrived within earshot just in time to hear Sir Lawrence say loudly, "I demand that you give me satisfaction, sir!"

Light sparkled on the rows of earrings in both ears as he turned slightly, making sure that the crowd heard him. His rapier handle was encrusted with tiny gems and the scabbard was inlaid with a dozen brilliant colors.

Shane said, in halting Dailian, "Your pardon, sir, I do not understand what you ask."

"You have offended my lady's honor!" Sir Lawrence informed him. "I demand satisfaction!"

The third person in this little drama stood off to one side, wringing her hands. She could not have been more than eighteen and looked as if she wanted to sink into the floor, die, and then have her body shipped somewhere very far away.

Shane's eyes lit up with relief when he saw Marguerite. *Possibly the first time he's ever been genuinely glad to see me.* "Thank the Saint," he said. "This man keeps asking me for something, but I don't know the word."

"Satisfaction," she translated.

His eyebrows lifted. "I don't know how to satisfy men. It's never come up."

Marguerite coughed to cover up the giggle that threatened to escape. "Vocabulary issue," she said, while the chevalier scowled at them both. "He's asking you for a duel."

"Oh. Your pardon, sir." Shane inclined his head to the chevalier. "This is not my language."

This explanation did not seem to mollify the man at all. "Understand this, then! I am calling you out!"

Marguerite was not an expert in fighting men, but could not see this ending well for the chevalier. The man was at least twenty years older than Shane and two-thirds his weight, if that. He was very tall and could look down on the paladin, which possibly had led him to over-estimate his chances, but Marguerite was guessing that Sir Lawrence had found courage in the bottom of a bottle.

"What seems to be the problem?" Marguerite asked. "This man is in my employ, and if he has offended, I wish to know how!"

Sir Lawrence drew himself up to his full height. "He cruelly rejected my lady's offer to dance, and then had the nerve to slander her character!"

"I didn't offer," mumbled the horribly embarrassed woman somewhere behind Marguerite. "I just said it might be nice to dance and then you said you would find me a partner and then you grabbed that man and I don't even *want* to dance now..."

Marguerite's heart bled for the poor girl, who had clearly been caught up in some misguided and possibly drunken chivalry on the part of Sir Lawrence.

"What man would speak of a lady so?" thundered the chevalier, drowning out the girl's explanations.

"He grabbed you, I take it?" Marguerite murmured to Shane.

"Yes. I shook him off. He shouted something in Dailian and kept pointing to the girl and he was talking so fast that I couldn't understand a word. It sounded like he was accusing me of something, so I kept shaking my head and saying no, I had never touched her."

Marguerite sighed. She could see how it had all fallen into chaos. "He was telling you to dance with the girl over there."

"That is *not* what it sounded like."

"Enough talk! I will not allow this insult against my lady to stand!" Sir Lawrence drew himself up to his full height, one bony hand settling over his sword hilt. "I challenge you to a duel!"

"No," said Shane.

There was a long pause. The chevalier was obviously thrown off stride. "What do you mean, *no?*"

"I will not fight you."

"But you will!"

"No." Shane gazed over the man's shoulder, his face impassive.

"Do you refuse to meet me, then?" The chevalier's lip curled. "Are you a coward?"

Marguerite had to translate that last word. Shane's expression did not change to any significant degree. "Sure," he said.

"What kind of man are you?" blustered Lawrence.

"One who does not fight duels."

"That is no kind of man."

"All right." Shane seemed unconcerned by this.

"Have you no care for your reputation?"

"Not...muchly? No." He murmured a quick question to Marguerite, who supplied the word. "Not *particularly.*"

The chevalier was clearly taken aback by this. "You *will* fight me, sir!"

"Will I?" Shane finally looked back to the chevalier. "Do you fight to first blood here?"

"For a matter of courtesy, most certainly." The man swept his arm toward the girl, who was trying to slink away. "Duels to the death are reserved for a matter of honor."

Shane listened to Marguerite translate the details on that, then nodded. "First blood, then?"

"So I have said."

Shane moved so quickly that Marguerite saw only a blur. The chevalier yelped and slapped his hand to the side of his head. Shane turned and carefully set a small object down on one of the little drinks tables scattered along the wall.

It was an earring. It was still snapped closed. Marguerite winced.

"You barbarian!" hissed the chevalier. Blood was leaking between his fingers, staining the fabric of his cuffs. The gathered crowd gasped excitedly.

"You will want to get that fix. Fixed? Fixed, yes," said Shane. "Ears always bleed...muchly?" And then he went back to staring over the man's shoulder.

"I...you..." The man grabbed for his sword, which was peace bonded into the scabbard. "You *dare!*"

"Was that not what was meant?"

Marguerite decided it was time to intervene, before Shane ripped another earring off of the man's head. "Sir Lawrence, I will thank you to stop badgering my bodyguard. This is clearly a misunderstanding."

"A lady's reputation is at stake!" the chevalier snarled, although this was deprived of some of its impact by the fall of lace across his face as he clutched his ear.

"The lady has left," said Marguerite. She stepped forward. Shane made a small disapproving noise and started to move after her, but she waved him back, annoyed. "Sir Lawrence," she said in an undertone, "no one can doubt that your heart was in the right place, but my bodyguard is more muscle than sense. He only barely speaks your language and had no idea what you were asking. He meant no insult to the lady."

"Nevertheless—"

"It would be *beneath* you to meet such a man on the field of honor," she said. "You spoke correctly when you said that he was a barbarian. He's from the northwest. Far northwest." She leaned in. "I found him wrestling ice-bears in the pit for spare change. He's got certain talents, but no comprehension of civilized honor whatsoever."

Sir Lawrence's gaze flicked from Shane back to Marguerite. Between the earring and the hypothetical ice-bears, he seemed to deflate slightly. "I have no concern for *my* honor," he said coldly, "but the lady's."

"I promise that I shall seek her out immediately and make amends for any insult that was given. He did not understand that you were only seeking a dance partner for her."

"Mmm." Sir Lawrence, clearly aware of the watching crowd, took the out that Marguerite offered. "I question your judgement bringing such a creature here, madam."

"It seemed like a good idea at the time," said Marguerite, with a sigh. "Thank you for your mercy, Sir Lawrence." She curtsied deeply to him, rather more deeply than was required for his relatively low rank. "I am grateful for your forbearance. As he will be, once I explain it to him."

Sir Lawrence sniffed haughtily and let his hand drop from the sword hilt. "Very well. See that it does not happen again." He turned and stalked away, like a disgruntled wading bird. The crowd began to disperse, clearly disappointed in the lack of further bloodshed.

"I caught something about bears," said Shane. "Do I want to know?"

"Probably not." Marguerite shook her head and rolled her eyes. "Come on, let's get you out of here before you cause another diplomatic incident."

They made their way toward the ballroom doors, pausing just long enough for Marguerite to get the name of the young lady who had been so dreadfully embarrassed. Unfortunately, word of the incident had clearly spread at lightning speed. Quizzing glasses were in favor this year, and so many people were peering through them that Marguerite felt as if she was moving through a sea of grotesquely magnified eyeballs.

Dammit, I don't dare run away from this. I've got to nip this in the bud or my name will be all over the keep by midnight.

Hating the necessity, she slowed her steps, stopping to chat with acquaintances, and doing her best to present the image of a woman who was not in full retreat.

It was Davith who came to their rescue. He intercepted her on the way out, full of apparent good cheer, and insisted that he bring her a cup of wine. Even though her feet were in agony, she accepted, while Shane tried to make himself look smaller, with no great success.

"So Lawrence tried to pick a fight with your boy there?" murmured Davith in an undertone, passing her the wine.

"Yes, indeed," she said quietly. "I'm hoping the fortress guard doesn't come down on us for unlicensed brawling."

Davith was too aware of the eyes on them to wince visibly, but she heard the indrawn breath. "Well, I suppose we should fix that."

"I'd like nothing better."

"Simplicity itself." He glanced at Shane and said, apologetically, "I'm sorry for what I'm about to say."

Shane shrugged philosophically.

"Lawrence was *how* drunk?" Davith roared, at top volume, and burst out laughing. "You're not serious!"

"Drunk as a lord," Marguerite confirmed, not quite as loud, but still in a carrying voice. She could practically hear ears pricking up all around them. She giggled into her wine. "And dragging the most unfortunate girl about, and then..." She waved a hand at Shane, who stared straight ahead, looking stolid and unimpressed.

"God's teeth, he thought she wanted to dance with your bodyguard? *This* oaf?"

"I *know!*"

"I mean..." He slapped Shane on the back. "You're not bad looking, my good man, but *can* you even dance?"

"I can do the Winter Dance," said Shane, more slowly than usual, "if I have a goat."

Oh, Lady of Grass... She had no idea what he was going to say next. Davith, however, had an unholy light in his eyes. "A live goat, or a dead goat?"

"Either works."

Davith's laugh this time was genuine, although Marguerite suspected that she was the only one who could tell the difference. "My god, Marguerite, where did you find this specimen?"

"What, and have everyone wanting one?" She scoffed. "Anyway, Davith, do be a dear and make certain Sir Lawrence is feeling better, will you? As much wine as he must have had...well, just tell him that no one holds anything against him, will you?"

"Of course, of course." He waved her off, and called the next words, deliberately, across the space between them. "At least I'll make sure he gets to his room and his valet can get his boots off."

She blew him a kiss and herded Shane from the ballroom, feeling somewhat like she was the one guarding him, and down the hall. It was not until they were most of the way back to their section of the palace that she finally relaxed. "Ooof. What a mess."

"I apologize," said Shane immediately. "I should not have—"

"No, no, no." She shook her head. "You did very well. He was trying to get you to agree to a duel."

"I suspect I would have won."

"Maybe." She pressed her lips together. "Or maybe someone saw a way to get rid of my bodyguard. I wouldn't be entirely surprised if he was paid to try to goad you into something."

Shane stopped dead in the middle of the hall. "I will find him and... ask."

"I'm pretty sure paladins aren't allowed to *ask* like that."

He started walking again, but reluctantly. "What happens now?"

"Now we hope that Davith has suitably muddied the waters that the fortress guard writes it off as a minor drunken mishap. Which *may* be all it was." She gnawed on her lower lip. Sir Lawrence had always been a bit of an ass, but would he normally pick a fight with a bodyguard? She would have sworn that it was beneath his dignity...then again, if the young lady *had* been looking at Shane... *And who could blame her?* "The problem with being both paranoid *and* having someone out to get you is that you start jumping at all the shadows, not just the real ones."

"Mmm."

They reached the suite and stepped inside. Marguerite was relieved to feel the door click shut behind them.

Wren was sitting in the chair in front of the fire. When they walked in, she sat up sharply. "There you are!"

"Is something wrong?" Shane asked.

"No, no." She was vibrating with barely suppressed excitement. "I think I've got something!"

CHAPTER 26

"It might be nothing," Wren said. "Really nothing. But I thought—well, it seems like something—"

"Tell us," said Marguerite, sitting down and pulling off her shoes, "and then we'll be able to tell you."

"Right." Wren cleared her throat. "Lady Coregator is *very* keen on connecting artists to patrons, and she invited me to meet with her again, because she said that she'd found some artificers for me to sponsor. A couple of them were hopeless, but there's one woman who's working on a new form of tidemill…it's actually pretty interesting, and if I had any money…" She trailed off with an embarrassed cough. "I wish I wasn't lying."

"If you give me her name, I think we can probably arrange something," said Marguerite. "Assuming we survive the next few weeks, of course."

"Right, right. Anyway, when Lady Coregator had me look over her list of artificers, I saw Magnus's name!"

"*Did* you now?" Marguerite leaned forward. Shane, who had been divesting himself of armor, stopped in mid-unbuckling.

Wren nodded eagerly. "I did! And there was a name written next to it!" She paused, and some of her enthusiasm faded. "Err…you're not gonna like it, though."

"Try me."

The paladin darted a glance at her brother-in-arms. "It was Baron Maltrevor."

Marguerite let out a whoop, jumped up, grabbed Wren by the forearms and hauled her to her feet, then swung her into an impromptu dance. Shane stepped back to let them go by.

"I guess that's good?" said Wren.

"Wren, you beautiful, marvelous, observant...*paladin,* you! It's wonderful!" Marguerite hugged her fiercely. "That's all I needed! That's more than I needed!"

"Click?" asked Shane.

"That wasn't a click, that was practically a smack." Marguerite grinned up at him. "Maltrevor is a dreadful human being, but he likes to be seen throwing money around. He's not the sort who would hire artists, though, unless they were attractive young women, and that's a different transaction. He's exactly the sort who would be an artificer's patron. I doubt he knows the first thing about what she's actually been working on, but that's not important."

"Would he agree to help her, though?" asked Shane. "When she had to go into hiding?"

Marguerite's feet were expressing strong disapproval of having started dancing again, even barefoot. She limped to the table and splashed wine into a cup while she considered Shane's question. "Maybe. If Magnus has been sensible enough to keep him in clockwork baubles, probably. But even if he didn't arrange it, if he's sending her regular payments, he's got to be sending them somewhere. Even if someone else is picking those up, we just have to find that person and track them back to Magnus."

"You mean we might be close?" asked Wren.

"We're about a thousand times closer than we were yesterday."

Shane frowned. "How do you mean to extract this information from the Baron?"

"He's already invited me to come see his collection of...yes, actually it was clockwork baubles, now that I think of it." *Although those are very common as novelties for the wealthy, so I can't blame myself for not jumping to assume that Magnus was responsible.* "I could hardly ask for a better opening. He'll name a time, I'll go to his quarters and try to steer the conversation in that direction."

"It's too dangerous," said Shane immediately.

"What?"

Shane took a deep breath. "Maltrevor is...not a good man. He might...attempt to take liberties."

Over the paladin's shoulder, Marguerite saw Wren cover her eyes and turn away.

"...Liberties," said Marguerite, not quite certain she'd heard correctly.

"Yes."

"*Sexual* liberties, you mean?"

Shane, to give him what credit she could muster, met her eyes squarely. "Yes. I am sorry to say, it seems likely."

"Good heavens," said Marguerite. "I was just going to suck his cock, then drug his wine, but if you think he might take *liberties...*"

The paladin's face became so expressionless that for a moment, Marguerite was afraid he might keel over in a dead faint. Wren sat down and put her face in her hands, shoulders shaking.

"...Ah," said Shane. "I see. I am a fool. I apologize, Mistress Marguerite, for having misunderstood the situation." He bowed his head, but not before Marguerite saw a flush spread across his cheeks.

"Out of curiosity," Wren piped up, "wouldn't it be easier to drug his wine first, and skip the rest all together?"

"You'd think that, wouldn't you? But it's only a little poppy milk and valerian. Much stronger than that and they figure out they've been drugged. You have to use a light touch or they get suspicious. Plus it makes some men unable to—ah—perform, and the dangerous ones are likely to get violent if that happens."

Shane made a wordless sound of protest. She took pity on him. "The job is the job, Shane. We need that information. And you've a job of your own, since you'll be accompanying me as far as the door."

The blush fled and was replaced with stark white. He stared at her, the ice blue of his eyes almost swallowed up by black, and then he straightened and put his shoulders back. "Yes. Of course. If there is a chance that you will be in danger, I must be nearby."

"Within shouting distance, anyway." She rose to her feet. "But you'll have another job. While I'm keeping him busy, you're going to be investigating his papers so I know what and what not to bother with."

"Of course. Anything you require. Just tell me what you need me to do."

Seducing Maltrevor was so easy that you could hardly call it seduction. He not only did all the work, he made it seem like his idea. Marguerite found the Baron at one of the endless gatherings, arranged to bump into him, and he brought up his clockwork collection without so much as a leading question.

"Oh, the most marvelous things," he said. "A golden grasshopper that hops about, and a beetle that flies on its own. Even a dog that rolls over when you snap your fingers." He squeezed her hand tightly.

"I *do* like things that roll over when I snap my fingers," murmured Marguerite.

"Naughty girl!" He waved a finger at her. "But truly this is something extraordinary. Clockwork animals are nothing new, of course—though I fancy these are particularly fine—but ones that respond to sound! That is quite out of the ordinary way."

"It really is." That wasn't even a lie. Having grown up in Anuket City, Marguerite was familiar with many clockwork creations, not to mention all the ways that they could go horribly wrong. (Ninety-nine times out of a hundred, it was an explosion. The hundredth time, it ran amok and stabbed innocent bystanders, and the artificer would be left standing there saying, "But I had to put blades on it, or how would it rake the leaves?" while the gutters filled up with blood.)

Little clockwork creatures were one of the more commercially viable things to come out of the Artificer's District. Marguerite had brokered more than one shipping deal involving them, and sabotaged more than one as well. But she'd never heard of any that responded to sound. Clearly there had been significant advances since she'd fled the city. *Hmm, if Magnus is responsible for that, there may be another opportunity there as well...I wonder what price they would fetch, and if Magnus has a dedicated agent yet?*

"I would love to see this clockwork," she told Maltrevor, with perfect honesty.

Baron Maltrevor licked his lips, and didn't even bother to hide the look he tipped down her cleavage. Marguerite resigned herself to an evening of being pawed and pretending to enjoy it. *All in a good cause.*

"Well, my dear," he said, patting her hand again, "I'm sure that can be arranged."

Wren was in an excellent mood that evening, which was good, because Shane looked as if he had swallowed a live porcupine and the spines were starting to work their way outward. *At least someone's happy.*

Marguerite herself looked forward to the evening in much the same way that one might look forward to digging a new pit for the outhouse—hard work, not exactly fun, possibly with some mildly disgusting bits. But, much like digging the pit, worthwhile in the end.

Wren twisted in the chair, put her feet up, and gazed into the middle distance with a vague, silly smile on her face.

"Seen your young man again?" asked Marguerite, amused.

Wren flushed. "He's not *my* young man," she said. "He's not...I mean...we haven't..."

A growl from the corner seemed to indicate that Shane's porcupine was not agreeing with him.

"But he has sought you out? Repeatedly?" Marguerite asked.

Wren nodded, the smile still on her lips. "He always finds me."

"Well, I can't speak to his background, but in the Court, that's certainly considered meaningful." Among a group like the Hundred Houses, that would be tantamount to a proposal, but without knowing where this Ian was from, Marguerite couldn't be sure.

"He might just be friendly," Wren said, apparently determined to bring herself back down to earth. "I mean, it's hard to make friends here, and I'm not very threatening. He could just want to talk."

"Uh-huh," said Marguerite. There were certainly young men in the world who simply wanted a friendly chat with a young woman. She had met at least five of them. *The other three or four hundred, on the other hand...* "Does he kiss your hand? Lingering looks? You glance over at him and he's looking straight at you?"

"Nmmmff," said Wren, turning scarlet.

The porcupine was definitely proving indigestible. Marguerite ignored the grumbling from the corner. "Does he ask you about you or talk about himself?"

Wren dug her shoulder blades deeper into the chair. "He wanted to know all about my life back home. And he asked me to go down to the lake with him, where all the shorebirds are nesting."

Is looking at shorebirds a euphemism now? Did I just miss it? "And did you see them?"

"The shorebirds? Yes. There's a spot where they all nest, so if you walk down the path, suddenly there's a dozen adult birds trying to convince you that they have a broken wing and running in all directions. It was completely ridiculous."

Regardless of Ian's intentions, Marguerite was pretty sure that Wren was infatuated with the man, if she was willing to risk the elevator just to look at strange birds. "You'll have to bring him by some time," she said. "I see the merchants more than the nobility."

"Except for Maltrevor," said Shane darkly.

"Yes, well. He isn't terribly welcome among the nobility with marriageable daughters, so he slums it with the merchants. Speaking of which..." She glanced at the water clock. "Probably time to get moving." She went into her bedroom, slipped into something that, while not terribly comfortable, was certainly minimal, then pulled a cloak on over it.

Wren took one look at her and started laughing. "Oh my god!"

"Subtle, isn't it?" Marguerite struck a pose. Out of the corner of her eye, she saw Shane turn the color of an overexcited tomato.

"Those shoes!" said Wren, sitting up.

"Dreadful, aren't they?" She bent down and rubbed her heel. "Fortunately there are no steep staircases between here and there, or I'd probably break an ankle."

Shane finally regained the power of speech and said, "You cannot—you can't *possibly*—you don't mean to—to—"

"To?" She pivoted to face him.

"Go out dressed like that!" He tried to demonstrate what he meant with his hands, ended up tracing an exaggerated hourglass figure, and turned, if possible, even redder.

Marguerite's eyes narrowed. "Are you getting moralistic on me, paladin?"

"I'm afraid you'll start a *riot!*"

She started laughing. She couldn't help it. "Thank you for the compliment. Don't worry, the cloak hides a multitude of sins." She adjusted it, pulling it closed at the front and pinning it in place. "There. I am as modest as a nun."

"Nuns don't wear shoes like that," said Wren.

"Lucky nuns." She leaned down to adjust the strap on one of the shoes. Shane threw his forearm across his eyes as if afraid that he would be struck blind. Marguerite snorted. Being judged by a knight ought to have been funny. *I'd think it was funny if Stephen was doing it, I bet.* Somehow, when it was Shane, it was irritating. *You know what I do for a living. You knew what you signed up for. You don't get to judge me for it.*

"Time to go," she said, settling the cloak back to respectability again.

Shane fell into step behind her. *Probably safer back there. Less chance of being blinded by cleavage.*

"Break a leg," called Wren. "Or...err...whatever you say in these circumstances."

Marguerite could think of at least a dozen options, most of them filthy. Sadly, Shane did not seem like the right audience. *If I turned and said, "Sprain a pelvis," I'm afraid he might faint.*

Oh, well. At least I keep myself entertained.

Hopefully I can keep the Baron entertained long enough to knock him out, too.

She pulled her cloak more tightly around herself and, paladin in tow, went to do her job.

CHAPTER 27

Shane stared around the Baron's outer chambers. It was not a place he'd expected to be. It was not a place he particularly wanted to be.

The room was not large. Even a baron did not rate much space within the fortress. Maltrevor merited several chairs and a small desk scattered with papers. There was an even smaller desk, almost a lectern, wedged in the corner, presumably for a personal secretary to take notes. The secretary did not rate one of the chairs, which were arranged around the desk for the Baron and any guests he might entertain.

Assuming, of course, that he was not entertaining them in the bedroom itself.

Shane closed his eyes. It had taken a lifetime of discipline not to intervene when Marguerite had greeted the Baron, her voice low and throaty with feigned desire. Maltrevor had pulled her hard against him, making her gasp, and Shane had taken an involuntary step forward.

"Don't mind *him*," she said, shooting Shane a sharp look. "All muscle, no sense. *He'll* be staying out here."

The Baron narrowed his eyes. He was not a complete fool, and doubtless he recognized that Shane could have chopped him in half without even breathing hard. "Why is he tagging along after you anyway?"

She stroked her fingers down the side of Maltrevor's jaw. "When you see what I'm wearing under this cloak, you won't wonder. The halls are safe, but not *that* safe."

The Baron's nostrils flared. The door slammed behind them and Shane was left alone in the tiny antechamber.

Marguerite's orders filled his head. He welcomed them, because otherwise he would have to listen to the noises from the next room, and he could not think of anything he wanted less.

Pick up each letter, read it, then place it back exactly where you found it. Test each drawer, quietly. If it does not open, do not rattle it and certainly do not force it. I will look everything over myself, but it will go much more quickly if you can tell me what is and is not a waste of time.

Rifling through a stranger's mail did not come naturally to him, but he steeled himself to the task. Marguerite was sacrificing a great deal for the mission, and he was not going to let that sacrifice go to waste.

The door to the main chamber creaked. Shane had not yet touched the papers, and was damned glad of it when a manservant poked his head around the corner. "The master'll be a bit," the man said in an undertone. "We've a game going, if you want to join us."

Shane shook his head. "Not good at cards," he said gruffly.

"No?"

One of the side effects of being handsome was that people assumed you couldn't be very bright. Shane leaned into it. "Can't keep the numbers straight. Always lose."

"You sure? We'll spot you ten points."

And then proceed to fleece the ignorant swordsman for all he's worth. Shane shook his head again. "Milady said to stay here, in case she calls for me."

The manservant's eyes flickered to the door. "Have a care you don't interrupt the master, then. Even if she screams."

Shane's gut turned over, but he only grunted. Grunts were useful that way. The servant closed the door and Shane heard muffled voices from the next room, and then another muffled voice from the room behind him. It sounded like the Baron.

The papers. The only things that mattered right now were the papers on Maltrevor's desk.

He scanned the first one, moved it aside, and scanned the one beneath it, then replaced the first one exactly where he'd found it. Invitations to dine with other nobles. Probably not important, but how would he know for certain? He scanned the next one, and the next, gleaning nothing more useful than the Baron's schedule for the next few days. There were no convenient letters stating, "Ashes Magnus has arrived at this address, and requests that you forward their mail."

Laughter on the other side of the door. Shane tested the drawers, holding his breath. Only one opened, and it contained nothing more exciting than writing equipment: quill and pen-knife, inkstone and blotter. He lifted the blotter, but did not find any letters tucked behind it.

He checked the lectern. It held a stack of papers, which was briefly exciting until he realized that they all said the exact same thing—"His Lordship Baron Maltrevor is pleased to accept your invitation." The secretary had clearly saved time by writing them up in advance, so that Maltrevor could grab one, sign it, and pass it to a page. Shane tucked one of the acceptances into his surcoat, on the off chance that it might come in handy. *Perhaps I will learn to think like a spy yet.*

Then there was nothing to do but wait.

And wait.

And wait.

And not listen.

There was a lot that he wasn't listening to.

Shane knelt in the middle of the floor and closed his eyes. Prayer. Prayer was what he had left. Not to the Saint of Steel, who he knew no longer heard. Nor to the Dreaming God, of whom Shane had not been worthy. He prayed instead to the White Rat, that practical god who solved problems and whose people tried so hard to make the world a better place.

White Rat, I owe Your people a debt I can never repay. I have no right to ask You for more, but please, let Marguerite be safe and well, and let us all get through this.

Whatever *this* was. It seemed like an enormous amount of trouble over mere salt. Still, both Marguerite and the Bishop thought that it was important, and he had faith that they understood the matter better than he did.

Shane wondered if the White Rat could hear thoughts tangential to prayers. Well, if He could, He had probably heard much worse. He tried to refocus. *Let the outcome, whatever it is, be the one that helps the most.*

And if nothing else, let us not make things worse.

The door creaked, very softly. Shane's eyes snapped open, but he knew the soft footsteps that came toward him.

"What do you have for me?" Marguerite whispered. "Anything useful?"

Her hair had slipped mostly loose from her braid, forming a disheveled knot, the ribbon dangling. He had a sudden intense urge to comb it out with his fingers and braid it back in place, midnight line over midnight line.

Of all the things that we do not have time for...

"Are you all right?" he whispered, because they had time enough for that.

"Fine, fine." She waved off the question. "What have you found?"

The first time that he'd killed a man, he'd wanted to be sick. The black tide had rolled back and he looked down at the corpse in front of him and his gorge had risen and then Stephen, who was only a little older but had been a soldier for a great deal longer, had grabbed his forearm and hissed, *"Later.* You aren't done yet."

And he had choked it down and lifted his sword and the tide had rolled over him again and he had cut down more of the enemy. And later on, Stephen had held his hair while Shane puked up everything he'd ever thought of eating.

Marguerite had been a spy for as long as he'd been a warrior. Undoubtedly she knew all about waiting until later. The least he could do was respect her composure. So Shane nodded to her and told her, in whispers, that it was all invitations and that only one drawer was unlocked.

"Good work." She pulled a thin metal implement from inside her bodice. "Extra boning," she said, at his glance. "At least, that's what it feels like on the outside." Shane went to the door, setting his back against it lest anyone try to enter, and waited.

He thought that he was calm and composed, until he heard Marguerite whisper, "Come on, baby, right there..." and nearly jumped out of his skin.

She was talking to the locked drawer. Of course she was. Certainly not to him. Certainly not those words, right now, when she'd just been pawed over by some titled brute.

"*There's* the spot," she murmured, and popped the lock.

There were two more locked drawers. Shane wasn't sure he'd survive if she had to talk to those locks, too.

What is wrong with you? How can you even think *such a thing right now?*

It was terribly wrong. The only thing he should be thinking right now was how to comfort Marguerite after an undoubtedly unpleasant experience and possibly how to murder the baron later.

I really need to figure out what that word for not feeling guilty enough is.

"Money," Marguerite muttered, sounding slightly disgusted by the concept, and closed the drawer again. She bent forward to work on the next lock and he squeezed his eyes shut, because only an unchivalrous monster would stare at her backside while she worked. "Now, then... come on...there we go...just a little bit more..."

With his eyes closed, it was impossible not to imagine her whispering those words in his ear. Impossible not to imagine what he might do that would have her saying such things.

She went to another man's bed to accomplish the mission, and still you're having these thoughts?

In his defense, they weren't exactly thoughts. More involuntary images. He risked opening his eyes, and saw with relief that she was sitting up again.

She shuffled quickly through the papers she'd found, eyes scanning over the pages, then stopped. Read the paper again. Her breath came out in a long sigh. "There," she said, with clear satisfaction. "That's what we needed."

She slid the papers back into the drawer and locked it. The third lock was almost perfunctory. She was clearly distracted—thank all the gods —because she did not attempt to sweet talk it. Instead, she cracked it open, rifled through the contents without much interest, and closed it up again. "Come on," she murmured, rising to her feet. "We got what we came for."

Shane opened the door to the suite and stood like a wall, shielding her from the curious eyes of the servants. Their card game was still going, it seemed. They looked up, saw Shane, then looked down again.

Not the first time that a woman has left these rooms in silence. Nor the last, I suspect. But at least we got what we came for.

He let the door close behind them and hoped that the price had not been too high.

Marguerite took a discreet path through the fortress, rather than a direct one. It was unlikely that anyone cared who warmed Malvertor's bed, as long as the woman was no one of consequence, but there was a slim chance that someone might be watching her. Davith, for example. *He does not entirely trust me, but how much does he know, I wonder?* So she took the long way around, using the corridors on the outside walls.

Shane walked beside her, rather than behind. Marguerite glanced up at his profile. She had thought that she had learned to read him a little, but tonight he might have been a carving made of ice.

Embarrassment? Disapproval?

He damn well better not disapprove. I've got the information, and all it cost me was about thirty minutes with an unpleasant man who smelled like he was trying to cover up sweat with sandalwood.

Irritation flared in her gut. She knew that it was mostly at Maltrevor, but he wasn't here and Shane was and the bastard wasn't even able to look at her. *Did he think I was as pure as he is? A virgin or a saint?*

Who gave him the right to disapprove of anything I do, anyway? Or who I choose to fuck? He's my bodyguard, not my chaperone. I could have a different man in my bed every night, and the only thing he has any right to do is check them for weapons at the door.

Chilly air puffed through the arrow slits on the outer wall. She wrapped her arms around herself more tightly. Her current outfit might turn her breasts into one of the wonders of the world but that was about all you could say for it, and the cloak had been chosen for concealment, not warmth. The night breeze cut right through the thin fabric and whipped it around her bare legs. Also, she'd taken off the damn shoes, which meant that her bare feet were becoming intimate with the flagstones.

Shane stopped and turned to face her.

"Marguerite..."

"What?" she asked crossly. "I chose to do this. Don't start getting cold feet now." *Swear to god, if he decides to read me a lecture about my behavior, I'll take that sword and give the stick up his ass some company.*

"I'm sorry you *had* to do it," he said. "I know there was no choice, but I'm sorry."

"Don't worry about it," she said. "It's just the job. I've done it before. It's all right."

"It's not—"

She groaned. She was *not* in the mood for this. "Shane, have you ever cleaned a privy?"

"Err...I've dug a latrine trench?"

"Close enough. Was it a horrible traumatic experience from which you will never recover?"

He blinked at her. "I can't say it was, no?"

"Was it a boring physical job that you didn't particularly enjoy but it had to get done?"

"Pretty much."

"Well, so is what I just did. A little soap and hot water and then I'm probably never going to think about it again."

Shane considered this. "A lot of people wouldn't feel that way about it," he said cautiously.

"Then they shouldn't go into my line of work." She pinched the bridge of her nose. "Shane, I understand you're trying to be delicate with my feelings, I realize that a lot of people would be horrified and conflicted and would need that, but frankly, *my* only feeling right now is that my goddamn feet hurt, okay?"

Shane nodded once, sharply. "I see." He pulled the heavy wool cloak from his shoulders and wrapped it around her. She blinked up at him, surprised, and then he bent down, slid his arm behind her knees and picked her up.

Wait, what?

Shane's chest was warm against her back and his cloak covered her completely. He smelled like ginger and spices, and she suddenly remembered Grace complaining that Stephen always smelled like gingerbread.

He looked down at her, and if there had been pity in his gaze, she would have punched him in the throat. But she saw something else instead, something she almost recognized. Then he lifted his head and it slipped away. "You did the job. Now I'll take you home."

It was the voice. He was using the voice and she could feel it everywhere she was pressed against him. Marguerite didn't know what to say.

Part of her still wanted to snap at him, but another part wanted to curl up and bask in that voice as if it were the sun.

Shane carried her away from the cold windows and down a flight of steps. Marguerite felt his weight shift and put her arms around his neck for balance. "Don't worry," he said. "I've got you."

I've got you. The words rang inside her as if she were a bell. They promised safety. She *knew* that it was only the voice, some trick handed down by an absent god, and yet she wanted desperately to believe in that promise. She had not felt safe for years. Not since the day that she learned there was a price on her head, because someone had come to collect.

Marguerite leaned her forehead against his shoulder, wishing that he would keep talking. *It's Shane. You're lucky he's not grunting at you again.* "Say something."

"What should I say?"

Tell me I'm safe. Make me believe it, just for a little while. "Anything. Tell me something about you. Something unimportant."

His breath hitched in something that was almost a chuckle. "Something unimportant? Hmm..." They passed the entrance to the bathing area, the smell of steam and mineral salts billowing out to meet them. Marguerite would have liked a bath, but that meant that Shane would put her down and she was not quite ready for this to end.

Several older women emerged, clearly having come from the baths. Shane nodded to them politely, ignoring their wide-eyed looks.

"Damn," one muttered appreciatively. He made it a dozen paces before muffled feminine laughter broke out behind them. Marguerite felt rather smug, even though she knew that the night was going to end with nothing more exciting than a debriefing about an artificer.

"Should I put you down?" asked Shane.

"Only if your arms are tired."

"Not at all."

"Then tell me something unimportant."

He went up the final flight of stairs. "I like cats. My favorite color is purple."

"I'm not sure those are unimportant enough."

"When I was eleven, I memorized the *Tragedy of Sir Pollux*."

"Why?"

"There was a tapestry in the temple. He had a very handsome horse."

Marguerite frowned. "Didn't he die horribly?"

"Extremely." He reached the door to their chambers and his grip on her shifted as he reached out to rap on it. "Pierced by a hundred arrows/Stabb'd through by a hundred swords."

"You'd think everything after the first dozen would be overkill."

"You would, wouldn't you?"

The door opened. Wren looked up at them, wide-eyed, and stepped back. "Oh. Uh. Hello."

"Get the door," said Shane, carrying Marguerite past her. To her surprise, he went to her bedroom before setting her down on her feet, just inside. She felt his lips brush her forehead, then he stepped back, over the threshold, putting a small but important space between them.

"Rest," he said. "Tomorrow will be soon enough to go over what you learned."

"Thank you," she said. The adrenaline from breaking into the Baron's desk was wearing off and Marguerite could feel the crash coming on. She lifted a hand and turned away, closing the door behind her.

Shane leaned his forehead against the doorframe and let his breath out in a long, long sigh.

"Is everything okay?" asked Wren. "Is Marguerite...?"

He straightened. "She says she's fine." *Almost certainly she is, too. She's a professional and you're a fool.*

Wren nodded. He had a brief, mad urge to drop to his knees and beg his fellow paladin to hear his confession, but the idea of pouring out his guilt and frustrated lust to Wren, of all people, was not to be borne. He'd die with his soul unshriven first. The gods would understand.

The ones with little sisters, anyway.

CHAPTER 28

Marguerite slept late the next morning, only waking up when the maid came to clean. She tumbled out of her room to let the woman work, and found the other two already awake and polishing off breakfast.

"Shane says you got something!" whispered Wren, bouncing in her chair.

Marguerite glanced over her shoulder, but it seemed unlikely that Ammy could hear her over the thumping sounds of the bed linens being changed. She nodded to Wren. "He had a letter from whoever he delegated handling the artificer to."

"So we need to find that person?"

"Thankfully, no." She gratefully accepted the mug of tea that Shane handed her. "We know where she went, so we can just go straight there."

"I can be ready within the hour," Shane said immediately.

Wren's excited expression faded so quickly that it might as well have been lopped off with a knife. "Oh," she said. "So we're going, then?"

It did not take the skills of a spymaster to guess the reason behind Wren's dismay. "I can help you write him a note," said Marguerite gently. "There's no reason you can't see him again when this is all over."

"I haven't exactly mentioned what I do," said Wren glumly. "And he probably doesn't think of me that way." She rubbed her forehead. "How long do we have?"

Marguerite shrugged. "Not long, I don't think. The letter said 'sent to the Nallans at the ford.'" She heard the maid approaching the door and hastened to finish up. "We just need to find the Nallan family and we're golden."

"Sorry, ma'am?" asked Ammy, popping her head into the room.

"Nothing, Ammy."

The woman frowned. "Thought I heard my name. Though no, of course you weren't calling me—you said Nallan and I haven't been a Nallan in thirty years."

Marguerite raised both eyebrows. "Nallan?" she asked. Hope mingled with suspicion. It couldn't possibly be this easy, could it?

"Aye, that was my maiden name. One of the Snowpeak Nallans, I was." She thumped her chest.

Shane caught her intention without having to be asked. "Where is Snowpeak?" he asked. "I don't know the highlands at all, I fear."

Ammy sniffed. "Fair distance from here. I don't get back as often as I'd like. In summer I'm working for you lot, and in winter—well, nobody goes to Snowpeak in winter."

"That's a shame," he said, with what seemed like genuine sympathy. "I'm sorry you can't get back to your family. The Nallans, you said?"

Marguerite's hopes soared. It was almost too convenient, but sometimes you did get lucky in this business. And even if Ammy was an enemy operative and trying to throw them off the scent, this sort of thing could be checked, although perhaps not until they were closer to Snowpeak.

"Oh, aye," said Ammy. "O' course, there's Nallans all over, you ken."

Soaring hope faltered. "There are?" Shane asked.

"Bless you, of course there are." Ammy swatted playfully at him with her dustcloth. "Comes from the old word for *warrior*, they say, which is why there's so many of us. Can't scarcely throw a pot of piss out the window without hitting one." She sniffed again, while Marguerite felt her hopes crash to earth. "'Course I wouldn't trust half the people who *call* themselves that. No better than lowlanders, some of 'em. No offense to yourself."

"No," said Shane, in his grave voice, as hope picked up a shovel and began to dig downward. "None taken."

"Not anybody's fault where they're born," Ammy continued magnanimously. "But there's Nallans everywhere you go. Why, I daresay we're in every county in the highlands!"

"I suppose I could seduce Maltrevor again," said Marguerite glumly, after the maid had left and they were all draped over chairs, nursing their disappointment. "Look for more letters, if there are any."

Shane looked up sharply. "I don't think that would be wise."

Irritation sparked. She knew that she was angry because their lead had proved so much less worthwhile than she'd hoped, but she couldn't keep the annoyance out of her voice. "Why? Because you don't approve?"

He might have been a statue carved in marble. "It is not my place to approve or disapprove."

Perversely, that made her angrier. *Damn him for not giving me a fight, even when I want one.* She took a deep breath. *Stop. It's not his fault that the lead dissolved. A good commander does not take her disappointment out on her people.*

"I am afraid that Maltrevor may be dangerous," said Shane. "There's a darkness in him. More than in a normal man."

Marguerite rolled her eyes. "And what do paladins know about darkness? Brothels are full of perfectly normal men who happen to like to spank their lovers or tie them up or whatever." She turned to Wren for backup, and met wide-eyed astonishment.

"Really?" said Wren. "I mean...that's a thing? *Really?*"

Oh gods above and below. Marguerite put her face in her hands. *This is what comes of having six older brothers who kill people for a living.* She briefly contemplated explaining recreational sadomasochism to Wren, then contemplated throwing herself from the battlements instead.

Though it might be worth it just to see if Shane expires of embarrassment on the spot...

And just like that, her anger and disappointment cracked apart, replaced by hilarity. Marguerite felt a laugh rising inescapably in her throat. "It's a thing," she assured Wren. "And some of those perfectly normal men will happily pay money to be the ones tied up and spanked. People are complicated."

"*Wow.*" Wren's eyes were as big as saucers. Shane stared fixedly at the ceiling, his face so absolutely blank that Marguerite was afraid that he was going to faint.

"Look," said Marguerite, standing up, "the thought of going back into the Court right now makes me want to tear my hair out. Let's go have a soak and I'll tell you all about it."

Shane reached out a hand as if to stop her, paused, and pulled it back. He looked from Wren to Marguerite, fraternal horror etched in every line.

"I'll be gentle," Marguerite assured him.

"But..."

"It'll be fine." She slid her arm through Wren's. "C'mon, let's get a bottle of wine sent over. It's noon somewhere, right?"

"Definitely."

She shut the door on the sight of Shane dropping his head onto his folded arms in utter despair.

They sat around the room that evening, making further inroads on another bottle of wine. The soak in hot water had been relaxing enough, but despite hours of heavy thinking (and another hour of heavy drinking) Marguerite was no closer to a solution.

"Maybe there aren't really *that* many Nallans?" Wren suggested hopefully.

"If anything, there are more," said Shane. "I visited the library."

Marguerite raised her glass in his direction. "Anything good?"

"Most of the recent novels were checked out before we got here, so I can't speak to the collection." A rueful smile flickered across his face. "Apparently nobility does not respect a waiting list."

"They wouldn't."

"However," the paladin continued, "it has a great many books on peerage and genealogy."

Marguerite nodded. "No surprise there. This is one of the biggest marriage marts around. You'd want a quick way to check up on any prospects and make sure they were who you thought they were."

Shane nodded. "The highland groups are not nearly so well-documented, I fear, but looking through what information there was, I found Nallans listed in nine separate counties. And that was just those that had attained ranks of minor nobility."

"Saint's balls," muttered Wren.

Marguerite poured the last of the wine into her cup. She was still depressingly sober. "Without knowing what county to start in, we're stuck checking every single ford. We'd practically have to go from door to door, convincing people to talk to us. It would take months." She snorted. "Mind you, the Sail won't have it any easier, it's just that they can field the manpower to knock on a lot more doors."

"Can they?" asked Shane. "Do they have the people?"

"Mmm." Marguerite rubbed the back of her neck. "That's a good question. They can certainly *get* that many people, and in short order, but I don't know how many are deployed in the highlands right this minute. Probably not that many. It's not a major market that they need to keep close tabs on, so few existing operatives, and if you have an army of strangers wandering around, you risk your quarry getting wind of it and relocating."

She rubbed her fingers absently over the cup. The ceramic glaze was smooth on the inside, but the exterior had a rough texture, in accordance with the local style. It was a pleasing contrast, if unexpected. "I've been trying to think how to narrow it down. All I can come up with is that we need to find out which counties Maltrevor has ties to. Sufficient ties that he could tell someone to hide his pet artificer there and they'd do it. But that probably gets us back to finding out who this middleman is, which probably means more time with Maltrevor—yes, I *know*, don't start—"

Shane was clearly going to start, no matter what she said, but before he'd gotten out more than two words, there was a knock at the door of the suite.

Saved at the last minute, Marguerite thought. She really wasn't in the mood for a fight right now.

The paladin got up, put a hand on the hilt of his knife, and went to the door. A man's voice spoke in low tones. Shane's answer was deep and, unsurprisingly, suspicious.

I know that voice, Marguerite thought, setting down her cup.

Shane moved aside and let the man enter, though he didn't take his hand off his knife. A familiar figure stepped into the room.

"Davith?" said Marguerite, at the exact moment that Wren said, "Ian?"

CHAPTER 29

There are some moments that seem to hang in the air forever. Marguerite felt everything fall into place inside her skull, pieces rearranging into a pattern that she knew and understood and desperately hated. She could almost hear the echoes of her own voice saying, "I don't know anyone named Ian...no, that's *good*, that means I don't know anything *bad* about him."

She was watching Davith and saw the moment that he realized that both women were there. Saw the flash of guilty understanding cross his face. Had he not known that they were all crammed into one suite? Had she not told him? Or had he simply hoped to arrive sometime when Wren was absent?

Now why do you assume he came to see you? Perhaps this is the next step in his seduction?

"Shane, Marguerite," Wren began, sounding so pleased and nervous that Marguerite wanted to weep, "this is—"

"Davith," Marguerite said crisply. This was a bandage that must be torn off as quickly as possible. Hesitation would be no kindness. "He is an operative of, among others, the Red Sail. He specializes in seducing women to obtain information from them."

Davith winced, but did not argue. She did not dare look at Wren, because then she might try to strangle him with her bare hands.

"Ah," said Wren, after a little silence. "I see. So I've been a fool, then."

She was trying to sound light and dry and amused, and almost, *almost* she succeeded, but there was the faintest tremor that betrayed her.

Because Marguerite was looking at Davith, she did not see Shane move until it was far too late. Instead she saw Davith's eyes suddenly widen and then Shane's fist cracked into the side of his face and Davith went sprawling across the floor, taking out a chair on the way.

"Get up," said Shane, so low and guttural that she almost didn't recognize his voice.

"Shane, *no.*" Wren got between them, hands lifted to stop him. "He isn't worth it."

Shane stared down at her, his expression almost puzzled. "No," he said simply. "*He* isn't. But you are."

Davith, very wisely, stayed on the floor.

Marguerite had, once or twice, had men fight over her, and thus remembered that, far from being romantic, it was actually among the more humiliating experiences of her life. She grabbed Shane's elbow and said, with all the command she could muster, *"Stop it."*

"I'm going to kill him," said Shane, almost conversationally.

So much for command. "You're going to *embarrass* her," Marguerite hissed. Wren was already turning scarlet and trying like hell to hide it. What had Beartongue said? *Wren will never tell you if she is injured or overmatched.*

Shane stared at his sister-in-arms as if he had never seen her before. "Ah," he said. "I beg your pardon, Wren."

"It's fine," she said. "It's fine. Just...just *don't.*"

"Before you kill me," said Davith, from somewhere around ankle level, "you might want to hear what I have to say. Since I actually came here to save your life."

Shane, with utmost courtesy, removed Marguerite's hand from his elbow, stepped around Wren, and picked Davith up by the scruff of the neck like a kitten.

"Rrrgh..." The spy broke into a coughing fit as soon as Shane set him down in a chair. He rubbed his throat, looking up at the paladin, then around the room. Finding no sympathy whatsoever, he coughed again reproachfully.

"Talk," said Marguerite. "And make it fast, because I'm not feeling particularly generous at the moment."

Davith's lip curled back. "I couldn't have guessed. Fine, the fast version? The local Sail representative figured out that you're *not* working for another branch and has decided to have you killed."

"Define 'you' in this context," said Marguerite.

"You." Davith waved a hand at her. "Presumably the mountain of meat here, too."

"Not Wren?"

He shook his head. "So far as they know, she's just someone you're using for cover. I imagine they'd kill her if she got in the way, but they aren't targeting her specifically." He glanced over at Wren, then looked away again. "I, uh, told them she wasn't important."

Wren made a sound that might have been "Heh!" or might simply have been a small explosion of breath.

Marguerite dropped into the chair opposite Davith, mind racing, and began absently running her fingertips over the woodgrain of the table. "Who's the local representative?"

"Calls herself Fenella. Fabric-buyer from Baiir. At least that's her cover."

Dammit. Marguerite had spoken to Fenella a half-dozen times, and while she was nearly certain that she hadn't spilled any damning information, she also hadn't even considered that the other woman might be an operative. *Getting old. Getting slow. Gods, what did we even* talk *about?*

Trading, mostly. Maltrevor. Pretty bodyguards. All of it innocuous, or so she'd thought. There might have been a recognition phrase in there that she hadn't responded correctly to. Then again, there might not have been. *I could have done everything right and still she'd have figured it out, if she could get word to the right people. Without knowing her chain of command...dammit, dammit, dammit.*

All of which meant that the odds of her talking her way out of the situation were distinctly low.

Panic tried to rise in her throat and she fought it back. *Yes, you're afraid. You hate any situation that's decided with steel instead of words. That's why you've got bodyguards. Two rather* unique *bodyguards.*

And what if one of them gets killed because someone on their side was smarter than you were?

Her gut clenched at the thought. *This is what comes of caring for people in the business.*

So stop whining and do what you can to make sure you don't *get them killed.*

She focused on Davith again. "So they're planning to kill me. How?"

Davith shook his head. "I don't know that. Just that she told me that your vicinity was likely to be—ah—*unhealthy* in the near future."

Unfortunately that left Marguerite with far too many options. *And I don't know if the Sail is willing to break their own cover or not. They could drop a corpse in here and frame us for murder, then discreetly garrote us in our cells, or they could simply have someone walk in, stab us, bundle us up in rugs, and pitch us off the side of the mountain into the lake. Or just stab us, let the maid discover the bodies, and sacrifice a pawn to take the fall if anyone connects the two.*

Damn it all, that's what that attack on Shane was, wasn't it? They were either trying to remove him, or testing to see what I'd do in response. And instead of going to the Sail and demanding answers, I did nothing.

Marguerite weighed the possibility that Davith himself was the assassin, and discarded it. Davith was, as the saying went, a lover, not a fighter. He could probably have overpowered her, but he was certainly no match for Wren, let alone Shane. *Although I doubt he knows that Wren is a paladin.*

Wren seems to have played her part better than I did.

"All right," Marguerite said. "If I send you with a message to Fenella—"

Davith was already shaking his head. "Marguerite, no." He started to reach out a hand, then yanked it back when Shane growled. "You can't negotiate your way out of this one, I promise you."

"You're saying Fenella doesn't have a price?"

"Everybody has a price." He carefully avoided looking at Wren. "I'm saying that you can't possibly meet it."

She narrowed her eyes. "How do you know that?"

"Because I know what the stakes are." He shook his head, then winced, lifting his fingers to his bruised eye. "The Sail believes that this artificer is a threat to their very existence. They aren't going to be put off for a few gold and a hot tip on what's selling in Delta next season. They're fighting for their lives, and they're going to kill anyone they think might get in their way."

It was what she had expected, but she didn't have to like it.

Marguerite drummed her fingers on the table. "So why did you decide to warn me, then? Can't have been safe."

Davith already looked uncomfortable, but now his expression resembled a man sitting on a tack. "You helped me out once," he muttered. "I owe you one."

"You expect us to believe in your honor?" said Shane, going from *standing* to *looming* with a minor shift of weight.

"I do have some, you know," Davith said. His left eye was rapidly swelling closed, but he managed to look wry nonetheless. "Valiantly as I have tried to squelch it. I don't much like Fenella, and I don't like seeing someone I've known for years slaughtered just because she's trying to get the same information that I am." He shook his head. "I want to beat you at the game, not see you dead."

"Well, there's that," said Marguerite. She believed him, strangely enough. Davith, for all his many flaws and deceptions, was neither bloodthirsty nor malicious. "Of course, now you're in almost as much trouble as we are, since the Sail undoubtedly saw you coming here."

Davith leaned back in the chair with a sudden grin. "Ah, but that fine shiner your bodyguard laid onto me will help enormously. And when you give me the information about where Maltrevor's pet artificer is holed up, that'll help even more."

Marguerite snorted. "And why exactly would I do that?"

"Gratitude, obviously." Davith spread his hands. "It's not like you can do anything with it now. We already know where Magnus is staying, we just don't know where exactly she is, and you know what these highland clans are like. You can't bribe them and you can't charm them and if you try to fight one, all his fifty cousins turn on you. The Sail's on their way there already, it'll just take them ages to search the place. Those hills have more holes than a good cheese. But you've got that information, don't you?"

Marguerite laughed. "How did you know?"

"Pfff, half the court knows that your bodyguard here carried you back from Maltrevor's rooms. The only reason you'd go to *his* bed is to get that information. Not, alas, a feat I can replicate." He clasped his hands together. "You give it to me, I give it to the Sail, they're so pleased with me that they overlook my possible indiscretion, you sneak out of the fortress and I take home a sack of coin."

"Brilliant," said Marguerite admiringly. "Really quite a fine plan. I salute you. There's just one tiny problem."

His good eye narrowed. "You're not going to tell me, are you?"

"Not a chance."

Davith sounded more resigned than upset. "You could be putting me in a very precarious situation."

"My heart bleeds," muttered Wren, not quite under her breath.

Marguerite's heart did bleed a little, mostly for Wren. She wasn't going to like this either. "We're running," she said. "But we're headed into the highlands. And you can either come with us, or we can leave you here."

"Hog-tied," added Shane.

Davith snorted. "My days of being tied up by attractive men are long past, knight." He drummed his fingers on the table. "What do I get out of this, again?"

Marguerite shrugged. "Your skin. Without that information, how charitable do you think Fenella is likely to be?"

Davith's scowl was all the answer she needed. "You're completely mad," he said. "Maybe you can sneak out of the fortress, but once you're on the road, they'll be hunting you clear to Cambraith."

Cambraith. Marguerite exulted internally. He'd just handed her the only piece of information she needed. She saw the flicker in Shane's eyes as he registered the name too. "Well, we'll burn that bridge when we come to it," she said lightly. "Right now, we need to get out of here. Fast."

Nobody said anything for a moment. Davith groaned and rolled his eyes. "Really? You're going to make me suggest the best way to kidnap myself?"

Shane's growl was so low as to be almost subterranean, but Davith was not a fool, no matter how often he acted like one. He held up his hands. "Right. I was just saying. So, there's two ways out. We either try to brazen our way through taking a lift, and risk them cutting the rope, or we go down to ground level through the cellars."

"Cellars," said Wren instantly.

"What, you don't favor being splattered across the landscape?" asked Davith.

Wren flushed. "The cellars it is," Marguerite said hastily. "Then we'll take a ship across the lake into the highlands."

Davith scowled. "Dodging the Sail's people, as I said, the whole way to Cambraith."

"Then think of all the chances you'll have to escape," said Marguerite lightly.

"I'm thinking of all the chances I'll have to catch a stray arrow, thank you very much."

"Do we go now?" asked Shane. "Will it be suspicious if we have full packs?"

"I think we can probably assume that we'll be observed leaving the room," said Marguerite. "They may attempt to stop us."

"They're welcome to try," the paladin said coolly.

Marguerite sighed. "And that will turn into unlicensed violence within the fortress, which will lead to both the Sail *and* the Court guards trying to stop us. And once we're in a jail cell, I don't see us all getting out alive again. I might be able to bribe or blackmail one of us loose, but probably not all three."

("Oh, I see how it is," muttered Davith.)

"We need a distraction, then," said Shane. "Something to allow us to get to the cellars unobserved, and to cover in case they do attempt to stop us."

Marguerite nodded. "We do. Hmm, let's see...who could I get a note to..." She nibbled on her lower lip, while Shane and Wren moved about the suite, shoving things into packs. Unfortunately there weren't that many people that both owed her a favor and would be able to cause a suitable distraction at a moment's notice. *And we have to figure that anything I write will be intercepted. Dammit.*

"I could stay behind and cause the distraction," Wren began.

"You're not staying behind," said Shane. "It's too dangerous."

She gave him an annoyed look. "You heard yourself that they don't consider me important. And I'm perfectly capable of taking care of myself in a fight."

"And once you demonstrate that fact, they will suddenly realize that you are very important indeed."

"Hate to say it, but he's right," said Marguerite. "And we don't even know that they believe Davith completely about that bit anyway." She considered. "On the other hand, it's probably less likely that they'll try to stop you if you leave here, so possibly you can carry a message for me."

"Or me," said Shane.

Marguerite's eyebrows went up. "You've got a plan?" *Has Mr. Communicates-in-Grunts actually made a useful contact or two when my back was turned? Or does the Temple have an operative here that has been carefully avoiding me?*

"I may." He looked sharply at Davith. "I don't want him to hear it, though. The less he knows, the better."

Davith rolled his eyes. "I'll go into the other room."

"You're not leaving my sight, *spy*."

"Oh for god's sake. What do you want me to do, put my fingers in my ears and hum?"

"...Yes. That is exactly what I want."

Davith stared at him. "You're not serious."

"I am entirely serious."

With a much put-upon expression, Davith shoved his fingers in his ears and began to hum a tune that Marguerite recognized as the one about the milkmaid and the wolverine.

"Can he read lips?" asked Shane suspiciously.

"Probably, yeah."

Shane made a little twirling gesture with his fingers and Davith rolled his eyes and turned his back. He began to sing the chorus. "Hmmm-mmm-mm-hmm, hmm-hmm...oh where are you going, my pretty little dear..."

"Lady Silver," said Shane. "If we send Wren to her and ask her to cause a distraction, I suspect she'd be willing to help."

"...with your milk buckets swaying to-and-fro..."

"Really!" Marguerite's eyebrows shot up at that. *Lady Silver? The diplomat? Gods above and below, she's been here as long as the Court has. They say she doesn't ever leave, just stays here writing letters to her nation and watching human politics.* "You know her?"

"...suppose I were to carry you up on my back..."

"We've met."

"...far far away from here..."

"And you think she'd help us?" Marguerite rubbed the back of her neck. "She doesn't play politics, so far as I know."

"I could be wrong. But at least if Wren goes to speak to her directly, there's less chance of a message being intercepted. Little as I like to send her off alone."

"...and with these great claws, why I'll scratch any itch..."

I can't imagine she works for the Sail. Though I suppose that I can just about believe that Bishop Beartongue knows her. "It's worth a try. If it doesn't work, I doubt it will put us in any more danger."

"...that troubles your skin so fair, my dear, that troubles your skin so fair..."

Shane tried to give Wren directions, which went badly. Davith warbling about how the wolverine successfully scratched the milkmaid's itch did not particularly help. "Just act like you're going to the baths," suggested Marguerite, "then find a page and ask them to lead you."

"Will do." She hurried out the door of the suite. It closed behind her and Marguerite tried to ignore the familiar lurch in her gut that happened every time she sent one of her people into potential danger. *At least Wren can defend herself. Better than I can, come to that.*

"...but the poor beast soon found that in scratching her itch..."

"Davith, you can stop now."

"...he'd acquired quite an itch of his own, aye, acquired quite an itch of his owwwwwwn..."

"May I hit him now?" asked Shane. "Just a little?"

"Tempting, but no." She poked the spy's shoulder just as he broke into a particularly impassioned hum.

Davith took his fingers out of his ears. "Hmm? Are we done?"

"For now." Marguerite went into her room and hastily threw the gear that she couldn't leave behind into a pack. She shoved her feet into her most comfortable shoes and returned before Davith could successfully needle Shane into murdering him.

"Why are we taking him again?" asked Shane.

"He's a dead man if we leave him here." Judging from the paladin's expression, this was not actually a negative, so she hurried on. "And he clearly knows more about the Sail's operation than I do."

"Ah."

CHAPTER 30

Wren returned within twenty minutes. Marguerite suspected, given her flushed face, that she'd had a bit of a cry on the way, and begrudged her none of it. "Lady Silver says that if we leave at exactly eleven, she will arrange a distraction."

Marguerite glanced at the water clock. Half an hour. The diplomat moved quickly.

It was a long, fidgety half hour. Wren packed with the same efficiency that Shane had. "I shall never have to wear those dresses again," she said, with enormous satisfaction. She was wearing one last dress, but had trousers on underneath, and a sensible shirt that was visible overtop of the low bodice. As fashion statements went, it was deplorable, but Marguerite hoped that no one would notice.

Shane, meanwhile, sat down in the corner and just...sat. He didn't fidget. He didn't fret. He just sat there. The man was as patient as a stone. Marguerite remembered the way he'd sat holding the bird, waiting for it to fly, and envied his coolness.

Other people were not nearly so calm. Davith stood up to pace back and forth, managed one circuit, encountered a look from Shane, and sat back down.

"May I have a weapon, in case someone tries to kill us?" he asked.

"No," said Shane from the corner.

"No," said Marguerite.

Wren swiped a whetstone over the blade of her axe with great enthusiasm.

"...Right." He paused. "An axe? Really?"

"I prefer them to swords," said Wren in a clipped voice.

"You have surprised me yet again, Lady Wren."

Marguerite saw Wren's expression and stepped in hurriedly. "While I'm thinking of it, give me all your money."

He spun around, eyebrows rising to his hairline. "You're *robbing* me?"

"I'm making sure you have fewer resources if you try to escape."

"It feels an awful lot like robbery."

"I'll write you a receipt."

Davith grumbled and handed over his belt pouch. Marguerite extracted a pitifully small handful of coins.

"You weren't lying about being hard up, were you?"

He shrugged. "We're not all blessed with wealthy patrons." His eyes strayed to Wren, and it suddenly occurred to Marguerite that Davith didn't know that she was a paladin. *Up until a few minutes ago, he probably didn't know she could fight at all.* And *he thinks that Shane is just a knight. Hmm.*

At precisely eleven, Shane opened the door, looked both ways down the hall, and gestured at the others to follow. Marguerite and Wren took the lead, while Shane brought up the rear, behind Davith.

The hall was empty except for a pair of pages. At the far end, a guard stood on duty, looking bored.

"If you attempt to alert anyone, I will stab you in the kidneys," Shane told Davith in an undertone. "Even if we are captured in the next moment, you will die of your wounds."

"Tell me, does your order surgically remove the sense of humor at birth, or were you simply born without one?"

Marguerite wanted to snap at the pair to shut up, but at that moment, someone in another corridor yelled, *"Fire!"*

The reaction was immediate. The guard's head snapped up and he half-turned. The pages both looked in the direction of the shout.

And...that was all.

"That's the distraction?" Davith asked no one in particular. "That's the least original thing I've ever heard."

"Fire!" the voice yelled again. *"Fire!"*

Marguerite agreed with Davith, even if she didn't want to say it. It couldn't possibly work. You'd get maybe ten seconds of distraction, no more. And no one working for the Sail would actually believe that there was a fire at such a convenient moment, so they wouldn't leave their post. *Oh crap, we're about to walk right into them, this is going to be such a mess...*

Then she smelled the smoke.

Sweet Lady of Grass, Silver actually started a fire? Inside the fortress?

A second voice joined the first one. "Smoke! Smoke! *Everybody out!*"

"Dreaming God have mercy," said Shane. "If that spreads up here, with all these people and so few exits—" He started to turn toward the cries.

"No time!" Marguerite hissed, redoubling her pace. The guard at the end of the hall left his post and broke into a jog.

"But—"

Of course he wants to go join a bucket brigade. Why did I think otherwise? "This is not the time to be knightly! *Come on!*"

Their progress slowed as doors began to open and groggy people emerged, many in nightshirts and bare feet. Shane stepped to the forefront and began pushing his way through with sheer bulk while Wren brought up the rear. "Where's the fire?" a woman asked. "Do we need to evacuate?"

"Can't hurt," Marguerite called back.

Shane paused again at an intersection, smelling the air. A line formed between his eyebrows. "Does that smoke smell odd to you?"

Marguerite sniffed. It smelled like smoke, although there was a peculiar, unpleasant undertone to it. "Errr..."

"Could be anything. The gods only know where the fire was started," said Davith. He glanced at Marguerite. "Unexpectedly ruthless of you, my dear."

Marguerite wanted to say that this wasn't her fault, but it had happened on her orders, which ultimately made it her responsibility. *If the Court of Smoke burns down because of me, the Sail may not be the only ones mad at me.*

There was a clot of bodies in the intersection ahead. A man standing in the middle was blocking traffic. As they approached, Marguerite heard him shout, "Don't be absurd, people. This is a stone building! Stone doesn't burn! We are in no danger!"

"Shane," said Marguerite, "I *know* I told you not to cause any scenes, but I suppose we're past that now. Can you move that idiot?"

"With pleasure." Shane pushed his way through the crowd, seized the man's upper arms, and picked him up.

"Unhand me, sir!"

"First of all," said Shane, pushing the man up against a wall so that the other three could move through the gap, "if you will look up, you will see that there are wooden beams holding the ceilings in place."

"Put me down!"

"Secondly, heated stone tends to crack and break."

"I said, *put me down!*"

The clot of traffic was slowing even further as people stopped to watch the show. Marguerite had to use her elbows to wedge her way through.

"I would like you to consider what will happen when a fortress made entirely of stone gets very hot. And begins to break."

Shane had a marvelously carrying voice. Someone in the crowd began to wail.

"You can stay if you like," the paladin said, "but I wouldn't." He set the man down, turned, and said, at a volume better suited to a parade ground than an enclosed hallway, *"Remain calm! Form orderly lines! Assist those who require aid!"*

To Marguerite's absolute astonishment, the panicked milling subsided somewhat. Shane pointed. "You there! You're a military man, aren't you?"

The man's back was as straight as an arrow and he ripped off a perfect salute, despite wearing a nightcap and gown. "Sir! Sergeant-at-Arms Kettler, formerly of the Fightin' Fifteenth, sir!"

"Good. You are in charge of this hallway. Make certain that everyone gets out of their rooms. Deputize anyone who can keep their head to lead groups to the stairs in an orderly fashion. Understood?"

"Sir!" Another picture-perfect salute, which Shane returned. The paladin came striding through the crowd, and took up his position at the front of the group again. Behind them, Kettler's voice rose, ordering people to form those lines and stop shoving.

"What the hell did I just watch?" Davith asked Marguerite.

"Amazing, isn't it?"

"If *I* tried to do that, those people would kill and eat me!"

"He's really good at the voice," Marguerite said.

The crowd thinned out substantially as they went. Marguerite steered them toward the stairs used to move deliveries between levels, rather than the broader set used by those guests who chose not to take the lifts. *I don't even want to think about what the approach to the lifts looks like right now.*

There were two more guards stationed ahead, who hadn't left their post. Marguerite slowed a little, not liking the suspicious way they eyed the group.

"There's a fire," said Shane.

"Good to know," said the one on the right. The one on the left grunted. Neither of them budged.

"We're taking the stairs down," said Shane.

"Not these stairs," said the one on the right. The one on the left was looking past them. There was an expectant edge to his gaze that set off Marguerite's internal alarms.

She turned, saw three men approaching, and inhaled sharply...and then wished very strongly that she hadn't.

A smell was flowing through the corridor like nothing she had ever experienced in her life. It was like rotten eggs and rancid meat and burning feathers had compared notes and come up with something that combined the most extraordinary parts of all three.

Also, for some reason, pumpkin.

The three men slowed. One doubled over and began to enthusiastically rid himself of his dinner. The other two staggered against the walls, wiping at their eyes. However strong the smell was at this end of the hall, Marguerite guessed that it was substantially worse at their end.

"What the hell *is* that?" Davith choked, flinging an arm over his face.

And then, to her absolute astonishment, she heard Shane laughing.

Marguerite turned back in time to see Shane lowering the lefthand guard to the floor, head lolling to one side. The righthand guard would probably have protested, but Wren had stepped up very close to him, holding her axe in an odd, low grip. "Do you have any children?" she asked pleasantly.

The guard swallowed hard. He seemed to be standing on his toes. "N-no, ma'am."

"Would you like to be able to?"

"Yes'm."

"Good answer."

Shane waved Marguerite and Davith down the stairs. Marguerite plunged downward, gulping fresher air with great relief. Wren joined them a moment later, wrinkling her nose. "That smell is getting worse. What the hell is it?"

"I believe it is a cynocephalic perfume," said Shane.

"A *what?*"

"Lady Silver is a member of a dog-headed race. I smelled one of her perfumes when I visited her, and it was remarkably similar." He shook his head, smile growing. "If she were to smash a concentrated vial, I imagine it would have much the same effect."

Marguerite glanced over her shoulder, as if somehow she would be able to see the spreading clouds of scent. "I wonder if the smoke was a perfume too. That would be a lot safer."

"I certainly hope so." Shane's smile faded. "I hope that it isn't traced back to her. I can't imagine that anyone would be happy about it."

"From what little I know of the lady," said Marguerite, "I suspect that she'll have taken precautions. Lady Silver isn't known for any intrigues whatsoever...and after a certain point, that lack begins to indicate almost superhuman skill."

"I hope you're right."

"Have faith," said Marguerite, and was rewarded with a startled smile.

They reached the next level down, which smelled of laundry and scrubbing powder. The alarm clearly hadn't reached this far yet. A pair of women appeared in the doorway, holding baskets of laundry. Judging by their expressions, they had not expected to encounter people carrying quite large weapons.

One shrieked and dropped her basket. The other, made of sterner stuff, narrowed her eyes and said, "I don't know what you're doing here and I don't want to know, but if you keep moving, no one will hear about it from me."

Shane inclined his head gravely. "Thank you, madam."

Not to be outdone, Davith swept off his hat and bowed so low that the plume touched the stairs. "Your discernment is matched only by your beauty, O Queen of Washerwomen—"

Marguerite reached over, seized him by the ear, and pulled. "Enough of that. We've got places to be."

"Ow...ow...ow..."

"Do you want me to let Shane do this instead?"

"He's taller so it probably wouldn't hurt as much!"

The next two floors were servant quarters and had the determined silence of people who only had a narrow window of time in which to sleep and were not going to waste any of it.

They were halfway to the next level when Shane paused and held up a hand.

"Problem?" asked Wren softly.

"People coming down the stairs. Fast." He started down the steps again, setting a much quicker pace.

"Evacuating?"

"I don't think so." He shot a quick glance back at Marguerite. "Fighting on the stairs heavily favors the higher ground."

Marguerite grimaced. "Next floors are storage. We may be able to hide?"

"I dislike being cornered."

"Go down one more," said Davith abruptly. "There's a separate stair in the back on that floor."

Shane gave him a deeply suspicious look. Davith rolled his eyes. "Will you just trust me? They're going to kill me too, you know!"

The paladin looked to Marguerite, his opinion stamped clearly across his face. *I don't trust him, but you are in charge.*

And to think that I used to find the man hard to read... Aloud she said, "We don't have much to lose."

They reached the floor in question, driven by the sounds of pursuit. Marguerite hoped like hell that it was just bouncing echoes that made their followers sound so close.

An immense storeroom opened in front of them, crates stacked high against the walls. Davith took the lead, sprinting across the open space toward the far corner. He ducked behind a wall of flour sacks and vanished from sight. Shane let out a growl and lengthened his stride to catch up.

Shouts went up from behind them. Marguerite risked a glance over her shoulder and saw men piling out of the door. They were carrying swords. Two were dressed as guards, but she was pretty sure that they weren't on the Court's payroll.

She and Wren rounded the wall just in time to see Davith yank a padlock off a small door and toss it aside. "Wine cellar," he said, stepping inside. "Come on."

Stairs went down sharply, obviously carved directly into the rock. Shane held the door open and waved Wren and Marguerite through, then yanked the door shut behind them.

"Did you pick that lock?" asked Marguerite. She knew that Davith had a certain facility with locks, but she wouldn't have thought that he could do it in a mere five seconds.

"You doubt me?"

"Frankly, yes."

He flashed her a smile. "Oh ye of little faith. Yes, I picked it...two months ago. Then I had a key made so that I could help myself to wine. It's amazing the doors that open if you're carrying a bottle, even if you don't have two coins to rub together."

Alcoves opened on each side, lined with rows of bottles. They were dimly lit compared to the other halls, the shadows deep. Marguerite followed Davith down as the steps twisted and turned, praying that she wasn't being led headlong into an ambush.

It would be an excellent place for one, but the Sail couldn't know that we'd take him hostage, and they certainly couldn't know what route we'd take.

The door slammed open above them.

Also they don't really need *an ambush at this point.*

Unexpectedly flat ground met her foot, and she stumbled. Roughly plastered walls met her gaze, a room perhaps a dozen paces across with a single large wooden door at the far end. A half-dozen more crates were stacked neatly against the wall, bearing the stamps of vintners from downriver.

Davith yanked out a key and tried to fit it in the lock, then let out a blistering oath.

"Doesn't fit, I take it?"

"Why have two different locks, I ask you...?" He went down on one knee.

Wren and Shane turned to face the stairs. Wren dropped her pack and revealed that her ill-fitting cloak had been concealing a round metal buckler strapped against her back.

Marguerite leaned toward Davith, not taking her eyes off the stairs. "Can you open the lock?"

"If I have enough time, yes."

"I do not believe that time is on our side," said Shane, as calmly as if he was observing the weather.

The two false guards reached the bottom of the stairs, followed by a wedge of men dressed as duelists. Their swords were clearly not peace-bonded. A big man in the clothes of a laborer brought up the rear.

"Seven of them," murmured Wren. Davith swore again. Both paladins ignored him, watching the men approach.

The false guards didn't say anything. They didn't gloat. They didn't threaten. They simply advanced. *Professionals,* Marguerite thought. Several of the duelists, however, grinned like sharks.

"I owe you, big man," one said. "You broke my brother's arm."

"Ah," Shane said. "So that *was* a test. I had wondered." He still sounded extremely calm.

Davith stopped trying the lock and stepped in front of Marguerite.

"Chivalry isn't quite dead, I see," said Marguerite. She felt numb. She was about to watch her friends cut down in front of her. Would they kill her as well, or drag her back to the Red Sail for questioning?

Could I talk my way out if they do?

Can I talk my way out of this before anyone *dies?*

"Gentlemen," she called, working hard to keep her terror locked down and out of her voice, "there is doubtless a solution here that does not involve bloodshed. I would be happy to negotiate for safe passage —"

One of the men spat on the ground. The brother of the man with the broken arm started to inform her, in quite crude terms, what he was planning to do before he killed her.

He got less than halfway through the speech when Shane's sword slid into his throat.

. . .

Marguerite knew that she shouldn't be surprised. She had seen the paladins fight before. She had seen them take down a demon steer, for god's sake. She knew what they were.

But she had never seen them when the battle tide took them, and it was extraordinary.

They were so goddamn *fast.* The men attacking them seemed like they were swimming in syrup. Wren—short, frumpy, frizzy Wren, who fretted about her hair and how to use her fan—blocked a sword with the handle of her axe, smashed her buckler into the wielder's head, ducked casually under a strike from another blade, opened the second man's guts up with a backhanded swipe, and then turned back and buried the axe in the first man's skull. Her expression of careful concentration never wavered once.

And Shane. Shane who was so guilty and so fretful under the surface calm, Shane with a voice so gentle and trustworthy that it cut Marguerite's heart...Shane blocked a sword slash with his own blade and drove his mailed fist into the man's throat, knocking him sideways into the man that Wren had casually gutted, then blocked another strike that had been aimed for Wren's head while she wrenched her axe free.

The big man dressed as a laborer had a hammer. He swung at Shane's head and the paladin stepped forward, not back, practically into the man's arms. The hammer shot past him and the man's forearm slammed into his shoulder. Shane didn't even seem to notice. He shoved forward and twisted and his sword slid out of the man's back. Shane caught the hammer-wielder as he fell, threw him into the remaining duelist, and Wren's axe opened up the last man's leg veins while his arms were full.

Gods above and below.

And just like that, their pursuers were dead. Shane and Wren stood back-to-back amid a wreckage of bodies. One of the men at their feet let out a long, rattling groan, and then was silent.

"My god," said Davith.

Wren twisted like a cat and locked eyes on him. Her eyes were flat as stones and her teeth were bared. "Wren...?" Marguerite said, even as her brain hissed a warning. *Has she not come out? Is she still berserk?*

Wren raised the axe and charged.

"Wren, *no!*" Marguerite flung herself sideways, trying to get out of

Davith's way. There was no way that he could fight off the paladin with his bare hands, but maybe he could get out of the way, run long enough for someone to talk her down—

Davith hesitated a moment too long, his mouth open in shock. Wren swung the axe high and brought it down.

Shane's sword blocked the blow. The blade broke. Davith fell backward. Wren hissed like a tea kettle, but Shane barreled into her, smashing her against the wall and pinning her with his weight alone.

She snarled, dropped her shoulder, and tried to lift him off his feet. Shane flung the broken sword aside and put himself between Wren and the others.

The stained axe blade lifted again, and Shane had no weapon in his hands. He lifted his arm, as if that might somehow stop an axe. He was going to die. Marguerite cursed herself for not being a warrior, for not having so much as a pen knife to her name, something that she could throw or maybe just hand to Shane or—

"Enough."

It was the paladin's voice like she had never heard. It was no longer trust and care and kindness. This was the voice of a prophet, not a priest. It sank into Marguerite's bones and demanded obedience from her very soul.

If she hadn't already been on her knees, she might have fallen to them. Davith, who had been trying to rise, sagged back against the floor.

Wren blinked. Some of the flatness left her eyes, and she looked from Shane to Marguerite to Davith, then back again. "Oh," she said, in a very small voice.

The axe fell to the floor. Shane stepped forward, wrapped his arms around his sister, and held her tight.

CHAPTER 31

Marguerite finished checking the last man's belt pouch and sat back on her heels. "Nothing," she said, in response to Shane's inquisitive glance. "Nothing useful, anyway. Not that I expected them to have signed orders from Fenella, but it might have been nice."

He nodded and took up his post at the foot of the stairs.

Davith, meanwhile, was trying to pick the lock on the cellar door. He looked almost normal but his hands were shaking in a way that Marguerite had never seen.

It was hard to say which of the two was more upset, Wren or Davith. Davith hid it better, perhaps. Wren, once Shane released her, picked up her axe and cleaned it, face blank and lifeless. Her eyes looked like holes in her skin.

Marguerite wanted to go to her, but cold practicality exerted itself. *Getting the door open will keep us all alive.*

"Davith," Marguerite murmured. "Do you want me to try that?"

"What are they?" he asked in a clipped whisper, ignoring the question.

"What?"

"*Them.* Those aren't ordinary bodyguards." One of the picks bent and he pressed his lips together until they went white.

"No." She thought about lying, but there didn't seem to be much point now. She glanced over her shoulders. Shane had picked up his broken sword and was studying it. After a moment, he slid what was left of it back in its sheath. "They're paladins of the Saint of Steel."

"The Saint of..." Davith rested his forehead against the door and gave a single bark of laughter. "Of course those would be your bodyguards. That's almost brilliant, in a twisted sort of way."

Marguerite did not feel particularly brilliant at the moment. "Move over," she said. "Let me give the lock a try."

He yielded. She worked the lock carefully. It wasn't difficult, but the mechanism was heavy and required a sure hand. She realized that she was holding her breath, a lousy habit, and took a deep, deliberate breath, whereupon the lock popped open as if it had been waiting for an excuse.

"I loosened that jar lid for you," muttered Davith.

"Sure you did," she said, rising to her feet. "Come on. I can't imagine they've got many more people to send after us, but I don't want to find out that I'm wrong."

Wren nodded mechanically and went through the door, her face still blank. Marguerite took a step after her, lifting a hand to touch her shoulder.

Shane caught her arm. His gauntlets were caked in gore, but Marguerite refused to flinch away. *This is what it looks like when men die. This is what the game you play costs. You don't get to look away.*

She looked from his mailed hand up to his face and waited for him to apologize for Wren, or for not stopping Wren, or maybe for not killing everyone even faster. He had that look that usually preceded an apology.

Instead he leaned forward, his lips almost at her ear, and said softly, "You asked me once what paladins knew of darkness."

Marguerite's breath went out in a long sigh and she felt unexpectedly ashamed. "I'm sorry," she said, almost inaudibly. "I knew, but I didn't understand."

He nodded and released her. Marguerite moved to the front of the party and glanced back to see him guarding the back, as remote and unreachable as a star.

No one tried to stop them on their way out. The door led to another storage room, and then another much larger one. There were several large elevators, apparently for moving supplies up from the docks, and several more sets of stairs. Laborers were working there by torchlight. Marguerite paused in the shadows, considering her options. *Sneak past? All those stairs are in use, can't imagine we'd make it. Pretend like we belong here? I've got two people covered in armor and other people's blood.*

"Right," she said, turning back to the others. "We're just going to brazen it out. You all with me?"

She met Wren's eyes in particular. The other woman took a deep breath and squared her shoulders. Marguerite could actually see her take the horror and shove it away somewhere else, a trick she recognized because she had done it herself so many times.

"I'm with you," Wren said. And then, to a space six inches to the right of Davith's head, "I'm sorry about what happened earlier."

Davith shrugged. "Eh," he said, "I probably deserved it. Let's just get out of here in one piece."

Marguerite didn't know if he genuinely meant it or if he was simply trying to appease someone who had come perilously close to putting an axe into his head. Probably it didn't matter. *People will remember that he was with us, so he's a dead man walking if the Sail gets to him.*

"Okay." She looked over the two paladins, both of whom were splattered with other people's blood. (Well, Shane was splattered. Wren looked as if she'd been bathing in it. It was something of an education in the difference between axe and sword fighting.) "Wren, take my cloak and try to hide some of that blood. Shane, you're going to be drunk. Davith, take one side of him. Wren, stick close behind us and look apologetic."

For some reason she expected Shane to argue about pretending to be drunk, but he nodded, slung his arm over Davith's shoulders, and leaned heavily on the smaller man.

"Ooof!" Davith said. "Are you a paladin or a side of beef?" Shane smiled and leaned harder.

Marguerite took Shane's other arm and led him directly toward the widest set of stairs. "Pardon," she said to the first person who noticed them, "but can you point me to the fastest way outside? My friend here *really* needs some air."

"M'fine," mumbled Shane.

"Buddy, you are so far from fine that you can't see fine from here," Davith told him.

The laborer looked from Shane back to Marguerite, who gave her most winning and apologetic smile. "He's had a bit much to drink."

"Have *not.*"

"How did you even get down here?" the man wanted to know.

"Stairs," said Davith grimly. "So many goddamn stairs. He refused to do the elevators, so I had to carry him—yes, I'm talking about *you*, you sod."

"M'*fine.*"

"I told you, man, she wasn't worth it. No woman's worth this."

Shane's grip on Davith's shoulders briefly resembled a headlock. Davith coughed. "Come on, man, your breath would kill a horse."

Marguerite didn't know whether to bless Davith or strangle him herself. "Please?" she said to the laborer. "He's a tame duelist and we really don't want his boss to see him like this."

"Oh, aye, I can see that." The man's lip curled and he waved an arm. "Take the left staircase. Don't want him getting underfoot on the main one."

"You are a life saver," said Marguerite fervently, and began steering Shane toward the stairs in question. The paladin stumbled a little too theatrically and she gritted her teeth.

No one else tried to stop them, although heads turned to watch their progress. Marguerite kept up a line of patter, not even listening to herself. "Come on, come on, you can do it, just a little farther, some fresh air will do you a world of good..."

And then, just like that, they were down the stairs and through the door and out of the fortress.

Out, thought Marguerite, with unspeakable relief, as the night air touched their faces. *Free. Now we just get to the docks, find a captain we can bribe to take us across the lake without dropping us over the side halfway through, and we'll be on the road and well away before anyone finds those bodies.*

They hurried along the narrow wharf, no longer bothering to be stealthy. Speed was more important now. Marguerite pointed, and they rounded a stack of crates, onto the dock dedicated to lake traffic.

She blinked. Behind her, she heard Shane swear.

Moonlight glinted on the surface of the lake, dancing on the small waves that broke against the pilings. She could see each wave clearly because the entire dock was empty and there wasn't a boat to be seen.

"It's the boatman's strike," said Shane grimly. 'I'm sorry. I should have remembered." He couldn't believe that he'd let it slip his mind. *Although it's not as if I haven't had anything else to distract me. Still, at the very least, I should have told Marguerite, and* she *would have remembered.*

He looked around helplessly, as if there might be a boat somewhere that they had simply overlooked. Unfortunately his night vision was getting worse the older he got. While the nearest boat mooring was clear enough, the far end of the dock dissolved into a blur. *Even if there* was *a boat, I'd be the last person to see it.*

It was cold consolation that apparently there wasn't anything to see.

Wren put her hands on her hips. "Dammit, we can't even *steal* a boat. Why would they take them all?"

"To prevent anyone from breaking the strike," said Davith. "If all the boats are at anchor on the other side, anybody trying to slip out will be immediately obvious. They'd be branded a scab."

"Community censure is a powerful incentive," Shane offered.

Davith gave him a wry look. "Particularly when they express displeasure by breaking your legs."

"Some forms of censure are more demonstrative than others." Shane still had a strong desire to censure Davith's face, but was determined not to embarrass Wren any further.

"That is...inconvenient," Marguerite said. She chewed on her lower lip. "Let's think this through. How are they communicating their demands, if there are no boats here?"

"There's one anchored off the dock," said Davith, pointing. "Most likely someone signals to it when they're ready to negotiate."

"And they'll likely be the last people amenable to a bribe to take us across."

"You don't break a *strike,"* said Davith, sounding somewhat shocked by the suggestion.

"We're not smuggling brandy, we're trying to keep from getting murdered," Marguerite shot back.

"Yes, but it's the principle of the thing."

"I have very strong principles about not getting murdered."

Davith folded his arms and looked obstinate. Shane took a casual step toward him. Davith unfolded his arms and muttered, "Fine, I just want it clear that I object."

"Your objection is noted. Anyway, it'll be moot if we can't find a boat."

Wren pointed over to the other dock. "I know those are all river boats, but could they cross the lake too? The river captains aren't the ones striking."

"I don't know," admitted Marguerite. "Boats aren't my specialty. I assume most of them have animals taking them upstream, but maybe there's someone with...errr..."

"Oars?" offered Shane.

"Those, yes." She glanced up at him. "Do you know how to work a boat?"

"Not even a little."

"Wren?"

"We don't have navigable rivers where I grew up."

"...Davith?"

"If I did, would I admit it right now?"

"Stealing one is right out, then." Marguerite nodded once to herself. "Right. It'll be fine. Bribery it is."

Bribery, alas, it was not. The vast majority of the riverboats relied on animals on shore for power, which was hardly feasible in a lake. The few boats at the dock that did not looked to belong to local fishermen. Most of them would have been very strained by four passengers, but Marguerite was willing to take a chance. After slipping some coins to stevedores, she managed to find one in a local tavern, who looked at her with a mixture of surprise and regret.

"Can't do it," he said.

Marguerite hefted a pouch, which made an inviting clinking sound. The fisherman gazed at it with clear lust, but shook his head sadly. "'S not the money. They'll shoot you on the other side right now."

"Shoot you?"

"Anybody comes from over here and goes back, they assume he's smuggling for the Court." The fisherman slugged back a drink. "Barbarians, the lot of 'em. Your man there's big, I grant you, but he's not bigger'n arrow in the neck. It's more than my life's worth to go over there."

"It's more than *my* life's worth to stay *here*," said Marguerite, exasperated. She didn't know the extent of the Sail's forces at the Court, but even if Shane and Wren could fight off everyone sent against them, the local authorities were bound to notice the piles of corpses eventually.

The fisherman wiped his mouth and looked at her blearily. "'Fraid I can't help. You'll have to go over the mountain."

"I can't fly, either," said Marguerite tartly.

He shook his head, surprising her. "There's a trail, o'course. Couple of 'em. How d'you think they get back and forth when the lake's all slush?"

Shane, who had been listening to all this in silence, said, "I would have thought sleds with runners."

"Oh aye, aye, once it's good and frozen. But we get about six weeks where it's just slop. Can't push a boat through it and you sink right through if you step on it." He jerked his chin in the general direction of the highlands. "You take the mountain road then."

"Bad season for it," said a man at the next table, turning. Marguerite stifled a sigh. Speed was more important than stealth, but she'd hoped not to have the entire tavern involved in the conversation.

Not that they wouldn't notice Shane anyway. The paladin stood out like a well-armed turkey in a hen house.

"Trail's still a mess from the spring thaw," the newcomer said. "Might be some bits washed out."

This just gets better and better. "Where does the trail start?"

The man shrugged. "Can't really miss it. There's a stable right there, handles the pack mules." Before Marguerite could ask, he added, "They won't sell you one now, in case you're trying to get around the strike."

She looked at Shane, who, predictably, grunted.

"Thanks for your help," she said to the two men. "I'll stand you a round. Guess I'll be heading downstream instead."

They both solemnly agreed that this was wise, and drank to her health. Marguerite and Shane went back outside, where Wren and Davith were watching each other with all the friendly feeling of a blood feud.

"Right," Marguerite said. "We're going to have to go through the mountains. Wren, I'm sorry. There's a trail, at least?" She decided not to mention it possibly being washed out, because there wasn't a damn thing anyone could do about it if it was.

Wren took a deep breath and squared her shoulders. "It has to be done. I just...won't look down, I guess."

Davith looked from one to the other. "Wait...Let me get this straight. You're named after a *bird*, and you're afraid of *heights*?"

Wren glared at him. "My parents weren't exactly warned in advance about that, all right? So that they could have named me for something suitably earthbound, like a toad."

Davith opened his mouth and Marguerite truly did not know if he was going to say something sardonic or actually apologize. Shane stepped between them. Davith closed his mouth again.

"It can't be that far," said Marguerite. "The other side of the lake is right there."

Wren rubbed the back of her neck. "That's not necessarily true. If the trail has to make a detour around a bit that's unclimbable, say..." She shook her head. "Even in my hills, the road's the best way, not the *shortest* way."

"Well," said Marguerite grimly, "I suppose we're about to find out."

CHAPTER 32

"That is not a trail," said Davith. "That is a goat track. For suicidal goats."

Privately, Marguerite thought that he was correct, but she wasn't going to show it. The trail wasn't even flat, but had a distinct sideways tilt, as if it might spill people off the side at any moment. "They take mules on it, so it can't be that bad."

Wren came to her aid. "I've seen worse. They've shored parts of it up, so somebody's repairing it. That's good."

"That it needs repair?" asked Davith.

"That it's in use, which means it's unlikely to run out or become impassable." She did not actually add *you asshole* to the end of the sentence, but it was strongly implied.

"Right," said Marguerite. "Let's go."

Shane insisted on going first to test the trail. Marguerite frowned at him. "Why you?"

"Because I'm the heaviest. If it will hold my weight, it will hold the rest of you. If it won't hold my weight, you'll find out before anyone else plunges to their death."

"I'd really prefer *no one* plunged to their death," she informed him tartly.

Shane shrugged, possibly indicating that plunging to one's death was a personal decision best left to the individual. Marguerite put her hands on her hips.

"I assure you, I will do everything in my power to avoid it," he promised her.

"You do that."

His eyes were the same color as the cold sky as he looked down at her, but then they shifted to something a little past her and softened. *He's looking at Wren,* she told herself. *It isn't you he cares about.*

Still, her heart twinged a little as he bent toward her. Stupid heart.

"Wren would be the logical one," he murmured. "She grew up in hill country, after all. But she cannot do it, and I do not trust Davith. That leaves you and I, and you are the one required for our mission to succeed. So I will go first."

He was right, and she knew he was right, but she glared at his broad back anyway as he led the way.

The trail was not so bad as all that...mostly. In places it was quite serviceable. But it seemed like every time they reached a switchback, the outer edge of the turn was crumbling away and dropped pebbles. Sometimes the entire turn was simply gone, and they had to scramble from the lower trail to the higher, up four or five feet of steep rock. It was not such a difficult proposition for Shane or Davith, but Marguerite was feeling her lack of height severely.

(Wren, despite her clear discomfort with heights, did significantly better, possibly because she was so much stronger. Given a good handhold, the younger paladin could simply pull herself up. Marguerite, who could not have done a single push-up even if her breasts hadn't rendered the issue largely moot, tried not to feel bitter envy.)

"What *happened* to this trail?" she grumbled, as Shane reached down, took both her hands, and pulled her up to the next switchback.

"People steal the bracing timbers," said Wren. She was pressed as far back from the edge as she could be, back firmly against the stone, and was staring up at the sky. "Same thing used to happen back home."

"They don't like having a path through the mountains?" Marguerite hazarded, wondering exactly what had happened to give Wren her fear of heights, and if it had to do with the trails in her homeland.

Wren glanced in her direction and managed a smile. "The trees up here are all pine," she said. "Softwood. These timbers are brought in from the lowlands, and they're much sturdier than anything up here.

People take them to build their own homes, or to brace up paths where they drive their animals to pasture."

"Seems short-sighted," said Marguerite, pushing away from the wall and following Shane upward again.

"Not really. They know that the clan lord will replace these eventually."

"The clan lord doesn't seem to know that," said Davith sourly.

Wren shrugged. "Maybe they've got a lousy clan lord."

"Judging by the map, this path is no longer regularly used," Shane called back. "Perhaps it is simply no longer worth the effort to keep it up." He paused for a moment, testing the ground in front of him. "The edge up ahead is crumbling. I suggest we keep hard to the wall. Wren..."

"I'm fine."

Davith straightened and looked at Shane over Marguerite's head. "I'll go after her," he offered.

"I don't need your help," Wren snapped.

"Nobody's helping you. I just would rather not have my back to you in a spot where accidents would be so convenient."

Wren's eyes narrowed. "Believe me, when I kill you, you'll know it wasn't an accident."

"I'm terribly comforted. Still, ladies first."

Marguerite had a pretty good idea that Davith was starting a fight with Wren so she'd pay attention to him and not the edge, so she bit down her instinct to rise to Wren's defense and began inching along the wall herself. Shane hadn't lied. If anything, he'd understated the case. There were spots where the path seemed to be held in place entirely by tufts of grass that had taken root in the rock crevices. In one or two places, there was barely six inches of path remaining at all.

"If mules are using this, it must be safe," Marguerite muttered, following Davith following Wren following Shane.

"Being safe for mules doesn't mean safe for humans," Davith said over his shoulder.

"Aren't we smarter than mules?"

He snorted loudly. "Sweetheart, I don't think I've known more than a dozen people in my life who were smarter than a mule."

"Oh look, something we agree on," Wren said.

"I thought you didn't like horses," said Marguerite.

"I like horses fine. Horses don't like berserkers. Mules are..." She frowned, obviously trying to think of a comparison. "Half of them won't come near us for love or money, and the other half go out of their way to let you know that they aren't impressed."

"I've known women like that," Davith said.

Fortunately, another treacherous switchback cut off Wren's reply. Shane reached down with both hands and pulled Marguerite up onto the next level. For a moment their bodies were pressed full-length against each other. They both hesitated a moment too long, and then Shane hastily stepped back, and Marguerite stood aside to let Wren and Davith pass.

"You remember how I told you once not to bed him?" Davith murmured, letting the other two get farther ahead and out of immediate earshot.

Marguerite flapped her hand toward his face, as if he were a mosquito she could swat away. "You may have said something of the sort. It was none of your business then, and it still isn't."

"I've changed my mind," said Davith, apparently unconcerned about whether or not it was his business. "You should definitely bed him at the soonest opportunity. In fact, once we hit the next wide spot in the trail, I'll happily turn my back and engage the other one in small talk."

She swatted at him again, narrowly missing his nose. He dropped back a step. Marguerite concentrated on her footing. Occasionally she'd glance up to see Shane's broad back, still reassuringly far ahead.

She wasn't going to ask.

She wasn't.

It was none of his business.

Goddammit.

"Fine," she hissed, twisting to glare at Davith. "Why the sudden change of heart?"

"Sweetheart, there's so much unrelieved sexual tension between you two that I'm surprised your clothes don't ignite. Bed him and be done with it before you grind your teeth into splinters."

Marguerite realized that she had been grinding her teeth and deliberately unclenched her jaw. "It's not like that," she muttered.

"The hell it isn't."

She grunted. A minute later she realized that it had been a pretty good version of a Shane-grunt, and had to unclench her jaw again.

"Cheer up," said Davith. "It could always be worse."

She grunted again. It was a lovely noncommittal noise that did not indicate either interest or agreement, and furthermore did not give the other person anything to work with. She was starting to see why Shane liked it so much.

Unfortunately it didn't work on Davith. "Sure it could. You could have been dragged out of your nice cushy job sleeping with beautiful women and made into a fugitive, all because you had a moment of ill-considered mercy. Instead *you* get to skip along this trail that would give a mountain goat heartburn without a care in the world, other than your libido."

"I am not skipping," said Marguerite, planting her feet with extreme caution and reminding herself that if she took a swing at Davith, he would very likely plunge to his death. That would be bad. Probably.

In theory, anyway.

"And at least the weather's nice," said Davith, gazing up at the mountain sky and the high white clouds.

Two hours later, it began to rain.

"You just *had* to say something about the weather," Marguerite growled at Davith.

"I didn't expect it to blow up so *fast.*"

"Flatlander," said Wren. The four had taken temporary shelter under a large overhanging boulder, which meant that they were only getting rained on when the wind gusted. Unfortunately, since they were on the side of a mountain, this was approximately every ten seconds. "Weather changes fast in the mountains and you can't see it coming."

"At least it isn't snow?" he said hopefully.

"Snow would be easier," Shane said. Marguerite was pretty sure that he was standing partly in the rain, using his bulk to shield the other three. It was all very noble and self-sacrificing and faintly annoying. It was also keeping her dry, or at least, less wet.

"Easier?" said Davith, in disbelief.

Both Wren and Shane nodded. Wren added, "You don't get wet as quickly. Being soaked through will kill you much faster than having snowflakes on your head."

"Aren't there...I dunno, avalanches and things, though?"

"There are..." Shane began.

"There, see? I don't want to get knocked off the trail by an avalanche."

"...but there are also mudslides," the paladin finished.

Davith threw his hands in the air, narrowly missing Marguerite's nose. "You know, given that I'm technically a prisoner, *I* should not have to be the optimist here!"

Shane and Marguerite grunted simultaneously, exchanged looks—his surprised, hers rueful—and then Shane gave about a tenth of a smile, clearly involuntarily, and looked hurriedly away.

"This isn't letting up," Wren said, after about twenty minutes. Shane nodded. Water dripped off the end of his nose.

"You've got more experience in this kind of territory than I do," said Marguerite. "What's our best plan?"

Wren sighed. "I hate to say it, but the longer we stand here in the rain, the colder we're going to get. At least if we're walking, we'll be a little warmer, and we may find a better stopping point." She rubbed the back of her neck. "In my country, there would be a shelter eventually, but I don't know if we can count on that here. But even a hollow out of the wind would be preferable to this."

"Right," said Marguerite. "You heard the lady. Let's go."

Shane set out with Marguerite behind him. She glanced back to see Davith and Wren waging a small psychological battle over who would bring up the rear. Wren won, probably because she had an axe and Davith didn't.

It was cold. It was wet. The trail didn't melt away underneath them, which was about the best that you could give it. Marguerite kept her eyes on Shane's back and realized that she was definitely, truly miserable because she wasn't even ogling his backside.

Our greatest weapon is useless. We're doomed. She didn't have the energy to laugh, but she snorted at herself, though no one could hear it over the wind.

She couldn't even tell if it was getting darker because of the hour or because of the clouds. *Have we been walking long enough for it to get dark? I don't even know.* It felt as if she had been walking for at least a century, but Marguerite knew just how easily time could stretch in such situations. *I think it's probably been an hour. That doesn't put us anywhere toward nightfall, does it? Certainly not in the middle of summer.*

She had absolutely no desire to be walking along this trail in the dark. It was bad enough in daylight. *And it'll get cold. Colder. And if we're not somewhere that we can stop, we'll be in serious trouble.*

They had passed several forks in the trail already, and each time had taken the branch that seemed as if mules could traverse it. Marguerite hoped that was the right choice. Wren seemed to think it was, but as the hours passed, Marguerite became less and less certain. *I honestly thought we'd be there by now. It's not like the lake itself is miles across.*

Life as a spy was frequently uncertain, and she'd had to hide out in the country before. It was just that the country was usually a lot flatter and had barns and churches and things. She'd managed to avoid crossing mountains before.

That was very smart of me. I wish I'd figured out a way to do it this time.

When the ground gave way under her, it did so quite slowly, which meant that at first she wasn't sure what was happening. Shane was suddenly about a foot higher up the hill than he had been, and she had the vague notion that he'd taken a step up. Then she was listing sideways unexpectedly and there was nothing under her right foot and she realized that the section of trail she was standing on was sliding down the mountain and taking her with it.

She let out an undignified squawk and grabbed for solid ground—and got two handfuls of mud instead.

She slid sideways down the hill, mostly on her side. Everything felt strangely slow, as if she was moving through mud. *Which I am. I just expected mud to be faster.*

She came to a squelching stop. Marguerite looked around, confused, and realized that she had actually slid down the hill to the next switchback, about ten feet down. Both her legs were encased in mud up to the knee.

Is it over?

She tried to pull herself out of the mud, onto the trail ahead. It did not go well. Mud oozed over the tops of her boots and she stopped, realizing that she was going to lose both boots. *Still, if I stay put, maybe one of the others can get to me and we can dig down—*

The second patch of trail gave way.

Either this section wasn't as solid or the weight of the mud was starting to add up, because it went a lot faster. Marguerite flopped forward on her belly, grabbing for anything solid that might slow her descent.

A small clump of sedge was the only handhold and she sank her fingers into it while the trail continued to pour out from under her, gaining strength and speed as it went. Mud pulled at her legs. One boot gave way.

"Shit," she said aloud. "Shit, shit, shit." Her voice sounded very calm as she said it. It would have been rather nice if someone had been impressed by that, but Shane probably couldn't hear her and Davith and Wren were presumably too busy trying not to slide down the mountain themselves.

Her focus narrowed down to her right hand and the sedge, which was now at the edge of the washed-out area. Possibly its roots were what was holding the remaining section of trail together. What was the weight-bearing capacity of a grassy tuft less than six inches wide?

"Good plant," she gasped. "*Sturdy* plant." Could she pull herself up? No, she could not. Was there another handhold? She groped for one along the exposed edge of the trail, and clumps of earth calved away under her fingers. *Shit.*

And then an arm seemed to materialize next to her face, and Shane got a grip on her coat and pulled her up. Marguerite got a face full of mud and the fabric cut into her armpits in a way that would probably leave bruises later, but she didn't care. Her arm went around his neck and she buried her face in his shoulder. *Good paladin. Sturdy paladin. Even better than the plant.*

He was saying something to her, in that marvelously soothing voice. She wanted to collapse into it and rest. Surely you would not be allowed to fall off a cliff while someone was talking to you like that.

...What was he saying, exactly?

"You have to let go," he repeated.

Let go? She couldn't let go. If she let go, she was going to fall. Still, he seemed insistent. Marguerite reluctantly tried to loosen her grip around his neck.

"No," Shane said, very patiently, "not me. Let go of the plant."

Marguerite looked down the length of her right arm. It seemed very long. She couldn't quite feel her fingers, but yes, there they were, dug into the sedge that was now very much worse for wear.

"Ah," she said, and told her fingers sternly to relax. *Thank you, good plant. I will make an offering to the Lady of Grass in your honor.*

Shane, on his knees, began to shuffle backward along the trail, still holding Marguerite, until they reached a spot that seemed to be more stone than mud. He got to his feet and set her down. "Are you injured?"

"I don't think so?" She tested her footing and excruciating pain failed to shoot up either of her legs. Her bare foot squelched. "I think I'm okay. Bruised, but nothing's broken."

"Good," he said.

A moment passed, during which Marguerite realized that her arms were still wrapped around his neck. It occurred to her that it would be somewhat difficult to walk in this position.

"I should probably let go of you."

"Only when you're ready."

She did not feel particularly ready, but another, more pressing thought struck her. "Wren! Davith!"

"They're fine. But we do have a problem."

Marguerite reluctantly let him go. As soon as she stepped back, the wind hit her again and the rain seemed to redouble. Rivulets ran down her face and her hair slapped wetly against the back of her neck.

Oh well, at least it'll wash off some of the mud... She pulled the hood of her cloak up and turned back to look at the trail.

She was glad that the hood hid her expression because the sight made her blanch. A good twenty feet had been washed out, gone in a churn of mud that looked more like a cattle wallow than a trail. *I rode* that *down?* Another cold wave of adrenaline shivered through her as she realized just how bad things could have been, if not for the sedge.

Up the hillside, on the next switchback, she saw Wren and Davith looking down. She waved up to them and both sagged in relief.

But if they're up there on the original trail...how did Shane get down here? "Did you get caught in the slide too?"

"No. I climbed down."

Given the steepness of the trail, it had probably been less of a climb and more of a controlled fall. She swallowed. "Are you hurt?"

"I'm fine. My armor could be better. Mud and chainmail is not the best of combinations."

Marguerite eyed Wren and Davith. Wren was facing toward the stone wall, and even with the lighting, Marguerite thought she looked remarkably pale. "How do they get over here?"

"I don't think they do. There's no way to cross that safely."

The others had clearly come to the same conclusion, judging by the hand gestures. Davith nodded glumly, then cupped his hands around his mouth. "We'll catch up with you!" he shouted, then turned back, tugging at Wren's sleeve.

"They'll have to backtrack to the last fork," said Shane. "Hopefully the two trails will reconnect somewhere lower down. I don't know how long that will take, but hopefully we can find shelter somewhere below and wait for them."

"Think they'll be okay?"

Shane watched the two, impassive. Davith appeared to be alternating talking and tugging Wren back down the path. "Will he take this opportunity to abandon her and escape?"

"Davith? No. I doubt it would even occur to him. He's a cad, but he's not actually a bad person."

"Then I doubt their risk is substantially greater than ours. I cannot imagine any pursuers would give chase in this weather."

Marguerite nodded. The Red Sail had deep pockets, but there were limits.

The pair vanished with a final wave. Marguerite dug into her pack and pulled out her spare pair of shoes. They were lighter, meant for court wear, and they were going to be absolutely ruined, but it was still better than going barefoot. She gazed at the embroidery with a touch of sorrow, then slid them onto her feet.

"Ready?" asked Shane.

She was cold and wet and miserable and shaky with adrenaline. She actually wanted to sit down in the middle of the trail and cry.

And if I do, he will use the voice and tell me that it's okay and I will believe him. And I'll probably feel better.

And then I'll still have to walk the rest of the way in the rain and the mud, except it will be darker and colder and wetter and I'll be embarrassed.

"Ready," she said, squaring her shoulders, and followed him into the storm.

CHAPTER 33

"I take back everything I said about the occupants of these hills," Marguerite said. "They are a noble people and I love them all."

The cause of her change of heart was a shelter built out of carefully stacked and fitted stones. It was dark and dusty and various animals had obviously been using it, but it blocked the wind and the rain and felt a good twenty degrees warmer inside than out.

The only furniture, if you could call it that, was a stone box built into the wall, topped by a metal lid. Marguerite dared to hope that it contained firewood. Shane flipped it up and pulled out a flattened, irregular disc of what looked like mud.

"Hmm."

"That tone fills me with dread," said Marguerite, slumping back against the drystone wall.

"Well," he said, "I suppose the good news is that we can make a fire."

Marguerite forced her tired eyes to focus. It was very dark inside, but nevertheless... "Oh god. That's dried cow poop, isn't it?"

"It might be sheep?"

"Is that better?"

"No, I think it's about the same." He took a few more of the patties from the box and set them in the soot-stained depression in the center of the shelter, then pulled out his tinderbox and set to work.

"I suppose beggars can't be choosers," said Marguerite philosophically. "It was good of them to keep the place stocked at all."

"Indeed. You should get out of those wet clothes. I'll build up the fire."

She had no doubt that he was legitimately concerned that she might die of hypothermia. It was just that it also kicked the sexual tension up by about five notches.

Impressive that I can even think about that, after a long hike and nearly sliding to my death down a mountain.

On the other hand, that would definitely *warm me up.* "Right," Marguerite said, and began stripping her soggy clothes off.

Painted orange by the fire, Shane's throat moved as he swallowed hard. Carefully not looking in her direction, he rummaged through his pack until he found a suitable length of cord and busied himself stringing it across the shelter to make a rough clothesline.

Marguerite wrung what water she could out of her cloak and stretched it out to sit on. Even damp wool was better than bare stone. The pungent smell of burning dung began to fill the small space, but so did the first stirrings of warmth. "Aren't you wet, too?"

"Um," he said. "I...yes. A bit." Marguerite draped her sodden shirt and tunic over the line to dry, then sat back to enjoy the spectacle of a man trying to remove armor in an enclosed space with his eyes closed.

Shane got the surcoat and chain hauberk off and finally opened his eyes to look at his mail. "I need to hang this," he muttered, "and oil it as soon as I can." He looked up at the clothesline, then back down at the hauberk.

"I don't think that'll support it," Marguerite offered.

He glanced toward her, probably involuntarily, and must have gotten an eyeful, because he jerked his gaze back so quickly that she was surprised he didn't get a neck spasm.

"No," he said. "No, it...err...no." He draped the chain over the stone box, looked at it, sighed, moved it a bit, then sighed again and sat back on his heels. "If the gods will it, we will be in the highlands tomorrow and I can treat it properly."

"From your lips to Their ears," said Marguerite. "How much fuel do we have for the fire?"

"Enough to get through the night, so long as we are not extravagant with it." He sounded apologetic. "That is, I do not think we can build it up much further than this."

"Ah, well," said Marguerite philosophically. "I suppose we'll just have to find some other way to keep warm."

Shane looked over at her, clearly startled. Then his eyes dropped below her collarbone, came back up immediately, and he cleared his throat several times.

If I sit around and wait for him to make a move, we'll probably both freeze to death. Hell with it, she thought, and kissed him.

His lips were ice cold as she flicked her tongue across them and for a moment she thought she had made a complete fool of herself, but then his mouth opened under hers and he was burning hot and his hands slid into her hair and tilted her face up toward his. His hands were also cold and her skin was cold and she pressed her cold breasts against his equally cold chest and the only warmth in the world was between their mouths, and for a little bit, that was all she needed.

When it finally ended—when her back wasn't going to let him bend her over his arm like that any longer, and when breathing through her nose was no longer enough air—he pulled back, his eyes wide and almost alarmed.

"I..." he began, and Marguerite put her fingers across his lips to stop whatever incredibly paladinly thing he was about to say next.

"If you shut up," she said, moving to straddle him, "and don't argue with me, we can get warm and incidentally have really *incredible* sex. Or you can keep wallowing in self-loathing and we can freeze to death. Your choice."

His eyes were a thin ring of ice around dark wells. He swallowed hard, and said, slightly higher-pitched than normal, "Am I allowed to wallow in self-loathing afterward?"

That was either a joke or an unexpected amount of self-awareness. "I wouldn't dream of trying to stop you," she said.

She was already out of her clothes, and fortunately he'd removed his chainmail already. She got his pants untied and lifted herself up on her knees long enough for him to wrench them off.

There was no question of readiness. He was already rock hard beneath her. Probably had been since the minute she kissed him. He hissed as her hand closed around his cock—well, no wonder, her fingers were probably like ice. His certainly were as he slid them across her breasts. She could have etched glass with her nipples even if he hadn't been touching her.

He lowered his head to cover one with his mouth. "Ah!" she said, feeling her breath go out in a gasp. "Sensible. Warming."

He made a small, amused noise and switched to the other one. Marguerite inhaled sharply and realized that she was in danger of losing control of the situation. *And I have no plans to give that up just yet.*

She lifted herself up on her knees again, worked him into place, and sank down his length with a purely hedonistic groan. *There. Now, let's see if I can make his eyes roll back in his head...*

She found the angle that pleased her the most and rode him ruthlessly while his fingers sank into her hips and he gasped her name. She wasn't sure if his eyes rolled back or not, because he had them tightly closed, head thrown back.

"Marguerite," he said hoarsely, "I can't...I'm going to..."

She smacked a hand down in the center of his chest and growled, "Don't you *dare,* paladin." His eyes snapped open in surprise and he stared up at her. "Not until I'm—*ahh!*—

done with you....*ahhh...*"

A great threat, and she didn't even last to the end of the sentence. She was too keyed up and her body was too desperate for release. And hell, she'd wanted the gorgeous holy bastard for far too long. Everything clenched suddenly, impossibly tight, and she fell forward against him, shuddering.

He must have felt it—*not surprising, people back in Archenhold probably felt* that—and taken it as permission because he bucked his hips hard against her, lifting her up and driving her back down, and then, with hilariously desperate courtesy, he said, "Excuse me—" and lifted her up, turning to spend himself away from her body. *Polite of him. Probably not necessary, but polite anyway.*

Then he curled up around her, no longer cold but deliciously warm. He had the presence of mind to grab his cloak and pull it over them both. It was still damp and steaming gently from the fire, but it held the heat in, and Marguerite fell asleep with her fingers still stroking the roughness along his jaw.

Shane wrapped himself around her, trying to keep the cold out with his own body, and knew that he had made a terrible, glorious mistake.

About five minutes as the crow flies, and about two hours as the crow walked, in a similar shelter partway down the mountain, two people sat as far apart as it was physically possible to sit. The fire box had not been so well stocked and the fire had lasted less than twenty minutes before guttering down to embers.

Finally, one of them cleared his throat and said, "It would probably be warmer if we—"

"I'd rather freeze to death."

"Fair enough."

Shane woke with his arms full of Marguerite, which was a marvelous way to wake up. He savored the moment as long as possible, until his lower back informed him that he was on a stone floor and if he didn't move *right this minute*, there would be dire repercussions.

He tried to shift unobtrusively, but Marguerite woke immediately. She blinked up at him, down at her state of undress, then said, "Huh!" in a tone that managed to be both surprised and smug.

"Sorry," said Shane reflexively.

She shook her head. "I'm not. Although I can think of better surfaces to do that on." She disentangled herself, while Shane tried to rub his lower back in as manly and attractive a fashion as possible.

It was past daybreak and the fire was cold. The sky was clear overhead, and Shane dared to hope that they wouldn't get rained on again. A bird called somewhere on the hillside, answered by another one, which seemed to offend it. They called back and forth, increasingly outraged, for several moments, while Shane dug through their supplies and produced a slightly squashed loaf of bread and a small, battered apple.

Marguerite felt the hem of her shirt, sniffed it and grimaced. "Well," she said, "it's dry, at least. Even if it smells like burnt sheep dung."

"Mine will, too," Shane offered. "So at least we won't offend each other."

She nodded and stretched to pull the shirt off the clothesline. It did fascinating things to her body. Shane's eyes traced her body downward, and paused at an unexpected row of lines across her hip. "Are those stretchmarks?"

He immediately wanted to sink into the floor of the shelter at his own tactlessness. "Not that they're—I'm not saying they're bad—I just noticed—"

Oh, well done. Perhaps you can map out all of her skin blemishes next.

Marguerite laughed and put a hand over one breast to hold it out of the way so she could look down at her hip. "Here?" She traced one of the silver-red marks. "They are, yes."

"Ah." He had a strong urge to drop to his knees and press his lips against one, but that seemed extremely presumptuous, given the circumstances.

One corner of her mouth crooked up. "In answer to the question you are carefully not asking, no, I've never been pregnant. It just happens sometimes. Surprised you noticed. Most men never look any lower than the breasts."

The word *pregnant* rang in Shane's brain, but was drowned out by the phrase *most men*. He had a sudden desire to go and talk to these other men. Perhaps bounce their heads gently off the pavement a few times.

Stop that, you ass. She took you into her bed once, that's all. You have no right to even expect it again, let alone feel jealousy.

"Ah," he said again. The word *pregnant* was still trying to get his attention, and finally did, accompanied by sudden panic. "Err...last night, we... I didn't...um... I tried not to...but that doesn't always..."

She laughed and dropped her shirt down over the marks. "I did. Silphium powder. I never take any risks with that."

No, of course she wouldn't. Nor would she trust anyone else to take them for her. The thought woke both admiration and an odd, diffuse kind of sadness in him. *Who does she have to depend on? Is there anyone?*

Perhaps she mistook his silence for concern, because she smiled at him. "It's very reliable. I am very much not cut out to be a mother."

"I would think that you could be almost anything you wanted."

Her laugh had a little roughness around the edges, but seemed genuine enough, if rueful. "Oh, I've tried. For a while there, I thought maybe I could just sell perfumes for a living. But something always drags me back." She paused, staring at nothing in particular. "Anyway, this would be no life for a child. Besides, I have an absolute horror of pregnancy."

Even Shane could recognize when it was time for the voice. "It can be very dangerous," he said gently.

"The original Marguerite died of it. Both her and the child. I decided early on that I didn't wish to tempt that fate."

There was a note of finality that Shane had no desire to push. "I... err...I don't have any children either. As far as I know." He cleared his throat. "That is, no one ever came to the temple to say that I might have fathered their child."

"Does that happen often?"

"Sometimes. After a battle, if you've helped people, some of them are grateful. Um. Very grateful." He realized, unaccountably, that he was blushing, which was completely ridiculous, given what they'd done the night before.

Marguerite's eyes danced and he knew she was about to say something hilariously cutting, when a familiar voice drifted up from the path to the shelter.

"If you're going to close your eyes, at least take hold of my hand so you don't walk off the damned cliff."

"I have no desire to hold anything of yours," another, equally familiar voice snapped back.

"I promise, I'm not going to enjoy it. I just don't want to see you splattered all over the landscape on my watch."

Wren's reply was too low for Shane to make out. "No, but that overmuscled brother of yours would," Davith said, clearly in answer, "and I'd rather not give him another excuse to punch me."

Marguerite sighed. "Well, it was fun while it lasted," she said, bending down to kiss Shane on the forehead.

What does that mean? That was fun, let's do it again sometime when other people aren't around? That was fun, now let us never speak of this again?

Davith's head crested the trail, followed a moment later by Wren. Davith looked up, saw the shelter's occupants, and let out a heartfelt groan. "Thank all the gods. You're here. Now this abominable child will be someone else's responsibility."

"Child?" Wren put her hands on her hips. "I'll have you know I've been widowed for longer than I was wed!"

"My congratulations to your husband on his excellent timing." Davith collapsed dramatically on the floor of the shelter. "I'm dying," he said, his eyes closed. "Please burn my body so at least I'll be warm."

"Are you hurt?" Shane asked, ignoring the man and focusing on Wren, who looked indignant but otherwise intact.

"We're fine," said Wren. She exhaled gustily. "Spent the night in a shelter a bit like this one on the lower trail. Ours had thatch, though. I'm pretty sure we can be out of the mountains in a couple of hours, though."

"Wren," said Marguerite, "you are my new favorite person." She brushed off her cloak. "I can't wait."

Shane hastily dragged on his armor. He'd have to sit down and go over it with oil and a stiff brush at the first opportunity, but getting out of the mountains sounded like a marvelous idea.

"You are well?" he asked Wren in an undertone. Despite Marguerite's assurances, he had worried for them.

"Sure," she said. He looked at her steadily and she finally rolled her eyes. "Fine. It was incredibly awkward and there is no good way to say, 'I think you're an asshole but I'm sorry I tried to kill you.' But we lived and nobody fell off a mountain and died."

Shane nodded. He was the last one out of the shelter, and paused on the threshold. "I wish there was some way to replace the fuel we used," he said. "Or pay for what we took."

"That's why it's there," Wren said. "It's for anyone who needs it, that's all."

"I know. Still. In case someone else needs it, I wish I could help."

He started down the trail. Ahead of them, Davith put one hand on Marguerite's shoulder, leaned down and murmured something in her ear. She gave a rueful laugh and swatted at him.

Jealousy struck Shane so hard that it felt like a sharpened stake piercing his chest, as if he might look down and see blood. He took a handful of deep breaths, trying to settle himself after the unexpected assault. *What is this? Why? I have no right. She is not mine. I am not hers.*

Like hell you're not, whispered the little voice that usually cried failure. *You are hers completely. She's just not* yours. *Best get used to it.*

He did not want to get used to it. He wanted to lay claim to her and snarl at any other man who came too close. It was nasty and primitive and it boiled in his chest, wonderful and horrible.

He had no right to feel that way. More than that, feeling it was dangerous. Jealousy was fear, plain and simple, fear of abandonment, fear that one would be judged in comparison and found wanting.

Can't imagine why I'd feel any of those *things,* he thought dryly. It was just a damn shame that knowing you *shouldn't* feel something didn't make the feeling go away.

The Dreaming God's people taught that jealousy was the kind of crack in a soul that a demon could exploit. The Saint of Steel, perhaps more practically, pointed out that a jealous berserker was a very dangerous thing.

I cannot afford to feel this. I cannot. Look at what happened when Davith broke Wren's heart. She nearly killed him, and I know they hadn't so much as kissed.

And if I snap because I'm jealous or heartbroken, who's going to stop me?

"You doing all right?" asked Marguerite, touching his arm. Her eyebrows rose as he jumped, startled. "Something wrong?"

"Just—ah—thinking." He hadn't even noticed her dropping back. *Saint's teeth, if this is what I do now when I bed a woman, it's probably for the best that I don't get much opportunity. We could be attacked by an army while I was staring off into space.* "Sorry," he added. "Distracted, that's all."

He wasn't sure if she believed him. He couldn't tell. *That's part of the problem, isn't it? You can't ever tell. She's too good at hiding her responses. You have no idea if she would like more or if that really was just two people staying warm.*

You could *just ask.*

What, right here, with Davith and Wren looking on?

"Are you *sure* you're all right?" Marguerite asked.

"Fine." He picked up the pace. "We should get going."

CHAPTER 34

Wren was not exactly wrong about getting out of the mountains in a couple of hours. It was just bad luck that those hours occurred sometime in the afternoon, and not actually when they set out.

"I knew that was the wrong direction," muttered Davith.

"It was the *correct* direction," grated Wren. "It was just that the rock-slide was in the way."

"Yes, but—"

"Children," said Marguerite wearily, "if you do not stop bickering, I will turn this escape attempt around, so help me god."

"Suits me," said Davith cheerfully.

"And I will tell Shane to kill you."

Shane did his best to look like a killer. He wasn't sure if it worked, or if he just looked constipated. Davith rolled his eyes.

"At any rate," said Marguerite, "there was a detour. A clearly marked detour, no less."

"Those were arrows painted on boulders."

"Yes. *Clearly* painted. And here we are. In the highlands." Marguerite made a sweeping gesture, taking in the expanse of rolling hills, the lush grass, and the absolute lack of other humans.

It pained Shane to agree with Davith in any way, but... "Unfortunately I'm not certain where we are in relation to the rest of the highlands. And the trail seems to have stopped."

Marguerite took a deep breath, squared her shoulders, and strode out across the green hillside. "It'll be *fine,*" she said. "We'll find someone and ask for directions."

It took an additional hour before they found someone. The light was starting to fade and Shane was beginning to look for anything that might work as shelter. It hadn't rained again, thankfully, but lacking even dried sheep dung to burn, it was going to be a long night.

Davith's insistence of asking directions of every sheep they passed wasn't helping.

"Are you certain we need him?" Shane asked, while the other man interrogated a ewe about which side of the hill to go around.

"Theoretically, he'll point out Sail operatives to us if he sees them," Marguerite said, with an expression that indicated that she wasn't certain if that was enough. "It's his skin too, and he knows that. Davith is a jackass, but he's not going to risk his neck out of spite."

"I could make it look like an accident," said Wren hopefully.

Shane just looked at her.

"An...axe-related...accident?"

"I can hear you, you know," said Davith, returning from the unimpressed ewe. "And once you're done plotting to kill me, you might like to know that there's smoke coming from over thataway."

He pointed. Shane couldn't see it, but Wren and Marguerite evidently could. "Oh thank the Rat," said Marguerite. "Civilization at last."

Civilization, in this case, turned out to be a solitary shepherd's hut, built of the same stone as everything else, but with a heavy thatched roof. Light leaked around the edges of the shutters and under the door. As they approached through the deepening twilight, Shane first saw a pen holding a flock of sheep, then heard a dog begin to bark from inside the hut.

"Dog," said Wren. She nodded toward the pen. "Flock protector, not the loud one."

Shane nodded, even though the sheep were now a white blur and he had no hope of picking a dog out of the flock, unless it happened to be, say, bright pink.

"Do you think they'd be willing to put us up for the night?" asked Marguerite. "Normally I'd ask if they had space in the barn, but..." She waved her hands, encompassing the lack of anything barn-like in the vicinity.

Shane had doubts that any of the locals would be willing to put up a small band of strangers, two of whom looked extremely warlike. "It doesn't hurt to ask," he said, and rapped on the door.

The dog inside lost its mind. Shane was just wondering if he should knock again when the top half of the door swung partway open, revealing an old man draped in sheepskins, holding a rushlight in a metal holder.

"Eh?" the man said. Bushy eyebrows drew together over small, bright eyes. "What's your business, strangers?"

"I apologize for disturbing you," said Shane, in the most soothing voice he could muster. "We've been lost for much of the day."

He half-expected Marguerite to step in at this point, but she didn't. When he glanced over at her, she nodded encouragingly to him. *Right. This is what I get for using the voice.* Well, it wasn't like it was the first time.

The old man lifted the rushlight, peering across the group, then back to Shane. "Lost, eh?" he said.

Shane bowed slightly. "I understand, sir, if you don't wish to let us in. I realize how we look. But if we could impose upon you to purchase some fuel...or perhaps a hot cup of tea..."

"I would commit mortal sins for hot tea," said Wren, which, while clearly heartfelt, probably did not put the shepherd at ease.

"Quiet!" the old man snapped. Shane immediately closed his lips on what he was going to say. "No, not you. The dog. Quiet, you!"

The dog did not stop barking, but at least began to space the barks out somewhat. The shepherd turned back. "Came over the mountain, did you?"

"Ah..." Shane glanced back at the other three, not sure how much to reveal.

"I ain't asking," the man said. "You must've come that way because if you came t'other way, dog down the way would have gone off when you went by."

"Ah," said Shane again. "Yes."

"Hmmph." He looked across the four again. "You ain't bandits."

"No, we're not," Shane agreed.

"'Course not. I know every bandit in the hills, and they know I ain't got nothing worth stealing but sheep. And you'd have just taken the sheep." He reached down and unbolted the lower door. "Might as well come in and get warm."

"Bless you," said Marguerite, as fervently as any priest.

They tromped into the little building, which filled up rapidly with all the extra bodies. Shane stationed himself by the door. Marguerite and Davith made a bee-line for the fire. Wren tried to help the old man make tea until he told her to sit down, he wasn't quite in the grave yet. The dog ran from one person to another, sniffing wildly, barked at Shane several times in apparent confusion, then shoved its head under Davith's elbow until he gave in and petted its ears.

"You have no taste," Wren told the dog.

Davith covered its ears with his hands. "Hush, you'll hurt her feelings." To the dog he said, "They just don't understand our love." The dog gazed at him adoringly and thumped its tail on the floor.

The shepherd passed around mismatched mugs filled with some brown tannic liquid that resembled tea more than it resembled anything else. The only thing that mattered was that it was hot. Shane suppressed a hedonistic groan. Marguerite didn't even try.

"S'pose you can stay the night," said the shepherd. "Ain't got blankets for the lot of you, but it's warmer than outside."

"We are very grateful," said Marguerite. She paused, then gave the shepherd a disarmingly frank smile. "As you guessed, we're not from around here. Is it acceptable to offer you money, or would it be offensive?"

Apparently elderly men were no more immune to Marguerite than anyone else. He didn't exactly smile, but the deep lines in his face rearranged themselves in a slightly less forbidding fashion. "You go handing out money willy-nilly, some people think you're saying they look poor. What you do if someone gives you a good turn is hand 'em a coin and ask 'em to offer a prayer for you in church."

"Ah." Marguerite nodded understanding and reached into her coin pouch. "So may I ask you to offer two prayers for me? One for your hospitality, and one for the good advice?"

The shepherd made a slightly awkward bow. "Be glad to do so, lady."

He paused, then added, "That advice wasn't worth a full prayer, so I'll also tell you this. You ladies prob'ly want to cover your hair. Not considered quite proper here if you're not married. I don't think worse of anybody, but there's those who'll make assumptions."

Marguerite nodded. "I understand. Thank you again."

"*I* don't understand," said Wren the next day, as they left the shepherd's hut. "What was he trying to say? Why do we have to cover our hair?"

"Because we're unmarried women and otherwise people'll think we're whores," said Marguerite, who had learned not to rely on euphemism around Wren.

"What?"

"I know, I know." She reached up to pat the shawl that she had draped over her own head. "But it's a common enough custom in this part of the world. Then you go a hundred miles east and people assume that if you cover your hair, you must *be* married."

"But why does it matter whether we're married or not? People don't have sex with their *hair,"* Wren said, sounding much aggrieved.

Davith had a sudden suspicious coughing fit and Shane immediately looked even more inscrutable than usual.

"Some places have very specific rules about clothes," Marguerite said. "So do we, frankly, we just don't notice them. If you ever find yourself around the Hundred Houses, for example, they find bare feet absolutely scandalous."

Wren clutched her forehead. "Feet? But people don't have s—"

"Actually, some of them do," Davith interrupted. When they all stared at him, he said, "Not *me.* I'm just saying." He paused. "Come to think of it, most of the fellows I knew who were very interested in a lady's feet were from the Hundred Houses. Lure of the forbidden and all that."

"How does that even *work?"* asked Wren, whose curiosity appeared to have briefly overcome her loathing of Davith.

"Well, I did know a fellow who always wanted to suck on his lady's—"

Shane's growl sounded like a volcano deciding whether or not it was quite dormant. Davith stopped in mid-sentence. "On second thought, that's a very boring story." He cleared his throat. "You know, perhaps I'll scout ahead a little way. Our charming host last night said that there were bandits."

"Do not think about running," said Shane.

Davith rolled his eyes and gestured at the vast sweep of highlands. "Where am I going to run to, exactly?"

"The bandits must be able to hide somewhere," Shane pointed out.

"Perhaps they're under a sheep."

"Or perhaps—"

"*Both of you* stop," snapped Marguerite. "Look!"

A narrow ribbon of reddish-gray wound across the opposite hillside. "Is that a road?" Wren asked.

Cart-track might have been a more accurate term. It was narrow, deeply etched with wagon ruts, and had grass growing down the center. It was also possibly the most beautiful thing that Marguerite had ever seen in her life.

Roads go from one place to another. Roads join up to larger roads. Larger roads mean towns and towns mean inns and inns mean hot baths and beds that are not packed earth with a dog trying to burrow in next to you.

"Which way do we follow it?" Shane asked.

"Cambraith is north," Marguerite said. "So we'll go north and hope that the road isn't squiggling around the hills until it ends up going south again."

"It's going downhill," said Wren, sighting along her thumb. "All else being equal, larger towns will tend to be downslope."

"The gods be praised," said Davith. "If I had to hike across another mountain, I'd ask the big guy to just kill me and be done with it."

"It would be my pleasure to assist you," Shane said.

"I'm going to assume that was your idea of humor, paladin."

"If you two don't stop sniping at each other, I'm going to gag you both."

There was a long silence, and then Wren leaned toward Shane and said, "She sounds just like Beartongue when she does that."

"I'm beginning to understand how she feels!" Marguerite snapped, and stomped down the road in the direction, the gods willing, of their destination.

CHAPTER 35

The road did indeed tend north and generally downhill. The hills became smaller, sprouted steep stone outcroppings, and immense boulders filled the landscape. There was even the occasional copse of trees.

The increased cover made Marguerite feel less exposed. Unfortunately, she wasn't the only one. They had just rounded a snakelike curve around the side of a hill when a voice called "Stand and deliver!" and Marguerite found herself gazing down a sword pointed very determinedly in her direction.

Oh for god's sake. Really? Now? Really?

She looked up the length of the sword to the man holding it. His skin was so weathered that it looked like old leather and his hair had gone mostly gray, but he did not look the slightest bit frail. Neither did the three bowmen standing at the edge of the road behind him.

Shane reached for his sword and one of the arrows moved very determinedly in his direction. "I wouldn't do that," the bandit said. "I fear that my associates are not known for their patience."

"Don't," Marguerite snapped at Shane. To the bandit, she said, "We're just travelers. We don't have anything worth stealing." *Please, White Rat, if you're listening, please let them not do something that makes Shane do something that makes them shoot him.*

The bandit looked her over thoroughly. He had brown eyes the color of beer, and Marguerite had to admit that his gaze was less lascivious than calculating. "You're lying," he said pleasantly. "I understand why, of course, but this will be much easier if you don't."

"No, no," Davith said helpfully. "We're as poor as churchmice."

"Then you are churchmice with chainmail and extremely good boots," the bandit said. "Please hand over your valuables—and your boots—and we can be done with all this."

"Oh no," said Wren. "You are *not* getting my boots. This is the only comfortable pair I own."

"Are they really worth your life?" asked the bandit, stepping toward her. His voice was pleasant and quite reasonable, the paladin's voice on a shoestring budget.

"Is that a threat?" asked Shane, sounding not at all pleasant or reasonable.

The bandit looked at him, then at the three bowmen, then back at Shane. "Yes," he said. "That *was* a threat. Well done."

Marguerite rubbed her temples. "Can I interest you in a token payment?" she asked. "Perhaps enough to...ah...offer a dozen prayers on our behalf?"

"Two dozen prayers, and I still want the boots."

"Two dozen, and nobody takes off their boots."

The bandit sighed. "Madam, I assure you that I am not stealing your boots merely for the fun of it. Footwear is the first thing to go in this accursed land. Between the rocks and the mud and the ground-wights..." In the tones of a man making a great concession, he added, "You may all keep your socks. We have plenty of socks. There is no shortage of wool locally."

Shane leaned toward her and murmured, "Give the word and I will end this."

"I am not letting you catch an arrow over boots!"

"You should listen to her," said the bandit.

"There's no glory in dying for footwear, paladin," said Davith, already starting to unlace his boots.

The bandit froze. Dust motes danced in the air over the roadway. One of the archers slowly eased the tension on her bowstring, but the tension in the air drew agonizingly taut.

"Beg pardon," the bandit said, sounding just slightly strained, "but did you say 'paladin?'"

Marguerite winced internally. *Of all the bandits in all the highlands, did we get one with a grudge against paladins?* "No, of course not," she said.

"Do you know, I'm fairly certain that he did?"

Marguerite speared Davith with a look. He coughed. "No, no. I said—err—*pal.* Of mine. We're pals." He inched across the road, laces trailing, and slung an arm around Shane. "*Great* pals."

"...Pals. Yes." Shane's smile was mostly gritted teeth.

The bandit pinched the bridge of his nose. "I definitely heard *paladin.*"

"I heard it too, boss," volunteered one of the archers.

"Thank you, Thea. My hearing is not going, even if my mind apparently is." He looked Shane over again, eyes lingering on the sword hilt. "Ah, hell," he murmured, almost to himself.

Marguerite prepared to dive out of the way of arrows.

"Good-looking if you like that sort of thing," the bandit said with a sigh, "sword that was probably gigantic before you broke it, no apparent understanding of irony. Are you by chance one of the Dreaming God's people?"

"No," said Marguerite.

"No?" said Wren.

"This guy? Ha!" Davith thumped Shane on the chest. Shane glowered.

"The one in back's got an axe, boss," said an archer.

"Yes. I see that. And chainmail under her cloak." The bandit studied Wren with narrowed eyes.

Please, Rat, if you have any love for your servants and the people trying to keep your servants alive...

"Paladin. Possibly two." The bandit nodded slowly to himself and took a step back. "You know what?" he said, to no one in particular. "I am capable of learning." He chopped his hand down. Marguerite flinched. Shane jerked forward, dragging Davith with him. The hilt of Wren's axe slapped into her hand.

The archers lowered their bows and stepped back behind the boulders. The bandit gazed at the four of them, shook his head, and reached into his belt pouch.

A coin landed at Marguerite's feet. She looked up into resigned beer-colored eyes.

"Offer a prayer for me," the bandit said, "the next time you're in church." And he too melted away into the hills, and left the four of them standing alone in the roadway.

"Pal. Of. Mine?" asked Shane, peeling Davith's arm off his shoulders.

"I'd like to see *you* do better under pressure, paladin."

"We could have taken them," grumbled Wren.

"Yes, and that's probably why he let us go," Davith said. He knelt and laced up his boot. "Sounded like he'd had a few bad experiences, didn't it?"

Marguerite bent down and picked up the coin. "I suspect we owe a prayer to the Rat for deliverance," she said.

Shane exhaled slowly, the tension leaving his shoulders, and turned toward her. "*Are* you going to pray for him?" he asked.

Marguerite rubbed the coin between her fingers, the metal cool and faintly slick. "I think I will," she said. "You never know who's going to need it."

The road continued to descend and by noon they stood overlooking a medium-sized village. It sat at a crossroads and boasted a public house, a general store, and a small stone church. Best of all, though, there was a bathhouse. Judging by the steam curling from the pools around it, it was built on a natural hot spring. A strong mineral smell filled their nostrils as they approached.

"I know we're in a hurry," said Marguerite, "but I am making a command decision. We're staying here tonight and having baths."

"I forgive you everything," said Davith fervently.

"What, all of it?"

"Well, most of it. Maybe not the kidnapping."

She snorted. Shane glanced at Wren and caught the edge of a glower, but she wiped it away as quickly as it had come.

His heart went out to her. She would never, ever admit that she'd been hurt, but it was obvious if you knew where to look. He wondered if his own feelings for Marguerite were as obvious to her.

By all the gods, living and dead, they better not be. His thoughts were not the sort that a man wanted his younger sister to know existed at all. Hell, if Shane had even *suspected* that a man harbored that sort of thought about Wren, he'd have bounced the fellow's skull sideways off a stone wall. Twice. With prejudice.

They reached the public house. The sign out front had no writing, only a peculiar illustration. Shane couldn't quite make out what it was supposed to portray. He paused to stare up at it, trying to work out what the brown thing in the mug of beer was supposed to be.

"Is that a turd?" asked Davith in an undertone.

"It does look like one," Shane was forced to admit.

"This makes me worry about the quality of the beer."

"The highlands are supposed to have excellent beer," Shane said. "I'm sure it's...fine."

"Ah yes. Sign of the Drowned Turd, everyone's favorite establishment."

"Both of you shut up," said Marguerite, pulling the door open.

"Welcome to the Happy Slug!" cried the innkeeper as they crowded in.

"Oh," said Davith and Shane together, then tried to pretend they hadn't.

Marguerite spoke to the innkeeper for five minutes, making expansive hand gestures, then returned to the group, her hands full of mugs and her face radiant with relief. "We have two rooms," she said, sliding the ale mugs across the table. "He'll bring out food. More importantly, there's another bathhouse just behind the inn, although he suggests we use it one at a time." She paused, looking at Davith. "Do I have to have someone stand watch over you? Are you going to run off?"

"Am I really going to say anything but no?" He raised a wry eyebrow at her. "*I* wouldn't trust me."

Which is exactly the sort of thing you'd say if you were trying to appear trustworthy, Shane thought. Marguerite evidently agreed. "Right. Shane, if you don't mind guarding the door?"

"Oh, he can come inside if he wants. I'm not shy."

She cut Shane's retort off with a look. "You know what? I'm going to go have a bath now," she said, sounding very calm. "Then I'll come back. Then I will have food. Then, perhaps, I will be able to deal with all of this without screaming and bashing your heads together. How does that sound?"

There was a long silence, broken only by the innkeeper rattling mugs.

"Can I go second?" asked Wren meekly.

"Yes. Yes, you may." Marguerite nodded to the group as if they were business associates, then turned and stalked back to the innkeeper. Shane watched her go, his eyes dropped to the shape of her hips through the concealing fabric. Even now, the memory of how they'd felt under his hands made his mouth go dry.

This was ridiculous. He knew how desire worked. You lusted after someone and then, assuming it was mutual, you fell into bed together and that took the edge off. Even if it was good...very, *very* good...your thirst was temporarily slaked.

And fantasy never quite lived up to reality.

And wanting was always more powerful than having.

Except now that he knew exactly what bedding Marguerite was like, he wanted her so badly that his back teeth ached. He took a long drink of his ale, which tasted much better than anything called The Happy Slug had any right to.

Marguerite finished her discussion with the innkeeper. He handed her a towel. She stalked out the door without so much as glancing in their direction. Wren followed hastily, either to keep potential enemies at bay or to make certain she got the second place in line.

"As a friendly bit of advice," Davith said, once she was gone, "if you don't stop ogling her like a piece of meat, she's eventually going to get annoyed."

Shane blinked at him, not sure whether to be angry or appalled at how easily the man had read his thoughts. "It is not your business," he said.

"Actually, it is very literally what I do for a living. Seeing someone doing it so badly offends my notion of craftsmanship." He lounged back in his chair, looking cool and amused and very much in need of a mailed fist to the face.

Lacking any better reply, Shane growled at him.

"Don't bother, paladin, I know you won't try to murder me in the middle of a pub. You know she'd be upset if you got us thrown out before she was done with her bath."

The fact that he was right did nothing to endear him to Shane.

"You don't like me very much, do you?" asked Davith.

"No."

He snorted. "Fine, I know I deserve that. But this is what I *do.* I'd ask you if I needed to know how to chop someone in half."

"I do not require the advice of a degenerate," Shane informed him.

He clutched his chest in mock anguish. "You wound me. Come now. It's no different than Marguerite cozying up to lords to raid their desks."

"It is," said Shane. "You do it to women."

"Are you saying women are somehow inferior?" asked Davith, raising both eyebrows. "Because I'd say Wren has more than proved that wrong."

Even knowing better, Shane put his hand on the hilt of his sword. Davith shook his head. "Don't bother," he said. "You could kill me in a heartbeat. So could she. I'm not going to fight back."

"That is," said Shane, "the safest thing you could do."

"Why do you think I'm doing it?" Davith leaned back on his stool and folded his arms. "I realize that we're never going to be friends, but we seem to be stuck with each other for a little while. If it helps any, I took no pleasure in deceiving Wren."

Shane thought about cutting out his heart and reluctantly dismissed it as impractical. "Your pleasure is no concern of mine."

"Damn, I can feel my nose hairs freezing up when you talk." Davith snorted. "Ask Marguerite if you don't believe me. We really are in the same line of work, she and I."

Shane gazed at him levelly. "Are you done?"

Davith sighed and his shoulders slumped a little, and suddenly he looked older and more tired. He took a swig of ale and set it down. "She can't love you, you know."

Shane blinked at him.

"Marguerite," Davith said. "She can't love you."

"I do not wish to listen to insults," said Shane, keeping his voice even despite the voice in his head screaming at him to pick the man up, turn him upside down, and shove him headfirst into the ground like a degenerate turnip.

"It's not an insult." Davith shook his head. "Look. You're a good man. Even I can see that. And you saved my life, so I'm telling you outright. When you do this sort of thing for a living—when manipulating people is your profession—you lose the ability. You can't. If you loved people, they'd be used against you, or you'd be too afraid to send them off into danger. She can't love you. All you can ever be to her is a weapon that she can use."

Shane met his eyes. "Then I am honored to be the weapon in her hand."

"Shit," said Davith softly, "you've got it bad." He got up and went to the bar, while Shane stared at his back and wondered if the man was actually right.

CHAPTER 36

In the morning, clean, fed, and having slept somewhere better than the floor, the four set out in the general direction of Cambraith. They had not bought horses, though their packs were much heavier with food, and Marguerite had finally acquired a map.

"Fortunately we can go from town to town," she said, consulting it. "We shouldn't have to sleep rough again, thank all the little gods."

"This would be faster with horses," said Davith.

"Yes, but then we'd have to take care of horses."

"I thought you were in a hurry."

"I am. That's why I don't want to deal with horses. I suspect we may be able to pay someone with a wagon to cut down on our travel time, and there's a river here,"—she traced a line with her fingertip—"where I'm told we can be ferried across by a riverman, unless we've got livestock, in which case we'd have to go a full day south to Wherryford to find someone with a raft."

"You're in charge," said Davith with a shrug. "I'm just a prisoner."

"He talks a lot for a prisoner," Shane observed, to no one in particular.

"I'd noticed that," Wren answered.

Marguerite pinched the bridge of her nose, stowed the map, and started walking.

The first few days were uneventful. The landscape was green and rolling, rolling and green. It was beautiful at first, then became monotonous. Occasionally it broke out in boulders, sheep, or small villages.

The villages were spaced several hours of brisk walking apart, roughly the distance that a laden wagon could make in half a day. They usually pressed on past the first one, and once or twice they did encounter someone with a wagon who was willing to take a coin to give them a ride somewhere. The inns were small but usually had at least two rooms available, even if the mattresses were of questionable quality. Marguerite asked indirectly about the Sail at every stop, but so far had turned up nothing suspicious.

"Are we ahead of them?" Shane asked.

She bit her lower lip thoughtfully. It was not meant seductively, Shane knew. Knowing that was surprisingly little help. He stared over her head at a distant hillside and reminded himself of the Lay of Sir Afrim, who had been walled up alive by his enemies and survived for fourteen days, being brought food and sips of water by a flock of sparrows. *That would be much worse than this. I have got to stop complaining.*

"I don't think so," Marguerite said. Shane blinked at her, trying to remember what question she was answering. "They should have a head start, but I suspect they took a different route. Although the boatman's strike may well have trapped them as effectively as it did us."

"Ah. Yes."

"Regardless, Cambraith is a large county and Magnus knows people are looking for her, so they may not have the easiest time searching. Highlanders are notoriously suspicious of strangers asking questions."

"Of course."

She smiled at him, reached up, and tucked a stray strand of hair behind his ear. He had taken direct blows to the head that staggered him less. "And if we get there too late...well, we'll figure out the next step once we get there."

"Yes. The next step. Certainly." His skin blazed where her fingers had brushed it. He half-expected the touch to have left blisters. *Sir Afrim. Sparrows. Fourteen days and nights.*

If any of the sparrows had been agonizingly attractive, the chroniclers had left those bits out.

"Are you all right?" Marguerite asked.

"Sparrows aren't attractive."

"Sorry, what?" She frowned up at him. "I think I misheard you."

"Fine," said Shane. "I'm fine."

Late afternoon of the third day. They'd gotten a wagon ride most of the way to the next village, rattling along between barrels that smelled strongly of salted fish. The trader had pointed over a rise and told them that if they crossed there, they'd cut a good half-hour off their time. Shane thanked her and she winked cheerfully at him before continuing on her way.

"Right," said Davith, as soon as the wagon was out of sight. "Find me a rock or avert your eyes, friends."

"The town's supposed to be right over there."

"Good for it. That wagon hit every single rock on the road and while I may have the stamina of a twenty-year-old, my bladder is significantly older."

"There's a very large rock over there," said Wren, pointing.

"So there is. Won't be a moment."

Shane sighed and set out alongside him. Davith slid a wary glance at the paladin. "Do you need the rock too, or are you worried I'll try to escape?"

"Both things can be true."

"Fair enough."

They were halfway back from the rock when Davith stepped into a hole, let out a squawk, and fell forward.

"Davith!" Shane grabbed for him, alarmed. He'd seen men break legs after stepping in concealed gopher holes, and while he had no particular fondness for the man, that wasn't something he'd wish on anyone. Also, Shane would probably have to carry him.

"Gah! Ah!" Davith levered himself upright. "Shit!"

"Is it broken?"

"No, it's stuck—*Ahhhh!*"

"You're stuck?"

"Something just bit me!" Davith sounded more outraged than hurt.

"*Bit* you?" Shane glanced up and saw the distant figures of

Marguerite and Wren hurrying toward them. "Here, let me look. Maybe you're trapped under a root."

"It is *not* a root, you armored jackass! I know the difference between a root and being bitten! Something is gnawing on my—*gah! Ah! Get it off!*"

Shane dropped to his knees, wondering what the hell could be biting from inside a narrow hole like that. *A rabbit? A gopher? Saint's teeth, let it not be a badger...*

He shoved Davith's cloak aside, looked down into the hole, stopped and stared.

It was not a badger. Actually, it wasn't any animal that Shane recognized. He wasn't even sure it was alive.

The hole was about twice the size of Davith's calf. A line of irregular pointed rocks the size of Shane's thumb ringed the top, set into slick brown earth. As Shane watched, the sides of the hole seemed to flex and it closed a little tighter, the rocks digging into Davith's boot. Deep gouges were already forming in the leather. Davith yelped as it tightened.

"Is it some kind of trap?" he panted.

"It's...uh...something." Shane drew his sword, not quite sure what to do next. They certainly looked like teeth, but what was he going to do, stab the ground?

He prodded the inside of the hole with the broken blade. The rocks that formed the teeth scraped along the metal. They were definitely rocks, too. He could see a thin thread of quartz sparkling through one, and though they were all sharp, it was the jagged sharpness of broken stone.

For lack of anything better to do, Shane did indeed try stabbing the hole next to Davith's boot. Clods of earth broke off and tumbled down into the dark. The stone teeth clenched again, tighter, and Davith's yelp turned into a hoarse yell.

"What the *hell?*" said Wren, dropping to her knees in time to see the hole bite down.

"I've never seen anything like it," Shane admitted.

"That is really not what I—*gahh!*—want to hear right now."

"If it's a trap, can you lever it open?" Marguerite asked.

Shane and Wren exchanged helpless looks. It was as good an idea as any. Shane pulled the heavy scabbard off his back. "This may hurt," he warned.

"That'll be a nice change from the general agon—AHHH!" Shane thrust the scabbard down, along the side of Davith's leg. Stone teeth ground against it. He pushed against the scabbard, trying to pry the hole apart, wondering if that was as bizarre as it sounded inside his head.

Astonishingly, it seemed to work a little. The earth walls flexed again, but didn't close any tighter. Wren reached down past him and struck at a tooth with the handle of her axe. She hit it twice and it broke free from the earth holding it. *Not gums. Don't think of it like gums.*

Wren started on another tooth and Shane stopped her. "Grab him," he said. "Get ready to pull. I'll see if I can get it to open a little farther."

"Right." She scrambled aside, hooked her hands under Davith's armpits, and set her feet. "Ready."

"Are you—*gah*—sure this is a good—"

Shane slammed his full weight against the scabbard and prayed that the hardened leather would hold. "Now!"

Wren pulled. Davith shrieked. Shane's feet slid as he tried to find something to brace against.

There was a loud *crack!* and Davith came free. Wren fell over backwards, still clutching him. Shane felt the scabbard twist as the hole snapped shut around it.

"Please tell me that wasn't your leg," said Marguerite, in the panting silence that followed.

"I don't know," said Davith. "It might have been."

"Get *off* me," growled Wren.

"I can't. I think my leg came off."

"It wasn't your leg," Shane said. The scabbard had split in half, the stone teeth buried in it. It stuck up from the ground at an absurd angle. Anyone stumbling over it would think that someone had tried to bury a sword in the ground and given up halfway through. He glanced over at Davith, who was missing his right boot. Dark red marks were already forming a ring halfway up the shin.

Davith rolled off Wren and grabbed for his leg. "My foot! My beautiful foot! It's attached!"

"Barely, by the look of things," Shane said. "Let me take a look."

"May I suggest that we first move off this patch of ground that appears to have random mouths in it?" asked Marguerite.

"Yes. Please, yes. I'll hop."

Davith leaned heavily on Shane as they made their way up the hillside. "Do you think this is far enough?" Wren asked, when they reached the summit.

"How would we even know?"

Shane checked the ground for suspicious holes or suspicious movements, but found nothing. Would the dirt need to move, though? Would the mouth tunnel like a mole, or would more dirt just open up? *Hell, for all we know, the whole hillside is alive and covered in mouths.*

This was an unpleasant thought. However, after half a minute of standing, nothing tried to swallow them. *Good enough.* The paladin helped Davith sit and felt his leg for breaks. "Does this hurt?"

"Yes, of course it hurts! The dirt bit me! *Dirt shouldn't bite people!*"

Shane reached, with some difficulty, for the paladin's voice. "Does it hurt like a break? Here? How about here?"

It was not broken, nor, thankfully, sprained. A bad sprain could have been worse than a break, as Shane knew all too well. "You're going to have a fantastic set of bruises," he warned.

"I don't suppose there's any way I can get my boot back?"

"Errr..." Wren held up the top half of what had previously been a rather expensive boot. "I went back. I think it's digesting the rest."

"Now we know why that bandit wanted our boots so badly," said Marguerite.

"I hate this place," said Davith, to no one in particular.

"Can you walk?" asked Shane. "The village isn't far."

"I can hop," said Davith grimly. "If it gets me away from that damned hole, I'll even crawl."

Ten minutes later, Shane pushed open the door to the inn. Davith limped through and didn't stop. He made a bee line for the bar, grabbed the edge to hold himself up, and hissed, "Do you know that there are holes that *bite people* here?"

The bartender gazed at him with clear astonishment. "Aye?" he said finally. "Ground-wights? Did you run afoul of one?"

"You *knew* about this." Davith's voice trembled with emotion. Shane started forward and Marguerite caught his shoulder.

"I think he's earned this one," she murmured. Shane relented.

"Aye?" The bartender glanced over at the other three, as if seeking backup. "They get a sheep now and again, so they do."

"...A...sheep."

"You pour water down the hole, they back right off. Do they not have ground-wights where you're from?"

Davith drew himself up as tall as he could without relinquishing his grip on the bar. "If you live in a country with holes that randomly eat you, you have to *warn* people," he hissed. Shane could not remember the last time he'd seen anyone so incandescently angry. Davith's finger stabbed against the bar. "You *tell* people. You tell *everyone.* There should be *laws.*"

The bartender gazed at him in silence for a long, long moment, methodically cleaning the mug in his hands. Finally he said, "Do you have badgers back home?"

"Yes," said Davith, with wonderful restraint. "We have badgers. Why?"

"Figured I'd warn you about 'em if you didn't, 'cos we've got those too." He set the mug down. "How about wolves?"

Davith hitched himself sideways onto a stool, put his head down on the bar, and whispered, "Whiskey. Neat."

Despite his general distaste for Davith, Shane found himself moved to pity. The man seemed genuinely broken. He turned to Marguerite. "If you'll arrange the rooms and the meals, I'll see if I can locate a cobbler."

"The town's probably too small for that," Marguerite said, "but I suppose we can't let him hop on one foot all the way to Cambraith."

"Oh, I don't know..." muttered Wren.

"It'd slow us down," said Shane.

"I suppose there's that."

"And here I thought that paladins weren't vindictive sorts," said Marguerite, clearly amused.

"I have no idea where you got that impression," Shane said.

"Hmm, now that you mention it, neither do I." She grinned at him and sauntered toward the bar. Mindful of Davith's advice about ogling, Shane took himself off into the dusk in pursuit of a replacement boot and a scabbard for what was left of his sword.

CHAPTER 37

Davith was hungover the next day, but kept pace nonetheless. "It was worth it," he said, even though his eyes were bloodshot and he had viewed breakfast with loathing. "I regret nothing. Except stepping in that damned hole." He eyed the side of the road suspiciously, as if it might suddenly open up to swallow him. "Predatory dirt. *What the hell.*"

Credit where it was due, Marguerite thought, Davith hadn't slowed them down significantly, even limping. Possibly he was afraid that if he didn't move fast enough, the ground would bite his other foot. Still, whatever the reason, they were only a day away from Cambraith, and there was still no sign of the Red Sail.

They stopped at the last inn before Cambraith proper. Marguerite drummed her fingers on the table, thinking. Were they ahead or far behind? Did the Sail know that they'd gone into the highlands instead of bolting to safety? What did they make of Davith's apparent defection?

The questions occupied only half her mind. She was watching Shane out of the corner of her eye. This was the third time in as many days that she had moved near him—not even touched him—and he'd started to lean toward her, then jumped back like a startled cat. It was getting on her nerves.

She wondered what was going on inside his head. Something, clearly. Probably something paladinly, god help them all.

If he's regretting rolling around on the floor with me, he could just say so. Or if he wants to do it again, he could just say that. *Though it's not like we can share a room anyway—I'd have to rent separate rooms for Wren and Davith, or they'd murder each other, and I don't want Davith left unsupervised.*

The thought that Shane might regret bedding her sent an unexpected pang through her. She stamped it down. *These things happen. Just because you want to do it again...as soon as possible...preferably several times, and preferably not on a stone floor...doesn't mean he's obligated to feel the same. Sometimes good and decent people just aren't interested in you.*

She snorted. Good and decent people probably *shouldn't* be interested in her. Spies and paladins did not mix. Most of the time, she knew that. *It's probably for the best if he isn't interested. But it would be nice if he didn't act like I was about to stick him with a pin.*

Assuming that's what he's thinking at all.

She laughed at herself. *Here we are, the future of the world's economy at stake, probably being chased by people with murder on their minds, and I keep thinking 'But does he like me?'"*

Probably that said something about the resilience of the human spirit, or at least its stupidity.

Regardless, I've got to get to the bottom of this, or I'm going to drive myself nuts.

As an experienced operative, Marguerite had a number of ways of extracting information from someone, with varying degrees of subtlety. Her old spymaster Samuel could have had one casual conversation about the weather with Wren and walked away knowing Shane's entire life story. Marguerite was not in that league, but she did have certain skills.

She weighed up the possibilities, considered her options, then decided on a plan of attack.

"So," she said, cornering Shane as he came back from the privy, "what the hell is going on with you, anyway?"

Shane said, "Um?"

She put her hands on her hips and glared up at him. The height difference was considerable, but Marguerite had always felt that this was a problem on their part, not hers. "You," she said. "You are acting strangely. You jump like a frightened rabbit when I get near you, and you haven't checked my room for assassins once. What is going on?"

He looked around, clearly uncomfortable. "Have there *been* any assassins?"

"Oh yes. Scads of them. Three at every stop. Wren fights them off with the chamber pot." She poked the center of his chest. "Is this about what happened the other night?"

He didn't answer that, but he didn't really need to. His agonized expression spoke volumes.

"Was it really that bad?" she asked ruefully.

"What? *No!*"

Well, at least I can be sure he's telling the truth. Beartongue had been right, the man was a terrible liar. "Oh good. I quite enjoyed it, myself."

The inn's back garden was dimly lit and under better circumstances, Marguerite would have considered it romantic. *The paladin is a decorative addition, or would be if he didn't look as if he was about to be drawn and quartered.*

"Yes," Shane said. "I…err…yes. As well." He rubbed his forehead. "I'm sorry. I'm doing this badly. I wasn't expecting to have this conversation right now."

Marguerite took pity on him. "It was just sex," she said gently. "It's fine. People do that. I'm not asking for your soul."

"No," said Shane with sudden bitterness, "no one's been interested in my soul for quite a while now." His lips twisted and he held up a hand. "Ignore that. I'm being more than usually self-pitying, it seems."

"Actually, I find it rather refreshing to see that you've got normal human flaws."

"I have *so* many flaws."

"So you say." There was a low bench against the wall and she sat down on it and patted the seat next to her. Shane gazed at it like a martyr witnessing the place of his imminent execution, then lowered himself down next to her.

"Any particular flaws troubling you at the moment?" she asked, since it seemed like he wasn't going to say anything on his own.

Shane gave a short huff, whether of surprise or dismay or simply because he didn't know where to start, she couldn't tell. "All of them. I don't know." He dropped his head into his hands, so the next words came out slightly muffled. "I'm going to choose the wrong thing. I always do."

"Mmm." Marguerite had a feeling they weren't just talking about sex anymore. "What about Lady Silver?"

"Huh?"

"You chose exactly the right thing there. We got away because of that."

"That's—"

"If you say 'that's different,' I shall cheerfully strangle you."

The huff this time had at least some laughter in it. "Fair enough, I suppose."

"Mmm. So what did you choose wrong, then?" She could make a pretty good guess, but there was always the chance that she was wrong.

"Well, we could start with my god."

"The Dreaming God, you mean? Was that really your choice?"

He snorted. "I chose to devote my whole life to training as one of His paladins, didn't I? And then..."

Marguerite was glad that he wasn't looking at her. She didn't want to see the expression in those pale blue eyes.

"Days, I waited," said Shane. His voice was as bleak as winter. "Weeks. Everyone else was chosen. And finally it was obvious. My god didn't want me."

Nearly two decades old, and the wound had only scabbed over, Marguerite thought, never healed. "What did you do?"

He sighed, looking faintly embarrassed. "I was young. I thought if I couldn't fight demons, maybe I could still do something worthwhile. Justify all the effort they'd put into me. Word came down that a gargath was in the woods—do you know those? No? They're more common around the Dowager's city, I think. Rather like a wolverine, but once it's killed something, it hollows it out and wears the remains around and...I don't know, fuses with it, somehow. Every kill means it gets bigger and bigger, just layering the bodies."

"That sounds *disgusting.*"

"Oh, very. The smell alone will knock you down. Gargath don't breed often, that's the only good thing. They're definitely magic but not demonic, but the Dreaming God's people will still try to take them down if they find them, because the smaller they are, the easier they are to kill." He rubbed his nose, probably at the memory. "I thought if I could kill the gargath, I'd be doing some good, and if it killed me, well...no great loss. So I went off after it by myself."

Marguerite put her head in her hands. "That is such a...a *you* thing to do."

"It was a bone-headed thing to do, if that's what you mean. Swords are not the optimal weapon for fighting a gargath. They can see out of the eyes of the fresher bodies, you see, and move their limbs, so you're fighting a ball of flailing rotten meat. I would have died and been added onto the pile if the Saint hadn't claimed me at that moment."

"I'm glad he did!"

"I'm not entirely sure I am." He sighed and scrubbed at his face, sitting up. "No, I'm being an ingrate. The Saint gave me purpose. I did a great deal of good in His service." He snorted. "Mostly because the battle tide didn't let me choose much of anything."

Marguerite leaned back against the bench. Part of her wanted to say, *Nope, no matter how pretty the man is, this is too much for me to deal with.* She'd never been particularly attracted to damaged men.

The other part of her was aware that she was sitting out in the open where an assassin could spot her, *knowing* that said assassins were in active pursuit—and she wasn't afraid. She wasn't checking every exit every few seconds. Her nerves weren't screaming at her. All because of the man sitting next to her.

(The smallest part of her was working out how to never be in the vicinity of a gargath, but it could probably be safely ignored for the moment.)

"You're doing a great deal of good now," she said.

"I am an excellent weapon." Another typically Shane delivery, no bravado, simply a statement of fact.

"You're more than that." Marguerite reached for something reassuring and uplifting to say, and instead heard herself blurt out, "I'm less broken when I'm around you."

Oh holy hell, I didn't mean to say that.

Shane went very still. Marguerite waited, wondering if she had just ruined everything past all mending. *What was I thinking?* Granted it was true, but her entire life's work hinged on weighing the truth out, grain by grain, not simply dumping it in someone's lap like a dead fish.

She wouldn't have blamed him if he ran away screaming, or at least the polite paladin equivalent of running away screaming, whatever that looked like.

Instead, he said, "I don't want to hurt you." Which, in most other men, she would have taken as a brush-off, but in Shane was probably nothing more or less than the truth.

"Physically or emotionally?"

"Errr..." He had to think about that. "I was mostly worried about physically. You, um...don't seem very vulnerable emotionally."

Marguerite's lips twitched despite herself. "You'd be surprised. But why are you worried?"

"Berserker. You know."

"Oh, is *that* all?"

Shane gazed into the night sky. "At least one religious order wanted us all killed after the Saint died, because they felt untethered berserkers were a public menace."

"I bet Beartongue *loved* that." She remembered Stephen's rampage through the city after Grace's arrest. It had been impressive, particularly in terms of property damage. "Should I be worried?"

"Nothing is ever certain," he said morosely.

Marguerite rolled her eyes. *Why am I attracted to this man? He can't go five minutes without sinking into despair.* "Are you worried about Grace?"

"What? No, of course not. Stephen would gnaw off his own sword arm before he'd lay a finger on her."

"And you wouldn't?"

He huffed. She waited. "Fine," he said, after a moment. "I'm being ridiculous."

"Not at all." Marguerite leaned back. "You're being cautious."

"I'm trying."

"And also, at a guess, you're afraid of getting your heart broken, so you're hiding behind being noble and self-sacrificing."

Shane turned his head to look at her. She gave the look right back, still with a slight smile, waiting.

"Damn," the paladin said finally. "Warn a person before you stab them like that."

"Am I wrong, though?"

He studied his hands. "*Are* you going to break my heart?"

"I might. Not deliberately, though. Are you going to break mine?"

His glance this time was wry. "Is that possible?"

"Oh, very much so."

"I've been informed that people in your line of work don't fall in love."

She snorted. "Whoever told you that was full of shit. We just try not to, because it might make someone a target. But as these things go, I'd say a berserker paladin is about as well-equipped as anyone to survive it."

"I suppose there *is* that."

Marguerite sighed. "You told me your story, so I'll tell you one of mine. When I was young and thought I was clever, I attempted to get information from a man who...well, let's just say that he learned far more from me than I did from him. Every question I asked, he worked out why I was asking it and traced it back to what I was trying to accomplish. By the time I figured out what was happening, his client had neatly cornered the market and mine was hemorrhaging gold."

Shane winced sympathetically, which Marguerite appreciated, even knowing that he probably didn't think money was nearly as important as undead-hermit-crab-wolverine monsters. *Which, granted, it probably isn't.*

"I went to Samuel, my mentor, and confessed everything. Exactly how foolish I'd been, and why I hadn't seen it sooner."

"That's never easy to do."

"No. The only thing worse would have been not confessing. I told him, and he made me recite every single conversation I'd had with the man, as close to verbatim as I could manage. And from that, he deciphered enough information to soften the worst of the blow. The client was even pleased. *He* thought we'd saved him from losing everything." She grimaced. "It was horribly embarrassing, and I expected Samuel to fire me on the spot, but he didn't. He said that I'd learned an important lesson about believing that I knew what was going on."

"If I've learned anything," Shane said, "it's that I have no idea what's going on."

Marguerite reached up a hand and stroked the back of his neck. He jerked slightly but didn't pull away, and after a moment, she felt the tension under her fingers ease.

Even the back of his neck was muscular. There ought to be a law against things like that.

"You know," said Marguerite gently, "one other thing he taught me is that some choices aren't wrong, no matter which you choose. They just *are.*"

"Hmmm," he said. Not a negative sound, but a thoughtful one. Marguerite let her hand drop, somewhat reluctantly, and decided that she'd pushed far enough and fast enough for one night.

"This is all a bit moot at the moment anyway," she said, glancing over her shoulder toward the inn. "It's not as if we could spend a night together, even if we wanted to."

"Dreaming God, *no.*" Shane blanched at the thought. "I'd never ask Wren to share a room with Davith."

"I was more thinking that Davith would be murdered in his bed, but it's the same thing."

Shane frowned. "Is it just me, or has he been quite...errr...*caustic* toward Wren? I have been wondering if I should step in."

"Yes, he has, and no, you shouldn't." Marguerite got to her feet. "It's the kindest thing he could do under the circumstances."

Shane looked blank. Marguerite sighed. "She fell in love with him, right?"

"Unfortunately."

"Yes. And now he is trying very hard to make sure that any feelings she had for him are gone. It's much easier to get over a total jackass than it is someone who's kind and decent and noble and..." She closed her mouth before she started describing Shane instead of Davith.

"Oh." The paladin digested this. "That is...yes. All right." He nodded. "I won't break him in half, then."

"I appreciate that," said Marguerite, and then, because he was still sitting down and thus was just about the right height, she leaned in and kissed him.

He said "Mmmf!"

It was a good kiss. It started to deepen into a great one, but Marguerite tore herself away. *This won't make anything easier, unless you want him to take you right now on this bench, which, actually—*

No. You've left Davith and Wren alone long enough. It's like that riddle with the goose and the fox and the corn, and if you don't stop now, you're going to find that the goose has beaten the fox to death with the corn.

"Think about it," she said. "Sooner or later we're bound to have separate bedrooms. Or we can just shove Davith in a locked closet for a night."

"I assure you," said Shane dryly, "I will be thinking about nothing else for days."

CHAPTER 38

"Well," said Marguerite, looking at the map, then across the landscape, "apparently this is Cambraith."

It looked exactly like everywhere else they had been. A river snaked across the rolling hills, and the endless green shaded toward blue to the north, where the hills turned into mountains.

"Just this valley?" asked Shane.

"This one, and the next one, and..." Marguerite consulted the map. "The next three after that."

They looked toward the hills. There were certainly a lot of them. Presumably they weren't quite so identical when you got up close, but Marguerite wouldn't swear to it.

"Maybe we should ask for directions," said Davith.

"So that the Sail can come up behind us and know exactly where we're going?" asked Wren.

"If the alternative is walking around knocking on doors asking if anyone's seen the artificer, yes."

"We'll have to ask someone," Marguerite said, "but we'll attempt to be subtle and unmemorable." She paused, studying the other three. "Which...ah...is easier said than done, I suppose. Wren, can you put your axe away long enough to come into an inn and look respectable with me?"

"Sure."

"I can look respectable," said Shane.

"No, you can't." Marguerite put the map away. "You look noble, which isn't the same thing. Respectable is subtle and boring. Noble isn't boring. Davith, don't start."

"Aww..."

"Right," said Marguerite an hour later, making sure that her hair was covered and adjusting her clothing. "We are traders of small valuable goods who are looking to finish our business as soon as possible and go back to the lowlands. Got it?"

"Got it," said Wren, who had handed her axes over to Shane at the outskirts of the village. It was a sizeable enough place, in that it had both an inn *and* a store. She pushed the door to the inn open, did a quick scan for assassins—none, unless they were disguised as chairs—and let Marguerite enter first.

Marguerite strolled up to the bar, which was manned by a middle-aged man with hair that had thinned considerably in front, but made up for it by descending over his bare shoulders. He wore an apron and the impersonally friendly expression of innkeepers everywhere.

"Can I help you?" he asked.

"God, I hope so," said Marguerite, with a broader accent than usual. "I'm looking for..." She dug through her belt pouch and came up with a scrap of paper. "A clan called the Kerseys? Maybe? Crest looks like a wolf?"

The innkeeper considered this. "Coupla Kerseys around these parts. Don't know about the crest, though. You might try over in Half-Stone, there's plenty of them there."

"Oh, thank the gods," said Marguerite, beginning to get into character. "The last time I asked, I got accused of being a bounty hunter, wanting to run someone in for banditry. I don't think they believed me when I said I was just supposed to make a delivery. I ask you, do I *look* like a bounty hunter?"

She did a little twirl. The innkeeper grinned. "No, ma'am. Though I ain't saying some of those Kersey boys don't get up to some mischief now and again, so I can see why they were worried."

Marguerite sighed heavily. "All I want is to settle this order. All right, what about..." She consulted the paper again, which was actually one of the leftover invitations to the perfume salon. "The Nallans? At a ford somewhere, I think?"

"That one's easy," said the innkeeper. "Nallanford's up the mountain, next valley over." He grinned again. "Word is the lord took a new bride not long ago, actually. Would that have anything to do with your delivery?"

"Oho, so *that's* the way the wind is blowing, is it?" Marguerite said. "*That'd* make sense." She patted her pack. "Wondered why my guild-master sent me all the way out here with fripperies, but if he's expecting to get another few orders from a new bride..."

The innkeeper gave her a conspiratorial wink. "I hear tell she's quite a bit younger, too. And Lord Nallan ain't poor."

"I'll keep that in mind." She knocked on the bar and bought two meat pies without more than token haggling. "Now, about these Kerseys...safe for two women to travel there with a hired guard, or should I be worried?"

The innkeeper was happy to give her directions to the respectable Kerseys, their less-respectable cousins, the Keirseys, which road was safe and which was asking for mischief of an unspecified variety. Marguerite listened, nodded, made ostentatious notes on her map, had him repeat directions twice, then swept out with Wren at her heels.

"What was all that about the Kerseys?" Wren asked in an undertone.

"Hopefully that's what he'll remember of the conversation," said Marguerite cheerfully. "Now, let's get to Nallanford before we're spotted."

"You think there's Sail people around?" Wren glanced around as if one might emerge at any moment and need to be dismembered.

"I can practically guarantee it."

They were halfway to Nallanford before the Sail finally caught up with them, or they caught up with the Sail, depending on how you looked at it. Marguerite went into a public house and came out again in a hurry, carrying several meat pies and looking remarkably grim about it.

"Trouble?" asked Shane, who didn't think she'd normally have that kind of expression over pastries.

"Two men," she said, in a clipped voice, shoving the meat pies at Davith. "I recognize one of them. I told the bartender we were looking for the Kerseys again." She was already walking briskly away from the pub, down possibly the only alley the village possessed, and around the back of a row of houses.

"Are they going to follow us?" Wren asked.

"Almost certainly."

"Do they know you saw them?" asked Shane.

"I don't think I gave us away, but if they're smart, they should know better than to trust me."

I should probably know better too, but that hasn't stopped me, either. Shane dipped his head in acknowledgment. In a city, he'd simply lie in wait until the men passed, but they were rapidly running out of village to wait in. The only thing left was the church and the graveyard around it. Judging by the number of graves, which exceeded the number of houses many times over, the town was either very old or very, very unlucky.

The two Sail operatives were also unlucky. They came around the side of the church, spotted Marguerite, Wren, and Davith walking away, and stepped into the obvious hiding place, between two tall obelisks leaning drunkenly together.

Shane stood up from behind the gravestone where he'd been crouched, grabbed them both by the hair, and bashed their heads together. Both men went limp. Shane dropped them behind the obelisks, dusted off his hands, and followed after the other three.

"Are they dead?" Wren asked.

"If they wake up again, no. If they don't, yes." At Davith's look, he said, "Head injuries aren't exactly precise."

A shutter seemed to roll down over Davith's face. "No," the man said, in a colorless voice. "That they are not."

Which was interesting in its own way, and Shane wished that he knew what to make of it.

"Right," said Marguerite. "If the gods are kind, they'll all think we went south. We're sleeping rough tonight, I think." She grimaced. "Let's hope it doesn't rain."

It did not rain, but the dew the next morning was so thick that everyone was soaked through anyway. Davith took off his shirt and wrung it out. Wren pointedly did not look at his bare torso. Shane did, long enough to determine that Davith was not a professional fighter of any kind. While he knew plenty of warriors who were slim rather than stocky—Galen, his fellow paladin, was built along almost identical lines —Davith's skin was as smooth and unmarked as a fresh sheet of vellum.

Not that I should assume. He could just be supernaturally lucky. I doubt it, though.

"See something you like, paladin?" asked Davith, striking a pose.

"You don't fight much, do you?"

"God, no!" Davith made a gesture to avert the evil eye. "I avoid it whenever possible."

"Afraid something will happen to your face?" asked Wren sweetly.

"Yes, as a matter of fact." Davith lifted his chin. "You see this nose? This nose is a *sculpture.* Breaking it would be a crime against humanity."

"It might give you character," Shane rumbled.

"*Character* is how you describe a building that's about to fall down. 'Oh, this place has so much character.' Then you get there and the roof's made of two sticks and a prayer. No, thank you."

"If you're done showing off, put your clothes back on and let's get moving," said Marguerite. "I have a dream that perhaps we'll get to Nallanford and I'll get to sleep in a real bed. Maybe with a real pillow."

"And sheets?" asked Wren.

"I don't dare dream that big."

Nallanford, at first sight, did not look like a place that you would find pillows, unless they were made out of rock. It appeared to be less a town than a sprawling compound inhabited by one enormous clan, a cross between a keep, a village, and a half-assembled rock pile. Many of the houses were obviously partly dug out of the ground, and what looked like mine entrances dotted the nearby hillsides. People came out of the houses to look them over, and two small children ran up as they approached.

"Be you traders?" asked the child with a clogged nostril.

"Be you minstrels?" asked the other, who had the kind of ground-in grubbiness that transcends both bathwater and parental care.

"Traders, yes," said Marguerite. "Of a sort. Where might I find your lord?"

Nostril pointed to the largest section of rock pile. Grubby bounced. "What've you got to trade? Is it good?"

"That's for your lord's ears first," said Davith. "Run along and tell him we're coming, will you?"

Shane gave him a sharp look. Davith rolled his eyes. "What? The whole town will know we're here in under five minutes. It's not like we could hide, even if we wanted to."

"Mmm." Shane was forced to admit the truth of this. "Could Magnus really hide here, then?"

"Maybe," said Marguerite. "Strangers will stick out like a sore thumb, so the Sail certainly won't be able to sneak up on her."

Shane glanced around the town as they walked through it. It looked prosperous enough. Most of the rock piles, on closer inspection were actually houses, with cut stone and timbers in the right places, and they looked to be in good repair. People wore good clothes, many with brightly colored scarves. Still, he was automatically suspicious of anyone that Baron Maltrevor would be inclined to trust.

It didn't help that the valley here actually had a good amount of trees. The river running through it held several millwheels and something—perhaps the added water, perhaps the shelter from the wind—meant that there was something resembling a wood on both slopes. Which of course meant that there might be a great many more people lurking than Shane could see.

Still, the Nallans didn't act nervous. Visitors were clearly interesting, but not frightening. *That bodes well that the Sail hasn't gotten here first.*

They followed the children to the keep, which initially looked like a walled courtyard built around a hole in the ground, with chimneys. A stoop-shouldered man, probably the castellan, came out to meet them. Shane listened to Marguerite dazzle the man with half an ear while mapping the defenses. Stubby stone towers at the courtyard's corners didn't rise much higher than the hill itself, but were manned by alert-looking sentries. The entrance had heavily reinforced double doors, and Shane suspected that they could withstand a siege engine. *Hmm, I'd probably try to find where the air intakes are and close those off...they're probably keeping fires burning there to draw air in...*

Indeed, as they entered the doors behind the castellan, air blew down the corridor behind them, pushing them deeper inside.

The castellan led them to a side chamber, appointed as a waiting area. The furniture had more wrought-iron than wood, but was fortunately heavily padded with cushions.

"I will inform Lord Nallan that you are here," said the castellan.

"Now," said Marguerite, as the door closed behind him, "if I was actually a double agent and planning on betraying you, this is about when I'd do it."

Shane and Wren looked at her with what Shane suspected were identical blank expressions.

She sighed. "Neither of you even thought of that, did you?"

"No."

"No."

"I did," said Davith brightly. "What do I win?"

"You already won. You're still alive."

"That's a pretty crappy prize."

"We could always rescind it," offered Shane.

"That joke wasn't funny the last ten times you made it."

"Maybe not to you."

"Children, *behave*," said Marguerite, running her hand over her face.

"He started it," said Davith, and winked at Shane, who wasn't sure how to feel about that.

Fortunately he didn't need to decide, because the door opened again and the castellan beckoned them through, down another corridor, to another room. The walls had been plastered and painted bright colors, but the lack of windows cast a certain gloom to the scene, particularly combined with the dark smoke stains across the ceiling.

"You will have to leave your weapons here," said the castellan, pausing in a large alcove.

"Haven't got any," lied Marguerite, "unless you count an eating knife."

"Haven't even got that," said Davith cheerfully.

Wren and Shane began stripping. It took a while. The castellan rocked on the balls of his feet and hummed, clearly no stranger to heavily-armed warriors with more swords than sense.

The meeting room itself had a higher ceiling and a fire in the hearth, and was plastered in freshly scrubbed white, and so managed to avoid feeling gloomy. A screen blocked off half the room. It was made of leather framed with more wrought iron, though an attempt had been made to make it decorative, with iron vines and a heavy iron rose.

Lord Nallan was tall, but had the stooped look common to miners everywhere. He wore a leather apron, like a smith, and an expression of cheerful skepticism. There was even a smith's hammer laid on the table, as if he'd been called away from working in a forge.

"Now, I know that I didn't buy anything from a trader," he said. "And I don't know who this Magnus person may be, but I didn't buy anything from them, either."

"No, you didn't," said Marguerite cheerfully. "May we?" She gestured to the chairs around the table. "We had a long walk to get here."

"Of course, ma'am. Not one to stand on ceremony, myself." He dropped into his own chair, watching them all with eyes that betrayed his wariness. *Not so cheerful as he seems. And if that hammer couldn't do double duty as a warhammer, I'll eat what's left of my sword.*

He also had a sneaking suspicion that there was someone behind the screen. They weren't making anything as overt as a sound, but he could feel a presence there nonetheless. *An advisor? A guard?*

"I'll be completely honest with you," said Marguerite. "I'm only posing as a trader, and I've really come to warn Ashes Magnus that the Red Sail is about to find her."

Lord Nallan's face was marvelously impassive. "I've told you, I don't know who that is."

Marguerite waved away his protests. "Baron Maltrevor's contact sent her to 'the Nallans at the ford' in Cambraith. I'm pretty sure that's you. If it isn't, I'm *very* sure that you know exactly who it is. You can't tell me that anything happens around here without you knowing about it."

Nallan was too good to let his eyes flick to the screen, but Shane was sure that he heard a sound from behind it. It sounded like a very quiet snort of amusement.

"I don't expect you to admit it to me," Marguerite continued. "I wouldn't, in your shoes. But the Red Sail is closing in. They already know she's in Cambraith, and if they don't know exactly where by now, it's a matter of days, not weeks."

The lord drummed his fingers on the table, looking displeased. "Even supposing I knew who this person was, what business be it of yours?"

"Let's say we're...interested investors," said Marguerite, leaning back in her chair. Nallan raised a skeptical eyebrow, and she grinned at him. Shane wondered how the man didn't melt like butter on the spot. "No, really. We're here from the Temple of the White Rat in Archenhold. These two are paladins. Magnus has an invention that could help a lot of people, and the Rat wants to make sure it gets in the hands of people who will use it, not lock it away in a vault somewhere to keep their profits up."

"That may all be well and good—" Lord Nallan began, but a voice cut him off from behind the screen.

"I've heard enough," she said. "I am Ashes Magnus."

CHAPTER 39

"Just as well, really," said the artificer, stepping around the edge of the screen. "Sitting on that stool was going to put a permanent crease in my backside." She made her way, slowly, to the small bench beside the table. Davith hastily jumped to his feet and pulled it out for her, bowing dramatically. This time her snort was clearly audible.

Ashes Magnus was seventy if she was a day. Shane thought that she might be older than she looked, because she was also very fat and had the sort of cherubic face that aged less quickly than her cohorts. She had immense sloping shoulders and nimble fingers so covered in ink and burns and small scars that it looked as if she were wearing patchwork gloves.

"Magnus," Lord Nallan said, clearly dismayed. "Be you sure about this? We can still send these outlanders off with a flea in their ear."

"No," said the artificer with a sigh. "You've been nothing but kind to me, Lord, and I don't plan to repay that by having your warriors killed for nothing. These Sail people are ruthless. It's best I leave while I still can."

"We don't fear any hired lowlanders," Lord Nallan said.

"They already burned my workshop. If they decide to burn your fields or start putting the outlying houses to the torch, your warriors will have their hands full."

The lord glowered, but didn't argue. His gaze lingered over the four outsiders. "And you be trusting these people?"

"Two of 'em are paladins. I'm not going to get a better deal than that. And the White Rat's people are as good as holy folk get, and better'n most. Besides..." She grinned at Shane and Davith. "The view won't be bad, at least."

Shane coughed. Davith swept another bow, this time brushing the floor with the back of his hand. "Madam Artificer, you will put me to the blush."

"Doubt anything's put you to the blush since you were out of split pants, my lad," Ashes said, firmly cementing Shane's good opinion of her observational skills.

"I can send warriors with you—" Lord Nallan began.

Ashes was already holding up a hand. "You've done enough and more than enough. I'm already bringing trouble here, and I feel bad about that. You've put me up on no more than the word of a man that I know you don't even care for, and don't think I don't know it."

"At first, maybe," Nallan said. "But Bryant tells me that that new chimney you showed him means we're burning a lot less fuel to keep the air going, and any fuel we don't have to use on that be more fuel for the forge. I'd ask you to stay for that alone."

"Bah, it's nothing," said Ashes gruffly. "Bryant would likely have figured it out himself with time, he's a quick lad."

"Mmm," said Lord Nallan, glancing in Marguerite's direction. "You be taking care of her, you hear?"

"I promise you that we'll put her safety above our own," said Marguerite.

"You've got paladins, so that's not saying much," Ashes said, elbowing Davith in the ribs. "You're not one though, are you lad?"

"No," said Davith pleasantly, "I'm the entertainment."

"Ha!"

Nallan shook his head. "If the Rat doesn't treat you right, you've got a home here, Magnus. As long as I'm lord, anyway, and if my son doesn't promise the same, he's not the man I raised him to be."

"Bah, don't talk like that. You'll outlive me by fifty seasons, I'm sure. But it's good to know, nonetheless." She leveled small, bright eyes on Marguerite. "The Rat's gonna give me the money to build another device? The Sail dropped my workshop's ceiling on top of the first one."

"You'll have to talk directly to the Bishop for that," said Marguerite, "but if she doesn't, she's not the person I think she is. I'll scrape up money for it myself, if I have to sell my body on the street."

Shane cleared his throat. Marguerite winked at him. "You're right, I'll sell your body instead."

"No one is selling anyone's body until we talk to the Bishop," said Shane firmly, then recognized the voice that was coming out of his mouth. It wasn't even the paladin's voice. It was... "Oh, Dreaming God, you've got *me* sounding like Beartongue now."

Marguerite looked as smug as a cat who had been dipped in cream. Lord Nallan rose to his feet, still looking skeptical, but increasingly resigned. "Very well. If this is what you choose, Magnus, I'll not be standing in your way."

For obvious reasons, Lord Nallan did not throw a feast to celebrate Ashes' leave taking, but he gave them full Nallan hospitality, which included fine food and, praise all the gods, *beds. Good* beds. In separate rooms, no less. (After a discreet word, a guard was posted outside of Davith's door, but given the sounds he made upon seeing the mattress, it seemed unlikely to be necessary.)

Marguerite lay in her extremely comfortable bed and pretended that she wasn't waiting for the door to open.

This lasted for about an hour, and then she pretended that she wasn't disappointed that the door hadn't opened.

It's fine. He gets to choose. It's fine.

It did not feel fine.

Goddammit.

The Nallan keep was built into the hillside and there were no windows, only a ventilation shaft with a decorative metal grille. Any assassin trying to get in would have needed to have their bones removed first. If someone made an attempt on her life, they'd have to come in by the door.

Not that she was worried.

Much.

She certainly wasn't going to use being worried as an excuse to go find Shane. That would be absurd. Wren was just as capable a bodyguard. If she was feeling paranoid, she'd go find Wren, since Shane obviously wasn't going to come here on his own.

Marguerite closed her eyes and told herself that she was being stupid and should go to sleep at once. The insides of her eyelids laughed at her.

There was no reason for anyone in Nallanford to attack her. Ashes Magnus had been here for over a month now, and if the Red Sail had an operative here, they'd have gone for the artificer already.

She should definitely go to sleep. In fact, she *was* going to sleep. Right now.

Sleep is occurring. For real this time.

Five minutes later, Marguerite got up, lit a candle, wrapped a dressing gown around herself, and went to the door. She pulled it open.

The interesting thing was that even though there was a looming figure in the doorway, she wasn't startled. Her nerves recognized Shane before her brain caught up.

He was fully clothed, one hand raised to knock. "Um?" he said.

"Oh, good," said Marguerite, and pulled him inside.

Less than thirty seconds after she'd gotten Shane undressed, Marguerite knew there was a problem. Not with his ability to perform...based on what was nudging against her leg, that was not going to be a problem... but in...well...

Actually, maybe 'performance' is the exact problem.

The man was as nervous as a new bridegroom, not that Marguerite had ever actually had one of those. He barely seemed to notice her touch. Instead, he was touching her and frankly trying to do too many things at once. The slightest hitch in her breathing made him freeze. "Is that good? Do you want me to stop?"

"Shane," she said gently, "this isn't an exam." She ran a hand down the muscles of his stomach and felt him quivering with what might be passion but was probably nerves. "Relax."

She tilted her head back and found those ice-blue eyes less passionate than frantic. "But I need to do this right. I want to make you feel..." He glanced away, probably not knowing himself how that sentence was supposed to end.

Just like a paladin. Needs? Paladins don't have needs! "Here to serve, ma'am. Just point me to the part of your anatomy that needs servicing." Hell, I'm probably lucky he doesn't salute.

Davith had been right, ages ago. She *did* like being in charge. But this didn't feel like being in charge, it felt like being an object of duty.

She curled her fingers around his cock and he hardly even seemed to *notice.*

Marguerite weighed her options. *Well, let's see. I can let him work himself into a lather trying to work me into a lather. I can kill him and dump the body in an open mineshaft. Or...*

She pressed her forehead against his. "Shane. Do you trust me?"

"Should I?"

"Probably not, but that wasn't the question."

"Yes."

"Then lie down on the bed." *And let's hope this works and he doesn't run away screaming or burst into tears, because that will be really awkward at breakfast.*

She turned away before she could see if he complied. The room did not come supplied with ropes or long scarves or anything of that sort, and anyway, they wouldn't have done any good. Marguerite was pretty sure that a berserker could snap anything short of iron chains, and she wasn't completely sure on that last one. But being tied up had nothing to do with the material and everything to do with what was inside a person's head.

She opened a side pocket on her pack, found the tiny sewing kit that had kept her clothes from turning into rags over the last week, and measured out two lengths of red thread.

When she turned back, Shane was lying on his back on the bed and no matter how awkward this second time was turning out to be, there was nothing awkward about the picture he made. It was all long bones and hard muscle and those extraordinary blue eyes, which were watching her, puzzled.

"Now, then," she said. "Grab hold of the headboard. However's comfortable."

It was, of course, more wrought iron. Shane clasped it obediently. "All right," he said, "but what are you—mmf!"

Marguerite straddled his chest and leaned forward. In that position, her breasts would have muffled better men than Shane. She carefully looped the thread around each wrist, leaving plenty of slack, tied them neatly, and then sat back.

Shane, breathing heavily, looked bright-eyed and slightly worse for wear after the time spent in her cleavage. "Um," he said. "Thread?"

"Thread," she agreed, looking down at him.

He pursed his lips. "This is a trifle more sophisticated than I'm used to."

"No, it's really very simple. If the thread breaks, we stop."

"Err..." He tested the slack. "Don't people usually use whips and chains and so forth?"

"Whips are a different thing. I haven't got any chains."

"Lord Nallan probably does." His lips twitched. "I suppose I could go ask."

"Not without breaking the thread you can't." She leaned back on her hands and watched his face carefully.

He swallowed and tested the slack again, then gripped the metal bars harder. "Are you sure? I wanted to please *you.*"

Marguerite grinned, feeling like the cat who had caught the canary and was about to fuck its brains out. "Oh, you're going to. Believe me."

"I...ah...expected I'd be using my hands."

"My dear paladin, there are a *remarkable* number of things you can do without using your hands. I'll show you." Her grin widened. "Don't think you're just going to lay back and think of Archenhold. *Just don't break the thread.*"

She actually saw the moment he relaxed. A tension in his arms and the line of his jaw eased, and then, slowly, was replaced by a different tension entirely. "Whatever my lady commands," he said hoarsely.

"Good."

In the end, they didn't actually do anything *terribly* sophisticated. If nothing else, they had an early start tomorrow. But once he was bound, even just by a pair of threads, it was suddenly easy. She positioned herself exactly as she liked, looking down at him, and he pressed his mouth against her flesh. She didn't let him stop until she was gasping and clutching the bedframe herself.

Not that he showed any signs of wanting to stop either.

"Very good," she said, when she could breathe again. "Very, *very* good. Now, I suppose I could untie you"—a tremor went through him at the words, and she wondered if it was eagerness or disappointment—"but I think I'll leave you just as you are for now."

This time, when she curled her fingers around his cock, he damn near levitated.

That's more like it...

It didn't take long at all. To Shane, it probably felt like an eternity, but that was all to the good. She only teased him for a moment, then rode him until he was panting, his eyes thin rings of blue around the pupils. She would have kept going longer, but her thigh muscles weren't going to last, so she leaned down and whispered in his ear, "*Break the threads. Now.*"

He hesitated for a gratifying heartbeat, then snapped them. An instant later, he rolled her over and took her, hard and fierce, frantic this time with his own need. She wrapped her legs around his waist and listened to the small sound, almost a whimper, at the base of each breath, and then he shouted her name loud enough to wake anyone in the next room and collapsed on top of her as if he'd been killed.

Marguerite stroked the back of his neck and felt ungodly smug about everything.

Several minutes after having come so hard that he wasn't sure he still had bones left, Shane said, "Dear *god,*" into Marguerite's hair.

"Mmmm," she said.

He propped himself up on his elbows, suddenly worried. "Was I too rough?"

"Not in the least." She stretched against him, which would have turned his mind to paste if it hadn't been already. "You were magnificent. Was I too...ah...*sophisticated?*"

"Dreaming God, no. I've never..." He raked a hand through his hair, not even sure what to say. "I...that is...no one's ever..." He swallowed and tried again. "I knew what I was supposed to be doing."

Which was a bizarre thing to say, he realized, even as he said it. But it was *true.* The Saint had given him certainty, which Shane had always lacked, and he felt that lack keenly every moment the Saint was gone. But with a length of red thread, she had given him a different kind of certainty. *Be here, right now. Touch me like I show you. Don't break the thread until the end.*

He'd heard about such things, of course, but the notion of being restrained had never struck him as interesting. He'd assumed those people enjoyed being immobilized. He'd had no idea at all.

It was terrifying and glorious and he hardly knew how to feel. Astonished that he had found what he needed. Appalled to realize how much he had needed it.

Marguerite did not laugh or scoff or demand that he explain himself. She simply nodded. "Good. And you did it perfectly," and it turned out that he had needed that, too.

A thought occurred to him suddenly and he turned toward her. "Should I be calling you Marguerite?"

"Hmm?"

"You, um, said it wasn't your real name. Would you rather I call you something else?"

Her body tensed just slightly. If he hadn't been pressed full-length against her, he likely would not have noticed. *Damn, that was the wrong thing to say.* He stroked the curve of her back hesitantly, hoping to soothe her and cursing his misguided impulse.

"I've used a number of names," she said. "Different names and different...personas...for different jobs. But Marguerite is the one that I've been the longest and like the most. Marguerite is the person I want to be."

Her back was smooth, the hollow of her spine leading to the warm curve of her buttocks, and Shane ran his fingers along it, trying to decide what he could say that wouldn't ruin the moment.

He wanted to say, *I am desperately in love with the person you are.* But he could not imagine that she felt the same way, and the thought of driving her away horrified him.

Marguerite stretched again and propped herself up on one elbow.

She had a slight, inquisitive smile on her face. "Better than a stone floor, I trust?"

Answer her, for the Dreaming God's sake, he ordered himself. *Say yes. Make a joke. Tell her she's beautiful. Say* something.

"I will serve you," he said hoarsely, "however I can. As long as you'll have me."

...or you could say that, I suppose.

Marguerite set her fingers against his lips. "That's a dangerous thing to promise," she said. "I might take you up on it, and then where would you be?"

He thought about answering her. Then he thought about just how badly words could ruin what lay between them, and instead he reached out and gathered her up in his arms, turning so that they lay curled together on the bed.

"Mmm," said Marguerite sleepily, and that, it seemed, was answer enough.

CHAPTER 40

It was difficult to tell the time of day underground, but it still seemed very early to Shane when someone tapped on the door. Marguerite had moved away from him in her sleep and was now a lump of covers that growled when he touched it.

"It's time to get up."

"Nnnrrrggg."

"We wanted to make an early start."

"Rrrrrrr."

"There are bad people after us."

"Ggghhh…" She shoved the covers back and scowled at him. "They're very bad if they're taking me away from this bed."

"No question there."

Her scowl softened. "You should do that more often."

"Do what?"

"Smile."

"Was I?"

"Yes. Don't deny it. I know what I saw."

"If you say so."

She threw a pillow at him, which he caught easily. "Right," she muttered. "Mornings. On the road. Dodging murderous thugs. I can do this."

The earliness of the hour was confirmed when the foursome trooped outside. Ashes Magnus was already up, inspecting a wagon and a pair of mules, under a sky the color of raw egg whites.

"Why is it so much earlier when you've been in a bed instead of sleeping on the ground?" asked Davith blearily, still drinking tea provided by Nallan's servants.

"Because when you're sleeping on the ground, you want to get up so you can stop," said Ashes. "At least, that's how I remember it. I've managed to avoid sleeping on the ground for the last twenty years or so."

"I can't swear that you'll be able to for the next twenty," said Shane apologetically.

The artificer sighed. "On the bright side, after a day or two of that, I may be downright grateful if the Sail tries to kill me."

There were two mules hitched to the wagon. They did not look any more pleased about the hour than Davith did.

"This is going to make us more visible," Wren murmured.

"Yes, but I don't think we have much choice."

"You most certainly don't," said Ashes, who apparently had extremely good hearing. "I can sleep in the wagon if I have to, but if you expect me to hoof it across the landscape, you're out of luck." She thumped her cane on the cobblestones by way of demonstration.

Privately, Shane thought that he'd be doing well to be in Magnus's shape by the time he was her age. He could already feel the ache of old wounds, and early mornings seemed to make it even worse. The Saint of Steel's chosen generally died in glorious battle and the few survivors went on to train the next generation, so he'd never given much thought to how his bones would feel once he was in his seventies.

If the last few days are any indication, not great.

Lord Nallan appeared, looking as if he'd been hard at work for an hour already. He helped Ashes up onto the wagon seat and said something to her that Shane didn't catch, but which made the artificer laugh.

"You've got supplies for a few days," said Nallan, patting the side of the wagon. "And I thought you might be wanting this."

It took Shane a moment to realize the man was talking to him. "What?"

Lord Nallan held a sheathed sword, lying flat across his palms. "Not as long as the one you be used to using," he said, nodding to the broken sword across Shane's back. "But a damn sight better than the one you be carrying now."

"You're not wrong," said Shane. "Thank you." He unslung the broken sword and traded it to Lord Nallan for the one in his hands. "I've had no chance to replace it, and I've felt half-naked for days."

Nallan nodded. Wren became very interested in the wood grain on the side of the wagon.

"Right." The lord lifted a hand. "Go well." Then he turned and went back inside, clearly not one for long goodbyes.

"Time to go," said Ashes Magnus. Shane climbed into the wagon and she clucked her tongue. The mules picked up their hooves, and they left Nallanford behind.

Despite everyone's eagerness to put the highlands behind them, instead of turning east and downward into the plains, they headed north along the road that hugged the mountains. Marguerite judged that it was more important to get out of Cambraith, rather than travel down through a valley that was guaranteed to be swarming with the Sail's people.

The northern road was a lonely one. Once they left the activity of Nallanford behind, the population thinned out to shepherd huts and the occasional prospector panning along a stream. Marmots with mottled coats sat on small rises and watched the wagon suspiciously, giving hoarse whistles of alarm whenever a human did anything that might be construed as a threat to marmotkind.

Despite Ashes' initial comments, she didn't complain about the long hours spent on the wagon seat, nor did she object to a night spent on the road. Some of that was probably because one of the bundles in the back turned out to be a very thick bedroll, which she unrolled in the wagon bed. "You youngsters have a good time with your dirt," she said. "Wake me up if anyone attacks us."

(To Lord Nallan's credit, there were also blankets for everyone else, so they slept warmer, if not that much more comfortably, than they had before.)

Shane, daring greatly, set his blankets close to Marguerite's and waited to see what she would do about it. She smiled archly at him, and while he would have been appalled at the thought of doing anything...

sophisticated...in front of other people, he did wake up with her pressed against his back, and her morning growl emanated from somewhere between his shoulder blades.

Neither Davith or Wren commented...much. Davith's eyebrows did the talking for him, and Wren whistled a tune that might or might not belong to a song with extremely bawdy lyrics. Shane chose to ignore them both.

Midway through the second day, Marguerite consulted her map and pronounced them officially Out of Cambraith. Everyone sighed in relief, except the mules. (Shane was not skilled at reading mule expressions, but they seemed to disapprove of everyone, except possibly Davith. Davith was the one who had rubbed them down and given them oats and told them that they were good and strong and pretty mules. This affirmation of equine self-image had earned him slightly more tolerance, though not by much.)

"Whew," said Ashes. "I feel less hunted already. Now where do we turn east?"

Marguerite consulted the map again. "As soon as we find a road going downhill. There's supposed to be one, but don't ask me how far it is. Parts of this map involve a lot of artistic license."

"Ah, well. It's pretty country, anyway." The artificer surveyed the green rolling landscape. A nearby marmot took that as a threat and sent up an alarm whistle. "Though to be honest, I'm near dying to see a color that isn't green. A wheat field ready for harvest would damn near make me cry."

"I may cry just thinking about it," Davith said. "No, wait, I'm thinking of what they make with wheat."

"Bread?" Wren asked.

"That, too."

Ashes snorted. "Don't start with me, lad. I've been drinking the stuff they brew up here for months now. At first I thought, oh, a nice rich dark beer, how lovely. Now I'd give my arm for something light enough to read a book through." She considered. "Well, somebody's arm, anyhow."

"Have you really been up here for that long?" asked Wren.

"Probably feels like longer than it was, but it *feels* like it's been years."

"When did you first realize the Red Sail was after you?" Marguerite asked.

"You might say that my workshop being burned to the ground was something of a clue." Ashes scowled. "Stupid bastards. They didn't realize that an artificer's workshop either blows up or melts down at least once every few years. I waited 'til the wreckage cooled, fished out the fireproof strongboxes, and dropped them off at the Guild for safekeeping. Still, it didn't seem healthy to stay around there. So I wrote to old Maltrevor, and he sent me out this way."

"Maltrevor's your patron, I hear," said Shane, attempting to keep his voice neutral.

"Dreadful old lecher, isn't he?" Ashes shook her head. "But he's got deep pockets and I haven't had to see him face-to-face in years. I ship him off some silly clockwork toy every few months and he's happy."

"He was showing them off at the Court," Marguerite said. "Like the little dog that moved when you clap. Amazing craftsmanship."

"Oh yes." Ashes slid a look in her direction. "Surprised he didn't try to show you some of the...other...clockwork toys..."

"He did mention something of the sort," Marguerite said dryly.

"Other toys?" asked Shane, puzzled.

In the wagon behind him, Davith had a sudden coughing fit.

"Oh yes. Vast market for that sort of thing, you know."

"What sort of thing?"

Ashes cocked her head and studied Shane thoughtfully. "Why are the pretty ones always dim?" she asked no one in particular. Davith's coughing fit worsened dramatically.

"He's a paladin," said Marguerite. To Shane she said, "They're...ah... erotic aids."

"Erot—" Understanding crashed over him. "You mean for the bedchamber? *Clockwork?*"

"It's a significant export of the artificer's district," Marguerite said. "I know at least two merchants who act as agents." Shane could feel his ears getting hot.

"I...see."

"Hang on," said Wren, breaking in. "You mean people put clockwork things in their—uh—*bits?*"

"On, in, against..." Ashes shrugged. "The primary problem is the waterproofing. The vibration's absurdly simple."

"But *why?*"

Davith appeared to have contracted consumption at some point in the last few minutes and was currently dying of it. Shane reached back and pounded him on the back with slightly more vigor than was necessary. Fortunately for his emotional equilibrium, this caused him to miss Marguerite's explanation to Wren.

"Huh," said his sister-in-arms when Marguerite had finished. "I never even thought about very fast wiggling."

Shane suddenly contracted Davith's cough and the other man pounded his back with retaliatory enthusiasm.

"It's not high art," said Ashes. "Once you've figured out how to rig the springs, they're rather boring to make. But it left me plenty of free time to invent the things I was really interested in."

A moment or two passed while everyone recovered themselves. Wren looked deep in thought. Marguerite's lips kept twitching every time she looked in Shane's direction. He cleared his throat and moved away from Davith to avoid any more thumping.

"So you invented a magic box that makes salt?" he asked, praying to the gods that this would lead to a change of subject.

"It's not magic," said the artificer. "There's a tiny bit of the mechanism that has to be done by a blacksmith-priest of the Forge God, but that's not exactly magic, is it? More of a miracle. Are miracles magic?"

The paladins of the Saint of Steel were primarily known for being unstoppable killing machines, and rather less for their grasp of applied theology. "Uh...I...ah...maybe?"

"Hmm, that would be an interesting question. At any rate, only one part of the box requires intervention beyond that of ordinary mortals, and that's the bit that moves heat from one part to another." She waved one surprisingly delicate hand. "It's really a very simple device. Fresh water freezes faster than salt, yes?"

"Yes," said Shane, back on firmer ground.

"Of course it does. That's one of the ways they harvest salt up in Morstone, they freeze off the fresh and concentrate it into brine. That's basically what my device does. Fresh water floats on top of salt because of the difference in specific gravity, we freeze the top, we output the ice, we freeze the top again, until we're down to a concentrated salt brine. Then we boil it. The really impressive bit happens after, if you ask me, since seawater is full of impurities and of course nobody wants to be putting dried fish piss on their potatoes."

Shane paused a moment to give this turn of phrase the attention it deserved, then frowned. "But if it is so simple, why are people not doing so already?"

"Oh, they can," said Magnus. "They did it all the time. That's the method behind a saltworks, usually, you have a series of brine tanks that are getting evaporated down. But in order to do it on a large scale, you need the right climate for it. Most of the coastline between Morstone and Delta is rock cliffs, you'd have to build floating platforms—and people do that, too—but of course one good howling windstorm through the Toxocan Straits and your saltworks is on the bottom of the ocean. And Delta's a marvelous city, but it rains five days out of six and on the sixth, the air is humid enough to chew." She grinned. "The food's amazing, though. One of my favorite cities."

"So how is your machine different, then?"

"Because you only need a little bit of heat to prime it. A log now and again. I was annoyed by the waste, you see. You need heat to evaporate the brine, but most of that heat is lost and not good for anything. And we want to take heat out of the water to make the ice. So why not just take the heat out of the water and store it and then use that heat to boil the brine with? So I invented a device to do that. The Forge God's people were very helpful, although I think I confused them. But once I convinced one to make an element that took out the heat and stored it, then put it back again, a couple of their brighter youngsters worked it out. It's just two little pieces of steel, although we had an exciting time working out the right sizes and shapes."

"And that's not magic?" asked Shane skeptically.

"Nah, it's just the trick they do to make steel heat evenly in the forge, only a bit more so. Their smith-priests learn to do it practically out of the cradle, or whatever the equivalent is for baby priests."

"Acolytehood," said Shane, on slightly firmer ground now.

"This is all quite fascinating," said Marguerite, scrambling forward to the front of the wagon, "but we have a problem."

"Problem?"

"We're being followed."

CHAPTER 41

Shane looked behind them, startled, and saw Wren sit up abruptly, though he could not make out anyone on the road behind them. Ashes only nodded. There was a sudden grim set to her lips. "The horseman from earlier?"

"I think so, yes." Marguerite scowled. "They've been very good about staying one turn back, but the few times they couldn't, it looked like him. And a few friends. I think...five."

"How do you know they're following us?" asked Shane. Too late, it occurred to him that might be taken as skepticism, and he hurriedly added, "I'm not doubting. Just curious."

She cast him a wry look. "On these roads? A group on horseback should have overtaken us within minutes. The only reason they haven't is because they're hanging back."

Ashes was already slapping the reins across the backs of the mules. "Time to move," she told them.

"Can we outrun them?" asked Shane, looking dubiously at the mules.

"Not a hope in hell," Ashes said. "But at least they'll have to work for it."

He scanned the landscape, looking for cover. If they had been in a forest—a city—even somewhere with decent bushes, he could have waited until they had pulled around a bend and the others could hide while he took the wagon on alone and drew pursuit. But there was *noth-*

ing. They had crossed a river not long before, which had actual trees, but now the shrubs were all knee-high heather that wouldn't hide a toddler. The only cover was occasional knots of boulders that had fallen from farther up the mountain, and it would be immediately obvious to any pursuer where their quarry must have gone to ground.

Far up on a distant hillside, he saw a cluster of buildings. Would the residents help?

"If I get off the wagon," he said slowly, "I can try to slow them. Maybe you can get to that steading up there."

"Slow them? On foot?" asked Marguerite dubiously. "How—no, never mind, I know how. That's suicidal! One man on foot against five horsemen?"

Shane shrugged. "After a point, a horseman is simply a larger target." He didn't enjoy killing horses, but the black tide did not distinguish. When the Saint of Steel had still lived...well, that was before and this was after and there was no point in dwelling on it.

"I'm more concerned that they aren't going to stop and fight you," said Ashes, her eyes still on the road. "You're not the one they're after. I expect a few of them will simply go around you. Possibly all of them."

"That is my fear," Shane acknowledged. "You'll have Wren here, but if they all break around me..."

Wren looked at Shane, then at Davith, then back at Shane. She nodded.

"Ah...you know, I think maybe I'll come with you," said Davith. "Buy the ladies some time, right?"

Marguerite put her hands on her hips. "You are *both* out of your—"

Something zipped by Shane's head with a crisp *zzzzzip!* and one of the mules let out a scream of pain and surprise. An arrow had buried itself in the animal's haunches. It bucked, kicking out wildly, then tried to run away from the pain, which set the wagon careening sideways.

Had it just been a matter of controlling the maddened mule, Ashes Magnus might have proved equal to the task. But the wagon went off the curve of the road and down the boulder-strewn hillside, and no amount of skill with the reins could overcome the massive stone looming before them.

"Bail out!" shouted Magnus, and with remarkable speed for her age, flung herself off the seat.

Shane swept Marguerite up in his arms and threw himself after. He saw Marguerite's mouth make an O of surprise, then the sky became the ground became the sky and he landed on his back and skidded, still clutching Marguerite in his arms.

Wood crashed somewhere nearby and the screams of the maddened mule ended abruptly.

There was a very long moment while the dust settled and then Marguerite said, faintly, "Ow."

"Are you hurt?" he asked.

"I don't think so?" She pushed herself up on her arms and looked down at him. Her lips curved in a sudden wry smile. "Ah, memories..."

Shane would have liked to take a moment to dwell on this, but the enemy had at least one archer. Marguerite appeared to remember this as well, because she sat up. This put pressure on several of his ribs which wanted him to know that they did not appreciate what had just happened. He grunted and Marguerite rolled hastily off him. "Are *you* hurt?"

"Bruised ribs," he lied. At least one was probably cracked, but they couldn't do anything about it now. He rolled to his knees and bit down on a hiss of pain. "Is everyone else okay?"

"Not dead," said Wren.

"You didn't need to throw me out, you know," Davith said, from somewhere nearby.

"You weren't moving fast enough."

"I was moving plenty fast, thank you, before someone put their elbow in my eye."

"If you'd like to get back in the wagon and try again, I'll be sure and let you crash this time."

Shane looked around, staying low in case the archer took another shot at them. Davith and Wren were both moving. Davith's left eye was red and already swelling, but that seemed to be his only injury.

He was most worried about Ashes. She was far too old to be flinging herself off wagons with aplomb. But when he turned, she was already up on her knees beside the shattered wagon.

"Are you hurt?" he asked, moving toward her. The boulders were going to be their only hope of cover. He gestured for the others to follow.

He couldn't see the horsemen from his position downslope, but he could hear hoofbeats.

Ashes glanced back at him. Blood was streaming down her face and he started forward, but she waved him away. "Nicked my scalp. I'm fine, it just looks like hell." She jerked her chin toward the mules. "Better than them, anyway."

One of the mules was clearly dead. The other was alive, but pinned flat by the weight of the shattered wagon on its harness. Ashes had a knife out and was sawing away at the traces to free it, while it tried to rise and then fell back, frightened and baffled.

"We've got to get under cover," he said. "These boulders—"

"Good idea." She kept sawing. Her knife was barely two inches long and possibly the worst sort of blade for the work.

He tried again. "If they shoot at us again—"

"Young man, if I leave this poor beast here to die, an arrow is the least of what I'll deserve."

Shane gritted his teeth. He approved in principle, but not when his job centered on keeping the artificer alive. "Get to the rocks," he said. "I'll cut her free."

She sat back on her heels and gave him a brief, searching look, then handed him the knife. Marguerite and Wren were already behind the rocks.

The mule heaved against her restraints. Shane didn't know enough about horses to know what exactly he was cutting, or if it was even the right thing, but having a half-ton animal thrashing around certainly wasn't helping.

"Easy, girl," he murmured, patting the animal's shoulder. "Easy. We'll get you loose. Just give me a minute..." She settled, but only slightly.

Davith appeared beside him and took the knife. "You keep talking," the man told him. "I'll cut."

Shane decided not to argue. The skin on the back of his neck was crawling, waiting for the next volley. *I might as well be wearing a sign on my back that says 'Insert Arrow Here.'*

"Good girl," he told the mule, petting her nose. "I know this is scary. It'll be over soon. Just a few more minutes..."

"If you'd like to pet my nose and reassure me next, I could really use it," said Ashes from the other side of the boulder. Marguerite laughed the loud, slightly mistimed laugh of someone under great strain.

An arrow shattered against a rock a few feet away.

"I hate this," Davith remarked, to no one in particular, but he didn't stop cutting.

"Good news," said Shane. "It's a crossbow."

"That's *good* news?"

"It explains why it's taking them so long to reload. They've probably only got one, and it's harder to do on horseback."

The mule bucked again and was suddenly free. She thrashed her way to her feet, while Davith and Shane retreated behind the boulders. Her flanks were scraped and bleeding, but all four feet were hitting the ground evenly. Shane could tell this because she immediately broke into a gallop, putting as much distance between herself and the hated wagon as possible.

"Well," said Davith, as the mule fled, "at least somebody's getting away."

Another bolt hit the ground. Shane pushed farther back into the tangle of stones. The crossbowman was going to have to circle around the stones to get a clear shot. *And if they're sensible, that's exactly what they'll do.*

Gods and saints, let them not be sensible.

He peered around the last stone again. If the crossbowman did circle around, his only choice would be to duck around the far side of the stones, probably into the waiting arms of the other four warriors. One person might be able to crawl into the wreckage of the wagon for cover, but not all five of them.

"So they have bows," said Ashes conversationally.

"Yes," Shane said.

"We don't have bows."

"No."

"Ah."

"*Why* don't we have bows?" asked Davith.

"We're berserkers," said Wren. The *you idiot* was silent, but clearly implied.

"Can't go berserk with a bow?"

"I absolutely can. I can break it over your head and then strangle you with the bowstring. Shooting arrows, not so much."

"I'm sorry I asked."

(While this was, indeed, a true answer, Shane was glad that Davith hadn't asked him. The truth was that Shane's martial talents did not extend to projectile weapons. On a good day, he could probably hit a barn, provided that the barn didn't make any sudden movements. The Saint of Steel had been a very close and personal god.)

Ashes leaned down and picked up a rock, tossing it in her hand. "I used to be a dab hand with a sling."

Shane didn't know why he bothered being surprised. Ashes was clearly a force to be reckoned with, despite her age.

"Sadly, my vision's not what it was. Still, I might be able to lug a few rocks at the moving blurs."

"Every little bit helps," said Shane.

"It'd help more if it was explosive. Hmm, I wonder..."

Davith cleared his throat. "Paladin?"

"Eh?"

"I'm a lover, not a fighter, and I know you don't trust me with sharp objects, but if you aren't using that dagger of yours, I can at least make it harder for them kill us all."

"Marguerite?"

"Do it."

Shane unstrapped his dagger and passed it back without looking. He felt someone take it. Meanwhile, the horsemen had stopped and were apparently discussing what to do next. They did not seem to be in any particular hurry.

Why should they be? They've got us pinned, and if we bolt, they can pick us off.

Seconds oozed by, like molasses cut with acid.

He felt someone press against his back, and recognized Wren by the solidity of mail and muscle. "Do we have a few minutes?"

"I think so."

He felt her take a deep breath against him. "Then shrive me, brother, for my heart is heavy."

Shane closed his eyes briefly. *We're all going to die, and she wants me to hear her confession?*

Of course, he answered himself immediately, *that's* why *she wants you to hear her confession.*

Which meant that he was probably going to have to confess himself, assuming the enemy held off that long, and yes, *fine,* there were a few things that he'd prefer to have off his soul before he died, but he didn't want to say them out loud in front of Marguerite and Davith. But not saying them would mean that he'd die with another lie on his soul, and...*oh hell, maybe I'll get lucky and take a bolt to the forehead before it's my turn.*

"The Saint hears you, sister," he said. Which was no longer true, so he added, "and the White Rat hears you," which he hoped like hell *was* true. *If not the Rat, perhaps Lady Silver's year-god will hear us, and look kindly upon two humans.*

"Is this really the time?" asked Davith in an undertone.

"This is exactly the time," Ashes told him.

"I have been wrathful," said Wren, pretending no one else had spoken. "I have used the Saint's gift for my own vengeance."

Ah. He'd been wondering what sins Wren could even have that merited confession, but that was fair. *She attacked Davith in a berserker fit. Of course that weighs on her, even if she didn't succeed in killing him.* No matter how justified, no matter how accidental, you did not use the tide for your own ends like that. It was part of the creed that was hammered into the Saint's chosen from the very first time the tide rose. *It is my duty to serve. I will be sword and shield for the weak against the strong. I will be a symbol for those who require hope. I will bear the burdens for those who cannot bear them. I will fight not for wealth nor glory but to safeguard the innocent. I am steel in the hands of the Saint. His will is mine.*

Which did not leave a lot of leeway for settling scores. *Or for taking up a lucrative career as a pit fighter, like Istvhan keeps threatening to do.*

"And have you made restitution for your sin?" Shane asked. *If Davith says a damn word right now, I'll kill him myself and make the whole thing moot.*

There was a lengthy pause. "Working on it," Wren said, in a small voice.

"I am unworthy," said Shane, "but I absolve you of your sin. The Sai—the gods forgive you your weakness."

"Thank you."

He risked a look around the edge of the rock. The horsemen had dismounted, and three of them were beginning to make a broad, wary circle around the outcropping. The crossbowman, who appeared to be a middle-aged woman, was still standing with the horses.

Checking to make sure we're here before sending their archer to pick us off. So we still have time. Dammit. "Shrive me, sister, for I have sinned."

"The gods hear you."

He closed his eyes. Closing his eyes was not very smart, with warriors circling them, but he needed, for just a moment, to be alone with the inside of his eyelids. "I have felt lust."

Davith snorted. Shane fantasized about bouncing his head off the stones. *It's not a sin if you don't actually do it.*

"I think we're allowed to feel that?" said Wren timidly. "It's not a sin?"

"It is if you do it right," said Ashes, not quite under her breath.

"It has led me to jealousy," said Shane, determined to get it all out, "and envy. And to act in fear." The tips of his ears felt hot.

"Ah." Wren cleared her throat. "Have you made restitution for your sin?"

"I have not."

"I am unworthy, but I absolve you of your sin. The gods forgive you your weakness, but They will require you to make restitution for your sins."

"Thank you."

He opened his eyes and checked the enemy's location. The four warriors—swordsmen, he saw—were standing a hundred feet away, watching them. *They know where we are, we know where they are...now they retreat and bring their crossbowman around, with all three of them guarding her, so that when we charge her because we have nothing left to lose, we won't cut her down easily. She'll aim for me first, then Wren if they're smart and Davith if they're not.*

He couldn't help but glance back toward the others. Marguerite was looking at him thoughtfully. He wished he knew what she was thinking. Was it about his confession?

Don't be ridiculous. She's probably wondering how I'm going to get them out of this mess. This is not *the time to be mooning about!*

Look, I wouldn't be if Wren hadn't...

And then he stopped thinking about lust or sin or confession, because an arrow had just appeared in one of the swordsmen's right eye.

CHAPTER 42

Shane was so surprised that he sat there gaping as the swordsman toppled over. Then he looked over his shoulder, halfway convinced that one of the others had pulled a bow out of thin air.

"What is it?" hissed Wren. "What's going on?"

"There's an archer somewhere!"

"Are they on our side?"

"I have no idea!"

He looked back, in time to see the remaining three running straight for their position. *They must think the arrow came from us, too. Crap.*

"Here they come," he said, drawing Lord Nallan's sword. Wren set her back against the stone, axe in hand.

Shane waited until the first one was almost upon them, then rushed to meet him. He hated to lose cover, but it was more important to keep the fighting as far from the noncombatants as possible. Dreaming God willing, the crossbowman couldn't get a clear shot through her comrade.

The black tide rose at once, and a good thing, too. His opponent had a shield. So did his opponent's friend, who arrived a second later. Shane blocked a strike and stepped out of the way of another, but even with the preternatural speed of the battle tide on him, it was all he could do to keep ahead of their blows.

...and dodge and duck under that one and cut for the legs and...

They fought as a pair, too. If he had been capable of conscious thought, he would have cursed. The Sail operatives back in the fortress had fought like a bunch of individual fighters. These two had clearly been working together for a long time.

...block that—no, duck, it's a feint!—and step around the side and cut...

He managed to slice one across the forearm, but he took a blow from a shield in return that made his collarbone creak. If Wren had been beside him, they could have made short work of the pair, but Wren was holding off the third swordsman, who had a lot of reach on her and kept trying to draw her away from the rocks and leave her charges exposed.

It occurred to Shane, in a distant fashion, that he might be about to die.

Then he saw it.

Five feet away, half-hidden in the grass, was a hole. A hole with a line of stones in it that might simply be stones, but which glinted in the afternoon light.

The tide rose higher. He blocked a strike from the swordsman on the left, saw the shield rising to bash him in the chest, and instead of trying to get out of the way, he charged directly into it.

He weighed more than his attacker, who gave ground, startled. Shane kept shoving, bearing his opponent's sword down, their faces so close over the top of the shield that he could see the whites around the man's eyes.

Then his opponent did what anyone would do in that situation, and put a foot back to brace himself against the ground. Probably he was thinking that his partner would swing in, any second now. Pressed against the shield, Shane might as well have been laid out on a cutting board waiting for the knife.

Except that the man's foot hit a hole and went in.

He let out a cry and fell backward. Shane dropped low, feeling a sword strike go so close over his head that it ruffled his hair, then scrambled back gracelessly. He had no idea where the crossbowman was any longer, and all he could do was keep moving.

The swordsman let out a shout of pain, tried to get up, and failed. Shane felt a rush of bitter satisfaction. Distracted by the cry, his partner was just a hair too slow getting his shield up, and Shane smashed the pommel of his sword between the man's eyes and watched him drop like a stone.

He made it back to the rocks a fraction of a second before a crossbow bolt slammed into the ground precisely where he'd been standing.

Wren's opponent was missing large chunks of his thighs where his femoral artery had previously been located, but was no longer in a position to be concerned about this. Shane shook off the remains of the battle tide, just in time to hear the trapped swordsman's shouts cut off abruptly.

Did the ground-wight...? He peered cautiously around the rocks and saw another arrow protruding from the man's neck. *Ah. I see. I don't know if they're friendly, but they seem to have helped us quite a—*

An arrow shattered against the rock an inch from his head.

Or not. Shit.

He looked around wildly, and saw, for the first time, three figures standing in the field, on the opposite side from the road. Two of them carried bows. As he watched, one notched an arrow and drew back the string.

"Don't shoot!" Marguerite shouted. "Don't shoot! We mean you no harm!"

The archer paused. The one who didn't have a bow said something, though Shane couldn't hear what it was.

On the other side of the rocks, he heard a voice say, "I surrender." He risked a glance around and saw the remaining Sail operative setting their crossbow on the ground and stepping back, hands in the air.

Marguerite elbowed him in the side. "Put your weapons down!" she hissed.

"There's only two archers," said Wren in an undertone. "We could—"

"You could get turned into a pair of pincushions is what you could do!"

They lowered their weapons.

"This is a misunderstanding!" Marguerite called. "We were attacked, not attacking! We don't mean you any harm!"

The trio approached, though the archers didn't lower their bows. Given the precision with which they'd shot, Shane was pretty sure they wouldn't miss a second time.

The closer they are, the quicker they have to move if we dodge. A few more yards, and it might be worth trying...

Their leader was a barrel-chested older man with a lined face and an unsheathed sword. "You're trespassing," he growled.

"We are *terribly* sorry," said Marguerite. "We didn't mean to. We were attacked and so we were trying to get away—"

"I am surrendering!" called the Sail operative again.

Neither of the archers have swords, so if Wren and I move together, and I grab the shield from the one Wren killed...

The leader rocked on the balls of his feet, then put two fingers to his mouth and whistled shrilly.

Five more people stood up from the grass. They must have been lying almost prone, given how little cover there was. All five of them carried bows.

"And what about you? Do you surrender?" the man asked, looking over Wren and Shane.

Dreaming God have mercy. "Yes," said Shane. "We do now."

They were not treated cruelly. Their hands were bound in front of them, and their weapons were taken, but that was all. At least two archers kept arrows on strings the entire time, and Shane had no doubt that they would use them.

"This is really a misunderstanding," said Marguerite.

"You can tell that to Wisdom," said the leader. "There's no point in telling it to me."

Shane glanced back toward the road, hoping for witnesses, but the only movement was an unsettling jiggling of the corpse in the groundwight's maw. It had gotten most of his leg down and showed no signs of stopping. Shane repressed a shudder. *Perhaps there was a reason this road was so empty.*

He glanced at Marguerite, who shrugged helplessly.

Their captors took the horses belonging to the Sail's people, and recaptured the remaining mule. The warrior that Shane had stunned was put on one of the horses, since he was still too groggy to understand what was happening. Everyone else was pulled into a line and marched across the field.

Their destination was the knot of buildings that Shane had noticed earlier. *Well, I suppose technically they did help...after a fashion.*

He looked back over his shoulder. Marguerite and Davith were uninjured. Wren was moving like she'd taken a blow to the ribs, but wasn't bleeding. The enemy crossbowman met his eyes and gave him a crooked what-can-you-do smile of acknowledgment.

"Here now," said the leader, "look where you're going."

"Sorry," said Shane, but as his captor tugged him back into line, a single thought pounded in his head.

Where the hell is Ashes Magnus?

Marguerite was fairly certain that this was not going down as one of her best days. Her shoulder ached from the fall off the wagon, her head ached from how badly everything had gone, and her heart ached from the fact that she had dragged her faithful paladins into this mess.

It would have ached even more, except that Ashes had somehow gotten away. She was pretty sure the artificer wasn't dead, but somehow, in the confusion, she just...wasn't there. Marguerite was actually quite impressed. Seventy-plus years old, best pace a slow amble, and the woman had vanished while everyone was still flailing around wondering where the arrows were coming from.

Now, if I could just convince these people to talk to me... They couldn't be bandits, surely? Half of the archers weren't old enough to shave. And they had been kind to the horses and the remaining mule as well. *Not that being a bandit makes you automatically cruel to animals, granted.*

They were led across the green sward toward a knot of buildings on a hillside. Marguerite paid attention to placing her feet more than their destination—the ground-wight was still devouring a dead man somewhere behind them—and didn't look up until she heard Shane grunt.

On the far side of the hill, a stone keep had been tucked into a rocky outcropping. It had the piecemeal look of a building assembled and added to over the centuries, and it had clearly suffered some neglect over the years, but it looked exceedingly defensible and showed signs of recent repairs. *Not bandits. Bandits might take over a keep, but they wouldn't patch the roof and replaster the walls.*

Not looking at the ground cost her. A stone worked its way into her shoe and she stumbled. One of the archers jerked an arrow toward her, and she held up her bound hands as peacefully as possible. "I'm not trying to escape. There's a rock in my shoe."

"Ah." The archer lowered her bow, and then, to Marguerite's mild surprise, said, "Right or left?" and helped her get the offending shoe off and the offending rock out before getting her back in line. Shane cast a quick glance over his shoulder to make sure that she was still there before continuing. Wren did as well, and Marguerite saw her brow furrow.

"Wait, where's A—"

Davith contrived to trip on a blade of grass and stumbled hard into her shoulder. Wren yelped and elbowed him. "Sorry," Davith grunted. "Clumsy of me. *Marguerite* is right behind us, though. *Since you were worrying.*"

"...ah," said Wren. "Yes, of course. Good to know."

Marguerite could have kissed Davith, but suspected that it would be misconstrued.

Their captors led them into the keep, through a maze of narrow corridors, and up a flight of stairs. Seeing the different textures of stone confirmed her opinion that the structure was the result of multiple architects, none of them on speaking terms. Claustrophobic staircases led to hallways where a pair of horses could have walked abreast. They had a brief glimpse of a large cobblestone courtyard, then went up a final flight of stairs into what appeared to be a great hall.

On the far end, in a chair that was rather less than a throne, was a tall, striking figure.

"Wisdom," said the man leading them, and bowed his head.

CHAPTER 43

The woman in the chair was very tall and very thin, her wrists and ankles sticking out from her cuffs. She did not look as if there was a single spare ounce of flesh on her body. Her eyes were very large in a narrow face.

"So these are the prisoners," she said.

"Yes, Wisdom," the leader of their captors replied. Marguerite felt Shane stiffen beside her. She turned her head slightly, but the paladin was still staring straight ahead, as still as a mouse under a hawk's shadow.

The woman called Wisdom rose to her feet. Her motions were strangely fluid, as if she had more than the usual number of joints. She bounced slightly on the balls of her feet, studying each of the prisoners in turn. Marguerite met her eyes squarely and said, "I believe there's been a misunderstanding, Your...Wisdom?"

"Probably," Wisdom agreed. She sounded rather amused by the possibility.

"We—that is, the four of us—were fleeing our attackers. We had no desire to trespass on your lands. We were running for our lives."

"Mmmm." Wisdom moved past, eyeing Shane with deep interest. His jaw was tight, his eyes absolutely blank.

"We meant no offense," Marguerite said, staring at the side of Shane's head. *Come on, use the voice. Back me up here.*

It was Davith who jumped in and said, "I don't blame you for being angry, Your Wisdom, but I assure you, we're harmless. Not terribly bright, but harmless." Marguerite was certain that he was giving Wisdom his most winning smile.

"That's a lie," said Wisdom, still sounding rather amused. "You've got two paladins with you."

How the hell did she know that? Marguerite flicked a glance at the two Red Sail operatives. *Have they talked? But* when *would they have talked? We haven't been out of each other's sight. Unless Wisdom's had her people spying on us.*

"Then you know paladins don't hurt the innocent," she said, trying to salvage the situation. "And they certainly don't raid villages or whatever you suspect us of doing. I promise that we mean you no ill-will whatsoever."

Now would be a great time to say something, Shane. Her eyes bored holes in the side of his head. Surely he could feel that?

"Ah yes, the...innocent." Wisdom moved on to Wren, giving her the same intent examination that she'd given Shane. "How many of us are truly innocent, I wonder?"

Rat and Forge and Lady of Grass, if any of you love me, please do not let us have fallen in with a group of religious fanatics. Marguerite steeled herself and threw the conversational dice. "Truly, we are sorry to have disturbed your people. If there's something that we can do by way of apology, please tell us. I'm certain that we can come to a resolution."

"Oh, I have no doubt of that," said Wisdom. She stepped back and gestured to the man who seemed to be leading their captors. "Erlick, take our guests to the cell. Politely."

Erlick bowed, then turned back. "Come on, you lot." He twitched the rope binding their hands together and led them back out of the room. Marguerite looked over her shoulder and saw Wisdom sitting back down in the chair, strange and supple as an eel.

Their captor took them down a set of stairs, waiting with surprising patience while they negotiated it without full use of their hands. The Sail operative on the end was slower than the rest, which gave Marguerite time to examine their surroundings. *Big place, but not all of a piece. They've been adding bits on here and there.* The mortar and the size of the stones changed from one wall to the next, and the depth of the stairs seemed to alter almost at random. *This is an old keep, and whoever lived here had money, once upon a time.*

Judging by the smell of cheap tallow and the flicker of rushlights, that time had passed.

The cell was, as advertised, a cell. It was about the size of an ordinary bedroom, with three stone walls and iron bars across the front. Marguerite suspected that it had probably been part of a stable once, since they passed by several deep alcoves that looked suspiciously like horse stalls. Rushlights burned in metal holders, illuminating a long wooden bench along the back wall, and a chamber pot in the corner. Incongruously, the pot was blush pink.

Erlick opened the cell door and gestured them inside.

"May we be untied?" asked Marguerite, with as much courtesy as she could muster under the circumstances.

"Once you're inside."

Lacking other options, Marguerite stepped inside. "Oh good, a prison," said Davith. One of the Sail operatives snorted. Shane and Wren were still as silent as the grave.

When they were inside, Erlick shut the door. The guard at the back of the line, who was carrying a crossbow, pointed it into the cell.

"Hold your hands out," Erlick said, "politely."

Marguerite offered her hands through the bars. The man untied her wrists with a few quick motions, then moved to the next. Marguerite thanked him, despite the pain of pins and needles in her hands. So did Davith and one of the Sail. The paladins did not.

"Right." Erlick looped the rope around his shoulder. "You lot behave yourselves, and there'll be water and as much food as we can spare. You don't, and there'll still be water, but we'll take the light with us. Understood?"

"Perfectly," said Marguerite, massaging her wrists. "Please tell Wisdom that I would be happy to negotiate any kind of settlement she wishes." She did not actually want to say *ransom,* even if it was accurate.

Erlick eyed her, snorted, then motioned to the other guard and walked away.

"Well," said Marguerite.

"That woman was *creepy,*" said Davith, as the sound of footsteps faded.

"She's obviously got some kind of cult," said Marguerite, "what did you expect? Normalcy?"

Shane showed expression at last, shaking his head and turning away from the door. "It's worse than that," he said grimly. "There's a demon in her."

"Are you sure?" Davith asked.

A hard, humorless bark of laughter came from Shane's throat. "I served in the Dreaming God's Temple until I was seventeen. Yes. I'm sure."

"...fuck," said Davith eloquently, tried to walk away, found the wall only two paces away, and dropped into the corner.

"She must be very strong," said Marguerite.

Shane rubbed his face. "Strong doesn't begin to cover it." He had felt the creature that called itself Wisdom tugging at him, reaching out with invisible hands to touch the shape of his mind. It was as far beyond the poor mad thing in the steer as Shane was beyond a mouse. "Strong and old and smart and...just...*more.*"

"I thought you couldn't sense the smart ones."

"You can't if they try to hide it. This one isn't bothering. I think it was amused that I knew about it."

"This is the cult then," Marguerite said. "The one that the Dreaming God's people warned us about."

"It must be." Shane felt his throat work around another humorless bark. "There couldn't possibly be two like this." He looked over at Wren, who had her arms wrapped around herself. "Did it try to talk to you?"

Wren shook her head. "I could feel it," she said, almost inaudibly. "It was like...like standing next to someone when the tide takes them. You feel it rising in them, even if they don't move. Except this wasn't just the tide." She looked up at Shane, her face very pale. "This felt almost like the *god.*"

Shane nodded. The Saint of Steel had been infinitely greater than a demon, but He had only poured so much into His paladins as mortal flesh could bear. The demon had no such concerns. *That woman it's riding must be as hollow as an egg by now.*

How long until it chooses another steed?

Shane was very afraid that he knew the answer.

Marguerite turned and looked at the two Red Sail operatives. One was a young man with a face like a shovel and a goose-egg turning purple between his eyes, and the other was an older woman who looked as if she should be running a bed and breakfast somewhere. Shane had watched her put a crossbow bolt two inches from his head. At a distance of at least forty yards.

"Soooo..." said Marguerite. "I realize you've both been hired to kill us, but given that we've been captured by a cult run by a demon, do you think we could set that aside for the moment?"

The younger one looked at the older one, who snorted. "Honey, we are not getting paid enough for *this.*" She swept her arm in a general motion that took in the keep, the cult, and presumably the demon. "So far as I'm concerned, bygones are bygones, at least until we're out of here."

"Which is exactly what you'd say if you were still planning to kill us," Davith pointed out.

"Nobody wants to kill *you,*" said the older woman, a bit rudely.

"Well, now I feel rejected."

"Anyway, I'm a sharpshooter, so unless they return our weapons, I'm reduced to hurling insults." She leaned back against the wall in the corner and closed her eyes. "Wake me when they come to kill us horribly."

There didn't seem to be much to say to that. Everyone took a piece of floor. The cell wasn't really large enough for six people, so there was a great deal of negotiating of leg placement.

Marguerite decided that discretion could go hang and leaned against Shane's chest. He looked down at her and she saw a brief flash of gratification cross through his unease.

"Can you exorcise her?" she asked.

Shane shook his head. "No priest or paladin would try to tackle this one alone. They'd send a small army, and expect to take losses. You see one like this once or twice in a generation."

Marguerite rubbed her face wearily. "Can we negotiate with it?"

She felt him stiffen against her back. "We *don't* negotiate with demons."

"We do if we don't want to all die horribly possessed," Davith snapped. Marguerite was glad that he'd said it so that she didn't have to.

"Realistically," said Wren, "I don't think we have anything that it wants. I mean, it's already *got* us."

"Bribes?" asked Marguerite, without much hope.

Shane was silent for a long moment. "I don't think so," he said slowly. "Though, I suppose if it's this smart, it probably understands money. But it could just possess one of us, take our knowledge, and get whatever it wants that way."

He didn't say that, in that case, Marguerite was the most likely target, since she was the one with a dozen accounts at banks and merchant guilds across the region. He didn't need to.

On that note, they settled into glum silence, and not even Shane's arm around her shoulders could warm Marguerite at all.

Shane didn't know how many hours passed before someone came. Candles burned down and were replaced, but from what he could see, they were mostly candle ends. Their guard had a chair and a crossbow and the ennui that descends on all prison guards regardless of their fundamental decency as human beings. He didn't move, but by the way he jerked occasionally, Shane was pretty sure he was sleeping with his eyes open.

Unfortunately there was no obvious means of escape. Despite having read many novels where the heroes cleverly snag the keys from a sleeping guard by means of braided rope and concealed hooks, Shane had failed to absorb what to do when the guard wasn't the one carrying the keys. The cell door hinges were old, and he and Wren could almost certainly have smashed their way out, but that would cause a great deal of noise and unless they knocked the door down on the first hit, the guard would wake up and get at least one shot off, at nearly point-blank range, directly into the cell.

Given what they were facing, Shane would almost have been willing to try it, except that there was a second archer stationed up a short flight of steps, who would also get at least one shot off, and who had already proved their lethal accuracy. There was a good chance that both he and Wren would be shot. With the battle tide, that might or might not matter.

Shane had once fought most of a battle with an arrow lodged in his thigh, but a headshot kills the berserk and the sane alike.

And then we fight our way through a keep we don't know, having made enough noise to let everyone know we're escaping, and the demon finds us anyway and decides to stop toying with us and do...whatever it's going to do.

No, the wisest thing to do was to wait until they were moved and hope for an opportunity. *If not to escape, at least for a clean death.*

Actually, the wisest *thing to do is probably to strangle each other right now and spare our souls.*

He was considering this depressing thought when footsteps rang on the stairs and the creature that called itself Wisdom entered the prison block, followed by Erlick and another archer.

Shane scrambled to his feet, dislodging Marguerite. Wisdom waved one hand. "No need to rise. I'm not royalty."

"I'm glad to see you," Marguerite lied. "I hope you've considered what we said. This is all a—"

"Misunderstanding, I know." The demon's voice shaded with amusement, just as a human's would. Shane wondered if it was doing so consciously, or if the creature had lived in a human body so long that it was second nature. Neither option was particularly comforting. "You've said. I'm afraid I don't actually care why you're here. The question is what to do with you now that you are."

Marguerite's gaze flicked to Shane, but he had no answer for her.

"I suppose I could have you all killed," Wisdom said. "But that would be a dreadful waste, don't you think?"

"Yes?" offered Davith hopefully.

"That was what humans call a rhetorical question."

"Sorry."

Erlick's eyes didn't so much as flicker at the word *human.* Shane had been wondering if they knew that their leader was a demon. Apparently they did. *Dreaming God have mercy, it really is a cult.*

He'd fought cults before. They died by swords like anyone else, but absent that, there was usually only one way to stop them. *Take out the leader, however you can.*

He took a deep breath and reached for the voice. It welled up in his throat, power and calm and ultimate authority, and it rolled out like the tolling of a great iron bell.

"Kneel," he ordered the demon.

Wisdom faltered. For just a moment, he thought that it might have worked, that perhaps this one time, the Dreaming God's power might be within his reach.

It put a hand on the bars and looked at him, and then it smiled. Alien intelligence flickered behind the host's eyes.

"You first, paladin," the demon said.

"Let the big one out of the cell," Wisdom said, nodding to the guard.

"What if I don't choose to come with you?" asked Shane.

Two archers stepped forward, bows drawn. The demon let out a very human sigh. "There are at least a dozen things that I could threaten your friends with that will force you to obey me. I know it. You know it. Must we really go through the motions?"

Shane swallowed. He did not want to accommodate a demon. Once you agreed to anything, no matter how innocuous, you were on a slope that wasn't just slippery, it was glazed with ice.

On the other hand, it was right.

He looked at Marguerite, who shrugged helplessly. "I'm afraid she's negotiating from a position of strength here." Wisdom chuckled softly.

It would probably try to possess him. Whether or not it could succeed, he truly did not know. He was, most likely, going to his death. But if nothing else, it would be forced to kill him well away from the others, and however long that took was time they might use to work up a plan.

I must keep it focused on me for as long as possible. Whatever that takes.

"Wren," he said, lowering his head, "it's your responsibility now."

Wren gulped, knowing what he didn't say aloud. She rushed forward, hugged him fiercely, and then turned away, straightening her shoulders.

And if I come back with a demon behind my eyes, sister, I hope that you will be able to kill me quickly.

And then, because he was going to die or worse and all his fears no longer mattered, he turned to Marguerite, put his hand beneath her chin, and kissed her.

Perhaps it would have been wiser not to. If it knew that he loved her, the demon could control him using Marguerite. But it could control him using Wren as well, and in Shane's heart of hearts, he could not believe that anyone looking at him could not tell that he was in love. Surely it was branded across his face for all the world to see.

It was not the time or place for a passionate kiss, but he put as much of that love into it as he had to give. Marguerite's fingers curled around his wrists as she responded.

He heard, faintly, the sound of the guard saying something, but Wisdom's voice was sharper overriding it. "Let the man say his goodbyes as he wishes, Erlick. We're not *monsters.*"

And then, reluctantly, he felt the end come. He stepped back and let his hand slip away from her cheek. Marguerite blinked up at him, then turned away, wiping at her eyes.

"Brother—" Wren barreled into him and he caught her reflexively.

"Take care of them," he whispered, and kissed her on top of the head. She clung to him tight enough to make his ribs creak, but he ignored the stab of pain. "I have to go."

"Dammit," she said, her face against the dusty fabric of his tabard. "Oh, dammit all to hell."

"I know."

She let him go and she too turned away, scrubbing angrily at her face. Shane nodded to Davith, who grimaced, then stepped up to the door and let the guards lead him away.

They took him, not to the great hall, but to a room in the keep's single tower. The stairs formed a tight spiral upward, with slits in the stone to let air through. Halfway up, a door opened into a wide, welcoming room, with whitewashed walls and a floor strewn with sweet rushes.

To his mild surprise, the demon waved the guards off and they went, closing the door behind. *If they're leaving us alone, they must not be worried that I'll attack. Or more likely, they're not worried that I'll be able to do any damage.*

"Well, well, well," said the demon. "A paladin delivered to my doorstep. Truly fate moves in mysterious ways."

"What is it you want?" Shane asked, folding his arms.

Wisdom met his eyes, clear and forthright. "It's very simple. I want to become a god."

CHAPTER 44

"A god," said Shane.

"That's right." The demon chuckled. "No need to look like that. Most demons would quite like to be gods, I imagine. It's just that most of us are terribly bad at it. I don't blame your priests for doing away with so many of us. I probably would too. We're dreadful nuisances when we're young and ignorant and haven't learned to share a body politely."

"Politely," Shane said, in disbelief, thinking of demon victims he had seen, their bones broken in unnatural ways, teeth splintered from trying to eat rocks as the alien intelligence controlling them tried desperately to answer the body's need for food.

"The young of your race aren't known for their courtesy either," Wisdom said. It picked up a carafe of water on the table and poured out a cup, then lifted it to its lips. "But we both grow older and learn civilized behavior. I would not judge you for what sins you may have committed as a toddler."

Shane shook his head, saying nothing.

"The difference, of course, is that your people *stop* growing." Wisdom made an up-and-down gesture indicating his height. "Mine have no equivalent. Given the chance, we can continue to grow in power, and become more than we are. Give me enough worshippers, give me the power of their faith, and I will be what even a paladin would consider a god."

"That is not how that works," said Shane, thinking, *Dreaming God, I hope that isn't how that works.*

"But it is. Several of what you consider gods began their lives as one of my kind." Wisdom laughed at his expression. "Why is that so hard to believe? Your saints are humans who become gods, and that takes a great deal more work, believe me."

I will not argue. No good will come of arguing with it.

...not much good will come of not *arguing with it, come to that.*

"If you want proof, consider this," Wisdom said. "The channel by which the god uses you is the same one that a demon could use to possess you."

"I don't believe that," said Shane, immediately breaking his resolution not to argue.

"I realize that belief matters when it comes to gods, but in this case it does not. Here." The demon reached out and he felt its touch inside him, shockingly intimate, as if it stroked the underside of his skin. It trailed up the inside of his ribcage as if he were nothing but skin stretched over hollow bone, and settled finally just beneath his heart, in the numb place where the god used to be.

"There," the demon crooned. "There we are. What lies inside you, paladin? Let's find out."

Shane jerked as ghostly fingers closed inside his chest. He could not tell if they were cold or hot, only that they burned.

"My, my...is this your soul? What's left of it, anyway. Hell's host, what did they *do* to you?"

To his horror, the demon began to stroke the burning place with its claws. It did not hurt. He wanted it to hurt, because he understood pain and did not fear it. This was something else. This felt like...sympathy?

It's a trick. That's all it is. He closed his eyes, not that it did much good.

The demon clucked its host's tongue, shaking its head. "Most people have scars on their soul, but yours has nearly been torn in half. I've never seen anything quite like it." The burning claws sank deeper. Shane twitched violently, involuntarily, feeling like a puppet yanked by unsuspected strings.

"Ahhhh... Your god died. That must have hurt."

Like nothing I've felt before or since. Worse than dying. Worse than failing. Worse than anything.

He did not say the words aloud, and yet the demon still nodded. Perhaps thought and speech were all mixed up in this place, or perhaps it could simply read his mind.

"The channel inside you is nothing but scars. It hasn't healed cleanly, has it?"

The understatement of a lifetime. "No."

"Scars and...is this faith?" It made a small, surprised sound. "Abandoned by two gods, and yet still you keep faith, like a dog waiting for its master to return. Astonishing." The claws sank deeper yet. "Greed? No. What about pride, hmm?"

He would have laughed if he had any strength. It was going to be sorely disappointed if it was looking for pride. He had little enough of that anymore.

"No," it agreed. "No, you were only ever a god's dog on a chain, and you knew it."

If that was meant to wound him, it failed. Shane had never thought of himself as anything else.

"I could take you," said the demon musingly. "I could break you into a thousand shards and jump to your body. But what a *waste* that would be."

Shane said nothing. He had seen what demons did to bodies they inhabited, had seen the shattered minds left behind. He had never seen what a clever demon could do, but he had heard the stories. The rampage of Lord Caliban through the temple in the Dowager's capital was a grisly cautionary tale.

Please, gods, he begged, to any god that might be alive and listening. *White Rat, Dreaming God if you still care—please, not that.*

"Or you could come to me," the demon said. "Willingly. As my champion, not as my host. The first paladin of a new god. What do you say?"

It was such an absurd offer that at first Shane couldn't believe he was hearing it. *It can't be serious. Why does it think I would ever agree to such a thing?*

The thought occurred to him that perhaps whatever it had seen inside him had made it think he was weak enough to be swayed by such a thing. If so, it would soon learn differently. He might have failed in every conceivable fashion, but not that one.

"No," he said. "Obviously."

"You haven't even heard me out," Wisdom said mildly, leaning against the table and folding its arms.

"What are you going to offer me?" asked Shane, his lip curling. "Offer to heal my soul? Give me everything I want?"

"No," said the demon, surprising him. "I can't heal you, paladin. All I can do is make the wounds not matter anymore. And I doubt you'd believe me if I offered you everything you wanted, would you?"

Shane grunted. The demon was right, but he didn't wish to admit it.

Wisdom's lips twisted up in a smile. "What can I offer you, paladin? How about the lives of your friends?"

His head jerked up. He tried to control the reaction, too late. *It's a trick. It's a trap.*

"No trick," Wisdom said. Whether it read his thoughts or simply guessed, he didn't know. "Your friends are of no use to me as worshippers, and I rather doubt I could hire your little paladin friend with gold. Agree to stay with me, and I will let them go. Free and clear." It spread its hands, the picture of reason.

"And if I say no?"

"Then I'll try again with the other member of your order, though I hold out less hope for her. And if—when—that fails, then perhaps I will consider that it may be time for a new host. This one is beginning to falter, I am afraid. She lasted a very long time, but the consumption that I have been keeping at bay is beginning to tax my strength." Wisdom examined its nails, the very picture of humanity. "You seem a fine, healthy specimen. I doubt much of your skill with a sword will be available to me—not after I am forced to shatter your mind—but your body is strong enough to last for years, with careful handling. But of course, I'll have no choice but to kill the others to keep my disguise intact."

Shane swallowed hard.

"Mmm. That might be the best plan after all. With a face like yours, I imagine I could attract a great many worshippers in short order." The demon ran its hands through its host's hair. "Although I must say that I have always preferred to live within women's bodies. I find them more congenial. No, no, not for any perverse reason!" It grinned at his expression. "No, honestly, it's your bodily functions. It takes a male host so much longer to urinate, and it's already fairly disgusting to endure."

From the face it made, Shane suspected that the demon was telling the exact truth. This was not a comfort.

"Mmm. A handsome face, or a more congenial host..." It made a weighing gesture. "The little paladin is strong, too, and I sense that she could endure a great deal..."

"No," rasped Shane, horrified by the prospect of Wren's soul ripped apart by a demon. *Kinder by far to put a knife to her throat.*

And your hand may be the one holding the knife, if the demon takes possession of you.

Wisdom folded its arms. "Their lives—or deaths—are up to you, paladin. With a champion, I need not exhaust myself defending my flock from those who besiege us. In that case, I could keep this body together for quite a bit longer, I expect."

He would be here. His soul, very likely, would be damned for eternity. But if the demon was true to its word, then Wren and Marguerite would escape, and they could get to a temple of the Dreaming God and warn them exactly what horror lurked in these hills.

My soul is worth little enough, but if there is a chance to stop this...

"How do I know you'll keep your word?" he said, and saw triumph flash across Wisdom's face.

"How do I know you'll keep yours?" it countered.

"I'm a *paladin.* You're a *demon."*

"Yes, and one of those two is known for dramatic acts of self-sacrifice." It frowned. "Perhaps I should keep one of your friends as a hostage, just in case."

"No. You let them all go, or there is no deal."

"And what keeps you from falling on your sword the moment they're safely away?"

Shane folded his arms in a mirror of the demon. "If you cannot convince your paladins to stay in your service, how do you expect to succeed as a god?"

"Ha!" Wisdom barked a laugh. "Well struck, paladin. Very well! But you must give me a chance to prove myself before you fling yourself from the battlements, yes?"

Shane hesitated. "I will need proof of their safety."

Wisdom sighed. "Very well. You, and none other, shall accompany them to the river that borders my lands. You may watch them go for as long as you like, to make certain that none of my men take potshots at them. You may even lock my fighting men in the prison cells below, if that will set your mind at ease. But you become my champion now. Tonight. I want you on my chain, paladin, before I risk letting you off the lead."

It was a monstrous bargain. A true paladin would never have made it, but he was not a true paladin any longer.

Perhaps he never had been. Perhaps, as it said, he had only ever been a dog on someone's chain.

"Agreed," he said.

It was wise enough not to gloat. It reached out and pressed its hand flat against his chest, a little below his heart, where the Saint of Steel had once filled him with holy fire.

"Then let me in, champion," the demon whispered.

Shane closed his eyes. His first god didn't want him. His second god was dead. He was a danger to the woman he loved.

Maybe it's better this way.

If the demon's touch had burned before, now it felt like a needle of fire thrust through his heart. Shane opened his mouth to scream, and then something tore, something he hadn't even known existed, and his scream turned into a ragged gasp for air.

It was as if there had been a festering wound deep inside him and Wisdom had lanced it. As if he had been in pain so long that he had forgotten there was anything else, until the demon had broken it open and set it to bleeding again.

An abscessed soul. Of course I'd get one of those. If souls could heal and souls could scar, it only made sense. He gave a short huff of laughter, startling himself. He'd heard dying men laugh like that.

Well. That made sense, too. Perhaps the wound in his soul had always been mortal. He had simply been too stubborn to fall down and die. Perhaps now he finally would.

"Not until I'm done with you," said the demon Wisdom, and used its host's body to smile.

CHAPTER 45

"It's taking too long," said Marguerite.

Wren lifted her head and looked at her with an expression so unexpected that it took Marguerite a moment to recognize it. *Pity? From* Wren, *of all people?*

"You still don't understand," said the paladin gently. "It's a *demon.* Five minutes would be too long. He's gone."

"He'd never give in to a demon," said Marguerite firmly. "It's *Shane.*"

Wren rubbed the back of her neck. "Normally I'd agree with you," she said. "But it's old. And powerful. When you get one like this, the temple sends out a dozen paladins and at least five priests, and they expect to lose people. Shane's just one man."

"I don't believe for a minute that he'd be possessed by a demon," said Davith. Marguerite turned gratefully towards this unexpected support, right up until he added, "He'd have to take the stick out of his ass to make room."

"Not helpful, Davith."

Wren wheeled around, teeth bared, and for a second Marguerite thought the other woman would strike him. "Don't you dare talk about him like that!" she hissed. "He saved your life! He could have let that ground-wight eat you—he could have let the Sail's people have you—but he's been ready to die for you every step of the way and he doesn't even *like* you! Because he is—he *was*—a good man! And he just sacrificed himself because...because...just *shut up!*"

Davith stared at her in astonishment and, to Marguerite's own private astonishment, obvious shame. "You're right," he said finally. "You're absolutely right. I'm sorry."

Marguerite had to swallow hard at Wren's use of past tense, but then she went and put her arm around Wren's shoulders. She could feel the paladin trembling.

And not that long ago, you were thinking of how you would sacrifice this girl to your cause if you had to.

Not that long ago, I watched her and Shane kill a half-dozen men in less time than it takes to tell it. It was easy to sacrifice an unstoppable killing machine. Less so to sacrifice a younger woman on the edge of tears.

She didn't say, "It will be all right," because neither Wren nor Shane had believed that it would be all right, and they knew more about it than she did. She could still taste the kiss he had given her, all sorrow and sweetness and leavetaking.

Gods of all things, what if he's really gone? What if the demon has already snuffed him out like a candle?

The thought did not have time to grip her, because she heard footsteps on the stairs and looked up and saw Shane and the creature called Wisdom descending the stairs.

Wren jerked free of her embrace and in an instant was a warrior again, balanced on the balls of her feet, as if they were about to be attacked. Marguerite watched Shane approach the bars. There was something different about him, something about the way he moved...

Wren backed away, shaking her head. "No," she said softly. "Oh no."

Marguerite met his eyes, and they were white ice and darkness.

Dread prickled her skin. "Shane?" she said. "Is that you?"

Shane reached through the bars and cupped her jaw. His fingers felt the same as ever, the same roughness of calluses against her skin, exactly the same pressure, as he tilted her chin up toward him.

"It's still me," he said, in the paladin's voice.

She stared into his eyes, trying to see past them, feeling as if she was trying to see the silver at the back of a mirror instead of the reflection.

Something wrapped around Marguerite's torso like a band of steel, and then she was being dragged back, away from the bars.

It was Wren. The other woman's breath was harsh in her ears, but she showed no sign of strain at having physically pulled Marguerite away. "It's not him," she said. "It's the demon."

"I am not possessed," Shane said, in the paladin's voice, low and calm. "You know that I can't lie like this."

"When a demon's involved, I don't trust *anything,*" Wren snapped.

"Really, that's fair," said Wisdom, mostly to the ceiling.

Shane sighed, and it certainly sounded like Shane sighing. A demon might imitate the voice and the expression, but could it really get the sigh right?

"You're free to go," said Wisdom. "The rest of you, anyway. Bruno, unlock the door."

"The rest of you?" Marguerite's gaze swung from the demon to Shane. "What does that mean?"

"I'm staying."

"Like hell you are!" Marguerite snapped.

Bruno cautiously stepped into the line of fire, unlocked the door, then hastily retreated.

"I have to stay," Shane said, not meeting her eyes. "That was the deal so the rest of you could go free."

"We'll return your friend's axes, too," said Wisdom. "Though you'll forgive me if we wait until after you're outside the building."

Shane pushed the door open. Wren immediately shoved Marguerite behind her and braced herself, clearly expecting a fight, even though Shane was doing nothing more threatening than standing there.

"We'll renegotiate the deal," said Marguerite. "You're not staying here."

"I'm afraid this particular detail is non-negotiable," said Wisdom. "Or rather, the deal is already done."

Shane finally met her eyes, and surely he couldn't be possessed, because no demon could have poured that much agony into a single glance.

"No deal is non-negotiable," Marguerite began, praying that it was true.

And then Wisdom's mask...slipped. Or, more likely, the demon simply stopped pretending to be human. Much later, Marguerite would wonder if it was trying to prove a point, or if it simply was tired of talking.

"This deal is," it said, and its jaw moved wrong and its eyes were wrong and its voice had a timbre that buzzed and crawled along the spine and drove needles in wherever it touched.

Marguerite stopped arguing. In the corner of her vision, she could see Davith pressed against the bars, trying to get as far away from that voice as he possibly could.

"Come on," Shane said into the silence that followed. "I'll see you as far as the river."

There was a moment, when Wren had her axes back, that Shane watched her think about attacking him. She didn't look at him and she didn't do anything so obvious as hefting the axes, but the battle tide hissed in his ears and told him to be ready.

"If you do it," he said tiredly, "Wisdom will probably insist on taking you instead. Please just...take this chance to get out of here. *Please.*"

In the end, he was fairly sure that the only reason Wren didn't attack was because she couldn't bear the thought that he might not fight back.

Marguerite wasn't looking at him either. He couldn't tell if she was furious or sick or sad. All three, maybe. He wasn't used to seeing it, and some tiny part of him thought *this is because of you* and then he felt even guiltier.

He'd thought there would be a little more time. Weeks. Months. Maybe even a year or two, if he was very lucky, before things fell apart. Not a few days on the road, and then...this.

"I'm sorry," he said. "It was the only way."

"It *can't* be," Marguerite said. "There has to be something we can do. You said you're not possessed. Then it can't control you, can it? You can come with us."

The channel in his chest burned. "I don't think so. The demon did something. I'm pretty sure trying to double-cross it would be a bad idea."

Marguerite pinched the bridge of her nose and stalked past him. Davith, who had been very carefully not saying anything, moved toward her, then apparently thought better of it.

"If you're not possessed," said Wren slowly, "then why do I still feel the demon in you?"

Shane rubbed his hand across his chest. "You know how it felt when the Saint was in you. That place?"

Wren nodded warily.

"Afterward, it was like a wound. A festering one. Like there was a pressure building up and I was so used to it that I had stopped noticing. And then the demon...I don't know, *lanced* it, somehow."

"And now you're fine?" asked Wren bitterly. "The demon healed you and everything is wonderful?"

Shane snorted. "God, no. It hurt like the devil. I think I might be bleeding to death. But the pressure, at least, is less."

"That doesn't sound like a good thing."

"I'm not sure it is. But also..." He swallowed, wondering if another paladin could understand. Wondering if anyone *but* another paladin could. "I don't feel hollow anymore."

The woman he thought of as a little sister sagged. "Oh," she said, as soft as a dying breath.

"I didn't know it would do that," he admitted. "I don't think the demon knew either. Otherwise it probably would have tried to tempt me with it, instead of threatening."

"You wouldn't have listened," said Wren, with the absolute faith that he probably didn't deserve.

"No," said Shane, pressing the heel of his hand hard against his chest. "I probably wouldn't have." And hoped that his voice did not express just how tempted he would have been.

It seemed like no time at all until they reached the river. It was shallow enough here that they could splash across it. The two Sail operatives hurried to do so, not looking back, and struck out for the road.

Shane turned to Marguerite and found that she was less than an arm's length away.

"We're getting you out," she said, her voice low and intense. "We aren't leaving you here. We'll go straight to the Dreaming God and drag them back here. I *swear.*"

The Dreaming God's people will want Wisdom stopped far more than they want me saved. Assuming I'm even still alive when they get here.

"That's the best thing you can do," he said.

She grabbed his forearms and stared up at him, as intent as she had been when they made love. Even with the demon burning a hole under his breastbone, the memory still made his mouth go dry. "I'm *not* going to abandon you," she said. "Don't think for a moment that I have."

He nodded. And then, because he knew he would never get another chance, he said, "I love you."

And maybe he didn't have the courage to know how she would answer, because he kissed her rather than hear whatever she said next.

It was both the best and worst kiss of his entire life.

"Please go," he said, when they finally broke apart. "Because I can't bear this."

Marguerite's face had the blank, set look of a woman trying not to cry. "I *will* come back for you," she told him.

Shane nodded, and kissed her forehead, and let her go.

He watched them wade across the river, the three of them, and he turned away after that, so that he would not have to watch them vanish out of sight.

It was the only way to keep her safe. I did what I had to do.

Cold comfort, but it was the only kind he had.

"You return," said Wisdom, as Shane entered the room. "Not that I doubted."

"Didn't you?"

It was a strange thing to think about a demon, but he thought that its sudden smile was genuine. "A little, perhaps, if I'm being honest. But I thought it was worth the risk."

"How did you know that I wouldn't simply ride off with them?"

"You gave your word."

He looked at it skeptically. "You cannot tell me that you trusted that I would honor a promise to a demon."

Wisdom chuckled. "No, not really. But I trusted that what I had given you would be enough."

Shane rubbed the heel of his hand against his chest. The scarred spot where the god had touched him was no longer numb. It burned again, though not as it had before. Acid instead of purifying flame.

Compared to the dead emptiness that he had carried for so long, it was a miracle of sensation.

But would that have been enough, by itself, to bring him back?

He tried to think like Marguerite, picking his way through a tangle of possible motivations, but gave up quickly. His mind was simply not that twisty. "I don't know if I believe you," he said.

"It's not as complicated as you think," said the demon, and Shane wondered if it was reading his mind again, or if he was simply so easy to predict. "You do not know the extent of my powers. You couldn't be sure that something terrible wouldn't happen if you broke faith with me. For all you know, if you'd betrayed me at the river, a horde would have risen up and taken you captive again and slaughtered your friends in front of you. Maybe I would have taken one of them as my new vessel, as I threatened to do. So you had to keep playing my game, just to make certain they were safely away."

Shane exhaled slowly. When he'd stood at the river, watching them go, he'd thought almost exactly that. Its accuracy was chilling.

"So yes, I trusted that what I'd given you was enough. The bond you bear...and the healthy fear of what I might be capable of." It flashed its teeth in a fox's grin.

"And would a horde have risen up?"

Wisdom snorted. "I suppose I could lie and say that I had archers hidden by the river, but you'll find out soon enough how few troops I really have. No, no horde. You would not have enjoyed the breaking of the bond between us, but then, neither would I."

So there was nothing standing in my way but my own fears.

Again.

In all the tragic novels and epic poems that he had read over the years, the key was that the heroes doomed themselves by their own flaws. *That's why it's a tragedy. Otherwise it's just a poem where people die.*

"Don't look so stricken," said Wisdom gently. "After all, if I do manage to become a god, you'd hardly want to be the person who double-crossed me, would you? I imagine that could be very unpleasant."

Shane raised an eyebrow. "Do you plan to be a vengeful god, then?"

The demon laughed. "I honestly don't know. I can't imagine that I'll actually care, once I'm a god, but I've never been one before, so perhaps

I'll care very much. Either way, surely it's safer to stay on my good side, yes?"

Shane shook his head. There was one immense, glaring flaw in Wisdom's logic. "You must know that they'll go straight to the Dreaming God's people to warn them about you." He strolled across the room to the window and looked out at the distant hillside, half-expecting to see an army already gathered.

"Of course they will."

"And you're not afraid?"

"I would rather see them coming than be blindsided." It leaned against the table. "Discovery was always inevitable. This way I choose the time of my discovery."

"They'll send an army against you."

The demon nodded. "Very likely. And if I am to survive that army, the thing I needed most was someone with an intimate knowledge of how the Dreaming God's people operate." It traced its fingers through the air in a symbol like a benediction, though one he did not recognize. "And that, my champion, is where you come in."

"Me?"

"You know the Dreaming God well. His mark is on your soul, if not so strongly as the Saint's. You will tell me how to face His people and survive."

"Like hell I will," said Shane, and threw himself out the window.

The courtyard below was cobbled with gray stone, which had gone almost pink in places where red mud had dried across it. There was a line of laundry stretched across one side and a half-dozen chickens pecked away in the corner. He had plenty of time to notice this, because he appeared to be hanging suspended in midair.

Well, shit.

"Levitation," said Wisdom behind him, its voice slightly strained, "is instinctive in demons. I believe it's an outgrowth of how we move in our birthplace." Shane felt a hand lock around his ankle and drag him backward into the room. "It's much more difficult to do to another person. Fortunately, the channel between us makes things easier."

It dropped him on the floor. Adrenaline washed through him, belatedly, setting his muscles trembling, and he felt the battle tide trying to rise. He pushed it down reflexively, then thought, *Wait, why? Perhaps I can force it to kill me.*

He'd been fighting the black tide for so long that it took a moment to make himself reach for it instead. But it rose around him at last, shot through with red, and he pushed himself to his knees as the world went slow around him.

Draw the sword and run at Wisdom. Hilt in the right hand, get its shoulder in the left. If you can get the blade around its back and run it through, then you can drive yourself onto it as well. There's a good two feet of blade left, it'll be enough to kill you both.

He lunged.

"Stop," Wisdom said, in the brisk, exasperated tone of someone telling their dog to get off the bed *this instant.*

Heat exploded inside his chest and burned the battle tide to ash. Shane felt as if he'd been kicked by a mule with hooves of fire. His charge turned into a stumble and he went to his hands and knees at the demon's feet, gasping for breath. Even his lungs felt seared and raw.

Wisdom sighed. He watched it walk away, then return. It knelt beside him and pushed a cup of water into his hands. "Drink."

He drank obediently. The pain subsided, but he didn't seem quite able to stand yet. He fell over on his side instead.

The demon gazed down at him, shaking its head. "I apologize," it said. "I have little experience with this yet, and I clearly used too much force. I did not actually mean to cause you pain."

Strangely, he believed it was telling the truth.

Wisdom crouched down and got an arm under his shoulders until he could sit up, back against the wall. On some level, he knew that the demon's touch should have made his skin crawl, but it only felt like human hands.

It got him another cup of water, then sat down cross-legged across from him. He drew a deep, rasping breath. It no longer hurt, but he could feel the connection burning like a brand between them.

"There are any number of ways that I could force you to serve me," Wisdom said. "But they are all unpleasant, and I don't particularly wish to be that sort of god." It gazed at him, thinking the gods knew what behind its host's eyes.

Shane rubbed a hand over his face and took a sip of water.

"Do you *want* me to hurt you?" asked Wisdom. It sounded almost plaintive, a question rather than a threat.

It came to Shane that the demon found him as baffling as he found it. He didn't know whether to laugh or cry. "No."

"Are you sure? You want so badly to serve, paladin. It's all right there." It cocked its head and he could actually feel the pressure shifting inside his chest, as if it was running its hands across his heart. "If I tortured you until you had no choice but to serve me, you'd...feel less guilty? *Really?*"

Shane opened his mouth, found that he had absolutely no words, and closed it again. The demon's question nudged up against things in his soul that he had always suspected were there and had spent his life carefully ignoring.

But oh god, he could imagine it so clearly. A baptism of agony, and then...then it would no longer be his fault. Not even the Dreaming God could blame him for having fallen from grace. No more guilt, no more gnawing fear, only a dark and near-infinite freedom to be what he was made to be, the weapon in the hand of something like a god.

It would be so very wrong to want such a thing as that.

The pressure eased. Through the connection between them, Shane realized that he'd managed to shock the demon.

They never warned us about that *in the Dreaming God's temple.* He could feel a laugh rising in his throat and fought it back. The temple spent a great deal of time on how demons would try to tempt you. They hadn't covered what to do when the demon hadn't expected to tempt you.

"I suppose if it's what you truly require, I *could* do it," Wisdom said uncertainly.

Shane closed his eyes. "No," he said, partly to Wisdom, partly to the darkness behind his eyelids, "I don't want that."

And then, so quietly that he wasn't sure if he heard the words or felt them through the channel: "Humans are so damn *complicated.*"

He shouldn't laugh, but he did. Probably that meant he was damned for real. "When you write your holy book," he said, "I suggest putting that on the first page."

CHAPTER 46

It was evening on the second day before they reached the town. Either the way was longer than the demon remembered, or—more likely—they were simply bone weary. Every step felt like a blow. Marguerite almost stepped into a ground-wight and was only saved because Wren was still far more alert than the rest of them.

She wasn't paying attention properly, that much was clear. Both because she was tired and because one thought kept running endlessly through her head.

You left him there.

I had no choice! she argued, and the thought didn't argue back. It just repeated, over and over. *You left him there. You left him there.*

Because there was really no argument to be made, was there? She had abandoned Shane as thoroughly as the Dreaming God once had. She had watched the demon unveil itself for an instant, and she had turned tail and run away, leaving Shane to bear the brunt.

The only thing that kept her moving at all was the belief that she would go back.

I don't care what it takes. I don't care if I have to drag the Dreaming God's people out by the ear. I will go back and I will get him unpossessed if it kills me.

That she was relying on a god who had already discarded Shane once was an irony that was not at all lost on her.

When they reached the town, the three of them stood, swaying, just outside it. It felt bizarre that there were still towns, and other people going on about their lives, untroubled by demons or hired killers or lost loves.

"Right," croaked Marguerite finally. "There's an inn. If I get a hot bath, I may be able to feel emotions again."

"Do you *want* to?" asked Davith.

She scrubbed at her face with her hands. "Not particularly, but I still want the bath."

The inn was called The Fig & Murder and showed a crow holding what could, with some imagination, be a fig. Marguerite wondered where they were getting figs in the highlands, briefly considered whether she could undercut them on shipping, then decided that she just didn't care anymore.

Shane's gone. Shane gave up his soul to save us. To save me. What is even the point? I can't buy him back from a demon.

Her uncaring lasted until she actually pushed the tavern door open, whereupon the first thing she heard was a familiar voice saying, "I know you people use all the dung. I'm not *asking* about the dung. I'm *asking* about *horse piss.* I need about a hundred gallons of it, and I'm willing to pay cash."

"Lady," said the bartender, who had backed away from Ashes Magnus until his spine hit the far wall, "I do not know anyone anywhere who has a hundred gallons of horse piss lying around! That is not a normal thing that people keep on hand!"

"Ugggh," said Ashes. "What about a tanner? Tanners keep all sorts of horrible things."

"Ashes?" whispered Marguerite. And then, louder, "Ashes!"

"What?" The artificer turned. "Marguerite?"

"You're alive!"

"I could say the same about you!" The artificer swung around and caught Wren and Marguerite up in a bear hug.

"But what happened?" asked Marguerite, when they had finished hugging and a few tears had been shed and wiped away. "How did you get here?"

Ashes grinned up and down at them. "The usual way. I walked. At least until I found someone with a farm cart, and I bribed him to take me to the next town." She waved an arm at the innkeeper. "And I've been sitting here, recovering from my bruises and trying to figure out what to do next." She peered over their heads. "I see the snarky one, but where's the pretty one?"

Davith, for once, didn't issue a sardonic rejoinder. He dug his hands in his pockets and looked away.

Marguerite took a deep breath. "He's still up there," she said. "And there's a demon with him."

Ashes was quiet for a long moment. "Shit," she said finally. "I can't fix that."

"I'm not sure anyone can." Marguerite rubbed her forehead. "How did you get away?"

"Oh, *that.*" Ashes looked vaguely embarrassed. "Pure cowardice, really. As soon as the Red Sail fellows got shot, I knew that somebody else had joined the fray, and I was pretty sure they weren't going to be friendly. Figured that maybe we'd crossed into the territory of someone who didn't like visitors. Lots of the clans up here don't, you know. And since I was already up against the wagon, looking for my gear—had some notion that I might have something explosive enough to make them think twice—I just dropped flat and wedged myself into the wreckage and pretended to be a corpse." She gestured toward her head. "The blood helped. Head wounds always look spectacular."

"And they thought you were dead," breathed Wren.

"Yep. One nudged me in the ribs, but I stayed limp, and thankfully they weren't interested in making sure. After they marched you all off, I worried someone'd be back to loot the bodies, so I made sure I wasn't there for it." She smiled sheepishly. "And so I've been sitting here for the past half-day, trying to figure out how to stage a rescue. Which fortunately you didn't need, because about all I could come up with was using a beer wagon full of black powder to take down a wall, and I didn't have that much black powder, which meant I needed a load of horse piss, which someone wasn't willing to provide." She glared at the barkeeper, presumably for his failure to stock large quantities of urine behind the bar. The man smiled weakly, clearly glad that someone had come along to distract the terrifying old woman.

"It's the thought that counts," said Marguerite.

"Not with explosives, it isn't," said Ashes, and on that point, Marguerite had to agree.

. . .

"Your task is simple enough," said Wisdom, tapping a spot on the map. "The steading here has been raiding us for the better part of a year. They take our sheep and sometimes our children. I want them eliminated."

Shane raised his eyebrows. "And you think I can do this single-handedly?"

"I have faith in you," the demon said. Shane didn't know if it was unconscious of the irony or simply chose not to acknowledge it. "There are perhaps two dozen people there. Only the warriors need to die."

"If there are only two dozen, why haven't you stopped them before?"

Wisdom laughed softly and went to the window. "Come here."

Shane approached warily. The demon pointed down, into the courtyard below, where a half-dozen people were drilling with swords. Erlick walked around the perimeter, shouting orders.

Shane looked the troops over with a practiced eye. Three of them were boys who probably didn't need to shave yet. One was a man who might be the boys' grandfather. The only two who might have crossed swords with him and lived for more than a moment were two middle-aged women with their skirts tied around their legs.

"Behold my army," said Wisdom, with a grand sweep of its arm. "Inspiring, are they not?"

"The prison guard—"

"Bruno. The only other man of fighting age here. He can see about ten feet in front of him, so long as the light is good."

Shane stared at the demon. "But when you captured us—"

"Archers. Nine of them, mostly under fifteen or over fifty, and Rory, born with a club foot, who cannot run. They also fill our stewpots with game." It smiled down at the troops and if it had been human, Shane would have believed there was fondness in its gaze. "Shortbows only. We had two crossbows in the entire keep. Now we have three, thanks to your pursuers. Though they killed Sebastian in the process, and put one of my best archers out of commission until her arm heals."

"I'm sorry," said Shane, almost absently. *My god. Wren and I could have taken this entire keep by ourselves. Hell, I could probably still take it by myself.*

Something tugged inside his chest and he looked up sharply. Wisdom raised its eyebrows at him. "Don't forget me," it suggested.

"No," said Shane. "I won't." He looked back down. "How did this happen?"

"This holding was in decline for years," Wisdom said. "Then a rival clan descended on it. They slaughtered all the warriors and many of the rest. Then they took what they wanted and left." The demon folded its arms across its chest, looking back down into the courtyard. "I found them a few days later. The survivors would not have lasted the winter, but I walked my host down to the nearest large town and jumped to a merchant. Then I drove all his stock here and told them that it was a gift from Wisdom." Its teeth flashed. "I did that three times. By the time I arrived in this body, calling myself Wisdom, the people were feeling very well-inclined toward me."

"So you killed three innocent merchants," said Shane.

"One was a cheat and a liar, and one was going to die soon no matter what I did. The third one...yes. I regret the third one, I admit. He was a fair man and he did not deserve to have his mind torn in half. But these people also did not deserve to starve." The demon stared broodingly out the window. "It is hard to be a god, and to make a god's choices."

"*Do* you actually regret it?" Shane asked. "Can you?"

"Does that surprise you, champion?" Wisdom looked at him unsmiling. "We pour ourselves into our hosts like whiskey into a barrel. You are not surprised when the whiskey tastes of the barrel, or the barrel smells of whiskey, are you?"

"Souls seem more complicated than whiskey."

Wisdom barked a laugh. "Don't tell Erlick that. He was a distiller before the raiders killed his family. But yes. First we must learn the lessons of physical bodies. Most of us are caught by your paladins then. If we live long enough or come back often enough, we may begin to learn other lessons. I know sorrow and regret and grief. And responsibility to my people."

"Yet you still want to become a god."

The demon smiled, showing teeth. "How else shall I best take care of my people? And how else shall I avoid taking these lessons back to the abyss with me, and dwelling for eternity on my failures?" It stretched. "My reasons are not entirely selfish, but neither are they entirely pure.

They are only entirely mine. And now I wish you, my champion, to go and make certain that these troublesome raiders no longer trouble me and mine."

Shane grimaced. "Do they have innocents among them?"

"Very likely." Wisdom smiled. "And that is where I come in. We'll see if a demon can stand in for a god, shall we?"

It took them five long days to reach the town that had an outpost temple of the Dreaming God. There was an easier route, the locals said, one with inns and traveler's rests, but it took twice as long. Marguerite thought of Shane in the hands of a demon and simply started down the shortest road. Not even Davith argued.

Dreaming God, if You are listening, let him hold on until we can save him. You owe him that much.

"You can leave me behind," said Ashes on the second day. "I know I'm not setting any speed records."

"No," said Wren, before Marguerite could speak. "We're not leaving anyone else behind."

Marguerite glanced at the paladin, who had been as silent as Shane used to be. The younger woman's face had aged a decade in a few days. *If we lost Ashes to the Sail, all this would be for nothing.*

It already felt like that. Vengeance was a stupid hollow thing and the only salt that she cared about any longer was the kind in blood and tears.

"We'll get him back," she said out loud, trying to convince herself as much as Wren.

Wren looked at her and looked away. "Of course we will," she said, but she didn't say it in the voice and Marguerite knew that she didn't actually believe it.

They were able to buy food at farms and Davith found a farmer willing to part with a dogcart and a pony and charmed both out of her at a decent price. Ashes rode in it and they made better time after that, but it was still a long and weary way. At night, they did not so much make camp as collapse where they stood.

Perhaps their luck turned. Perhaps the Dreaming God, absent from His duties where Shane was concerned, had belatedly turned an eye toward them. Regardless, they were still almost half a day out from the town, at Marguerite's best guess, when they heard hoofbeats.

Looking up, Marguerite saw a trio of remarkably handsome people atop moderately handsome horses. They wore armor and white tabards with a closed eye.

Paladins, she thought. The word drifted through her head and she knew that she was supposed to do something, but she was so very tired.

It was Wren who stepped forward, waving her arms. "*Jorge?* Is that you?" She broke into the first smile that Marguerite had seen from her since they'd been captured by Wisdom's people.

"Wren?" One of the paladins laughed aloud and swung himself off his horse. He was tall and muscular and something about the way he held himself reminded Marguerite very much of Shane. Jorge's skin and hair were much darker and a scar cut rakishly through his right eyebrow, but he moved the same way and the massive sword slung across his back was a twin to the one that Shane had broken. "Dreaming God save us, what are you doing this far from Archenhold?"

"It's a long story." Wren looked back at Marguerite, as if for orders. "A very, very long story."

"It must have been." Jorge eyed their party sympathetically. Marguerite glanced back herself, seeing the layers of caked-on dust, torn clothes either hastily mended or covered with cloaks, and the fading bruises on Ashes' face. "Please, let us offer you the hospitality of the temple. You can tell me all about it on the way."

Davith spoke up. "Will there be baths?" he asked.

The paladin laughed. "I think we can manage that. But come, Wren, introduce me to these lovely ladies, will you?"

Wren rolled her eyes and made the introductions. Jorge bowed over Marguerite's hand and kissed the back like a chevalier. "Charmed," he told her.

"Tired," she told him.

To his credit, he bowed just as deeply over the hand of Ashes Magnus and if anything, lingered longer on the kiss. Ashes snorted, but there was an appreciative glint in her eye. "You're lucky I'm not twenty years younger, paladin."

"And yet I find myself feeling deeply *unlucky*."

Marguerite heard Davith mutter something under his breath about goddamn amateurs.

"Jorge, stop flirting and let us get these poor people to hot water and beds," said one of the other paladins.

"Yes, of course. Forgive me." He turned away from Ashes, (who definitely eyed his backside as he did) and picked up his horse's reins, leading the animal on foot. "So, what brings you so far from Archenhold?"

Wren took a deep breath and looked at Marguerite for permission. Marguerite nodded to her. *If we have to worry about the Dreaming God's paladins working for the Red Sail, we are so utterly and comprehensively fucked that we might as well slit our wrists and be done with it.*

"We came looking for Ashes. Some other people were, too. It got messy. But that's not the important bit." She waved a hand. "You've heard the rumors about a demon with followers in the hills?"

Jorge's face went grave. "We have, yes."

"We found them."

The three paladins of the Dreaming God all reached for their sword-hilts simultaneously, probably unconsciously. It would have been amusing if Marguerite had any amusement left in her.

"Shit," said Jorge, letting his hand fall away. "It's true, then? How many? Did you see the demon itself?"

"At least twenty people," said Wren. "Maybe more. Not many fighters, I don't think. Lots of kids and old people with bows, though. We saw the demon when they captured us."

The paladin who hadn't yet spoken until now slid off her horse, and grabbed Wren's chin, staring into her eyes. Wren bore this patiently. Marguerite had only a moment's warning before Jorge had her by the shoulders and was dipping his head to meet her eyes as well.

His eyes were deep, velvety brown, framed with fine laugh lines, and he was very handsome. Lucky, too, if the scar through his eyebrow was any indication. It picked up again on his cheek, which meant that he'd come within a hair's breadth of losing that eye. Marguerite noted all this dispassionately. *I must be tired. Normally I'd at least wonder if he was single.* She found that she could not possibly care less. Behind her, she heard Davith squawk indignantly as the third paladin manhandled him.

Jorge nodded to her and stepped back, glancing at his fellows. "I don't see any sign," he said, "but if the demon's as old and smart as they say, it could probably hide." His lips twisted ruefully. "Forgive me, ladies, gentleman, this is extremely rude of me, but...*KNEEL.*"

His voice wrapped around her spine like a mailed fist. The paladin's voice, no longer kind and patient but as implacable as winter. Marguerite's knees tried to buckle under her, but she caught herself and glared at him.

"Son, I don't care if you're a paladin, I'm too old to kneel for anything less than a god," Ashes said. Behind her, in honeyed tones, Davith invited Jorge to eat shit and die.

"Thank the Dreaming One," Jorge said, stepping back. He clapped his hands together. "I'm *very* sorry about that. We don't dare take any chances."

"What did that prove?" Davith asked.

"If you held a demon, you would have knelt," said Jorge simply. "Even if it resisted, we would have caught something of its shape when it did." He looked back at Wren. "Forgive me, sister. We had to know." He sighed. "I suppose it would take a berserker to escape such a demon's clutches. How many did you kill?"

Wren paused, and Marguerite thought that she braced herself, as if expecting a blow. "We didn't escape. Shane bargained for our lives and stayed behind."

Jorge missed a step and nearly stumbled. The other paladins went gray. "Shane?" Jorge began to shake his head. "No. That's not possible. Not Shane. He was one of us. He would *never* have bargained with a demon."

"It's the only reason we're alive," Marguerite said.

Jorge looked at her, all humor and flirtation gone. "Forgive me, madam," he said. "But all of you should be dead, then."

"You know, I can probably find a bath somewhere else," said Davith. Marguerite was beginning to agree with him.

"No," said Wren quietly. "He's right. I should never have left Shane there."

"We had no choice!" Marguerite snapped. "He sacrificed himself, and now we have to go back and get him. As soon as possible." She faced Jorge, feeling anger starting to rise inside her, the sort of hot red anger that she always tried to avoid. "You're paladins, you fight demons, bring an army and help us *save* him."

"If he went with a demon willingly," said one of the other paladins, in a voice as cold and clear as broken glass, "then it has taken him as a host. A berserker paladin, with all that entails, ridden by a demon so old and canny that it has eluded us for years."

"And in that case," said Jorge softly, "an army might not actually be enough."

CHAPTER 47

The raiders' holding consisted of a dozen rough stone huts. Shane watched it from the cover of an outcropping high on the hillside, Erlick at his side. The holding was not built for defense, but it didn't need to be. The landscape was doing all the work for them.

He glanced up and down the length of the valley. It was not a geographically appealing piece of land, little more than a slot in the rock between high hills. The northern end was choked with trees, and he could see flashes of a stream between them. Shane could actually tell exactly where the winds came funneling through the hills by the growth of the trees, which grew thick near the base, then turned into thin gnarled trunks, like bony hands sticking out of full sleeves.

"I'm surprised no one's logged that," he said.

Erlick spat. "No use. That's all mushpine." At Shane's raised eyebrow, he said, "You don't know 'em?"

"Forestry wasn't my god's usual remit."

Erlick snorted. Shane couldn't tell if he was amused or thought that gods who didn't pay attention to trees were beneath contempt. "It's no good. They'll grow on bare rock if they have to, but you cut one down and the wood rots out by the time you get it home. Nasty, runny rot, too. Whole log turns to paste with some bark on. People've tried all kinds of ways to get use out of it, but about the best you can say is that if you pour the paste out flat and let it dry in the sun for a couple months, it'll burn."

He spat again. "'Course, it smells like a dead fish shoved up a dead sheep's arsehole if you do."

"That was an extremely vivid description. Thank you."

A smile might have flicked across Erlick's face, but Shane couldn't be sure. He went back to studying the holding.

Defensible, but no one else wants it. From what he could see, there was precious little flat ground that one could till, and even the hardy highland sheep probably didn't want a meal of mushpine. *If you weren't raiding your neighbors when you moved in, you'd have to start so that you didn't starve to death. Hmm.*

All the roofs were in poor repair, though from lack of craftsman or simple lack of materials, Shane couldn't say. They were made of sod, he thought, or maybe thatch so old that it had grown grass. He wondered if they would prove flammable.

After an hour on the hillside, he counted ten obvious fighting men, a few who were obviously not, and a handful who might pick up cudgels in defense of their holding. It seemed a small force to be such a thorn in Wisdom's side, but then again, Wisdom had so few people.

"These're outcast from one of the other clans," Erlick explained. "Fought over who was going to be the leader, and those who threw in with the loser didn't fare well. A few of them dragged their families along. More the fools they." He scowled.

"And your archers could not stand them off?"

Erlick spat. "They'd have to get close enough to hit. They're too canny for that. They take our sheep when they're out to graze, and they take the shepherds too, if they can."

Shane grimaced. A berserker of the Saint of Steel could kill a dozen men, or be killed by a single one. Shane wasn't fool enough to simply run into the middle of the holding and start swinging. *Although the thought is not without its charm.*

Am I really going to do this? Truly? Kill a dozen people on the word of a demon?

He'd cleared out nests of bandits and raiders before. The Saint of Steel's people had been in great demand for that, for their ability to kill the enemy and leave the innocent. Wisdom had said that it would handle that part. Shane had very grave doubts. *Still, is this so different from what the god would have had you do?*

"They got my niece last month," said Erlick quietly. "She's fourteen. I don't know if she's still alive."

Shane exhaled slowly. Not so different at all, it seemed. "Very well," he said. "I'd rather not bring anyone with me. If I die, they won't know where I'm from, but they might recognize one of your people."

Erlick scowled. "I don't say you're wrong, but I'm coming with you. I'll stay back in the woods, right enough, but I've got a score to settle with these bastards myself. And I'm the best archer we've got."

"But—"

"I'll use the arrows those Sail fellas brought. They won't trace the fletching back to us. I'll dress in the Sail's clothes, too. If I die, they'll think I'm from somewhere else."

Shane grunted. "And if they capture you?"

"They won't," Erlick said, patting his dagger. "Not alive, anyhow."

I should probably talk him out of this, but I don't think I can. And I'm not sure I should. There was a light in Erlick's eyes, or perhaps an absence of light, that said a great deal. Erlick did not plan to live a great deal longer, but he meant to do a great deal of damage to the enemy before he died.

"Right," said Shane. "Then here's what we'll do..."

"I'm sorry that we are meeting under such circumstances," said Jorge. "I don't blame you for being annoyed with us. We are...um...single-minded about demons."

"I noticed," said Marguerite. She thought about saying, "It's fine," then thought there was no damn reason to let him off the hook, then thought, *I do not want to antagonize these people, I want their help,* and said it anyway.

Marguerite was riding double with Jorge, and Davith was with one of the others. Wren had joined Ashes in the dogcart, since the paladins' horses had made it abundantly clear that they did not like Wren, would never like Wren, and would prefer that Wren was somewhere far away, preferably with a hoofprint on the back of her head. Wren had been philosophical, and the shaggy pony that pulled the dogcart appeared almost embarrassed for its brethren's behavior.

"It's not fine," said Jorge with a sigh, "but it's what we are. Though we usually manage to be slightly more tactful about it. I apologize. The hospitality of the temple will be open to you, and though it is not lavish, I trust that you will find it better than either the ground or a jail cell."

He was using the voice, Marguerite realized. He was good at it, though not so good as Shane. She told herself to stop being soothed. Her traitorous nerves relaxed anyway.

The temple, when they finally reached it, was a utilitarian-looking building, and Marguerite expected everything else about it to be utilitarian as well. The décor certainly didn't change her opinion—plastered stone, plain white with only a small line of decorative paint near the floor. She was just thinking, *Paladins!* with a certain amount of smugness when they reached the baths, and then her opinion underwent a dramatic reversal.

It wasn't ostentatiously luxurious, the way that the Court of Smoke's baths had been, but soap and hot water was plentiful, and afterward there were deep pools for soaking. Judging by the mineral smell, the water was piped from another of the region's hot springs. Marguerite settled with a groan somewhere between bliss and agony.

"*Tell* me about it," said Davith. The baths were not divided by sex, though he'd taken his own pool in deference to modesty. *Wren's modesty, specifically, I bet...*

She felt guilty wallowing in such pleasure when Shane was undoubtedly suffering. *But not wallowing isn't going to help him in the slightest. You don't get to package up your virtuous forbearance and send it to him. And possibly it will be important later that my back isn't permanently kinked.*

Ashes required a hand into the water, but then sank down to her chin. "The artificers keep trying to do this in Anuket City," she said, eyes closed. "But none of us can ever agree on how to run the boilers. It's come to blows, and once, a murder attempt."

"Was it a serious attempt?" asked Marguerite, after digesting this for a moment.

"There was a hammer involved."

"I see."

"And a small explosion, although that may not have been deliberate."

"Ah."

When they had soaked long enough that Marguerite's fingers were starting to prune, they hauled themselves out of the water and were led to the main hall. Jorge was waiting, along with three other people, one of which was clearly a paladin and the other two of which looked like priests. They were all significantly older than he was, and had a look of seniority about them.

"If you can talk while you eat, we can make this as quick as possible," said Jorge, giving the other three a sharp glance.

"No need to glare, Jorge," said one of the priests, an older woman with dark skin and her hair worked into dozens of tiny braids. "We can see that they're about done in. We won't keep them answering questions until they drop."

And answer questions they did. Most of the interrogation was directed at Wren, who confirmed that it was definitely a demon, that she had felt it herself, and that it was far and away the most powerful one that she had encountered.

Marguerite listened and interjected occasionally, but this seemed like a case where specialized vocabulary was called for, which Wren had and she didn't. The food was simple—bread, cheese, and spiced meat—but the quality was very high. The Dreaming God's people clearly favored simplicity, but not necessarily austerity.

She was almost lulled into complacency by the food and the bath and the hum of conversation when the senior paladin asked, "How difficult will it be to kill this man?"

Marguerite's head snapped up. "Whoa! Wait a minute, now!"

"We must plan for the worst," the senior paladin said.

"Obviously this isn't knowledge that any of us wish to use," said the priestess, giving her colleague a quelling glare. "But it is important to know."

Wren looked sick. "Hard," she said. "We're former Saint of Steel. If he's berserk, he, um. Would be very hard." She pushed the rest of her food away. "He's very strong." She took a deep breath, and then her voice flattened out and assumed the odd, almost dreamy tone that Marguerite had heard before, when discussing assassins in the fortress. "Shane prefers a two-handed sword and will be slower as a result of it, but you must assume that any hit he lands is likely to be a lethal one. He compensates for the slowness by wearing heavy gauntlets and he will punch with them. His reach is what you would expect from a man of his height. His distance vision past about twenty feet is poor. He is right-handed. He has an old knee injury on the left side that troubles him in bad weather, and it takes him a few minutes to work the stiffness out in the morning. Once he is berserk, it is impossible to guess how he will fight. It will be brutal, efficient, and unpredictable. If he's been unable to obtain a replacement two-handed sword, he may try to compensate with a shield." Wren paused and swallowed and sounded a little more like herself. "He was never terribly good with a shield, though."

Dead silence filled the hall. Davith had stopped eating and looked as ill as Marguerite felt.

"Well," said the senior paladin finally. "That was an extraordinarily clear and concise report."

Wren nodded, still staring at her plate.

"I think," said the priestess gently, "that we have kept you all awake long enough. Beds have been prepared for you. In the morning, we'll talk more."

Wren nodded again, rose, and saluted. There was a mechanical quality to her movements, as if her body was running on old instinct and the real Wren was locked away somewhere inside. *Probably not far from the case.*

Marguerite took her arm as they left the hall. "It will work out," she said, and the beauty of not being a paladin was that she could lie.

CHAPTER 48

The first raider that Shane saw had large, dark eyes that might have been called soulful if they had been in a less murderous face. He was watching over a group of a half-dozen children who were struggling to wash clothes in the stream, though his air was far more that of a prison warden than a nanny.

The sounds of laundry slapping against rocks covered the sound of Shane's approach. *And if they were ordinary children, they should be loud enough for an elephant to sneak up on them. That they aren't shrieking and laughing and trying to drown each other is not a good sign.*

The raider had his arms folded and his back to a tree. His chin had sagged to his chest, though he lifted it every few minutes to glare at his charges. Shane judged the distance he'd have to cover to reach the man and grimaced. The Saint of Steel had not chosen His warriors for stealth.

Even if Wisdom keeps me from accidentally hurting one of the kids, I don't trust this fellow not to decide to use one as a shield.

It would have been an excellent situation for Erlick's bow, but the older man was working his way down the hillside overlooking the steading, where Shane would presumably need him rather more.

Right. If I creep around through the woods, perhaps I can get behind...shit!

One of the children left the stream and went toward the bushes where Shane was lurking. Shane froze, trying not to breathe. Had he been spotted? Would the child raise the alarm?

The boy couldn't have been much more than eight or nine, and he proved without a doubt that he was a boy by unbuttoning his trousers and pissing about eighteen inches to the left of Shane's hiding spot. Shane stifled a sigh.

The boy turned slightly from side to side, apparently trying to hit a particular section of shrubbery. Shane closed his eyes, waiting for the inevitable.

It didn't come. Instead he heard a gasp and opened his eyes to see the boy staring directly at him.

It was very, very hard to use the paladin's voice in a single whisper, but Shane did his best. *"Shhhh."*

The child's eyes were huge. Shane risked a whisper. "I'm here to help."

"I…I…" The boy darted a glance over his shoulder at the raider. Shane winced. *Might as well hold up a sign saying, "I Am Doing Something Wrong Over Here."*

The raider caught it immediately. "Hey! What're you doin' over there?"

"Nothing!" squeaked the boy, an answer guaranteed to spark paranoia in the most trusting adult.

Heavy footsteps heralded the raider's approach. Shane tensed, hand closing over his dagger.

"Nothing, eh?" The man stalked up and dealt a stinging slap to the side of the boy's head. "You're supposed to be working, you little snot."

The child fell down. The raider turned to face him, drawing his foot back, which left him both off-balance and with his back to Shane.

Stabbing a man in the kidneys was a remarkably good way to make him think about his life choices, but he only had a second or two to do so before Shane followed up by cutting his throat. He shoved the man to one side so that he didn't fall on top of the startled boy and waited glumly for the screaming to start.

It didn't. All six of the children stared at him in silence, round-eyed, like a line of little owls.

Shane wiped his dagger off and pulled the boy to his feet. "Do any of you have somewhere to go?" he asked.

The oldest looking of the children, a girl of perhaps eleven, said, "'M from Hangman's Glen."

"Do you think you can get back there on your own?"

She shrugged. "Can try."

Shane wanted desperately to herd them away himself, but if he did, they would wind up with Wisdom's people, and he couldn't bring himself to feed children into the demon's maw. *It's summer and warm enough. They won't freeze at night, and they undoubtedly know the area better than you do.* "Go north," he said, "and circle around the hills. Go now. Take the others with you. I don't know how long the raiders will be distracted."

The girl nodded. She grabbed the smallest child by the hand and beckoned to the others. "C'mon, you lot. Keep quiet."

The boy wiped his nose, looking up at Shane. "You gonna kill the rest of them?"

"I'm going to try."

"Good." He directed a kick at the dead raider.

"Get going," said Shane. The others were already crossing the stream and vanishing into the brush. "Stick together. And, lad...?"

"Eh?"

"Button up your trousers."

The raider holding hadn't been much to look at from above, and wasn't much to look at from ground level, either. The huts all shared stone walls where possible, leaving two semi-circles flanking a straggling central area, with the stream on one side and a stone cliff face on the other.

In theory, such a layout should have been defensible and well-protected.

In practice, Shane simply walked up to the half-asleep guard, cut his throat, and ducked back around the edge of the farthest hut.

Someone eventually came out to check on the guard, and Shane cut *his* throat as well, then dragged the body back out of view. He had a vague urge to find whoever was in charge and yell at them about the value of redundancy in guard posts.

Probably he could have kept doing this for all dozen raiders, except that a woman came past, saw the dead guard in the chair and froze. Her eyes shot to Shane, who gave a tiny wave and put his finger to his lips.

She let out a shriek to wake the dead, and Shane sighed.

The woman stumbled back, still shrieking. A gabble of voices went up from the holding, mostly in the vein of "Who's yelling?" and "What *now?*"

If I was a little less chivalrous, I would hit her over the head. But that might kill her and she isn't attacking me, so I suppose I'm doing this the hard way.

He lifted his arm over his head and swung it in a short circle, hoping Erlick could see him.

"Attack!" the woman finally screamed, taking to her heels. "We're being attacked!"

The gabble immediately changed in tenor. Shane sheathed his dagger and drew his sword.

He hacked through the first man that came charging to see what the problem was, empty-headed and empty-handed. Shane might have felt guilty for taking down such an obviously unwise opponent, but he remembered the faces of the children at the stream and yanked his sword loose with a vicious twist.

Three down. Who's next?

It was two of them this time, and they were smart enough not to simply come barreling around the corner. They stayed well out of range, took his measure, and one spat on the ground. "Who're you with?"

"No one you know," said Shane pleasantly. The black tide was rising inside his head, drunk on bloodshed, and he knew that he could move forward and take the larger one in the gut with the sword, grab his shoulder, turn and block the smaller one's blow with the big one's body, throw the dying man into his companion as he pulled his sword loose, and then whichever way the small one went, Shane would be waiting with a blade...

The world jogged sideways and he discovered that he'd already done it and the smaller one was on one knee, staring up at him in astonishment. Unfortunately Shane's sword was hung up on his collarbone and since the other raiders might be right behind him already, Shane was forced to slam his knee into the man's face and pry him off the point. *Four...five...*

Something went *zzzip!* and Shane turned to find that yes, there was another man coming up behind him, and behind that man was an archer. Fortunately Erlick had gotten his shot off before the archer had.

Shane noted this and appreciated it for half a heartbeat before he threw himself at the next opponent.

Time jumped sideways around him. There was a body at his feet. Which number was it? Was the archer out completely? He'd lost count. The tide didn't care. The tide flowed forward, carrying him with it, and he heard another arrow and something hit his shoulder and it hurt but pain didn't matter and it was the left shoulder, he didn't need the left, he could still swing with the right, and the swing went through a raider's face who had an axe but didn't use it nearly as well as Wren did.

Darkness swept in on both sides as he entered one of the huts. Empty. He tried the next one. The center of the holding was full of bodies. Someone in the distance was still screaming. Shane should probably go see why they were screaming. That was his job, protecting people who were screaming and running away. Yes. Another hut. There was a man in this one. He had a table. He seemed to think that the table would keep Shane back. He learned his mistake too late to have much time to contemplate it.

More empty huts, and then another pile of furniture and he pulled it away and someone was there and the tide hissed and he raised his sword and Wisdom's voice stabbed through his chest like a white-hot needle saying, *No.*

Shane froze.

The tide receded like water down a drain. Shane listened for a moment and heard nothing that sounded like an attacker.

He looked down at the person before him. A young woman or an old child, or both. Her hair was matted and her nose had been recently broken, but he could see the resemblance around the eyes.

It worked. It really worked. Wisdom stopped me.

He did not know if what he felt was horror or exultation or both together. His mind was full of red threads.

The girl moved and broke his thoughts. It was wrong of him to stand lost in his own head while she waited to be struck down.

Shane lowered the sword, reached out a hand to help her up, and said, in a voice that shook only a little, "Forgive me, but would you happen to be Erlick's niece?"

. . .

Marguerite would give the Dreaming God's people this much—they didn't try to shut her out of the planning. Possibly it was simply expediency, since they needed Wren and anyone with eyes knew that Wren would tell Marguerite everything, but she suspected that it simply didn't occur to them to leave her out. Paladins everywhere, it seemed, were cut from the same straightforward cloth.

Somewhere on this earth is a paladin of an order of twisty-minded little bastards, and if the gods are kind, I will meet them before I die. Just so I can say "Ha! I knew it!"

Simmering in the back of her mind was a suspicion that she much preferred her own pair of uncomplicated paladins, but she refused to drag that out into the light of conscious thought.

The council of war was held at noon in the hall where they had dined the night before. Davith and Ashes were there as well, and the only thing Marguerite had to contribute was to help Wren draw a map of the keep, as best they could remember it.

"It looks like a maze inside," muttered a heavily bearded priest named Burnet. Marguerite had been a bit surprised to discover that he wasn't a paladin, given that he exuded the air of someone with multiple knives stashed on their person at all times. *Then again, even their priests must frequently encounter more than just spiritual combat...*

"It pretty much was," said Wren glumly. "We saw one way in and one way out, but there could be dozens. And I suspect I'm missing a couple of cross-corridors, but we didn't get a lot of time for sightseeing."

"Any approaches to the keep that might be less guarded?" asked the senior paladin, whose name, judging by how others addressed him, might as well have been "Sir."

"If so, we didn't see them," said Wren. "They spotted us a long way off, too. I suspect they've got either very good sightlines or a lot of sentries."

"They have a lot of archers, anyway," said Marguerite.

"They're all carrying those little horn bows the locals use," Wren added.

Sir and Jorge both grimaced at that. Burnet nodded. "Those have range all out of proportion to their size," he said. "The local shepherds use them against wolverines. Even if the archers aren't otherwise warriors, those bows could stop us before we get anywhere near the keep."

"A night attack?" asked Jorge.

"I hate night attacks," said Sir. "Everyone tripping over everybody else's feet. Half the time you end up doing more damage to your side than the enemy does."

"We may have no choice, sir."

"Dawn by preference, then. If we can close the distance before the archers can take too many shots at us, then we'll at least be able to see what we're hitting before too long."

"Well," said Ashes, speaking up for the first time, "if you can get me a hundred gallons of horse piss—"

It was probably a good thing that the conversation was interrupted by the sound of the door opening. Three newcomers entered the hall, their clothes mottled with road dust.

"Well," said Jorge, "it seems that the gods are looking out for us in some small way, at least." He raised a hand and one of the newcomers waved in return. She was a tall, lean woman with red-brown hair and an oddly expressionless face.

"Judith?!" cried Wren, and then, to Marguerite's astonishment, the paladin flung herself forward, charging across the open space. Marguerite half-expected the newcomer to brace for an attack, but then Wren skidded to a halt, wrapped her arms tightly around the other woman's torso, and burst into tears.

Davith made a small noise and made as if to rise from his seat, then stopped himself. Marguerite glanced over at him and saw an expression she could not read, quickly hidden.

"Dear heart," said the tall woman gently, stroking Wren's hair. "This isn't for me, is it?"

"Yes," sobbed Wren. "No. But yes." She took a gasping breath and stepped back, wiping furiously at her eyes. "What are you *doing* here?"

Judith shrugged one shoulder. "I had to get away. Everything I looked at was a reminder. I needed to see different walls. The Dreaming God's people can always use a fighter who follows orders, particularly one who's faced demons before. I had been working my way from temple to temple and ended up here." One corner of her mouth twitched down in a tiny frown. "But why are you crying? Did we lose someone?"

"It's Shane. A demon's got him."

Judith's eyes widened a fraction. "No."

"Yes."

"When do we ride?" Judith asked.

"That's what we're discussing," said Jorge.

"We must wait," said Sir. "I don't wish to, believe me. But we need bowmen. At least a half dozen, more if we can get them. Reynaud is out trying to scare some up from the local lords."

"Bowmen?" asked Marguerite. "Why bowmen, specifically?"

All of the Dreaming God's looked people at her. Marguerite, who prided herself on always being a step ahead, felt a stab of annoyance at their obvious pity. She spread her hands. "Pitched battles aren't my forte. But they've got a keep, and I'd think you'd need something other than archers to take a keep. Isn't it hard to shoot people from the ground?"

"It's not for the keep," said Judith, her voice oddly gentle. "It's for Shane. They mean to kill him at a distance."

"What?"

"It's the only way," said Jorge. He had the decency to look miserable. "If we can kill him, the demon will have to jump to someone else, and then we can exorcise it."

"Why can't you exorcise it from him?" Marguerite felt as if she was listening to the conversation from the other side of a pane of glass, as if she were shouting and no one could hear her. "Do that—that thing you do. Yell at him to kneel and pull the demon out!"

"Because we don't know if the voice will *work* on him!" Jorge yelled back.

Marguerite inhaled sharply. Jorge sighed and rubbed his temples. "He was almost a paladin of our god," he said, more quietly. "And he would have been a great one. He can do the voice better than I can. When one of *our* paladins is possessed, they seem able to shake off the commands. We all remember Lord Caliban's rampage in the temple. He killed at least three nuns who could speak in the imperative mode. It only ended because someone managed to bash him over the head. We could walk right up to Shane and speak the words and he might not even *notice."*

"If the battle tide has risen for him, he might kill you all and still not notice," said Judith. "We become...very hard to kill."

"But he *wasn't* possessed," said Marguerite, ready to pull her hair out. Was no one listening? "Not when we left him." She waved a hand at Wren. "That creature that called itself Wisdom was standing right there. She was *definitely* still the demon. She moved wrong. You saw it."

"That's true," Wren admitted, but Jorge was already shaking his head.

"How long do you think that will last? If the demon has access to a paladin host?"

Marguerite didn't know how to answer that. Wren's shoulders hunched up, a picture of misery. "And it did *something* to him. I could feel it. Like there was a shadow over him, even when we were at the river. Only not a shadow. Something weird and...I don't know. Jittery."

The paladins of the Dreaming God all nodded in grim recognition at that description. Marguerite forced herself to sound calm, even though she wanted to bash all their armored heads together. No one listened when you sounded hysterical, even if you had a damn good reason. "It was still *him*, though. Not the demon."

She had not kissed a demon at the end. She would have staked her life on it. The lips that had moved on hers had belonged to Shane and no one else. *And if I say that out loud, they will all look at me with profound pity, and probably they'll try to make me kneel again, just in case I'm dealing with some kind of residual possession. They'll just think I'm in denial because I'm in love.*

...shit. I am in love, aren't I?

What a lousy goddamn time to figure that out.

"If we can make the demon jump to someone else, we might have a chance," Jorge was saying.

"But if he's not possessed—" Marguerite began again.

"We can't risk it. I'm sorry." He swallowed. "Shane saved my life once. He's my friend, too. If I thought that I could save him, I'd walk into that keep alone, even if I knew I wouldn't come out again."

Marguerite put her face in her hands. "There has to be another way," she whispered.

"If you think of it," said the Dreaming God's champion, "let me know."

CHAPTER 49

"The plan is simple," Wisdom said. "The Dreaming God's people will come here, and they will tear this keep apart to reach me, correct?"

Shane nodded. That was about the shape of it.

"Most of my people cannot fight, and I will not ask it of them. They are leaving even now. First to the raider's camp you cleared, then on. Better to be refugees than casualties."

Shane licked dry lips. "The Dreaming God's paladins wouldn't..." he began, and then stopped. He'd never dealt with a demonic cult before. It had never come up in his time with the temple. He was sure that they wouldn't put everyone to the sword—almost sure—but they probably weren't going to send them on their way with a stern lecture either. At the very least, Wisdom's followers would find themselves in a very uncomfortable position, and it was likely that some of the leaders would be treated as heretics or accomplices or both.

Even in the very best case, families would be split up and people held as the priests attempted to sort the innocent from the guilty.

He thought of Erlick and his niece and his heart sank.

"Exactly," said Wisdom, reading his thoughts. "I will not gamble with the lives of my followers. We have gathered enough here that they need not go completely penniless into the world. That encampment you cleared will serve as a staging ground for those who cannot travel quickly. The rest will spread out as they can, and spread the word of a god called Wisdom." It laughed, a little ruefully. "It is my hope that my worship will continue long enough for me to find a way back if I am banished again."

"Do you expect to be banished?"

Wisdom spread its hands. "It does me no good to run. They will follow like bloodhounds, and I risk leading them directly to my people. So I am going to stay here, as are you. As are enough of my people to make a good showing fighting back. And when we have fallen back, you and I shall make a very dramatic show."

"And what is my part in this show?"

"Simple." Wisdom grinned its slightly-too-wide grin. "You're going to kill me, where everyone can see."

"You know, I could just kill you now and tell everyone that I did," said Shane. "It would save a lot of steps."

Wisdom rolled its eyes. "Yes, and they *might* believe you. But what they'll actually think happened is that I jumped to someone else, and they'll round up anyone that might have been associated with this keep, which puts us back where we started. The only way that this will work is if I do enough demonic tricks to convince them that I am very much present, and then you kill me. Preferably where they can see it."

Shane opened his mouth to say, *But they'll think you jumped to* me, and then closed it again. "Ah," he said instead.

"Now you understand."

"And they will capture me, and you will have left enough of a demonic taint through the bond between us to be convincing."

"Precisely." Through the bond, he felt a wash of something like... regret? Apology? He would not have thought that a demon could feel such things. "Though they may choose to kill you outright, of course, and try to bind me with your death. I am sorry for that."

Shane shrugged. *I have been a dead man walking since I left that cell for the first time.* "And you plan that they should be binding the wrong person."

"Exactly. I will already be gone, back to hell but unbound. From there, I *think* that I can follow the faith of my people back."

"You think? You're not sure?"

"It's not as if I can test it. The only thing I know is that no demon comes back once the Dreaming God's people bind them to hell. This is the only way that I can think of that keeps both myself and my people free."

Unspoken between them was that Shane would be in a great deal more trouble if he *was* taken alive. The punishment for a paladin convicted of heresy was burning at the stake. It didn't happen often, but Shane had read too many tales of martyrs not to have some idea how that would work. *Better to die fighting.*

He only hoped that he didn't take too many of his old brethren with him when he did.

"Right," Marguerite said, late that night. She and the others had gathered in Magnus's quarters. The artificer had been given a large room on the ground floor, in deference to her difficulty with stairs. She had brewed a pot of tea and Marguerite had already checked the door twice to make sure no one was listening.

No one was. The Dreaming God's people were apparently even worse than the Saint of Steel about subterfuge. *No wonder they can't spot demons that are good at lying. Though I suppose if you're mostly expecting levitating cows, you don't have much experience.*

"Are we doing what I think we're doing?" asked Judith, in her almost eerily calm voice.

Marguerite eyed her warily. The new paladin was the wild card, and Marguerite still didn't know what to make of her. "Give me your word that what I say does not go beyond this room."

"Mmm." Judith considered it. "No."

Marguerite blinked at her. She wasn't used to flat denials like that. Usually people at least tried to lie. "What?"

"I said no." She crossed her hands over the hilt of her sword. "I will not give my word to that. Do you want me to leave?"

"No, I *want* your assistance." Marguerite rubbed her forehead and looked at Wren. "Help me here, Wren."

Wren screwed her face up in thought, then said, "Can you promise not to tell anyone for at least a day?"

Judith considered this. At least, Marguerite thought that she was considering it. Hadn't she thought Shane was hard to read once? Compared to this woman, he was an open book. Printed in large block letters. With accompanying illustrations.

"Very well," Judith said. "I will swear not to reveal what you say for a full day, unless it is necessary to save a life." She inclined her head to Marguerite. "Will that serve?"

"It'll do," said Marguerite fervently. "Since I'm trying to save a life here. Maybe you can help."

"Mmm. I assume that you wish to stage a suicidal raid on the demon's stronghold in order to extract our possibly-possessed brother before the Dreaming God's people kill him?"

Marguerite paused, her teacup halfway to her lips. "That was... succinct."

Judith raised one shoulder in a bare approximation of a shrug. Davith snorted into his tea.

I suppose it's not like it was hard to guess. I just hope that Jorge doesn't guess it too.

"I am not actually opposed," Judith said. "But do you truly believe that he is still in there?"

"It's *Shane,*" said Marguerite, frustrated that she didn't have a better argument to muster. "You *know* what he's like. Do you think he wouldn't fight against possession tooth and nail?"

"Fighting will not always serve," Judith said. "And having borne a demon is not easy. Do you think he would wish to survive?"

To Marguerite's surprise, Ashes Magnus was the one who spoke up. "I knew a paladin who was possessed once," she said. "Or had been possessed, anyhow. Nice lad. Ridiculously good-looking, and thicker than a short plank of wood, mind you." She pursed her lips. "Had an ass you could bounce a coin off."

There was a brief pause while everyone gave this comment the attention that it was due. Davith made a choking sound and took a hasty swig of tea to drown it.

"Anyway," said Magnus, "he's most of the reason we don't have clocktaurs anymore." She dropped a dollop of honey into her teacup and swirled it, ignoring all the eyes on her.

"After he was possessed?" Wren asked.

"*Because* he'd been possessed before," Magnus said. "Couldn't happen to him twice, apparently. Demons don't share or something like that." She gave a vast, almost tectonic shrug. "Don't ask me to explain it. I make machines. Demons are somebody else's problem."

"And this paladin was...happy?" Judith wanted to know. Marguerite looked up, slightly surprised by the question.

"Either happy or completely miserable," Ashes said. "But that was because he was madly in love, and like I said, thicker than a short plank of wood. That bit didn't have anything much to do with the demon either way."

Judith leaned back in her chair, expressionless once more.

"I'm just saying, don't write the lad off just because he's possessed. You never know."

"I'm not even sure it's the same sort of possession," Wren said. "He said it felt more like when the Saint would touch people. In his soul, not his mind. And the demon was still in somebody else's body. We saw it."

"If he's not really possessed, do you think they'll let him live?" Marguerite asked.

Judith and Wren looked at each other, then back at her. "Maybe," said Wren. "I won't swear that they won't shoot first and ask questions later."

"They are deeply committed to their purpose," Judith added.

"You can say that again," muttered Marguerite. She absolutely believed Jorge when he said that Shane was his friend, and she also absolutely believed that he would put a sword through the other man's heart without hesitation.

The truly infuriating thing was that she knew exactly why the Dreaming God's people were doing it, and under other circumstances, she would probably have agreed that it was the right thing to do.

Judith tapped her fingertips together. "Given what you say, I think there is a chance—a slim one, but a chance—that Shane can be saved from the demon. It is much more difficult to save someone from an arrow in the eye." She nodded. "I will help you."

Marguerite sagged with relief. There was something about Judith that inspired...not confidence, exactly. *She feels like a power. A strange, rather damaged power, to be sure, but one that I would much rather have on my side.*

"Right," said Marguerite. "Judith, Wren, we'll leave tonight. Davith..."

She glanced at him, shaking her head. "Go where you please. Any debt you owed me is long since paid. I'd prefer you didn't go running to the Sail to tell them about Ashes, but if you do, I suspect the paladins will be more than able to handle it."

"Oh, don't worry about me," said Ashes. "They loaned me a scribe this morning. There are three sets of instructions for my salt-maker already, and the scribe promised to make another dozen tonight. We'll send copies to every temple of the Forge God within a hundred miles." She looked more than a little smug.

Davith scowled fiercely, looked at Marguerite, looked at Wren, then looked at the ceiling. "Fine. That's fine. That's just fine. *Gaaaaah.*" He rapped his fingers on the arm of the chair, stood up, kicked over a footstool, set it back upright, then dropped into his chair again and muttered something almost too low for Marguerite to hear.

"What was that?" she asked.

"I *said,"* Davith growled, enunciating every word, *"I'll come with you."*

"What?" said Marguerite.

"What?" said Wren.

"Heh," said Ashes.

Judith said nothing, but one of her eyebrows lifted a fraction.

"The stupid armor-plated bastard saved my life, okay?" said Davith. "And I'm not saying I like him, but..." He made a frustrated gesture that was somehow both meaningless and surprisingly eloquent.

"My god, Davith, is that *guilt* I'm hearing?" asked Marguerite.

He glared at her. "I try to pay my debts. Besides, there's something you're forgetting."

"Oh?"

His annoyed expression vanished under a broad smile. "You're going to want to move fast, and I know for a fact that I'm the only one here who knows how to take care of a horse."

CHAPTER 50

"This plan is far too complicated," muttered Shane, looking over the battlements atop the single tower. "It has too many moving parts. Plans like that fail too easily."

Wisdom leaned against the stone beside him. "Probably," it agreed. "Are any of them fixable?"

The paladin sighed. It was an odd thing, but when he looked away from Wisdom, his body did not register the presence of another being beside him. His eyes and ears said that the demon existed, but his skin and his nerves did not.

"Probably not. What do you plan to do if they kill me before I get back to you?"

"There will be an archer stationed up here to shoot this body," said Wisdom tranquilly. "That, at least, I can plan for. And if the archer is lost, I will dash myself against the stones. But I would prefer to have you do it."

"Thanks," said Shane. "I think."

Wisdom grinned at him. "Take it as a compliment, paladin. Very few people are chosen to kill a god."

Which put him in mind of Lady Silver and Beartongue and the Saint. He hoped that Wren would be able to carry the news to the Temple of the Rat in his stead.

She'll do it. You know she'll do it, as long as she has breath in her body.

Worry about something you can control instead, like our defenses. What little there are of them.

Five of Wisdom's people were staying behind with him to present the illusion of a force defending the castle. Shane had been surprised to find Erlick among them.

"You're staying?"

"Got a cousin taking my niece," the older man said, clearing his throat. "She's good with kids. An' just good in general. She'll do right by her. Better'n I would. I ain't...I ain't good at that sort of thing."

"But—"

Erlick met his eyes, and Shane saw the dead light in them and closed his mouth.

The other five were much the same. One older man with a pronounced limp, who slapped his bad leg and said, matter-of-factly, that he was in so much pain that it would be a relief. Shane could see something seeping through the bandages on the man's foot and knew better than to ask. Two middle-aged women with eyes like Erlick's, who only grunted, and one very old grandmother who said that she was about dead anyway but by god, she could still put an arrow in a man's eye, just see if she couldn't.

The fifth was a young woman named Kasha, who had too-bright eyes and the hard, hacking cough of a consumptive. Wisdom informed him that she was to be the archer stationed on the roof.

"The plan may go badly if she has a coughing fit when she's supposed to be shooting you," Shane warned the demon.

"Have faith," Wisdom said, and laughed at the look the paladin gave her.

It took less time to reach Wisdom's keep than it had to leave it, partly because they had horses, partly because they were driven by panic. Their pace was limited mostly by Wren's mount, who was, without question, a plowhorse. Marguerite was fairly certain that Davith hadn't left money for it, and glumly added horse-theft to the tally of their crimes.

"Oh, don't worry," Davith said when she asked. "I told them I was taking it on the authority of the Dreaming God, and that the paladins behind us would make good."

"That's not any better."

"On the contrary, it's *marvelous.*"

Judith, who seemed as humorless as a stone, actually snickered, so Marguerite gave up. *It's not like we can get in any hotter water with the temple. They must know that we're going to warn him.*

It's a good thing they don't have access to divine horseflesh, or we'd be in so much trouble right now.

As it was, they used the horses badly, and Marguerite felt badly for it. "I will make it up to you," she told her mount. They alternated walking and trotting, getting off to walk alongside, over and over, as long as daylight lasted. The hills were green and rolling and beautiful and Marguerite hated them for it. "When this is over," she said, "I am going to find a forest. Or a desert. Or the ocean. Anything but this." A marmot whistled at her in alarm. "Sod off," she told it.

Wren snorted. So did Davith. Judith smiled her small smile that did not rearrange any of her facial features in any way.

Somehow, after an eternity, they found themselves at the river that marked the edge of Wisdom's territory.

"Right," said Davith. "How are we going to approach them, anyway? Seeing as the last time, a bunch of people got turned into pincushions."

"White flag," said Marguerite. She dug out a handkerchief that had been white once and now might, with charity, have been called grubby cream. "I'll need a flagpole."

"Ah, yes," said Davith, looking around the landscape. "I'll just cut one from one of these many, many trees, shall I?"

Judith, more practical or at least less sarcastic, dismounted and chopped at one of the scruffy bushes that clung to the river's edge. The resulting flagpole was about two feet long and less than half an inch thick. Marguerite felt as if she was waving a toy flag at a parade. Nevertheless, she hoisted her flag high as they approached the keep. *And here's hoping that white flags mean peace here, and not, "We've come to murder everyone down to the sheep."*

No one shot them. That was, she felt, a positive sign.

They drew up in front of the large double doors and waited.

And waited.

"Do you think they know we're here?" asked Davith.

"They know," said Judith flatly.

They waited longer. The stone walls were too thick to hear activity. Marguerite scanned the outbuildings, looking for signs of life. *They can't have moved, can they? I mean, the demon must know that the Dreaming God's people will be coming, so moving might be* sensible, *but...*

She had just started to run through the ramifications of having stolen horses from the Dreaming God's temple in order to aid and abet a demon, only to find no demon to aid and abet, when one of the doors opened and Shane strode out to meet them.

He looked surprisingly well. The demon apparently hadn't been torturing him. The blue hollows under his eyes were deeper, and he'd stopped shaving and now had a few days growth of badger on his face, but he didn't have the half-dead look that, say, the possessed bull had had.

Shane walked up to Marguerite's horse, caught her stirrup, and she gazed into his eyes, feeling her heart melt, feeling *I love you* waiting on her tongue, and then he said, in horrified tones, "You can't be here!"

Marguerite swallowed the *I love you* and felt it burn on the way down.

"*Judith?!* Did they rope you into this, too?"

Judith shrugged eloquently. "You know how it is."

"Yes—no—oh, Dreaming God have mercy." He pinched the bridge of his nose. "You have to go. You can't be here."

"The Dreaming God's exactly who isn't going to have mercy," said Marguerite tartly, sliding off her horse. He caught her reflexively and his body still remembered how to hold her, even if his mouth was saying foolish things. "They're probably no more than a day or two behind us, and they're coming with archers because they plan to *shoot* you."

"Sensible of them," he said. Her ear was pressed against his chest and he had his arms around her. She closed her eyes, feeling as if a weight had lifted off her, which was ridiculous because things were, if anything, worse than ever. Fighting the Red Sail was one thing. Fighting the Dreaming God was another, and there was no way that she was on the right side and she knew it, but at the moment, it didn't seem to matter.

"I told you I'd come back for you," she said.

Judith also dismounted, stepped up, and leaned forward until she was staring into Shane's eyes and was an inch from squashing Marguerite between them. "Um," said Marguerite.

"You're not possessed, exactly," said Judith slowly, "but there *is* something..."

Shane sighed. "No. And yes. It's like the channel with the god was. In the same place. Except that it's Wisdom on the other side of it." He gently released Marguerite and rubbed his face. "It's not the same as the god, but...Judith, Wisdom stopped me from killing an innocent when the tide rose. Exactly the same way."

"Hmmm," said Judith. "Interesting." And while Marguerite hadn't yet learned to read Judith's expressions—the paladin was a book not just closed, but locked and barred and possibly encased in lead—she thought that there was something rather more than interest in her tone.

"But you have to leave," said Shane, gathering himself. "You have to get away from here. They're going to come and kill Wisdom and if you stay, you'll get yourselves killed. And they'll probably think you're possessed in the bargain."

"But they're going to kill you!" said Marguerite indignantly.

"I *know* that!"

Wren cleared her throat. "If we knock you out, we can maybe just convince them to exorcise you?" she said hopefully.

Shane groaned. "You don't understand. I have to stay. It's the only way to make sure that—" He clamped his teeth on whatever he was about to say next, to Marguerite's frustration.

"That *what?*"

"It doesn't matter. It's fine. I know what the risks are. And you can't stay here."

Marguerite threw her hands in the air. "We pretty much sold out the Dreaming God to come talk to you, so you better figure something out!"

His skin, already pale, went the color of skim milk. "You what?"

"Stole horses and everything," said Wren, with unholy cheer.

"I left a note," said Davith.

Shane's mouth worked but no sound came out.

"Just let us rescue you!" hissed Marguerite.

"You *can't* rescue me!" He raked his hands through his hair. "Don't you understand? Even if I went with you, the Dreaming God's people would hunt me to the ends of the earth! We'd have to flee to—to—I don't know, to Morstone or Toxocan or Lady Silver's homeland!"

"Fine! Then let's go there! I don't have any pressing reasons to stay around here!" Which, thinking of Grace, was a lie, and the gods only knew what she'd do for money, but those were problems for a future Marguerite to deal with.

Shane's eyes flickered, and for a minute, she thought he might actually agree. "Oh Dreaming God," he said, as if the words were dragged out of him. "And they warned us that *demons* might tempt us..."

"Please," she said. "I need you." She drew a deep, shuddering breath. "I feel safe when I'm with you."

His eyes were the color of frost but the heat in them seared her to the bone. "Marguerite..."

A voice called over the battlements, "Hey! Do we shoot 'em?"

"No!" Shane grabbed Marguerite and hefted her back into the saddle. Since her options were to sit on the horse or fall off the other side, she chose to sit on the horse. "I will do anything to keep you safe," he told her. "And right now, you have to leave. Wisdom's coming." He pressed the heel of his hand against his sternum as if it pained him.

"But—"

He gripped her calf and took a shuddering breath. "It means the world to me that you came back," he said. "I don't know what I did to deserve such loyalty. From any of you." His gaze swept the group, lingering briefly on Davith. "I'll keep out of easy arrow shot. I'll carry a shield. But you have to *go*. It isn't safe here, and it's about to be much worse."

Marguerite would have kept arguing, but Judith leaned forward, caught her horse's reins, and tugged on them. "Right," the tall woman said. "We're going." She nodded down at Shane. "I can't wish you luck, but I hope you know what you're doing."

"So do I," said Shane grimly. "So do I."

She'd come back for him. Shane could hardly believe it. She hadn't abandoned him, even though it would have been the smartest thing she could possibly do. She'd come back to try to save him.

The thought made him giddy, made him want to run in circles and laugh and dance and weep and maybe punch something. It felt like falling in love for the first time, and even though it was hopeless and useless and he knew that he was going to die in the next few days and that she'd put herself in terrible danger, he couldn't help but feel it.

If I'm going to die, at least I won't die abandoned. Maybe it wouldn't matter at all, once he was dead, but it mattered now.

"You're in a good mood," Wisdom said, as he entered the keep.

Much of his giddiness drained away. "Oh. Um."

"Relax," the demon said. "I have no intention of snatching your lady love and your friends back. You're the only one I wanted."

"It was too dangerous for them to be here," Shane said. "The Dreaming God's people are coming." He sighed, remembering what Marguerite had said. "And they're planning on just shooting me from a distance if they can."

"Well, then," said Wisdom. "We'll just have to make sure they won't get the chance, won't we?"

"That rescue could have gone better," Davith said.

"Davith," said Marguerite, with marvelous calm, "if you say one more word, I am going to *slap* you off that horse."

He held up his hands in surrender. Marguerite hunched down in the saddle, feeling as if there was a ball of ice in her gut. It wasn't as if he was wrong. She'd made a mess of everything. Shane hadn't wanted to be rescued. He'd rather stay with a demon than with her. Because of duty, no doubt. *God forbid a paladin ever be happy when there's duty about.*

Worse, she'd dragged the others down with her. The Dreaming God's people were going to be furious.

Well, Marguerite had her own sense of duty. She'd fall on that sword, say that she'd forced them. Wren, at least, was sworn to her service and ought to get off lightly, and she could claim to have been blackmailing Davith. Judith...she wasn't quite sure what to do about Judith. It would come to her, though. She'd come up with a story, and then the Dreaming God could bring her up on charges or have her thrown in the stockade or whatever they did. Whatever a stockade was. She supposed she'd find out.

These thoughts kept her company as far as the river, where she stopped and looked up, because there was a small army waiting on the far side.

They were, very politely, taken into custody. Jorge came up, accompanied by Sir, and Marguerite immediately said, "This is my fault."

"Oh, we figured," said Jorge. Sir snorted explosively.

The bearded priest that they had seen before, Burnet, looked closely in their eyes, then back at Jorge and Sir, and shrugged. "If I saw them on the street, I wouldn't think they were possessed. But this is a very old and very subtle one, and if it went into one of them willingly, I can't swear that I'd know. I'd suggest taking them back to the temple to be sure, assuming that we don't find it lurking in someone else."

"Mmm," said Sir. "The two paladins, would you clear them to fight alongside us?"

Burnet considered this. "I would, actually. If they are possessed, better we find out when there's a half-dozen paladins with drawn swords around them."

"You make a very valid point." Sir looked to Wren and Judith. "Will you help us winkle your brother out of this shell?"

"As long as you don't mind if I hit him on the head instead of running him through," said Judith.

"I'd consider that fair." He gestured to the people around him--six paladins, two priests, four crossbowmen and a half-dozen grooms, plus an inordinate number of horses. "Given how few we were able to field, I won't turn down your help."

"Then I won't refuse it," said Judith. Wren looked up from where she was picking nervously at her nails, gave a bare nod, and looked back down again.

"But how did you get here so *fast?*" asked Marguerite. "We rode as fast as we could and we didn't spend more than ten minutes at the keep..."

"Remounts," said Jorge, waving to the horses. "Three each. We picked up the bowmen on the way. But you say you've actually been to the keep?"

"I'm sorry," said Marguerite, "but I had to try to get Shane away."

"I take it you didn't succeed?" asked Jorge.

"No. He wouldn't come with us and he wouldn't let us in. He said it was too dangerous to be there."

"Either the demon's smart, or he is," said Sir, and walked away to shout at one of the grooms for something horse-related. Jorge shrugged.

"Err...you're not mad?" asked Marguerite.

Jorge heaved a sigh. "Let's say that I'm exasperated. But you haven't taken holy orders *and* you're civilians. You'll have to stay with us long enough for the priests to be absolutely certain that a demon didn't jump to you." He grimaced. "Some of the others are pretty mad. I...well, I understand why you tried."

"But we stole your horses!"

"It's fine," said Jorge, "Davith left a note."

"See, I *told* her..."

Marguerite squared her shoulders. "Then I'm going into the fight with you."

"Like hell you are."

"Shane won't hurt me."

Jorge scowled at her. "Which, if we were just fighting Shane, might be important. But an arrow doesn't care who it hits."

"You'll take Wren and Judith, though?"

"Wren and Judith are trained fighters. You're a trained..." Jorge trailed off, apparently realizing that he had no idea what Marguerite did.

"Negotiator," said Marguerite, which was only adjacent to a lie, not the real thing.

It was, unfortunately, the wrong thing to say. "We don't negotiate with demons," said Jorge stiffly.

"Fine, then use me as a human shield once we're inside!"

Jorge looked appalled at the very suggestion. So did Wren. Judith looked like Judith, but there was something slightly tighter in the set of her mouth.

"I'm actually fine with staying back," Davith volunteered.

"Listen," said Marguerite desperately, "you still have to make sure we aren't possessed, right?"

"Ideally, yes."

"So you'll either need to leave someone to guard us—and you *know* you haven't got enough people—or you let us follow along. Because otherwise Davith and I are going to light out of here and lead you on a chase through the hills for *weeks.*"

"This woman does not speak for me," Davith said.

Jorge's scowl deepened to consume his whole face. "Unless we hogtie you and carry you over the saddle."

"I believe my bodyguard would object to that," said Marguerite, elbowing Wren in the ribs.

"Huh?" said Wren. "Oh, yes. I would. Very much."

Jorge appeared to be marshalling further arguments when Burnet the priest slapped him on the back. "Let them come," he said. "If your paladin friend has as many archers as they say, they may hold back for fear of hitting them, and that's all to the good."

"Or they may catch a stray arrow!"

Burnet shrugged. "They're adults," he said. "Madam, may I assume that you know that you may well die if you insist on accompanying us?"

"You assume correctly."

"Again," Davith began, "this woman does not—"

"Our job is to exorcise demons," Burnet said, "not to stop people from doing foolish things. Madam Florian appears neither hysterical nor deluded, and there is a chance her presence will help." He inclined his head.

Jorge's expression indicated that he hated every bit of this, but he nodded grudgingly. "As you say, then. Marguerite, Davith, you may accompany us, but stay *back.* And don't get in anyone's way." He stalked away, stomping hard enough to make his armor jingle.

"Don't mind him," said Burnet. "His sense of chivalry is overdeveloped when it comes to beautiful women." He winked at Marguerite. "He doesn't much like priests being in the first wave either, but fortunately these days I outrank him. I, too, will be in the back. I suggest you stay close to me."

"But..." Davith said.

"And now," said Burnet, "I suggest you get a meal and as much sleep as you can, because night attacks are the worst."

CHAPTER 51

Burnet was right. Night attacks were the worst. It was too dark for the horses to see, so they walked, except for one draft horse decked out in plate mail and carrying an oddly shaped burden across its back. One of the paladins in the lead had a long pole that he swept back and forth, checking for ground-wights.

Marguerite only hoped that it was also too dark to be shot.

As it turned out, she was mostly right, because they had started up the incline toward the keep itself before the first arrow came zipping out of the dark and embedded itself in the ground.

"Shields up!" called Sir, and the paladins lifted large shields over their heads and continued forward. Wren and Judith had been issued similar shields of their own, though Wren's was nearly as tall as she was. The armored horse seemed unconcerned by any of it.

Burnet had a smaller shield, which he held up like an umbrella, and Marguerite and Davith tried to fit under it. "I hate shields," the priest said cheerfully. "But it's so hard to knife an arrow."

More arrows landed around them. Some hit the shields. One lucky shot got through and took a crossbowman in the shoulder. He swore. So did Sir.

"I love this shield," said Davith. "Deeply. Fervently."

Marguerite hated all of it. This was the sort of thing she feared the most—death landing at random, impossible to talk to or negotiate with. She wanted to stand up and shout, "Everyone stop! Let's discuss this!" but she didn't because that seemed like an excellent way to be the target of every archer atop the keep.

They reached the front door without losing anyone else, though one of the paladins was clutching an ear that bled from an arrow graze. Under a roof of shields, the horse was relieved of its burden, while everyone else pressed against the walls to present the worst possible angle for anyone shooting down. Wren came over to offer what little cover she could with her shield, which helped, but Marguerite still felt as if her knees and elbows were not only exposed but glowing. Possibly with writing that said, "Shoot here."

An arrow thunked into Burnet's shield and he winced. "Would one of you like to hold this for a bit?" he asked. "My arms are incredibly tired." Davith took it. Marguerite settled practically into his lap to take advantage of the cover, and her only consolation was that Davith probably wasn't enjoying it either.

The horse had been carrying a small battering ram. Four paladins grabbed it, and the fifth, still bleeding from his ear, shuffled the horse out of the way. Marguerite hoped that even in the gritty gray light of predawn, the archers on the roof wouldn't target the animal.

Thunk. The ram hit the doors, which shuddered. *Thunk.*

Why am I even here? What am I hoping to do?

Stupid question. She was hoping to find a way to negotiate. To leap in at the last minute between Shane and the crossbow bolts and demand that they talk to each other. Which, realistically, she had very little hope of doing. *But if I was sitting back at the river, I'd have no hope at all. And Shane* won't *hurt me. And even these people won't shoot through me to get at him. I think.*

Thunk.

An archer leaned out too far and one of the crossbowmen shot them. There was a shriek of pain, but no falling body.

"If you throw down your arms and surrender the demon, you will be treated fairly!" roared Sir.

The voice that came back over the wall was thin and wavering, clearly an old woman's voice, but her words came through clearly. "Go piss up a rope, you armor-plated son of a bitch!"

Thunk. Thunk. Thunk.

"On the bright side," said Burnet, "they don't seem to have had time to boil any oil."

"Was that a *possibility?*"

"Oh yes. If they aren't through in a few minutes, we'll probably at least get some tea kettles worth of boiling water dumped on us."

Davith began to pray with more sincerity than Marguerite had ever heard him express about anything.

Crash!

The doors gave way and the paladins poured inside the keep, followed by the crossbowmen, followed, with much trepidation, by two priests, and Marguerite and Davith.

The paladins split into two groups as soon as they were inside the keep, taking a priest and two crossbowmen with them. Marguerite and Davith clung to Burnet's side, in the group that included (thankfully) Jorge and Wren and did not include (thankfully) Sir. They also had the injured bowman, who had wrapped his shoulder but was obviously not going to be shooting anyone any time soon.

Judith had gone with the other group, as Sir apparently did not wish to leave the two potentially possessed berserkers together. Marguerite's group went up a flight of steps, reached a landing, and then someone shot across the top of the stairs, fired an arrow down, and kept going. A paladin let out a strangled sound, snapped off the shaft of the arrow that had pierced his forearm, and growled, "No, don't worry, I'm fine. Keep going."

Jorge glanced back at the group and nodded once. The crossbowman said, sounding surly, "No, I didn't have time to get a shot off, not with you lot in the way. They were firing blind and got lucky, that's all."

At the top of the stairs, they faced a corridor running in both directions. Whoever was in charge—Marguerite was no longer sure—took them right. Through the press of bodies, she could see doors being opened, presumably in a fashion that minimized being unexpectedly murdered, and the rooms checked for people.

Two more arrows were fired at them, one from either direction. "Hold!" Jorge snapped, when it looked as if a paladin might run after one of the archers. "If we get separated and led into a trap, we're done for."

Which was good tactical advice, no doubt, but one of the arrows passed so closely by Wren's head that Marguerite let out a startled yelp and Wren herself jerked back and nearly bashed the back of her head into the wall.

I hate this, I hate this, I hate this so much...

Stop that. Get hold of yourself. You've sent people into danger before, you can damn well deal with it yourself. It's only right.

Marguerite took a deep breath and told herself that she was firmly in control of her emotions, whereupon the world slewed sideways as Wren kicked her feet out from under her, vaulted over her falling body, and buried an axe in the face of the man who had just leapt out of a side room that was supposed to be empty. He dropped his sword across Marguerite's shins, fell heavily backward, and died.

Marguerite gave herself up to the panic for a moment. Davith and Burnet hauled her to her feet and someone was saying something that she couldn't hear through the ringing in her ears. Were there more stairs? There must have been, because when she could focus again, they weren't in the same hallway and there wasn't a dead man at her feet, though Wren was still splattered liberally with someone else's blood.

The smallest voice in the back of Marguerite's mind said, *If you can't save Shane, you're going to have to hire Wren as your permanent bodyguard or you're never going to feel remotely safe ever again.*

This wasn't the most appealing prospect. Marguerite liked Wren quite a lot but there were very few people she didn't get tired of after weeks on end. Actually, the only ones she could think of were Grace and...Shane.

Which is why you're here. Doing a dreadfully unsafe thing. So that you can feel safe.

The absurdity of that made her snort and she shook herself off, feeling as if she was stepping out of cold water. "Thanks," she said to Wren.

Wren grinned briefly. "It's what you pay me for."

"I haven't been paying you, but I'll double it."

"Heh."

There was a short flight of steps leading down at the end of the hallway. Which made no sense at all, but Marguerite had lost track of the architecture by now. Sloppy. Her days of lifting paperwork had taught her better than that, surely.

Once down the stairs, the paladins started opening doors again. The rooms were all empty, but Marguerite's stomach clenched with every door, until she was almost ready for another arrow, just to break the tension.

Then they opened a door and a man lunged out with a knife in each hand.

Marguerite had an instant to recognize Erlick before he swiped at the lead paladin. The man swung his shield around to deflect, and to Marguerite's horror, Erlick threw himself sideways, blades flashing—directly onto the paladin's sword.

The paladin had no time to appreciate his victory. He had moved his shield and that mistake proved fatal. Two arrows came from farther down the hall. One took him in the throat and the other buried itself in the uninjured crossbowman and dropped him like a stone. His weapon fired when it hit the ground, the bolt shattering against the far wall.

"*Got* you, you son of a bitch," whispered Erlick, and then blood poured out of his mouth and he died.

"Shit!" Jorge reached for his comrade, saw at once that it was hopeless, and turned to the other man. Burnet was already rising, shaking his head.

For the first time, it occurred to Marguerite that possibly it wasn't Shane who had needed rescuing.

Davith picked up the dead paladin's shield, but it was a smaller and more nervous party that went forward after that. Marguerite felt horribly guilty, even though she knew that there was nothing she could have done.

The sound of clashing metal reached them, and Jorge's head jerked up. "This way!" he said, and broke into a run. The others followed behind him, Wren in the rear, her eyes shining with that odd, flat light that presaged the battle tide.

By the time they reached the source of the sound, the fight was over. Two paladins and a crossbowman stood there, along with Judith and a very worried looking priest. One of those paladins was kneeling on the floor with a crossbow bolt in his back, holding himself in the peculiar stillness of a man who, if he doesn't move an inch, hopes to live a few minutes longer.

"What the hell happened?" demanded Jorge.

"Your *friend* happened," spat the uninjured paladin, slinging his warhammer back over his shoulder. "Trisk had him blade to blade when Wylie here took his shot, and the bastard moved like a snake and yanked Trisk in front of him, then ran off."

"I am *extremely* sorry," said the unfortunate Wylie.

"Nothing you could have done," breathed the even more unfortunate Trisk.

"Where's the marshal?"

"Took an arrow in the thigh." The uninjured paladin looked even more disgusted. "Missed anything vital, but if he tried to walk out on it, it wouldn't stay that way for long. We stashed him in a room with the other fellow with the crossbow."

"...Right." Jorge nodded. "Which way did Shane go?"

The paladin pointed. "We've taken out two archers," he said. "You?"

"Two armed men."

"How they can use those bows in this tight little space..."

"They know the place. We don't." Jorge squared his shoulders. "All right. Frederick, stay here with the wounded." The injured bowman nodded. "Everyone else, with me. Three of us, one bowman, two priests, two berserkers. And one of him. Let's go."

They didn't have to go far. Shane was waiting at the top of the next staircase. Blood had sheeted down the side of his head and though he stood stock-still, the air around him seemed to vibrate.

"Shane," said Jorge, very calmly, "you don't want to do this."

"You're right," said Shane. "I don't. But it doesn't seem like we have much choice."

At the foot of the staircase, Jorge held up his sword like a cross and said, *"KNEEL."*

Shane staggered sideways and caught himself against the wall. The two remaining paladins charged up the steps, weapons at the ready, but

Shane was already back on his feet. He lifted his head, his face a bloody mask, and roared, *"Come and make me!"*

In the silence that followed, Marguerite heard Jorge say, not very loudly, "Dammit, I really wanted that to work."

The crossbowman next to her lifted his weapon and took aim, waiting for a clear shot. "No!" Marguerite hissed.

He jerked back, startled. "What?"

"You'll kill him!"

"That's the idea, yes!"

The other bowman didn't waste time arguing. Marguerite's heart clenched at the loud thrum of the string, and was inordinately relieved when it struck Shane's shield instead.

She didn't get long to be relieved. Shane threw his shield down the steps, into the face of one of his opponents, slashed at the other one, then turned and ran.

Baying like hounds, the three remaining paladins of the Dreaming God gave chase.

Come on...come on...just a little farther... Shane's breath was coming in sharp pants, but he was almost there. If he could avoid taking a bolt long enough to reach the courtyard, he'd be in place for the final act of Wisdom's little play.

It had been far too easy to play his part. He had dreaded crossing swords with his counterparts, until Kasha had staggered into his arms, coughing up blood even as she reported that two of her fellow archers were dead. Suddenly it had seemed a great deal easier. He only hoped that she'd made it to the roof in time.

Only one flight of steps and a corridor remained. The corridor was the worst. If Jorge had any sense, he'd order—

A crossbow bolt sizzled past his ear, close enough to tug at his hair.

—that.

The tide took him, sending him careening like a drunk down the hallway, harder to hit. They had to follow him, but he wasn't going to do any good if he was full of holes by the time he got there. *Just a little farther...*

He turned the last corner, led on by the inexorable tug of the demon on his soul, and—*there!*

Shane raced through the archway into the courtyard and stumbled. Wisdom hung suspended in the air, arms outstretched, unnaturally still as only a demon could be. Even knowing what to expect, his first instinct was to freeze in his tracks.

With the Dreaming God's people in hot pursuit, that would be tantamount to suicide. He caught himself and went forward instead. One quick glance upward, and he saw the archer standing there, arrow nocked and ready.

Wisdom hung in midair as he circled her. He heard the moment that the paladins arrived, heard the shouts of dismay and the stumble of feet as they halted.

Slowly, slowly, the demon descended. Shane caught it just as its feet touched the ground, and it sagged back into his arms. Across the channel, he felt the demon signal its readiness.

Not yet...not yet...

He looked over the demon's shoulder to the paladins standing at the entrance to the courtyard. In another life, they might have been his brothers.

In this life...

Shane took a deep breath and shouted "Be prepared to bind it!" and rammed the sword low through Wisdom's body. Through the gut, where it would be fatal, but not, potentially for hours.

"I'm sorry," he whispered in the demon's ear, as he turned himself to shield against a shot from the archer on the roof. "I will save your people, but I cannot let you go unbound."

My god broke faith with me, but I will not break faith with my god.

He waited for pain, for punishment, for agony. Through the channel came a wash of sadness instead. Sadness—but no surprise.

The Dreaming God's paladins ran toward him. Shane eased the falling body down and looked up into their ranks. Three paladins, with faces like avenging angels. "Bind it now," he urged them. "That blow won't kill it, but I can't swear it won't try to jump."

For a moment, they stood frozen, and then Jorge moved. He dropped to his knees next to Shane, slapped his palm against Wisdom's forehead...and stopped.

"What?" said Shane. "What's wrong?"

Something was wrong. It wasn't the Dreaming God's people. It wasn't the channel with Wisdom. It was the body itself, so unnaturally still in his arms, not the stillness of a demon but a different stillness entirely.

He grabbed the tip of his glove in his teeth and yanked it loose, laying his hand alongside Jorge's. The other paladin didn't flinch, merely gazed at him steadily. His skin was hot, slick with sweat, but the skin beneath both their palms was the same temperature as the surrounding air.

"It's dead," Shane said numbly. "It's already dead."

I knew you'd never actually turn on them, Wisdom whispered through the channel.

"Where is it then?" said Jorge. "Where did it jump?"

"I..." Shane shook his head slowly. "I don't know. It said it wanted me to kill it so that it could get back to hell without being bound. But it knew I was going to betray it. It *knew.*"

Jorge ground his teeth together, then slumped. He leaned forward, looking deeply into Shane's eyes for a moment, then reached out and gripped his shoulder. "You should have known better than to deal with a demon," he said, almost gently.

"I did know," Shane said. He could already feel its presence draining away. "It was the only way to save the others."

"I know why you did it. The Dreaming God prevent me from ever having to make the same choice...*NOW STAND.*"

Shane felt only the reflexive twitch of obedience that any ordinary human felt. He stayed on his knees. Jorge sighed and rubbed his forehead. "I can't tell," he muttered. "Dreaming God help me, I can't tell. The taint is there, but I don't see the demon in you, but it was old and subtle and we were friends..."

"We were," said Shane, acknowledging the past tense.

"We have our orders," said one of the other paladins. Shane didn't recognize him. *No surprise there, really, it's been a long time and there were always far more servants of the Dreaming God than the Saint.*

"Right." Jorge took a deep breath. "The priests felt that you were too dangerous to leave alive. Probably I should kill you now. But you've surrendered, and so I must give you the choice. The water or the sword."

A clean death, or being drowned over and over until I die and the demon leaves me. But there is no demon in me. The thought of his own death no longer had much power to move him, but where had Wisdom gone?

And then, suddenly, he knew. Shane lifted his eyes, past Jorge, past the other paladins, to the roofline, where the archer was already gone.

CHAPTER 52

The demon that called itself Wisdom hurried through the empty hallways of the keep. It was fairly certain that the paladin would keep his brethren busy for some time, whether he intended to or not.

Wisdom bore the human Shane no ill will. Indeed, it had rather liked him. He was so desperately confused, and yet so doggedly persistent that every time he did manage to work something out, it wanted to cheer. He reminded Wisdom of the demon's own early, faltering steps in the world, when everything was new and terrible and strange, when every feeling registered with blinding intensity.

Well, it had done the best it could. It rather hoped that Shane would survive. Humans did such terrible things to each other, and it regretted having to leave him to his brethren's mercies. But that was nothing compared to what they did to demons, and Wisdom would not allow itself to be bound to hell forever.

It was just congratulating itself on its escape when something came out of nowhere and sliced through the tendons in the back of its host's legs. Pain flared through its consciousness, pain so intense that it felt like another sense had opened up and drunk in a thousand shades of agony. Wisdom wrenched itself back from the pain, shutting down its host's senses as fast as it could. *No more pleasant for her than me,* it thought. It was currently ascendant in the body, of necessity, but it would have been cruel to let its host feel pain that Wisdom itself could shut out.

When the pain was shut down, the demon became aware of the next sense, which was cold stone against the host's cheek. It rolled and sat up gingerly. Its host's head did not feel right. *We slammed into the floor very hard. The skull has moved in ways it should not.*

It knew already that it could not run. Its attacker had cut vital tendons. Many injuries could simply be ignored once you knew how, but this was not one of them. The legs no longer worked right. It would have to crawl.

Damnation, it might even have to kill its host and go back to hell after all. What a miserable thought.

Its vision was not working well, but it managed to focus its host's eyes on its attacker, which loomed over it like an avenging angel.

The human was female, taller than its current host, with hair that tinted red-brown in the light. Her soul was strange. It did not extend far enough past her skin. Wisdom's experience with humans was that their souls surrounded them like the corona of a star. Shane's, for example, had blazed out in a halo of silver and violet, a good six inches from his body.

This human's was tightly compressed inside herself, barely a glow along her own skin. When Wisdom reached out, she felt...*dense.* As if there was too much soul clamped in too tightly. How very odd.

Still, humans were odd and Wisdom knew it had not encountered even a tenth of the variations among them. This was just another kind, it seemed. Wisdom ran its senses over the strange new human and saw something unexpected. A channel, just above her heart, as scarred and closed as Shane's had been. *Another paladin? You do find them flocking together, like sheep or sparrows.*

"Listen to me," said the new paladin, her voice flat and cold. "You are going to do what I say."

"Am I?" asked Wisdom. "You seem very sure of that."

"You will," said the paladin, "because if you do not, I will sever your spine *here.*" A cold kiss of blade against the skin that covered its host's upper vertebrae. The body wanted to shudder and Wisdom allowed it. "Then I will summon the Dreaming God's people, while you remain trapped, and they will bind you."

Wisdom considered this. It was a fine threat, but it failed to account for one particular possibility. It wondered if it should bother pointing this out to the human. Wise or unwise? Was the human being foolish or did she have some other plan? Did she think that she could prevent herself from becoming possessed? *Perhaps against one of my lesser brethren your will would be enough, but I am something else entirely, human.*

In the end, it spoke simply because it was curious how she would react. "You realize, do you not, that I could simply jump to your body?"

"Yes," the human said, leaning in. The point of the knife stroked underneath its body's chin. "That is exactly what I am counting on."

This was unexpected. Wisdom was fascinated and also, it had to admit, somewhat charmed. "I am listening."

"The first thing you are going to do," Judith said, "is let my brother go."

"Please," said Jorge pleadingly. "Choose. The water or the sword?"

"Perform the rite," said one of the others. "We're wasting valuable time." He carried a warhammer instead of a sword and there was blood splattered across his gauntlets. Shane wondered which of Wisdom's faithful had bled and died for that.

"He has the right to—" Jorge began.

And then something happened inside Shane's chest, something so sharp and shocking that he looked down, expecting to see that Jorge had simply stabbed him after all. Except that there was no blade and no blood and the sensation was horribly familiar, something that he had felt once before, on the day that the god had died.

For two heartbeats it didn't even hurt. It was almost too big to hurt. Then his heart squeezed a third time and pain tore through him and he screamed.

Like a barbed arrow in the soul. That was how it was usually described, having a demon torn out of you. He'd even used that description himself. Now Shane marveled at the sheer uselessness of it. This hurt like being ripped in two, like dying or being born, on and on, forever.

He kept screaming, of course. No amount of pride would have stopped him. Pride could not have touched a pain like this. The last time it had happened, the tide had risen and he had attacked someone, then lost consciousness. There was no tide now, no merciful unconsciousness, only Wisdom leaving and tearing him apart in its wake.

And then, as suddenly as it had come, it was over. Shane collapsed backward, his breath coming in thin rasps. The inside of his chest felt as if it had been scalded raw, and the memory of pain was so vivid that it was almost pain itself.

Jorge was half on top of him. It didn't occur to Shane to wonder why until the other paladin sat up, one arm still pinning his chest. *Was I having a seizure? Perhaps I was.*

"That," Jorge said grimly, "was a demon leaving the hard way, I think."

"Or that's what it *wants* us to think," said the one with the warhammer.

Jorge ignored him. "Shane? Can you hear me?"

"I hear you," Shane croaked. Blackness edged the corner of his vision, but it seemed that he still was not allowed to faint. He managed to lift a hand—Warhammer took a step forward—and rubbed his chest. "Feels like...I...drank hot lead..."

"Can you sit up?"

"Stop this." Warhammer loomed over them both. "Jorge, we have our orders. I know he's your friend, but the kindest thing you can do is end it quickly."

"If the demon's gone, there's no need—"

"And what if it isn't?" Warhammer folded his arms. "Do you really want another massacre on your hands? A berserker Caliban?"

Jorge bit his lip.

"It's fine," Shane rasped. He had been hollowed out and the most he could feel was a distant pity. *Perhaps once I'm dead, it'll stop hurting so much.* "Do what you need to do."

And then he heard a familiar voice and Marguerite catapulted across the space between them, her hair flying around her face, shouting, *"Don't you dare!"*

Jorge put his face in his hands. Marguerite dropped to her knees next to Shane. Shane looked over at her, which meant that he was mostly looking into her cleavage. He was aware that at some other point in his life, he would have appreciated that very much. It was a shame he couldn't feel much of anything right now.

Then Warhammer grabbed Marguerite's shoulder and Shane found that he was, in fact, still capable of feeling something.

The tide was less of a tide and more of a thin trickle of darkness. If he sat up, he could grab Warhammer's ankle and *pull* and then *wrench* and the man would fall back and then...then it wouldn't matter because he probably couldn't sit up.

Jorge reached out a quelling hand. "Matthias, let her go."

"Are we sure the demon didn't jump to her instead? She's the only one here who isn't one of us."

"I swear by all that's holy," said Marguerite, in a clear, cold voice, "I will make you *eat* that hammer if you don't stop acting like a jackass."

Oh Dreaming God, no. If they thought Wisdom had jumped to Marguerite, then it would be her turn to choose the water or the sword. *Dreaming God, please, I know that I failed You, but please, please,* listen—

And then, quite suddenly, Shane was somewhere else.

The air was made of silver fire. Shane stood within it, sheathed in flame, and knew that he should be burning, but was not. It encircled him like fog, bright and cool and blinding.

Little brother, said a voice that he heard inside his chest and through the soles of his feet as much as with his ears. *It has been too long.*

He knew that voice. It had never spoken to him, and yet he had heard it echoing behind the words of others for the first seventeen years of his life.

"Dreaming God?" he whispered.

Yes.

Shane went to his knees, or perhaps he had already been on his knees. It was hard to tell. There was no ground, only the cool silver fire in every direction.

"Lord," Shane choked out, then stopped. What could he say? He had willingly consorted with a demon. *Any* holy order would find such a thing anathema, but for the Dreaming God, Whose paladins existed solely to root out demonkind wherever they were found... Shane stared at the silver light between his hands and closed his eyes against it.

Why do you not speak, little brother?

"Lord, I have done terrible things."

Yes.

"I bargained with a demon to save my friends."

I know.

"I fought Your chosen to buy time for the demon's followers to escape."

I know.

There was no censure in the god's voice, only statement of fact. Shane felt the silver light blazing against his eyelids and opened them again. "Why aren't You *angry?*" he cried, and realized that he *wanted* the god to be angry with him, because...because...

Because you are angry with Me, little brother.

Part of Shane knew that he had no right to be angry with a god. Part of him knew that people cursed the gods when they had no one else to blame.

Those parts were shoved aside as he cried, *"Why did You abandon me?"*

Little brother, I did not.

"I waited for You! For weeks! You called the others, why not me?"

Because I could not. Silver fire flowed past his fingertips and lost itself in light. *From the hour of your birth, you were promised to the Saint. I had no claim on you.*

"Oh," Shane said, which seemed woefully inadequate, given the circumstances. He stared into the fire. A priest had suggested to him that this was the case, and he had hoped desperately that it was, but he had never quite made himself believe it.

He believed it now.

"I'm sorry."

As am I. We did not mean to cause you pain.

It occurred to Shane, finally, to ask the question that he should have asked first. "Am I dead?"

You are not.

Shane rubbed his face. He was increasingly unsure if this was his real body, but it *felt* like his hand and his forehead and the gesture made him feel slightly better. "Then what...*how*... Forgive me, Lord. I did not think that You spoke to mortals." The Saint had certainly never spoken to him in words, only in fire and glory.

Fire and glory, and, if Shane was being honest, being pointed in the proper direction and shoved. There were never any explanations afterward, but then, he had never expected them.

It is rare that any of Us can speak to mortals. The channel that lets Us touch a mortal soul is a narrow one. To force it open is no kindness.

The raw wound in Shane's soul twinged at that, as if someone had breathed across it.

The Saint's passing scarred that channel closed for you, little brother, or else I would have claimed you then. The demon's passing has ripped it open again, though those same scars protected you a little.

"A demon could get in, but a god could not?" asked Shane. The bitterness in his voice horrified him, but the Dreaming God did not seem to notice.

Can you set the bones of a chick still in the egg?

"No," Shane admitted.

Nor can I, no matter how well-inclined I may be toward the chick. There are subtle gods, but I am not among Them. The flames danced briefly, as if with rueful laughter. *I am not used to owing a demon a favor. It is not a comfortable thought.*

Shane almost said, "*Tell* me about it!" but that seemed like an unwise thing to say to a god. The flames began dancing again though, and he had a suspicion that the Dreaming God knew perfectly well what he was thinking.

Very well, said the Dreaming God. *Because of what has happened, because of what you have done, it is given to you to choose.*

"Choose? Choose what?"

Your soul will heal in time. If you wish, I will withdraw, and it will scar over again, as it was before.

"Or?"

Another breath across the raw places inside his heart. *Or I will stay, and you will become one of My paladins, as you once wished to be.*

Shane sat down hard, before he remembered that he was already on his knees. It didn't seem to matter. The flame obligingly rearranged itself so that it felt like he was sitting.

"*Your* paladin? After what I did?"

Would you cast aside a fine sword merely because it had been used, however briefly, by your enemy?

"I doubt Your priesthood will feel the same."

My priests are very dear to Me, said the Dreaming God musingly, *but they do not dictate My choices. They will recognize Who you serve, even if they wonder at it.*

"I didn't think You explained yourself to Your swords," Shane said. "They taught us not to expect that."

Generally I cannot. There is a door in most mortal souls that stands between you and the divine. Some of Us can whisper through the keyhole, but as I said, I have never been a terribly subtle god. I could only blast the door open and cause such pain as would be no kindness. But the door in your soul has been broken already, between the demon and the Saint, and you have already borne the pain.

Though I must warn you, little brother, that I will not continue to speak to you like this. Only saints can bear the voice of a god for long, and I fear that you are not quite a saint.

Shane snorted. "Definitely not." But if the Dreaming God's servants were not an issue, what of Shane's own comrades, of Wren and Istvhan and Stephen and all the rest? Surely it was not right that he accept something that was denied to them?

The flames bent sideways in a divine sigh. *Truly, little brother? You would deny yourself healing because someone else may be in pain? Even if your suffering helps them not at all?*

"Well, when you put it like that, it sounds stupid," Shane muttered. "But it's not..." He stopped himself before he said that it wasn't fair. He *knew* that life wasn't fair, but having a god confirm it was a blow that he did not think he could survive.

But the Dreaming God, for all that He claimed not to be subtle, had a different strategy. *Would your brothers and sisters* want *you to give this up for them?*

A painful laugh tore itself out of Shane's chest. "They'd kick my ass," he admitted. He could almost hear Istvhan yelling at him, and Stephen would give him the not-in-anger-but-in-sorrow look and Galen would just punch him in the head a few times and then they'd probably tell the Bishop and the Bishop would drag him back to the Dreaming God's temple and demand he try again and...well, it would be ugly.

They love you, little brother, said the god. *They will not love you less for being whole.*

It was Shane's turn to sigh. It was a hard thing to admit that a noble sacrifice wouldn't do any good, and that the people you were sacrificing for would think you were an idiot.

The silver flame seemed to retreat a little way, as if the god was stepping back. Shane wondered if the god was giving him time to think.

Did he *need* time to think?

To be a paladin of the Dreaming God had been his greatest desire for as long as he could remember, and once it seemed impossible, his greatest source of bitterness. Now it seemed, impossibly, that he was being offered that again.

But…

What about Marguerite?

Laying down his life for her had been an easy choice, but somehow it seemed that he was going to survive.

I will serve you however I can, for as long as you'll have me, he'd told her.

All he had to offer her was his service. If even that was promised to another, what did he have left to offer? *My humor, warmth, and charm?* He snorted at himself.

Davith had tried to warn him once. *All you'll ever be to her is a weapon.* And he'd blithely replied that at least he would be *her* weapon, not realizing that there would ever be another choice.

He thought about it. He thought about it for what seemed like a very long time, sitting there in a haze of divine light.

And what if she does not want you after all? What if even your service is not enough for her?

How could you *ever be enough?*

Perhaps he couldn't be. But he was enough for a god.

Shane laughed softly, painfully to himself, and sank his head in his hands. Gods, it seemed, were easier to serve than mortals.

Either she wants me for what I am, or she does not. And since I have not managed to be other than what I am—despite years of trying!—that is her decision, not mine.

I can only choose for myself.

He got to his feet. "Lord," he said aloud. "I know what I have to do."

He did not have to say anything more. The god knew. Perhaps the god had always known what his choice would be.

The silver fire swept in, wrapped him up, and made him whole.

CHAPTER 53

Shane woke up in a whitewashed room that smelled of lavender. It took a moment for his eyes to focus, and when they finally did, it was on a short, dark-haired woman sitting in a chair, frowning furiously at a stack of papers.

"Marguerite?" he whispered.

She lowered the papers and glared at him. "Do you have any idea," said Marguerite, in a voice that etched like engraving acid, "how tragically *inept* the Dreaming God's people are at intelligence gathering?"

This was not exactly the greeting he had been expecting. "Are they?" he asked, because it was hard to know what else to say.

"Did I say inept? This borders on the apocalyptic." She tossed the papers down on a side table, leaned over and kissed his forehead, then went to the door and shouted something into the hall. Shane didn't quite catch what it was, because the kiss had left him breathless, despite being as chaste as a nun.

A man in the pale robes of an acolyte came inside and the next few minutes were spent getting Shane to sit up, drink a bitter concoction of herbs and then a much sweeter one, and help him to the chamber pot. Marguerite absented herself for this last operation, and Shane snatched the opportunity to ask, "What's wrong with me?"

"You've been asleep for three days," said the acolyte.

"Three days!"

"Yep. You'll feel shaky for a day or two until your muscles get used to moving again. Food will help."

"But what happened?"

The acolyte paused. "You don't remember?"

"I..." Shane touched his forehead. "I thought the Dreaming God spoke...but...?"

"Oh, He did all right," said Marguerite, coming back inside. "I had just finished threatening that oaf Matthias when you stood up and said *something* and every paladin in that courtyard suddenly looked like they'd been hit with a board." She paused, rubbed the back of her neck, and added, "I'm not saying I was much better. If that's what a god passing by feels like, I wouldn't want to experience that more than...oh...once a decade or so, at the most."

The acolyte clapped him on the shoulder and helped him to the chair that Marguerite had been sitting in. "I'll send in a senior," he said. "Everyone is very concerned with your recovery." (Marguerite muttered something that Shane didn't quite catch, and wasn't sure he wanted to.)

The idea of the god speaking through him was so large that he could hardly grasp it, but fortunately, there was a more pressing concern. "The others! Are they okay?"

"They're fine. Wren's here. Judith rode out before the dust was even settled, but Davith saw her go and said she was fine. He left yesterday." Marguerite snorted. "Said to tell you that you and he are square now, and he'd prefer never to see any of us again."

Shane slumped back in the chair, relieved. "And...the others? At the castle?"

"Mmm." Marguerite studied the ceiling. "*So* odd. I could have sworn there were a great many more people there. Clearly I was mistaken, because the paladins were quite embarrassed to discover they'd been laying siege to a castle with all of five defenders. I'm afraid the old lady is the only one who made it, other than you. The priests say she's not possessed and if anyone starts asking her about the other people there, she starts telling them stories about her youth. Very *spicy* stories, I'm told."

Shane's breath went out in a long sigh. Wisdom's people had done what they set out to do. He might mourn for Erlick and the others, but they had chosen their path, and because of it, their families were together, and free.

Guilt stabbed him. If he was a paladin of the Dreaming God, surely he should tell the priests about the settlement?

And then, like an echo under his heart, *I am not used to owing a demon a favor. It is not a comfortable thought.*

No. My God knows what I did. It was the right thing, or as close to the right thing as I was capable of. Wasn't it?

He reached for the presence of the god, suddenly frightened that he had misunderstood everything.

Silver fire under his heart. The feel of some great Other, just on the far side. He couldn't hold the touch for long—everything still felt raw and scalded—but it was enough.

Oh Dreaming God. It was real. You *were real.*

Marguerite silently passed him a handkerchief and he mopped his cheeks. "It was real," he said hoarsely. "It was all real."

She squeezed his hand. "It was." She turned her gaze to the ceiling, the dark beams cutting across the plaster. "Everyone's been worried. The healers said it was just strain, but you were asleep for so long." She snorted. "Wren's been going out of her mind. She eventually took over the kitchen here and started baking things. I didn't even know she could bake."

Shane turned his hand to grasp hers, and she didn't pull away. "Were you worried?" he asked, needing desperately to hear the answer but afraid of what it might be.

"I wasn't," she said. And then, before his heart had time to sink, "I knew you'd come back to me."

"Oh," said Shane, feeling very much as if he, too, had been hit with a board.

The door opened and two people came in. One wore the rumpled robes of an acolyte but the vestments of a very senior priestess, and the other was Jorge.

Jorge let out a shout, thumped him enthusiastically on the shoulder and probably would have done more, except that the priestess said, "If you're going to beat my patient, I'll have you thrown out."

"Sorry, sorry." Jorge shot her an apologetic look then turned back to Shane. "I'm just relieved that you're here and your brains aren't scrambled." He froze. "Um…they aren't, are they? There was kind of a lot going on."

The priestess sighed in a manner that reminded Shane faintly of a god. "Tact, as always, is your strong suit, Jorge." She waved him away. He joined Marguerite sitting on the bed, and the priestess took Shane's hand, curling her fingers over his wrist. "Still, it's a good question. How do you feel?"

"Intensely hungover," Shane admitted.

She snorted. "Yeah, that's normal. Being god-touched may be good for the soul, but the body still has to carry that soul around." She sat back. "I'm Gwen. I'm in charge of the infirmary here, for my sins. How many fingers am I holding up?"

"Four."

"Good. Are you hearing gibbering demonic voices in the back of your head?"

"No?"

"Even better. Feeling hungry?"

Shane had to think about that one. "I'm not sure. I think if I had food in front of me, I would be?"

"Right." She stood up, made a futile attempt to smooth down her wrinkled robes, then gave up. "I'll have something sent up. You're probably going to sleep more for the next day or two, and I'm sure you're sore as hell from that battle, but you should be fine."

"Are they still going to try to exorcise me?" he asked warily.

"God, no!" She made a warding gesture. "We only do that to drive a demon out. I'm told a demonic taint *was* clinging to you, but it's gone now. Wish *I* knew how to do that."

"And…ah…" He touched his breastbone. "The god is there, but everything feels raw."

Gwen folded her arms and leaned against the wall, her lips twisting. "So far as I can tell from what everyone has said, you had part of your soul ripped out a few years ago, then a demon forced its way in, then the Dreaming God ripped *that* out *and* claimed you as a paladin *and* briefly made you His avatar so He could shout at everyone. And you're surprised that things are a little sore?"

Marguerite snickered. Shane stared at the priestess, too worried by the word *avatar* to even protest.

"You'll be fine. You just...I don't know, sprained your soul. Stay off it for a few weeks." Gwen waved her hand. "If it doesn't stop hurting, come talk to me. Quit snickering, Jorge, or I'll tell everyone about that 'personal problem' I cleared up for you last year."

Jorge immediately clammed up. The priestess shook her head and bid them farewell.

"I *like* her," said Marguerite.

"She's superb," Jorge said. "You couldn't be in better hands." He turned back to Shane. "I'm very glad you're feeling better. I wanted to apologize to you."

"Eh?" Shane blinked at him. "I should be apologizing to you. You had to storm a keep because of me."

"Yes, but..." Jorge raked his hands through his hair. "But that was because of the demon. But then, after...I might have let them kill you!"

"You didn't, though."

"But I didn't *stop* them. Hell, I offered you the sword."

"Which was probably the right thing to do at the time," Shane pointed out. "It's not like you knew that the Dreaming God was going to take a personal interest. *I* certainly didn't."

Jorge looked unconvinced. Shane cast a look of mute appeal at Marguerite, who did not let him down.

"If you want to be ashamed of something, be ashamed of this intelligence network of yours. Wisdom was up there for years and you *missed* it? And it's not as if it was hiding all that well. The locals all knew there was something weird going on."

"Uh..." Jorge was not expecting this sudden flank attack. "I...well...I mean, we asked around..."

"You *asked,*" said Marguerite in obvious despair. "You asked and then you believed what they told you, didn't you?"

Jorge's eyes darted back and forth. "Were we not supposed to do that...?"

"*Paladins.*" She dropped her head in her hands. "And if that's not enough, your recordkeeping looks like the sort of thing a drunken mercenary would scribble down to justify his bar tab. Do you know that your people *lost* a whole entire possessed paladin? Just *lost* him?"

"What?" said Shane.

"What?" said Jorge.

"This Lord Caliban person that you all speak in such hushed tones about. I went looking to see what happened to him." She thumped the stack of papers. "There's a trial record, he's remanded to local custody, somebody scrawls a note that says, *Ask the captain of the guard*, and then absolutely nothing. Your cautionary tale could be running around loose somewhere, and *nobody* has ever followed up?"

"Uh," said Jorge. "Um. This isn't really my field. I just kill demons. You want to talk to one of the senior priests—"

"Who do you think I got the papers from?"

Shane started to laugh. His ribs were sore but he didn't care.

"Right." Jorge stood up. "I should probably go...uh...check on something..."

"Wait," said Shane, a thought striking him. Jorge paused and raised his eyebrows inquiringly. "In the courtyard. Marguerite said that I said something. But what was it?"

An odd light flickered in Jorge's eyes. "You don't...no, of course you don't know. Everyone heard something different."

"Oh." Shane hadn't expected that. "That's why you knew it was the Dreaming God speaking?"

"We would have known that it was the God anyway." Jorge rapped his knuckles on the doorframe. "There was no doubt at all. I'll go check on that food, shall I?"

Shane sagged back in his chair, feeling suddenly exhausted despite having been awake for less than an hour. "Huh."

"He's right, you know," said Marguerite. "There really wasn't any doubt. You're good at the voice, but not *that* good." She rose to her feet. "Most of the paladins who were there won't tell anyone what they heard. Just that it was for them alone."

"Huh." It made a certain kind of sense. Perhaps if You could rarely speak directly to mortals, You seized the opportunity when you had it. A little rawness in his soul was a small price to pay for that, surely.

"Did you hear something too?" he asked. "You don't have to tell me what it was."

"I did," said Marguerite. To Shane's surprise and delight, she sat on the arm of the chair and leaned against him, her hip against his side and her cheek against the top of his head. "He told me to have faith."

CHAPTER 54

"You have a visitor, Mistress Florian," said the very young acolyte of the White Rat. "She's waiting in the small courtyard."

"A visitor?" Marguerite raised her eyebrows. "Me?"

"I did not realize anyone knew that you were here," Shane murmured.

She glanced up at him and felt an involuntary smile curve her lips. *Look at me, mooning around like a teenager. It must be positively disgusting to watch.* "Oh, a few people do, I'm sure. It's not as if it's a secret. But I don't know anyone who would need to be announced, instead of just showing up."

"She did not give her name," the acolyte said. Marguerite and Shane followed him through the bustling halls of the temple, dodging law clerks and supplicants.

Marguerite would not have expected to enjoy spending time in a temple, but the last few weeks had been surprisingly peaceful. They had escorted Ashes to Archenhold, accompanied by multiple paladins, and then the Bishop had extended the Rat's hospitality until, as she said, "the Sail realizes just how much trouble it's in." Marguerite had been touched, and more than a little grateful. She could have stayed with Grace, of course, but she did not want to put her friend in any danger—and the Rat's temple, as she knew well, was surprisingly difficult to infiltrate.

I would probably feel different if it was a temple of the Dreaming God. I'm still a little miffed at them. Although I swear to their god, I'm going to fix that spy network if it kills me.

...oh, who am I kidding? I could probably be happy in a temple of the Hanged Mother, if Shane was there with me.

He reached out and took her hand as they walked, and she felt a by-now familiar rush of affection. She kept waiting for the feeling to wear off. It kept not doing so.

The acolyte halted at the entrance to the small courtyard and bowed them through. Marguerite took two steps inside and stopped as if she'd run into a brick wall. Her fingers closed tightly on Shane's.

"Peace," said Fenella, raising one hand. "I'm only here to talk." The older woman sat at a little table, sipping a cup of tea, her embroidered shawl loose around her shoulders, exactly like the fabric-buyer from Baiir that she had pretended to be in the Court of Smoke. Perfectly relaxed and perfectly harmless: Marguerite doubted either one was true.

She dropped Shane's hand and sat down across the table, already cursing herself for having let her alarm show. "I admit that I am surprised to see you here," she said.

"I was in the area," Fenella said, taking a sip of tea. "I thought perhaps we might speak."

"Mmm." Marguerite wished that she had a teacup to sip from, but would not have trusted anything served to her. She sensed Shane taking up his accustomed guard position and took comfort from it. "What shall we speak of, madam?"

"Salt." Fenella set her cup down and steepled her fingers. "It would seem that there is soon to be a great deal more of it about."

"I've heard rumors to that effect, yes."

One corner of Fenella's mouth crooked up. "I think there's little point in either of us being coy. You won, we lost. That's all there is to it."

Marguerite inclined her head, accepting this tribute. "It was a near thing," she said, "and hinged entirely on luck."

"Luck is what you make it. No, I think you played the game better than I did." Fenella pulled her shawl more tightly around her shoulders. "It would not have occurred to me to hide an artificer among demonslayers. I daresay that was inspired. We could not move against them, or risk every man's hand turned against us."

"Also luck," Marguerite repeated. "It did not occur to me either, until there was an actual demon."

"Ah. Not *good* luck, then."

"Not precisely, no." Marguerite glanced toward the entrance to the courtyard. The acolyte was still standing there, just out of earshot. He looked bored. *Good, someone to run for help if she suddenly whips out a dagger and stabs me.*

"Mmm." Fenella took another sip of tea. "At the end of all this, I find that the only question I have is 'Why?'"

"Why?"

"Why put yourself in such mortal danger for such a risky proposition? Why oppose us so fiercely at all?" Her eyes were hooded, but not hostile. "I have dug through everything we know of you, Marguerite Florian, which is a good deal. Yet I can find no secret backers, no master who you might serve. Except perhaps the Rat—" she gestured toward the walls of the courtyard, "—and they would not have masterminded something like this. So I decided that I would ask you. Why?"

"Because I wanted the Sail to leave me alone. That's all."

Fenella's lips twitched. "One is reminded of stories of using a siege engine to swat a fly."

"I tried other ways to swat that fly," Marguerite said. "I assure you, this was not my first plan. But after several years of trying, it became clear that your organization was simply unable to grant me amnesty. No matter how many of the Sail's people were grateful for my aid, no matter how much amnesty I was promised, there would always be another faction who thought of me as only a loose end."

"Ah." Fenella's look of disgust was clearly unfeigned. "The right hand does not know what the left is doing. And the right hand, I fear, is often an idiot."

Marguerite snorted, though not without sympathy.

"I have long thought that we were far too large to manage ourselves effectively." Fenella shook her head. "Being proven right is somewhat gratifying, I admit, for all the good it does. You have destabilized us quite effectively, Mistress Florian. The Red Sail will not survive this as we are. What remains in a few years' time will look very, very different."

"What if the machine doesn't work?" Shane asked.

If she was surprised at being addressed by a bodyguard, Fenella gave no sign. "It will work. If not this machine, then the next one, or the one after that. Magnus's blueprints are in the hands of the Artificer's Guild now, and they love nothing more than tweaking machines and making them more efficient." She shrugged. "Had we stopped Magnus completely, it might have been another hundred years before someone thought to create such a machine. But once the idea is out, we shall have a dozen copycats before year's end. More than that, we shall have governments investing in such machines rather than in the Sail's ships. Investors who have backed us because we were quite literally the only option are already pulling out, now that another possibility presents itself. No—Shane, was it?—if your client stays out of sight for another year, I suspect she will find that neither the right or left hand will have the resources to swat at her. We shall be too busy scrambling to find a foothold in this new world."

"I shall do my best to lie low," said Marguerite.

Fenella rose to her feet. "They will not learn your whereabouts from me, at least," she said. "I have never been particularly interested in revenge. In fact...I don't suppose you'd be interested in working for me?"

Shane made an incredulous sound. Marguerite chuckled. "Your organization could not protect me against itself when it was at the height of its power. I fear I can't trust that it will do so in its death throes."

"No, quite right," Fenella said. She draped her shawl more comfortably. "But if things proceed as I suspect they will, there is an excellent chance that I will not be working for the Sail much longer myself. And should that day come to pass...well. One always has need of extremely talented people."

Marguerite rose as well and bowed to her. "If that day does come to pass, then I would be happy to revisit this conversation."

"Then I hope that we shall find ourselves speaking again, Mistress Florian." Fenella ambled toward the entryway, found the acolyte, and tucked her arm through his. "Thank you for the tea, young man. Now, if you can show me how to get out of this great maze of a temple, I shall be *eternally* grateful..."

The acolyte cast a long-suffering glance back at Shane and Marguerite, and suffered himself to lead the clearly dotty older woman away. Marguerite rocked back on her heels and let out a long sigh.

"After all that—after everything—she offered you *a job?*" Shane raked his hands through his hair. "And actually thought you might take it?"

"I might," said Marguerite. "In a few years, anyway, depending on how things fall out."

"But she tried to kill you!"

"Yes, and the Dreaming God's people tried to kill you," Marguerite pointed out. "You forgave *them.*"

His eyebrows drew together. "That's different."

Marguerite just looked at him.

"...I'm pretty sure it's different?"

"I'm not, but never mind. That's all a long way off, if ever." She scowled. "Besides, I'll need something to do after I fix the Dreaming God's intelligence network."

"Are you going to do that, then?"

"Oh, you laugh, but I might. If only so it doesn't cause me physical pain whenever I hear about it." Despite her tone, a knot was forming in her stomach. "Of course, now I really do have to lie low for a year or so."

And I don't expect you to come with me. Why would he? Shane had his god now. Even if he wanted to stay with her, the obligations of a demon-slayer undoubtedly took precedence over one small spy with a price on her head.

Marguerite had always known this moment would come, but she had hoped to have a little more time. She stared at the flowers on the edge of the courtyard so that she would not have to look at his face.

It's fine.

No, it's not fine, but I'll deal with it anyway. He wants to do good more than anyone I've ever met, and I have to let him. Trying to keep him with me instead of off fighting demons would be like asking a working dog to be a lap dog instead.

The thought made a yawning chasm open up in her guts. She had been avoiding it for weeks now, but it seemed that she couldn't ignore it any longer.

Doing the right thing for someone else's good. How very noble of me. Almost paladinly. Shit.

"All right," Shane said. "Where are we going?"

"I haven't—wait, *we?*"

He looked down at her, clearly baffled. "Yes, of course. Did you think I wouldn't come with you?"

"I thought..." Marguerite swallowed. The knot in her stomach seemed to have changed and become a lump in her throat. "I didn't think you'd want to come with me."

He made an impatient gesture. "Where you go, I go."

"Are you sure?"

"If the Sail is still going to try to kill you, you'll need a bodyguard."

"But..." Marguerite pinched the bridge of her nose. She hadn't seen this coming.

Pile it on all the other things I didn't see coming, I suppose. Samuel would give me such a lecture. But it was too good to be true, it was what she wanted, and things that were too good to be true were suspicious.

"Shane, you have other duties. I know that. And I really don't want to come between you and your god."

His eyes were the blue of a very hot flame. "You both came back for me. But you came back first."

"Yes, but...Shane, He's a *god.* Won't He want you to go...I don't know... chop up bulls that are speaking in tongues?"

"There's no reason I *can't* do that while we're on the move, is there?"

Marguerite had to stop and think about that one. Was there a reason? Granted, slaying demons wasn't quiet or subtle, but any sensible operative would be running in the other direction. Demons weren't profitable for anybody. *Frankly, if we're tracking down demons, the Sail will be trying to get as far away from us as possible. And nobody can predict where they'll show up, and if we're moving from temple to temple, the Sail sure can't buy off anyone there.*

"Good god," she said. "That might actually work."

Shane stared intently into her face for a moment, and then, to her surprise, began to laugh.

"What? What's so funny?"

"Sorry," he said, immediately getting himself under control. "I'm sorry."

"You'll be *really* sorry if you don't tell me why you were laughing."

His lips were twitching and he couldn't quite meet her eyes. "It's just that you looked like someone had just hit you with a board. And I thought, oh hey, that must be how *I* look nearly all the time..."

Marguerite dug her elbow into his ribs. "Very funny. And how are you going to explain to the temple here that you have to go roam about the countryside with no forwarding address?"

"I thought I'd just tell them."

Her eyebrows went up. "Seriously?"

Shane rubbed the back of his neck. "I realize I'm not as good at this as you are, but I was an avatar of the god for a minute or two, and they're all still a little worried about that. But that won't last forever. Every time I go over to the Dreaming God's temple, I get the feeling that a lot of the priests would like me to go away. Not *die,* you understand. Just go be someone else's problem. Does that make sense?"

"That makes a *lot* of sense, actually. We might make an operative of you yet."

He made a hasty warding gesture and Marguerite laughed. The lump in her throat had gone, and left her feeling strangely light. Maybe she didn't have to be noble and self-sacrificing after all. "I did promise to do something about their intelligence network. But are you sure? Really sure? I know you don't always approve of everything I do."

He looked uncomfortable, and she suspected that he was thinking of Maltrevor. "Who am I to approve or disapprove?"

"You're the man I love, for one thing. And you're the only man I've ever known who makes me feel safe."

He wrapped his arms around her, but not before she caught sight of the smile spreading across his face.

"We'll work something out," he said. "I'm told you're a master negotiator."

She leaned against him, feeling safe, blessedly safe, like she felt nowhere else. Thinking of how he looked, reading by rushlight, with spectacles perched on the tip of his nose, and how he felt in her arms, wrists bound by a fragile length of thread.

"If you're sure," she said. "But swear to me that you'll tell me if something's wrong. You won't just suffer in martyred silence. Because I love you, and I want this to work."

"I'll tell you," he said. "I love you, and I want it to work, too." And he said it in the voice, so she believed him.

EPILOGUE

Bishop Beartongue leaned on the upper railing of the warehouse, watching the work going on below. A machine the size of a small room was being slowly assembled on the floor of the warehouse, by a dozen harried-looking apprentices and two acolytes of the Forge God. Ashes Magnus sat on a chair in the center of the chaos, directing the streams of activity and occasionally shouting things like, "No, other way 'round!" and "If you hook that up there, your eyebrows won't grow back in a hurry, my lad!"

"So you're building it," said Rigney, her assistant, coming to stand beside her. "I wasn't actually sure that you would."

"Neither was I," Beartongue admitted.

"And will it work?"

"The Forge God's people say it should. We won't know until it's built. And even then, we won't know if it's cost-efficient." She waved her hand at the machine. "We're having to bring in barrels of sea water for this one, which pretty much kills the budget, but if it does work the way Magnus thinks, we'll put a much larger one in Delta. *If* it works."

Rigney knew her far too well to be put off by that. "You think it will, though."

Beartongue blew air out in a long sigh. "I do. That will make the most problems, so of course that's what will happen."

Rigney folded his arms and gazed down at the controlled chaos below. "It will disrupt a great many things if it does work."

"I know." Beartongue gave a short, humorless laugh. "Do you know that the damned thing makes ice too? Ashes didn't care about that bit. Said it was just a byproduct and wasn't that interesting."

Rigney's eyebrows shot up. Ice was expensive and had to be stored in sawdust underground through the summer months. In a city like Archon's Glory, where the water table was never very far below the surface, that made it a rare luxury item. "The Rat have mercy," he muttered.

Beartongue could see him doing figures in his head. "I know, right?" She rubbed her face. "Yes. It will change a ridiculous number of things, I expect. Probably even a few that no one's thought of yet. But at least if we're the ones building it, we can ease the world into it as gently as possible, instead of abruptly crashing a few national economies overnight. Some of which may well deserve to be crashed, but it's never the people on top who bear the brunt."

Rigney nodded. "I'll prepare a report," he suggested, "on what we can expect."

"Do that," said Beartongue. "Then you can be the one to read the report and summarize it for me."

He laughed softly. "Naturally."

The Bishop pushed away from the railing and moved toward the door, trailing Rigney like a tall shadow. Behind them, metal clanged and Ashes Magnus yelled, "Lad, if you can't be more careful with your fingers, you don't deserve to keep them!" and Beartongue shook her head and muttered something under her breath that sounded like a prayer.

And a long way away, on the edge of the dry, dusty plains of Charlock, a tall, auburn-haired woman stood looking across the desert.

She no longer had a horse. The horse hadn't much cared for berserkers, and it cared even less for what this one carried. They had parted with much mutual antipathy.

<The desert, then?>

"Do you dislike the desert?" Judith asked aloud. She didn't need to, but speaking out loud made it easier for her to keep track of what was her and what was...not.

<I have never formed an opinion.>

"You will," Judith promised. "No one who goes into the desert comes out of it without one." She considered for a moment, then, in the interest of honesty, added, "Most people hate it."

<We are not like most people> said the demon called Wisdom.

Judith laughed. Her fellow paladins would have been surprised to hear it. In the years since the Saint of Steel died, she might chuckle, but she had thought that her old, full-throated laugh had been buried along with her god.

"No," she said, pulling her scarf up to cover her face from the sun. "We most definitely are not."

The heat haze drifted over their tracks and magnified them briefly, before the relentless wind pulled them apart and left no trace of their passage behind.

ABOUT THE AUTHOR

T. Kingfisher is the vaguely absurd pen-name of Ursula Vernon, an author from North Carolina. In another life, she writes children's books and weird comics. Her work has won the Hugo, Nebula, Locus, Sequoyah, Dragon, Alfie, WSFA, Mythopoeic and Coyotl awards.

This is the name she uses when writing things for grown-ups. Her work includes horror, fantasy romance, fairy-tale retellings and odd little stories about elves and goblins.

When she is not writing, she is probably out in the garden, trying to make eye contact with butterflies.

x.com/ursulav

patreon.com/ursulav

ALSO BY T. KINGFISHER

As T. Kingfisher

Thornhedge

Nettle & Bone

Paladin's Strength

A Wizard's Guide To Defensive Baking

Paladin's Grace

Swordheart

Clockwork Boys

The Wonder Engine

Minor Mage

Nine Goblins

Toad Words & Other Stories

The Seventh Bride

The Raven & The Reindeer

Bryony & Roses

Jackalope Wives & Other Stories

Summer in Orcus

Horror Novels:

The Twisted Ones

The Hollow Places

What Moves The Dead

A House With Good Bones

As Ursula Vernon

From Sofawolf Press:

Black Dogs Duology

House of Diamond

Mountain of Iron

Digger

It Made Sense At The Time

For kids:

Dragonbreath Series

Hamster Princess Series

Castle Hangnail